I0523803

Frances Elliot

The Italians

A novel

Frances Elliot

The Italians
A novel

ISBN/EAN: 9783337000622

Printed in Europe, USA, Canada, Australia, Japan

Cover: Foto ©Andreas Hilbeck / pixelio.de

More available books at **www.hansebooks.com**

THE ITALIANS:

A NOVEL.

BY

FRANCES ELLIOT,

AUTHOR OF

"ROMANCE OF OLD COURT LIFE IN FRANCE," "THE DIARY OF AN IDLE
WOMAN IN ITALY," ETC., ETC.

NEW YORK:

D. APPLETON AND COMPANY,

549 AND 551 BROADWAY.

1875.

TO

THE REAL ENRICA,

WITH

THE AUTHOR'S LOVE.

CONTENTS.

PART III.

PART IV.

THE ITALIANS.

CHAPTER I.

LUCCA.

WE are at Lucca. It is the 13th of September, 1870
—the anniversary of the festival of the Volto Santo—a
notable day, both in city, suburb, and province. Lucca
dearly loves its festivals—no city more; and of all the festivals of the year that of the Volto Santo best. Now the
Volto Santo (*Anglicè*, Holy Countenance) is a miraculous
crucifix, which hangs, as may be seen, all by itself in a
gorgeous chapel—more like a pagoda than a chapel, and
more like a glorified bird-cage than either—built expressly
for it among the stout Lombard pillars in the nave of the
cathedral. The crucifix is of cedar-wood, very black, and
very ugly, and it was carved by Nicodemus; of this fact
no orthodox Catholic entertains a doubt. But on what
authority I cannot tell, nor why, nor how, the Holy Countenance reached the snug little city of Lucca, except by
flying through the air like the Loretto house, or springing
out of the earth like the Madonna of Feltri. But here it
is, and here it has been for many a long year; and here it
will remain as a miraculous relic, bringing with it blessings
and immunities innumerable to the grateful city.

What a glorious morning it is! The sun rose without

a cloud. Now there is a golden haze hanging over the
plain, and glints as of living flame on the flanks of the
mountains. From all sides crowds are pressing toward
Lucca. Before six o'clock every high-road is alive. Down
from the highest mountain-top of Pizzorna, overlooking
Florence and its vine-garlanded campagna, comes the hermit, brown-draped, in hood and mantle; staff in hand, he
trudges along the dusty road. And down, too, from his
native lair among the pigs and the poultry, comes the
black-eyed, black-skinned, matted-haired urchin, who makes
mud pies under the tufted ilex-trees at Ponte a Moriano,
and swears at the hermit.

They come! they come! From mountain-sides bordering the broad road along the Serchio—mountains dotted
with bright homesteads, each gleaming out of its own
cypress-grove, olive-patch, canebrake, and vine-arbor, under which the children play—they come from solitary
hovels, hung up, as it were, in mid-air, over gloomy ra-
vines, scored and furrowed with red earth, down which dark
torrents dash and spray.

They come! they come! these Tuscan peasants, a trifle
too fond of holiday-keeping, like their betters—but what
would you have? The land is fertile, and corn and wine
and oil and rosy flowering almonds grow almost as of
themselves. They come—tens and tens of miles away,
from out the deep shadows of primeval chestnut-woods,
clothing the flanks of rugged Apennines with emerald
draperies. They come—through parting rocks, bordering
nameless streams—cool, delicious waters, over which bend
fig, peach, and plum, delicate ferns and unknown flowers.
They come—from hamlets and little burghs, gathered beside lush pastures, where tiny rivulets trickle over fresh
turf and fragrant herbs, lulling the ear with softest echoes.

They come—dark-eyed mothers and smiling daughters,
decked with gold pins, flapping Leghorn hats, lace veils or

snowy handkerchiefs gathered about their heads, coral beads, and golden crosses as big as shields, upon their necks—escorted by lover, husband, or father—a flower behind his ear, a slouch hat on his head, a jacket thrown over one arm, every man shouldering a red umbrella, although to doubt the weather to-day is absolute sacrilege!

Carts clatter by every moment, drawn by swift Maremma nags, gay with brass harness, tinkling bells, and tassels of crimson on reins and frontlet.

The carts are laden with peasants (nine, perhaps, ranged three abreast)—treason to the gallant animal that, tossing its little head, bravely struggles with the cruel load. A priest is stuck in bodkin among his flock—a priest who leers and jests between pinches of snuff, and who, save for his seedy black coat, knee-breeches, worsted stockings, shoe-buckles, clerical hat, and smoothly-shaven chin, is rougher than a peasant himself.

Riders on Elba ponies, with heavy cloaks (for the early morning, spite of its glories, is chill), spur by, adding to the dust raised by the carts.

Genteel flies and hired carriages with two horses, and hood and foot-board—pass, repass, and out-race each other. These flies and carriages are crammed with bailiffs from the neighboring villas, shopkeepers, farmers, and small proprietors. Donkeys, too, there are in plenty, carrying men bigger than themselves (under protest, be it observed, for here, as in all countries, your donkey, though marked for persecution, suffers neither willingly nor in silence). Begging friars, tanned like red Indians, glide by, hot and grimy (thank Heaven! not many now, for "New Italy" has sacked most of the convent rookeries and dispersed the rooks), with wallets on their shoulders, to carry back such plunder as can be secured, to far-off convents and lonely churches, folded up tightly in forest fastnesses.

All are hurrying onward with what haste they may, to

reach the city of Lucca, while broad shadows from the tall mountains on either hand still fall athwart the roads, and cool morning air breathes up from the rushing Serchio.

The Serchio—a noble river, yet willful as a mountain-torrent—flows round the embattled walls of Lucca, and falls into the Mediterranean below Pisa. It is calm now, on this day of the great festival, sweeping serenely by rocky capes, and rounding into fragrant bays, where over-arching boughs droop and feather. But there is a sullen look about its current, that tells how wicked it can be, this Serchio, lashed into madness by winter storms, and the overflowing of the water-gates above, among the high Apennines—at the Abbetone at San Marcello, or at windy, ice-bound Pracchia.

How fair are thy banks, O mountain-bordered Serchio! How verdant with near wood and neighboring forest! How gay with cottage groups—open-galleried and gar-landed with bunches of golden maize and vine-branches—all laughing in the sun! The wine-shops, too, along the road, how tempting, with snowy table-cloths spread upon dressers under shady arbors of lemon - trees; pleasant odors from the fry cooking in the stove, mixing with the perfume of the waxy flowers! Dear to the nostrils of the passers-by are these odors. They snuff them up—onions, fat, and macaroni, with delight. They can scarcely resist stopping once for all here, instead of waiting for their journey's end to eat at Lucca.

But the butterflies—and they are many—are wiser in their generation. The butterflies have a festival of their own to-day. They do not wait for any city. They are fixed to no spot. They can hold their festival anywhere under the blue sky, in the broad sunshine.

See how they dance among the flowers! Be it spikes of wild-lavender, or yellow down within the Canterbury bell, or horn of purple cyclamens, or calyx of snowy myrtle,

the soft bosom of tall lilies or glowing petals of red cloves
—nothing comes amiss to the butterflies. They are citizens of the world, and can feast wherever fancy leads them.

Meanwhile, on comes the crowd, nearer and nearer to
the city of their pilgrimage, laughing, singing, talking,
smoking. Your Italian peasant must sleep or smoke, ex-
cepting when he plays at *morra* (one, two, three, and
away!). Then he puts his pipe into his pocket. The
women are conversing in deep voices, in the *patois* of the
various villages. The men, more silent, search out who is
fairest—to lead her on the way, to kneel beside her at the
shrine, and, most prized of all, to conduct her home. Each
village has its belle, each belle her circle of admirers.
Belles and beaux all have their own particular plan of di-
version for the day. For is it not a great day? And is it
not stipulated in many of the marriage contracts among
the mountain tribes that the husband must, under a money
penalty, conduct his wife to the festival of the Holy Countenance once at least in four years? The programme is
this: First, they enter the cathedral, kneel at the glistening shrine of the black crucifix, kiss its golden slipper, and
hear mass. Then they will grasp such goods as the gods
provide them, in street, *café*, eating-house, or day theatre ;
make purchases in the shops and booths, and stroll upon
the ramparts. Later, when the sun sinks westward over
the mountains, and the deep canopy of twilight falls, they
will return by the way that they have come, until the coming year.

.   .   .   .

Within the city, from before daybreak, church-bells—
and Lucca abounds in belfries fretted tier upon tier, with
galleries of delicate marble colonnettes, all ablaze in the
sunshine—have pealed out merrily.

Every church-door, draped with gold tissue and silken
stuffs, more or less splendid, is thrown wide open. Every

shop is closed, save *cafés*, hotels, and tobacco-shops (where, by command of the King of New Italy, infamous cigars are sold). Eating-tables are spread at the corners of the streets and under the trees in the piazza, benches are ranged everywhere where benches can stand. The streets are filling every moment as fresh multitudes press through the city gates—those grand old gates, where the marble lions of Lucca keep guard, looking toward the mountains.

For a carriage to pass anywhere in the streets would be impossible, so tightly are flapping Leghorn hats, and veils, snowy handkerchiefs, and red caps and brigand hats, packed together. Bells ring, and there are waftings of military music borne through the air. Trumpet-calls at the different barracks answer to each other. Cannons are fired. Each man, woman, and child shouts, screams, and laughs. All down the dark, cavernous streets, in the great piazza, at the sindaco's, at college, at club, public offices, and hotels, at the grand old palaces, untouched since the middle ages—the glory of the city—at every house, great and small—flutter gaudy draperies; crimson, amber, violet, and gold, according to purse and condition, either of richest brocade, or of Eastern stuffs wrought in gold and needle-work, or—the family carpet or bed-furniture hung out for show. Banners wave from every house-top and tower, the Italian tricolor and the Savoy cross, white, on a red ground; flowers and garlands are wreathed on the fronts of the stern old walls. If peasants, and shopkeepers, and monks, priests, beggars, and *hoi polloi* generally, possess the pavement, overhead every balcony, gallery, terrace, and casement, is filled with company, representatives of the historic families of Lucca, the Manfredi, Possenti, Navascoes, Bernardini, dal Portico, Bocella, Manzi, da Gia, Orsetti, Ruspoli—feudal names dear to native ears. The noble marquis, or his excellency the count, lord of broad acres on the plains, or principalities in the mountains,

or of hoarded wealth at the National Bank—is he not Lucchese also to the backbone? And does he not delight in
the festival as keenly as that half-naked beggar, who rat-
tles his box for alms, with a broad grin on his dirty face?

Resplendent are the ladies in the balconies, dressed in
their best—like bands of fluttering ribbon stretched across
the sombre-fronted palaces; aristocratic daughters, and
dainty consorts. They are not chary of their charms.
They laugh, fan themselves, lean over sculptured balustrades, and eye the crowded streets, talking with lip and
fan, eye and gesture.

In the long, narrow street of San Simone, behind the
cathedral of San Martino, stand the two Guinigi Palaces.
They are face to face. One is ditto of the other. Each is
in the florid style of Venetian-Gothic, dating from the beginning of the fourteenth century. Both were built by
Paolo Guinigi, head of the illustrious house of that name,
for forty years general and tyrant of the Republic of Lucca. Both palaces bear his arms, graven on marble tablets
beside the entrance. Both are of brick, now dulled and
mellowed into a reddish white. Both have walls of enormous thickness. The windows of the upper stories—quad-
ruple casements divided, Venetian-like, by twisted pillar-
ettes richly carved—are faced and mullioned with marble.
The lower windows (mere square apertures) are barred
with iron. The arched portals opening to the streets are
low, dark, and narrow. The inner courts gloomy, damp,
and prison-like. Brass ornaments, sockets, rings, and torch-
holders of iron, sculptured emblems, crests, and cognizances
in colored marble, are let into the outer walls. In all else,
ornamentation is made subservient to defense. These are
city fortresses rather than ancestral palaces. They were
constructed to resist either attack or siege.

Rising out of the overhanging roof (supported on wood-
en rafters) of the largest and most stately of the two pal-

aces, where twenty-three groups of clustered casements, linked by slender pillars, extend in a line along a single story—rises a mediæval tower of defense of many stories. Each story is pierced by loop-holes for firing into the street below. On the machicolated summit is a square platform, where in the course of many peaceful ages a bay-tree has come to grow of a goodly size. About this bay-tree tangled weeds and tufted grasses wave in the wind. Below, here and there, patches of blackened moss or yellow lichen, a branch of mistletoe or a bunch of fern, break the lines of the mediæval brickwork. Sprays of wild-ivy cling to the empty loop-holes, through which the blue sky peeps.

The lesser of the two palaces—the one on the right hand as you ascend the street of San Simone coming from the cathedral—is more decorated to-day than any other in Lucca. A heavy sea of Leghorn hats and black veils, with male accompaniments, is crowded beneath. They stare upward and murmur with delight. Gold and silver stuffs, satin and taffeta, striped brocades, and rich embroideries, flutter from the clustered casement up to the overhanging roof. There are many flags (one with a coat-of-arms, amber and purple on a gold ground) blazing in the sunshine. The grim brick façade is festooned with wreaths of freshly-plucked roses. Before the low-arched entrance on the pavement there is a carpet of flower-petals fashioned into a monogram, bearing the letters " M. N." Just within the entrance stands a porter, leaning on a gold staff, as immovable in aspect as are the mediæval walls that close in behind him. A badge or baldric is passed across his chest; he is otherwise so enveloped with gold-lace, embroidery, buttons, trencher, and cocked-hat, that the whole inner man is absorbed, not to say invisible. Beside him, in the livery of the house, tall valets grin, lounge, and ogle the passers-by (wearers of Leghorn hats, and veils, and white head-gear generally). This particular Guinigi Palace belongs to Count Mario Nobili. He bought it of the Marchesa Guinigi, who lives opposite. Nobili is the richest young man in Lucca. No one calls upon him for help in vain; but, let it be added, no one offends him with impunity. When Nobili first came to Lucca, the old families looked coldly at him, his nobility being of very recent date. It was bestowed on his father, a successful banker —some said usurer, some said worse—by the Grand-duke Leopold, for substantial assistance toward his pet hobby— the magnificent road that zigzags up the mountain-side to Fiesole from Florence.

But young Nobili soon conquered Lucchese prejudice. Now he is well received by all—*all* save the Marchesa Guinigi. She was, and is at this time, still irreconcilable. Nobili stands in the central window of his palace. He leans out over the street, a cigar in his mouth. A servant beside him flings down from time to time some silver coin among Leghorn hats and the beggars, who scramble for it on the pavement. Nobili's eyes beam as the populace look up and cheer him: "Long live Count Nobili! Evviva!" He takes off his hat and bows; more silver coin comes clattering down on the pavement; there are fresh evvivas, fresh bows, and more scramblers cover the street. "No one like Nobili," the people say; "so affable, so open-handed—yes, and so clever, too, for has he not traveled, and does he not know the world?"

Beside Count Nobili some *jeunesse dorée* of his own age (sons of the best houses in Lucca) also lean over the Venetian casements. Like the liveried giants at the entrance, these laugh, ogle, chaff, and criticise the wearers of Leghorn hats, black veils, and white head-gear, freely. They smoke, and drink *liqueurs* and sherbet, and crack sugar-plums out of crystal cup on silver plates, set on embossed trays placed beside them.

The profession of these young men is idleness. They

excel in it. Let us pause for a moment and ask what they do—this *jeunesse dorée*, to whom the sacred mission is committed of regenerating an heroic people? They could teach Ovid "the art of love." It comes to them in the air they breathe. They do not love their neighbor as themselves, but they love their neighbors' wives. Nothing is holy to them. "All for love, and the world well lost," is their motto. They can smile in their best friend's face, weep with him, rejoice with him, eat with him, drink with him, and—betray him; they do this every day, and do it well. They can also lie artistically, dressing up imaginary details with great skill, gamble and sing, swear, and talk scandal. They can lead a graceful, dissolute, *far niente* life, loll in carriages, and be whirled round for hours, say the Florence Cascine, the Roman Pincio, and the park at Milan—smoking the while, and raising their hats to the ladies. They can trot a well-broken horse—not too fresh, on a hard road, and are wonderful in ruining his legs. A very few can drive what they call a *stage* (*Anglicè*, drag) with grave and well-educated wheelers, on a very straight road—such as do this are looked upon as heroes—shoot a hare sitting, also tom-tits and sparrows. But they can neither hunt, nor fish, nor row. They are ready of tongue and easy of offense. They can fight duels (with swords), generally a harmless exercise. They can dance. They can hold strong opinions on subjects on which they are crassly ignorant, and yield neither to fact nor argument where their mediæval usages are concerned All this the golden youths of Young Italy can do, and do it well.

Yet from such stuff as this are to come the future ministers, prefects, deputies, financiers, diplomatists, and senators, who are to regenerate the world's old mistress! Alas, poor Italy!

The Guinigi Palace opposite forms a striking contrast to Count Nobili's abode. It is as silent as the grave.

Every shutter is closed. The great wooden door to the street is locked; a heavy chain is drawn across it. The Marchesa Guinigi has strictly commanded that it should be so. She will have nothing to do with the festival of the Holy Countenance. She will take no part in it whatever. Indeed, she has come to Lucca on purpose to see that her orders are obeyed to the very letter, else that rascal of a secretary might have hung out something in spite of her. The marchesa, who has been for many years a widow, and is absolute possesssor of the palace and lands, calls herself a liberal. But she is in practice the most thorough-going aristocrat alive. In one respect she is a liberal. She despises priests, laughs at miracles, and detests festivals. "A loss of time, and, if of time, of money," she says. If the peasants and the people complain of the taxes, and won't work six days in the week, "Let them starve," says the marchesa—"let them starve; so much the better!"

In her opinion, the legend of the Holy Countenance is a lie, got up by priests for money; so she comes into the city from Corellia, and shuts up her palace, publicly to show her opinion. As far as she is concerned, she believes neither in St. Nicodemus nor in idleness.

A good deal of this, be it said, *en passant*, is sheer obstinacy. The marchesa is obstinate to folly, and full of contradictions. Besides, there is another powerful motive that influences her—she hates Count Nobili. Not that he has ever done any thing personally to offend her; of this he is incapable—indeed, he has his own reasons for desiring passionately to be on good terms with her—but he has, in her opinion, injured her by purchasing the second Guinigi Palace. That she should have been obliged to sell one of her ancestral palaces at all is to her a bitter misfortune; but that any one connected with trade should possess what had been inherited generation after generation by the Guinigi, is intolerable.

That a *parvenu*, the son of a banker, should live opposite to her, that he should abound in money, which he flings
about recklessly, while she can with difficulty eke out the
slender rents from the greatly-reduced patrimony of the
Guinigi, is more than she can bear.   His popularity and
his liberality (and she cannot come to Lucca without hearing of both), even that comely young face of his, which she
sees when she passes the club on the way to her afternoon
drive on the ramparts, are dire offenses in her eyes.   Whatever Count Nobili does, she (the Marchesa Guinigi) will do
the reverse.   He has opened his house for the festival.
Hers shall be closed.   She is thoroughly exceptional, however, in such conduct.   Every one in Lucca save herself,
rich and poor, noble and villain, join heart and soul in the
national festival.   Every one lays aside on this auspicious
day differences of politics, family feuds, and social animosi-
ties.   Even enemies join hands and kneel side by side at
the same altar.   It is the mediæval " God's truce " celebrated in the nineteenth century.

.   .   .   .

It is now eleven o'clock.   A great deal of sausage and
garlic, washed down by new wine and light beer, has been
by this time consumed in eating-shops and on street tables ;
much coffee, *liqueurs*, cake, and bonbons, inside the palaces.

Suddenly all the church-bells, which have rung out
since daybreak like mad, stop ; only the deep-toned cathe-
dral-bell booms out from its snowy campanile in half-minute
strokes.   There is an instant lull, the din and clatter of the
streets cease, the crowd surges, separates, and disappears,
the palace windows and balconies empty themselves, the
street forms are vacant.   The procession in honor of the
Holy Countenance is forming ; every one has rushed off to
the cathedral.

CHAPTER II.

SAN MARTINO, the cathedral of Lucca, stands on one side of a small piazza behind the principal square. At the first glance, its venerable aspect, vast proportions, and dig-nity of outline, do not sufficiently seize upon the imagination; but, as the eye travels over the elaborate façade, formed by successive galleries supported by truncated pillars, these galleries in their turn resting on clustered columns of richest sculpture forming the triple portals—the fine inlaid work, statues, bass-relief, arabesques of fruit, foliage, and quaint animals—the dome, and, above all, the campanile—light and airy as a dream, springing upward on open arches where the sun burns hotly—the eye comes to understand what a glorious Gothic monument it is.

The three portals are now open. From the lofty atrium raised on broad marble steps, with painted ceiling and sculptured walls—at one end a bubbling fountain falling into a marble basin, at the other an arched gate-way leading into grass-grown cloisters—the vast nave is visible from end to end. This nave is absolutely empty. Every thing tells of expectation, of anticipation. The mighty Lombard pillars on either side—supporting a triforium gallery of circular arches and slender pillars of marble fretwork, delicate as lace—are wreathed and twined with red taffetas

bound with golden bands. The gallery of the triforium itself is draped with arras and rich draperies. Each dainty
column is decked·with flags and pennons. The aisles and
transepts blaze with gorgeous hangings. Overhead saints,
prophets, and martyrs, standing immovable in the tinted
glories of the stained windows, fling broad patches of purple, emerald, and yellow, upon the intaglio pavement.

Along the nave (a hedge, as it were, on either side) are
hung curtains of cloth of gold.

The high altar, inclosed by a balustrade of colored marble raised on steps richly carpeted, glitters with gemmed
chalices and crosses. Behind, countless wax-lights illumi-
nate the rich frescoes of the tribune. The Chapel of the
Holy Countenance (midway up the nave), inclosed by a
gilded net-work, is a dazzling mountain of light flung from
a thousand golden sconces. A black figure as large as life
rests upon the altar. It is stretched upon a cross. The
eyes are white and glassy; the thorn-crowned head leans
on one side. The body is enveloped in a damascened robe
spangled with jewels. This robe descends to the feet,
which are cased in shoes of solid gold. The right foot
rests on a sacramental cup glittering with gems. On either
side are angels, with arms extended. One holds a massive
sceptre, the other the silver keys of the city of Lucca.

All waits. The bride, glorious in her garment of needle-work, waits. The bridegroom waits. The sacramental
banquet is spread; the guests are bidden. All waits the
moment when the multitude, already buzzing without at
the western entrance, shall spread themselves over the mosaic floor, and throng each chapel, altar, gallery, and transept—when anthems of praise shall peal from the double
doors of the painted organ, and holy rites give a mystic
language to the sacred symbols around.

Meanwhile the procession flashes from street to street.
Banners flutter in the hot mid-day air, tall crucifixes and

golden crosses reach to the upper stories. In the pauses the low hum of the chanted canticles is caught up here and there along the line—now the monks—then the canons with a nasal twang—then the laity.

There are the judges, twelve in number, robed in black, scarlet, and ermine, their broad crimson sashes sweeping the pavement. The *gonfaloniere*—that ancient title of republican freedom still remaining—walks behind, attired in antique robes. Next appear the municipality—wealthy, oily-faced citizens, at this moment much overcome by the heat. Following these are the Lucchese nobles, walking two-and-two, in a precedence not prescribed by length of pedigree, but of age. Next comes the prefect of the city; at his side the general in command of the garrison of Lucca, escorted by a brilliant staff. Each bears a tall lighted torch.

The law and the army are closely followed by the church. All are there, two-and-two—from the youngest deacon to the oldest canon—in his robe of purple silk edged with gold —wearing a white mitre. The church is generally corpulent; these dignitaries are no exception.

Amid a cloud of incense walks the archbishop—a tall, stately man, in the prime of life—under a canopy of crimson silk resting on gold staves, borne over him by four canons habited in purple. He moves along, a perfect mass of brocade, lace, and gold—literally aflame in the sunshine. His mitred head is bent downward; his eyes are half closed; his lips move. In his hands—which are raised almost level with his face, and reverently covered by his vestments— he bears a gemmed vessel containing the Host, to be laid by-and-by on the altar of the Holy Countenance. All the church-bells are now ringing furiously. Cannons fire, and military bands drown the low hum of the chanting. Every head is uncovered—many, specially women, are prostrate on the stones.

Arrived at the basilica of San Frediano, the procession halts under the Byzantine mosaic on a gold ground, over the entrance. The entire chapter is assembled before the open doors. They kneel before the archbishop carrying the Host. Again there is a halt before the snowy façade of the church of San Michele, pillared to the summit with slender columns of Carrara marble—on the topmost pinnacle a colossal statue of the archangel, in golden bronze, the outstretched wings glistening against the turquoise sky. Here the same ceremonies are repeated as at the church of San Frediano. The archbishop halts, the chanting ceases, the Host is elevated, the assembled priests adore it, kneeling without the portal.

It is one o'clock before the archbishop is enthroned within the cathedral. The chapter, robed in red and purple, are ranged behind him in the tribune at the back of the high altar, the grand old frescoes hovering over them. The secular dignitaries are seated on benches below the altar-steps. *Palchi* (boxes), on either side of the nave, are filled with Lucchese ladies, dark-haired, dark-eyed, olive-skinned, backed by the crimson draperies with which the nave is dressed.

A soft fluttering of fans agitates feathers, lace, and ribbons. Fumes of incense mix with the scent of strong perfumes. Not the smallest attention is paid by the ladies to the mass which is celebrating at the high altar and the altar of the Holy Countenance. Their jeweled hands hold no missal, their knees are unbent, their lips utter no prayer. Instead, there are bright glances from lustrous eyes, and whispered words to favored golden youths (without religion, of course—what has a golden youth to do with religion?) who have insinuated themselves within the ladies' seats, or lean over, gazing at them with upturned faces.

Peal after peal of musical thunder rolls from the double

organs. It is caught up by the two orchestras placed in gilt galleries on either side of the nave. A vocal chorus on this side responds to exquisite voices on that. Now a flute warbles a luscious solo, then a flageolet. A grand barytone bursts forth, followed by a tenor soft as the notes of a nightingale, accompanied by a boy on the violin. Then there is the crash of many hundred voices, with the muffled roar of two organs. It is the *Gloria in Excelsis.* As the music rolls down the pillared nave out into the crowded piazza, where it dies away in harmonious murmurs, an iron cresset, suspended from the vaulted ceiling of the nave, filled with a bundle of flax, is fired. The flax blazes for a moment, then passes away in a shower of glittering sparks that glitter upon the inlaid floor. *Sic transit gloria mundi* is the motto. (Now the lighting of this flax is a special privilege accorded to the Archbishop of Lucca by the pope, and jealously guarded by him.)

CHAPTER III.

MANY carriages wait outside the cathedral, in the shade near the fountain. The fountain—gushing upward joyously in the beaming sunshine out of a red-marble basin—is just beyond the atrium, and visible through the arches on that side. Beyond the fountain, terminating the piazza, there is a high wall. This wall supports a broad marble terrace, with heavy balustrades, extending from the back of a mediæval palace. Over the wall green vine-branches trail, sweeping the pavement, like ringlets that have fallen out of curl. This wall and terrace communicate with the church of San Giovanni, an ancient Lombard basilica on that side. Under the shadow of the heavy roof some girls are trying to waltz to the sacred music from the cathedral. After a few turns they find it difficult, and leave off. The men in livery, waiting along with the carriages, laugh at them lazily. The girls retreat, and group themselves on the steps of a deeply-arched doorway with a bass-relief of the Virgin and angels, leading into the church, and talk in low voices.

A ragged boy from the Garfagnana, with a tray of plaster heads of Victor Emmanuel and Garibaldi, has put down his wares, and is turning wheels upon the pavement, before the servants, for a penny. An old man pulls out from under his cloak a dancing dog, with crimson collar and bells, and collects a little crowd under the atrium of the cathedral. A soldier, touched with compassion, takes a crust from his pocket to reward the dancing dog, which, overcome by the temptation, drops on his four legs, runs to him, and devours it, for which delinquency the old man beats him severely. His yells echo loudly among the pillars, and drown the rich tide of harmony that ebbs and flows through the open portals. The beggars have betaken themselves to their accustomed seats on the marble steps of the cathedral, San Martin of Tours, parting his cloak—carved in alt-relief, over the central entrance—looking down upon them encouragingly. These beggars clink their metal boxes languidly, or sleep, lying flat on the stones. A group of women have jammed themselves into a corner between the cathedral and the hospital adjoining it on that side. They are waiting to see the company pass out. Two of them standing close together are talking eagerly.

"My gracious! who would have thought that old witch, the Guinigi," whispers Carlotta—Carlotta owned a little mercery-shop in a side-street running by the palace, right under the tower—to her gossip Brigitta, an occasional customer for cotton and buttons, "who would have thought that she—gracious! who would have thought she dared to shut up her palace the day of the festival? Did you see?"

"Yes, I did," answers Brigitta.

"Curses on her!" hisses out Carlotta, showing her black teeth. "Listen to me, she will have a great misfortune—mark my words—a great misfortune soon—the stingy old devil!"

Hearing the organ at that instant, Brigitta kneels on the stones, and crosses herself; then rises and looks at Carlotta.

"St. Nicodemus will have his revenge, never fear."

Carlotta is still speaking. Brigitta shakes her head prophetically, again looking at Carlotta, whose deep-sunk eyes are fixed upon her.

"Checco says—Checco is a shoemaker, and he knows the daughter of the man who helps the butler in Casa Guinigi—Checco says she laughs at the Holy Countenance. Domine Dio! what an infamy!" cries Carlotta, in a cracked voice, raising her skinny hands and shaking them in the air. "I hate the Guinigi! I hate her! I spit on her, I curse her!"

There is such venom in Carlotta's looks and in Carlotta's words that Brigitta suddenly takes her eyes off a man with a red waistcoat whom she is ogling, but who by no means reciprocates her attention, and asks Carlotta sharply, "Why she hates the marchesa?"

"Listen," answers Carlotta, holding up her finger. "One day, as I came out of my little shop, *she*"—and Carlotta points with her thumb over her shoulder toward the street of San Simone and the Guinigi Palace—"*she* was driving along the street in her old Noah's Ark of a carriage. Alas! I am old and feeble, and the horses came along quickly. I had no time to get into the little square of San Barnabo, out of the way; the wheel struck me on the shoulder, I fell down. Yes, I fell down on the hard pavement, Brigitta." And Carlotta sways her grizzly head from side to side, and grasps the other's arm so tightly that Brigitta screams. "Brigitta, the marchesa saw me. She saw me lying there, but she never stopped nor turned her head. I lay on the stones, sick and very sore, till a neighbor, Antonio the carpenter, who works in the little square, a good lad, picked me up and carried me home."

As she speaks, Carlotta's eyes glitter like a serpent's. She shakes all over.

"Lord have mercy!" exclaims Brigitta, looking hard at

her; "that was bad!" Carlotta was over eighty; her
face was like tanned leather, her skin loose and shriveled;
a handful of gray hair grew on the top of her head, and
was twisted up with a silver pin. Brigitta was also of a
goodly age, but younger than Carlotta, fat and portly, and
round as a barrel. She was pitted by the small-pox, and
had but one eye; but, being a widow, and well-to-do in the
world, is not without certain pretensions. She wears a
yellow petticoat and a jacket trimmed with black lace. In
her hair, black and frizzly as a negro's, a rose is stuck on
one side.—The hair had been dressed that morning by a
barber, to whom she paid five francs a month for this adorn-
ment.—Some rows of dirty seed-pearl are fastened round
her fat throat; long gold ear-rings bob in her ears, and in
her hand is a bright paper fan, with which she never ceases
fanning herself.

"She's never spent so much as a penny at my shop,"
Carlotta goes on to say. "Not a penny. She'd not spare
a flask of wine to a beggar dying at her door. Stuck-up
old devil! But she's ruined, ruined with lawsuits. Ruined,
I say. Ha! ha! Her time will come."

Finding Carlotta wearisome, Brigitta's one eye has
again wandered off to the man with the red waistcoat.
Carlotta sees this, watching her out of her deep-set, glassy
eyes. Speak Carlotta will, and Brigitta shall listen, she
was determined.

"I could tell you things"—she lowers her voice and
speaks into the other's ear—"things—horrors—about Casa
Guinigi!"

Brigitta starts. "Gracious! You frighten me! What
things?"

"Ah, things that would make your hair stand on end.
It is I who say it," and Carlotta snaps her fingers and
nods.

"*You* know things, Carlotta? You pretend to know

2

what happens in Casa Guinigi? Nonsense! You are mad!"

"Am I?" retorts the other. "We shall see. Who wins boasts. I'm not so mad, anyhow, as the marchesa, who shuts up her palace on the festival, and offends St. Nicodemus and all the saints and martyrs," and Carlotta's eyes flash, and her white eyebrows twitch.

"However"—and again she lays her bony hand heavily on Brigitta's fat arm—"if you don't want to hear what I know about Casa Guinigi, I will not tell you." Carlotta shuts up her mouth and nods defiantly.

This was not at all what Brigitta desired. If there was any thing to be told, she would like to hear it.

"Come, come, Carlotta, don't be angry. You may know much more than I do; you are always in your shop, except on festivals. The door is open, and you can see into the street of San Simone, up and down. But speak low; for there are Lisa and Cassandra close behind, and they will hear. Tell me, Carlotta, what is it?"

Brigitta speaks very coaxingly.

"Yes," replies the old woman, "I can see both the Guinigi palaces from my door—both the palaces. If the marchesa knew—"

"Go on, go on!" says Brigitta, nudging her. She leans forward to listen. "Go on. People are coming out of the cathedral."

Carlotta raises her head and grins, showing the few black teeth left in her mouth. "Are they? Well, answer me. Who lives in the street there—the street of San Simone—as well as the marchesa? Who has a fine palace that the marchesa sold him, a palace on which he has spent—ah! so much, so much? Who keeps open house, and has a French cook, and fine furniture, and new clothes, and horses in his stable, and six carriages? Who?— who?"

As old Carlotta puts these questions she sways her body to and fro, and raises her finger to her nose.

"Who is strong, and square, and fair, and smooth? Who goes in and out with a smile on his face? Who? —who?"

"Why, Nobili, of course—Count Nobili. We all know that," answered Brigitta, impatiently. "That's no news. But what has Nobili to do with the marchesa?"

"What has he to do with the marchesa? Listen, Madama Brigitta. I will tell you. Do you know that, of all gentlemen in Lucca, the marchesa hates Nobili?"

"Well, and what then?"

"She hates him because he is rich and spends his money freely, and because she—the Guinigi—lives in the same street and sees it. It turns sour upon her stomach, like milk in a thunder-storm. She hates him."

"Well, is that all?" interrupts Brigitta.

Carlotta puts up her chin close to Brigitta's face, and clasps her tightly by the shoulder with both her skinny hands. "That is not all. The marchesa has her own niece, who lives with her—a doll of a girl, with a white face— puff! not worth a feather to look at; only a cousin of the marchesa's husband; but, she's the only one left, all the same. They are so thin-blooded, the Guinigi, they have come to an end. The old woman never had a child; she would have starved it."

Carlotta lowers her voice, and speaks into Brigitta's ear. "Nobili loves the niece. The marchesa would have the carbineers out if she knew it."

"Oh!" breaks from Brigitta, under her breath. "This is fine! splendid! Are you sure of this, Carlotta? quite sure?"

"As sure as that I like meat, and only get it on Sundays.—Sure?—I have seen it with my own eyes. Checco knows the granddaughter of the man who helps the cook—

Nobili pays like a lord, as he is!—He spends his money, he does!—Nobili writes to the niece, and she answers. Listen. To-day, the marchesa shut up her palace and put a chain on the door. But chains can be unloosed, locks broken. Enrica (that's the niece) at daybreak comes out to the arched gate-way that opens from the street into the Moorish garden at the farther side of the palace—she comes out and talks to Nobili for half an hour, under cover of the ivy that hangs over the wall on that side. Teresa, the maid, was there too, but she stood behind. Nobili wore a long cloak that covered him all over; Enrica had a thick veil fastened round her head and face. They didn't see me, but I watched them from behind Pietro's house, at the corner of the street opposite. First of all, Enrica puts her head out of the gate-way. Teresa puts hers out next. Then Enrica waves her hand toward the palace opposite, a side-door opens piano piano, Nobili appears, and watches all round to see that no one is near—ha! ha! his young eyes didn't spy out my old ones though, for all that—Nobili appears, I say, then he puts his hand to his heart, and gives such a look across the street!—Ahi! it makes my old blood boil to see it. I was pretty once, and liked such looks.—You may think my eyes are dim, but I can see as far as another."

And the old hag chuckles spitefully, and winks at Brigitta, enjoying her surprise.

" Madre di Dio ! " exclaims this one. " There will be fine work."

" Yes, truly, very fine work. The marchesa shall know it ; all Lucca shall know it too—mark my words, all Lucca ! Curses on the Guinigi root and branch ! I will humble them ! Curses on them ! " mumbles Carlotta.

" And what did Nobili do ? " asks Brigitta.

" Do ?—Why, seeing no one, he came across and kissed Enrica's hand ; I saw it. He made as if he would have knelt upon the stones, only she would not let him. Then they whispered for, as near as I can guess, half an hour—Teresa standing apart. There was the sound of a cart then coming along the street, and presto!—Enrica was within the garden in an instant, the gate was closed, and Nobili disappeared."

Any further talk is now cut short by the approach of Cassandra, a friend of Brigitta's. Cassandra is a servant in a neighboring eating-house, a tall, large-boned woman, a colored handkerchief tied over her head, and much tawdry jewelry about her hands and neck.

"What are you two chattering about?" asks Cassandra sharply. "It seems entertaining. What's the news? I get paid for news at my shop. Tell me directly."

"Lotta here was only relating to me all about her grandchild," answers Brigitta, with a whine.—Brigitta was rather in dread of Cassandra, whose temper was fierce, and who, being strong, knocked people down occasionally if they offended her.

"Lotta was telling me, too, that she wants fresh stores for her shop, but all her money is gone to the grandchild in the hospital, who is ill, very ill!" and Brigitta sighs and turns up the whites of her eyes.

"Yes, yes," joins in Carlotta, a dismal look upon her shriveled old face. "Yes—it is just that. All the money gone to the grandchild, the son of my Beppo—that's the soldier who is with the king's army.—Alas! all gone; my money, my son, and all."

Here Carlotta affects to groan and wring her hands despairingly.

The mass was now nearly over; many people were already leaving the cathedral; but the swell of the organs and the sweet tones of voices still burst forth from time to time. Festive masses are always long. It might not seem so to the pretty ladies in the boxes, still perseveringly fan-

ning themselves, nor to the golden youths who were divert-
ing them; but the prospect of dinner and a siesta was a
temptation stronger than the older portion of the congregation could resist. By twos and threes they slipped out.

This is the moment for the three women to use their
eyes and their tongues—very softly indeed—for they were
now elbowed by some of the best people in Lucca—but to
use them.

"There's Baldassare, the chemist's son," whispers Brigitta, who was using her one eye diligently.

"Mercy! That new coat was never cut in Lucca. They
need sell many drugs at papa-chemists' to pay for Baldassare's clothes. Why, he's combed and scented like a spice-
tree. He's a good-looking fellow; the great ladies like
him." This was said with a knock-me-down air by Cassandra. "He dines at our place every day. It's a pleasure to
see his black curls and smell his scented handkerchief."

A cluster of listeners had now gathered round Cassandra, who, conscious of an audience, thought it worth her
while to hold forth. Shaking out the folds of her gown,
she leaned her back against the wall, and pointed with a
finger on which were some trumpery rings. Cassandra
knew everybody, and was determined to make those about
her aware of it. "That's young Count Orsetti and his mamma; they give a grand ball to-night." (Cassandra is standing on tiptoe now, the better to observe those who pass.)
"There she goes to her carriage. Ahi! how grand! ' The
coachman and the valet with gold-lace and silk stockings.
I would fast for a week to ride once in such a carriage.
Oh! I would give any thing to splash the mud in people's
faces. She's a fine woman—the Orsetti. Observe her
light hair. Madonna mia! What a train of silk! Twelve
shillings a yard—not a penny less. She's got a cavaliere
still.—He! he! a cavaliere!"

Carlotta grins, and winks her wicked old eyes.

"She wants to marry her son to Teresa Ottolini. He's a poor silly little fellow; but rich—very rich."

"Who's that fat man in a brown coat?" asks Brigitta. "He's like a maggot in a fresh nut!"

"That's my master—a fine-made man," answers Cassandra, frowning and pinching in her lips, with an affronted air. "Take care what you say about my master, Brigitta; I shall allow no observations."

Brigitta turns aside, puts her tongue in her cheek, and glances maliciously at Carlotta, who nods.

"How do you know how your master is made, Cassandra mia?" asks Brigitta, looking round, with a short laugh.

"Because I have eyes in my head," replies Cassandra, defiantly. "My master, the padrone of the Pelican Hotel, is not a man one sees every day in the week!"

A tall priest now appears from within the church, coming down the nave, in company with a rosy-faced old gentleman, who, although using a stick, walks briskly and firmly. He has a calm and pleasant face, and his hair, which lies in neat little curls upon his forehead, is as white as snow. One moment the rosy old gentleman talks eagerly with the priest; the next he sinks upon his knees on the pavement, and murmurs prayers at a side altar. He does this so abruptly that the tall priest stumbles over him. There are many apologies, and many bows. Then the old gentleman rises, dusts his clothes carefully with a white handkerchief, and walks on, talking eagerly as before. Both he and the priest bend low to the high altar, dip their fingers in the holy-water, cross themselves, bend again to the altar, turning right and left—before leaving the cathedral.

"That's Fra Pacifico," cries Carlotta, greatly excited— "Fra Pacifico, the Marchesa Guinigi's chaplain. He's come down from Corellia for the festival."—Carlotta is proud to show that she knows somebody, as well as Cassandra.—

" When he is in Lucca, Fra Pacifico passes my shop every morning to say mass in the marchesa's private chapel. He knows all her sins."

" And the old gentleman with him," puts in Cassandra, twitching her hook nose, " is old Trenta—Cesare Trenta, the cavaliere. Bless his dear old face! The duke loved him well. He was chamberlain at the palace. He's a gentleman all over, is Cavaliere Trenta. There—there. Look!" —and she points eagerly—" that's the Red count, Count Marescotti, the republican."

Cassandra lowers her voice, afraid to be overheard, and fixes her eyes on a man whose every feature and gesture proclaimed him an aristocrat.

Excited by the grandeur of the service, Marescotti's usually pale face is suffused with color; his large black eyes shine with inner lights. Looking neither to the right nor to the left, he walks through the atrium, straight down the marble steps, into the piazza. As he passes the three women they draw back against the wall. There is a dignity about Marescotti that involuntarily awes them.

" That's the man for the people!"—Cassandra still speaks under her breath.—" He'll give us a republic yet."

Following close on Count Marescotti comes Count Nobili. There are ease and conscious strength and freedom in his every movement. He pauses for a moment on the uppermost step under the central arch of the atrium and gazes round. The sun strikes upon his fresh-complexioned face and lights up his fair hair and restless eyes.—It is clear to see no care has yet troubled that curly head of his.—Nobili is closely followed by a lady of mature age, dark, thin, and sharp-featured. She has a glass in her eye, with which she peers at every thing and everybody. This is the Marchesa Boccarini. She is followed by her three daughters; two of them of no special attraction, but the youngest, Nera, dark and strikingly handsome. These three young ladies, all matrimonially inclined, but Nera specially, had carefully watched the instant when Nobili left his seat. Then they had followed him closely. It was intended that he should escort them home. Nera has already decided what she will say to him touching the Orsetti ball that evening and the cotillon, which she means to dance with him if she can. But Nobili, with whom they come up under the portico, merely responds to their salutation with a low bow, raises his hat, and stands aside to make way for them. He does not even offer to hand them to their carriage. They pass, and are gone.

As Count Nobili descends the three steps into the piazza, he is conscious that all eyes are fixed upon him ; that every head is uncovered. He pauses, casts his eyes round at the upturned faces, raises his hat.and smiles, then puts his hand into his pocket, and takes out a gold-piece, which he gives to the nearest beggar. The beggar, seizing the gold-piece, blesses him, and hopes that " Heaven will render to him according to his merits." Other beggars, from every corner, are about to rush upon him ; but Nobili deftly escapes from these as he had escaped from the Marchesa Boccarini and her daughters, and is gone.

" A lucky face," mumbles old Carlotta, working her under lip, as she fixes her bleared eyes on him—" a lucky face ! He will choose the winning number in the lottery, and the evil eye will never harm him."

The music had now ceased. The mass was over. The vast congregation poured through the triple doors into the piazza, and mingled with the outer crowd. For a while both waved to and fro, like billows on a rolling sea, then settled down into one compact current, which, flowing onward, divided and dispersed itself through the openings into the various streets abutting on the piazza.

Last of all, Carlotta, Brigitta, and Cassandra, leave their corner. They are speedily engulfed in the shadows of a neighboring alley, and are seen no more.

CHAPTER IV.

THE stern and repulsive aspect of the exterior of the Marchesa Guinigi's palace belied the antique magnificence within.

Turning to the right under an archway from the damp, moss-grown court over which the tower throws a perpetual shadow, a broad staircase, closed by a door of open iron-work, leads to the first story (the *piano nobile*). Here an anteroom, with Etruscan urns and fragments of mediæval sculpture let into the walls, gives access to a great *sala*, or hall, where Paolo Guinigi entertained the citizens and magnates of Lucca with sumptuous hospitality.

The vaulted ceiling, divided into compartments by heavy panels, is profusely gilt, and painted in fresco by Venetian masters; but the gold is dulled by age, and the frescoes are but dingy patches of what once was color. The walls, ornamented with Flemish tapestry, represent the Seven Labors of Hercules—the bright colors all faded out and blurred like the frescoes. Above, on the surface of polished walnut-wood, between the tapestry and the ceiling, are hung suits of mail, helmets, shields, swords, lances, and tattered banners.

Every separate piece has its history. Each lance, in the hand of some mediæval hero of the name, has trans-

fixed a foe, every sword has been dyed in the life-blood of
a Ghibelline.

At the four corners of the hall are four doorways corresponding to each other. Before each doorway hang
curtains of Genoa velvet, embroidered in gold with the
Guinigi arms surmounted by a princely coronet. Time
has mellowed these once crimson curtains to dingy red.
From the hall, entered by these four doors, open out endless suites of rooms, enriched with the spoils of war and
the splendor of feudal times. Not a chair, not a table, has
been renewed, or even shifted from its place, since the fourteenth century, when Paolo Guinigi reigned absolute in
Lucca.

On first entering, it is difficult to distinguish any thing
in the half-light. The narrow Gothic casements of the
whole floor are closed, both those toward the street and
those facing inward upon the inner court. The outer wood-
en shutters are also closely fastened. The marchesa would
consider it a sacrilege to allow light or even outer air to
penetrate in these rooms, sacred to the memory of her
great ancestors.

First in order after the great hall is a long gallery
paneled with dark marble. It has a painted ceiling, and a
mosaic floor. Statues and antique busts, presented by the
emperor to Paolo Guinigi, are ranged on either side. This
gallery leads through various antechambers to the retiring-
room, where, in feudal times, the consort of the reigning
lord presided when the noble dames of Lucca visited her
on state occasions—a victory gained over the Pisans or
Florentines—the conquest of a rebellious city, Pistoia perhaps—the birth of a son; or—the anniversary of national
festivals. Pale-blue satin stuffs and delicate brocades,
crossed with what was once glittering threads of gold,
cover the walls. Rows of Venetian-glass chandeliers,
tinted in every shade of loveliest color, fashioned into col-

ored knots, pendants, and flowers, hang from the painted
rafters. Mirrors, set in ponderous frames of old Florentine
gilding, dimly reflect every object; narrow, high-backed
chairs and carved wooden benches, sculptured mosaic tables
and ponderous sideboards covered with choice pottery from
Gubbio and Savona, and Lucca della Robbia ware. Sunk
in recesses there are dark cupboards filled with mediæval
salvers, goblets, and flagons, gold dishes, and plates, and vessels of filigree and silver. Ivory carvings hang on the walls
beside dingy pictures, or are ranged on tables of Sicilian
agate and Oriental jasper. Against the walls are also placed
cabinets and caskets of carved walnut-wood and ebony
inlaid with lapis-lazuli, jasper, and precious stones; also
long, narrow coffers, richly carved, within which the *corredo*,
or *trousseau*, of rich brides who had matched with a Guinigi,
was laid.

Beyond the retiring-room is the presence-chamber. On
a dais, raised on three broad steps, stands a chair of state,
surmounted by a dark-velvet canopy. Above appear the
Guinigi arms, worked in gold and black, tarnished now, as
is the glory of the illustrious house they represent. Overhead are suspended two cardinals' hats, dropping to pieces
with moth and mildew. On the wall opposite the dais, between two ranges of narrow Venetian windows, looking
into the court-yard, hangs the historic portrait of Castruccio
Castracani degli Antimelli, the Napoleon of the middle
ages, whose rapid conquests raised Lucca to a sovereign
state.

The name of the great Castruccio (whose mother was a
Guinigi) is the glory of the house, his portrait more precious than any other possession.

A gleam of ruddy light strikes through a crevice in a
red curtain opposite; it falls full upon the chair of state.
That chair is not empty; a tall, dark figure is seated there.
It is the Marchesa Guinigi. She is so thin and pale and

motionless, she might pass for a ghost herself, haunting the ghosts of her ancestors!

It is her custom twice a year, on the anniversary of the birth and death of Castruccio Castracani—to-day is the anniversary of his death—to unlock the door leading from the hall into these state-apartments, and to remain here alone for many hours. The key is always about her person, attached to her girdle. No other foot but her own is ever permitted to tread these floors.

She sits in the half-light, lost in thought as in a dream. Her head is raised, her arms are extended over the sides of the antique chair; her long, white hands hang down listlessly. Her eyes wander vaguely along the floor; gradually they raise themselves to the portrait of her great ancestor opposite. How well she knows every line and feature of that stern but heroic countenance, every dark curl upon that classic head, wreathed with ivy-leaves; that full, expressive eye, aquiline nose, open nostril, and chiseled lip; every fold in that ermine-bordered mantle—a present from the emperor, after the victory of Altopasso, and the triumph of the Ghibellines! Looking into the calmness of that impressive face, in the mystery of the darkened presence-chamber, she can forget that the greatness of her house is fallen, the broad lands sold or mortgaged, the treasures granted by the state lavished, one even of the ancestral palaces sold; nay, worse, not only sold, but desecrated by commerce in the person of Count Nobili.

Seated there, on the seigneurial chair, under the regal canopy, she can forget all this. For a few short hours she can live again in the splendor of the past—the past, when a Guinigi was the equal of kings, his word more absolute than law, his frown more terrible than death!

Before the marchesa is a square table of dark marble, on which in old time was laid the sword of state (a special insignia of office), borne before the Lord of Lucca in public processions, embassies, and tournaments. This table is now covered with small piled-up heaps of gold and silver coin (the gold much less in quantity than the silver). There are a few jewels, and some diamond pendants in antique settings, a diamond necklace, crosses, medals, and orders, and a few uncut gems and antique intaglios.

The marchesa takes up each object and examines it. She counts the gold-pieces, putting them back again one by one in rows, by tens and twenties. She handles the crisp bank-notes. She does this over and over again so slowly and so carefully, it would seem, as if she expected the money to grow under her fingers. She has placed all in order before her—the jewels on one side, the money and the notes on the other. As she moves them to and fro on the smooth marble with the points of her long fingers, she shakes her head and sighs. Then she touches a secret spring, and a drawer opens from under the table. Into this drawer she deposits all that lies before her, her fingers still clinging to the gold.

After a while she rises, and casting a parting glance at the portrait of Castruccio—among all her ancestors Castruccio was the object of her special reverence—she moves leisurely onward through the various apartments lying beyond the presence-chamber.

The doors, draped with heavy tapestry curtains, are all open. It is a long, gloomy suite of rooms, where the sun never shines, looking into the inner court.

The marchesa's steps are noiseless, her countenance grave and pale. Here and there she pauses to gaze into the face of a picture, or to brush off the dust from some object specially dear to her. She pauses, minutely observing every thing around her.

There is a dark closet, with a carved wooden cornice and open raftered roof, the walls covered with stamped leather. Here the family councils assembled. Next comes a long, narrow, low-roofed gallery, where row after row of portraits and pictures illustrate the defunct Guinigi. In that centre panel hangs Francesco dei Guinigi, who, for courtesy and riches, surpassed all others in Lucca. (Francesco was the first to note the valor of his young cousin Castruccio, to whom he taught the art of war.) Near him hangs the portrait of Ridolfo, who triumphantly defeated Uguccione della Faggiola, the tyrant of Pisa, under the very walls of that city. Farther on, at the top of the room, is the likeness of the great Paolo himself—a dark, olive-skinned man, with a hard-lipped mouth, and resolute eyes, clad in a complete suit of gold-embossed armor. By Paolo's side appears Battista, who followed the Crusades, and entered Jerusalem with Godfrey de Bouillon; also Gianni, grand-master of the Knights Hospitallers of St. John—the golden rose presented to him by the pope in the corner of the picture.

After the gallery come the armory and the chapel. Beyond at the end of the vaulted passage, lighted from above, there is a closed door of dark walnut-wood.

When the marchesa enters this vaulted passage, her firm, quick step falters. As she approaches the door, she is visibly agitated. Her hand trembles as she places it on the heavy outside lock. The lock yields; the door opens with a creak. She draws aside a heavy curtain, then stands motionless.

There is such a mist of dust, such a blackness of shadow, that at first nothing is visible. Gradually, as the daylight faintly penetrates by the open door, the shadows form themselves into definite shapes.

Within a deep alcove, inclosed by a balustrade, stands a bed—its gilt cornice reaching to the ceiling, heavily curtained. This is the nuptial-chamber of the Guinigi. Within that alcove, and in that bed, generation after generation have seen the light. Not to be born in the nuptial-chamber, and in that bed within the ancestral palace, is not to be a true Guinigi.

The marchesa has taken a step or two forward into the room. There, wrapped in the shadows, she stands still and trembles. A terrible look has come into her face—sorrow, and longing, and remorse. The history of her whole life rises up before her.

"Is the end, then, come?" she asks herself—"and with me?"

From pale she had turned ashy. The long shadows from the dark curtains stretch out and engulf her. She feels their dark touch, like a visible presence of evil, she shivers all over. The cold damp air of the chill room comes to her like wafts of deadly poison. She cannot breathe; a convulsive tremor passes over her.

She totters to the door, and leans for support against the side. Yet she will not go; she forces herself to remain. To stand here, in this room, before that bed, is her penance. To stand here like a criminal! Ah, God! is she not childless? Why has she (and her hands are clinched, and her breath comes thick), why has she been stricken with barrenness?

"Why, why?" she asks herself now, as she has asked herself year after year, each year with a fresh agony. Until she came, a son had never failed under that roof. Why was she condemned to be alone? She had done nothing to deserve it. Had she not been a blameless wife? Why, why was she so punished? Her haughty spirit stirs within her.

"God is unjust," she mutters, half aloud. "God is my enemy."

As the impious words fall from her lips they ring round the dark bed, and die away among the black draperies. The echo of her own voice fills her with dread. She rushes out. The door closes heavily after her.

Once removed from that fatal chamber, with its death-like shadows, she gradually collects herself. She has so long fortified herself against all sign of outward emotion, she has so hardened herself in an inner life of secret remorse, this is easy—at least to outward appearance. The calm, frigid look natural to her face returns. Her eyes have again their dark sparkle. Not a trace remains to tell what her self-imposed penance has cost her.

Again she is the proud marchesa, the mistress of the feudal palace and all its glorious memories.—Yes; and she casts her eyes round where she stands, back again in the retiring-room. Yes—all is yet her own. True, she is impoverished—worse, she is laden with debt, harassed by creditors. The lands that are left are heavily mortgaged; the money received from Count Nobili, as the price of the palace, already spent in law. The hoard she has just counted—her savings—destined to dower her niece Enrica, in whose marriage lies the sole remaining hope of the preservation of the name (and that depending on the will of a husband, who may, or may not, add the name of Guinigi to his own) is most slender. She has been able to add nothing to it during these last years—not a farthing. But there is one consolation. While she lives, all is safe from spoliation. While she lives, no creditor lives bold enough to pass that threshold. While she lives—and then?

Further she forbids her thoughts to wander. She will not admit, even to herself, that there is danger—that even, during her own life, she may be forced to sell what is dearer to her than life—the palace and the heirlooms!

Meanwhile the consciousness of wealth is pleasant to her. She opens the cupboards in the wall, and handles the precious vessels of Venetian glass, the silver plates and golden flagons, the jeweled cups; she examines the ancient bronzes and ivory carvings; unlocks the caskets and the inlaid cabinets, and turns over the gold guipure lace, the rich mediæval embroideries, the christening-robes—these she flings quickly by—and the silver ornaments. She uncloses the carved coffers, and passes through her long fingers the wedding garments of brides turned to dust centuries ago—the silver veils, bridal crowns, and quaintly-cut robes of taffetas and brocade, once white, now turned to dingy yellow. She assures herself that all is in its place.

As she moves to and fro she catches sight of herself reflected in one of the many mirrors encased in what were once gorgeous frames hanging on the wall. She stops and fixes her keen black eyes upon her own worn face. "I am not old," she says aloud, "only fifty-five this year. I may live many years yet. Much may happen before I die! Cesare Trenta says I am ruined"—as she speaks, she turns her face toward the streaks of light that penetrate the shutters.—"Not yet, not ruined yet. Who knows? I may live to redeem all. Cesare said I was ruined after that last suit with the chapter. He is a fool! The money was well spent. I would do it again. While I live the name of Guinigi shall be honored." She pauses, as if listening to the sound of her own voice. Then her thoughts glance off to the future. "Who knows? Enrica shall marry; that may set all right. She shall have all—all!" And she turns and gazes earnestly through the open doors of the stately rooms on either hand. "Enrica shall marry; marry as I please. She must have no will in the matter."

She stops suddenly, remembering certain indications of quiet self-well which she thinks she has already detected in her niece.

"If not"—(the mere supposition that her plans should be thwarted—thwarted by her niece, Enrica—a child, a tool—brought up almost upon her charity—rouses in her a tempest of passion; her face darkens, her eyes flash; she clinches her fist with sudden vehemence, she shakes it in the air)—"if not—let her die!" Her shrill voice wakes the echoes. "Let her die!" resounds faintly through the gilded rooms.

At this moment the cathedral-clock strikes four. This is the first sound that has reached the marchesa from the outer world since she has entered these rooms. It rouses her from the thralldom of her thoughts. It recalls her to the outer world. Four o'clock! Then she has been shut up for five hours! She must go at once, or she may be missed by her household. If she is missed, she may be followed—watched. Casting a searching look round, to assure herself that all is in its place, she takes from her girdle the key she always wears, and lets herself out into the great hall. She relocks the door, drawing the velvet curtains carefully over it. With greater caution she unfastens the other door (the entrance) on the staircase. Peeping through the curtains, she assures herself that no one is on the stairs. Then she softly recloses it, and rapidly ascends the stairs to the second story.

That day six months, on the anniversary of Castruccio's birth, which falls in the month of March, she will return again to the state-rooms. No one has ever accompanied her on these strange vigils. Only her friend, the Cavaliere Trenta, knows that she goes there. Even to him she rarely alludes to it. It is her own secret. Her inner life is with the past. Her thoughts rest with the dead. It is the living who are but shadows.

CHAPTER V.

THE marchesa was in a very bad humor. Not only did she stay at home all the day of the festival of the Holy Countenance by reason of the solemn anniversary which occurred at that time, but she shut herself up the following day also. When the old servant (old inside and out) in his shabby livery, who acted as butler, crept into her room, and asked at what time "the eccellenza would take her airing on the ramparts "—the usual drive of the Lucchese ladies—when they not only drive, but draw up under the plane-trees, gossip, and eat sweetmeats and ices—she had answered, in a tone she would have used to a decrepit dog who troubled her, "Shut the door and begone! "

She had been snappish to Enrica. She had twitted her with wanting to go to the Orsetti ball, although Enrica had never been to any ball or any assembly whatever in her life, and no word had been spoken about it. Enrica never did speak; she had been disciplined into silence.

Enrica, as has been said, was the marchesa's niece, and lived with her. She was the only child of her sister, who died when she was born. This sister (herself, as well as the marchesa, *born* Guinigi Ruscellai) had also married a Guinigi, a distant cousin of the marchesa's husband, belonging to a third branch of the family, settled at Mantua.

Of this collateral branch, all had died out. Antonio Guinigi, of Mantua, Enrica's father, in the prime of life, was killed in a duel, resulting from one of those small social affronts that so frequently do provoke duels in Italy. (I knew a certain T—— who called out a certain G—— because G—— had said T——'s rooms were not properly carpeted.) Generally these encounters with swords are as trifling in their results as in their origin. But the duel in question, fought by Antonio Guinigi, was unfortunately not so. He died on the spot. Enrica, when two years old, was an orphan. Thus it came that she had known no home but the home of her aunt. The marchesa had never shown her any particular kindness. She had ordered her servants to take care of her. That was all. Scarcely ever had she kissed her; never passed her hand among the sunny curls that fell upon the quiet child's face and neck. The marchesa, in fact, had not so much as noticed her childish beauty and enticing ways.

Enrica had grown up accustomed to bear with her aunt's haughty, ungracious manners and capricious temper. She scarcely knew that there was any thing to bear. She had been left to herself as long as she could remember any thing. A peasant—Teresa, her foster-mother—had come with her from Mantua, and from Teresa alone she received such affection as she had ever known. A mere animal affection, however, which lost its value as she grew into womanhood.

Thus it was that Enrica came to accept the marchesa's rough tongue, her arrogance, and her caprices, as a normal state of existence. She never complained. If she suffered, it was in silence. To reason with the marchesa, much more dispute with her, was worse than useless. She was not accustomed to be talked to, certainly not by her niece. It only exasperated her and fixed her more doggedly in whatever purpose she might have in hand. But there was

a certain stern sense of justice about her when left to herself—if only the demon of her family pride were not aroused,
then she was inexorable—that would sometimes come to
the rescue. Yet, under all the tyranny of this neutral life
which circumstances had imposed on her, Enrica, unknown
to herself—for how should she, who knew so little, know
herself?—grew up to have a strong will. She might be
bent, but she would never break. In this she resembled
the marchesa. Gentle, loving, and outwardly submissive,
she was yet passively determined. Even the marchesa
came to be dimly conscious of this, although she considered
it as utterly unimportant, otherwise than to punish and to
repress.

Shut up within the dreary palace at Lucca, or in the
mountain solitude of Corellia, Enrica yearned for freedom.
She was like a young bird, full-fledged and strong, that
longs to leave the parent-nest—to stretch its stout wings
on the warm air—to soar upward into the light!

Now the light had come to Enrica. It came when she
first saw Count Nobili. It shone in her eyes, it dazzled
her, it intoxicated her. On that day a new world opened
before her—a fair and pleasant world, light with the dawn
of love—a world as different as golden summer to the winter of her home. How she gloried in Nobili! How she
loved him!—his comely looks, his kindling smile (like sunshine everywhere), his lordly ways, his triumphant prosperity! He had come to her, she knew not how. She had
never sought him. He had come—come like fate. She
never asked herself if it was wrong or right to love him.
How could she help it? Was he not born to be loved?
Was he not her own—a thousand times her own—as he
told her—"forever?" She believed in him as she believed
in God. She neither knew nor cared whither she was drifting, so that it was with him! She was as one sailing with
a fair wind on an endless sea—a sea full of sunlight—sail-

ing she knew not where! Think no evil of her, I pray you. She was not wicked nor deceitful—only ignorant, with such ignorance as made the angels fall.

As yet Nobili and Enrica had only met in such manner as has been told by old Carlotta to her gossip Brigitta. Letters, glances, sighs, had passed across the street, from palace to palace at the Venetian casements—under the darkly-ivied archway of the Moorish garden—at the cathedral in the gray evening light, or in the earliest glow of summer mornings—and this, so seldom! Every time they had met Nobili implored Enrica, passionately, to escape from the thralldom of her life, implored her to become his wife. With his pleading eyes fixed upon her, he asked her "why she should sacrifice him to the senseless pride of her aunt? He whose whole life was hers?"

But Enrica shrank from compliance, with a secret sense that she had no right to do what he asked; no right to marry without her aunt's consent. Her love was her own to give. She had thought it all out for herself, pacing up and down under the cool marble arcades of the Moorish garden, the splash of the fountain in her ears—Teresa had told her the same—her love was her own to give. What had her aunt done for her, her sister's child, but feed and clothe her? Indeed, as Teresa said, the marchesa had done but little else. Enrica was as unconscious as Teresa of those marriage schemes of her aunt which centred in herself. Had she known what was reserved for her, she would better have understood the marchesa's nature; then she might have acted differently. But heretofore there had been no question of her marriage. Although she was seventeen, she had always been treated as a mere child. She scarcely dared to speak in her aunt's presence, or to address a question to her. Her love, then, she thought, was her own to bestow; but more?—No, no even to Nobili. He urged, he entreated, he reproached her,

but in vain. He implored her to inform the marchesa of
their engagement. (Nobili could not offer to do this himself; the marchesa would have refused to admit him within
her door.) But Enrica would not consent to do even this.
She knew her aunt too well to trust her with her secret.
She knew that she was both subtle, and, where her own
plans were concerned, or her will thwarted, treacherous
also.

Enrica had been taught not only to obey the marchesa
implicitly, but never to dispute her will. Hitherto she had
had no will but hers. How, then, could she all at once
shake off the feeling of awe, almost terror, with which her
aunt inspired her? Besides, was not the very sound of
Nobili's name abhorrent to her? Why the marchesa should
abhor him or his name, Enrica could not tell. It was a
mystery to her altogether beyond her small experience of
life. But it was so. No, she would say nothing; that was
safest. The marchesa, if displeased, was quite capable of
carrying her away from Lucca to Corellia—perhaps leaving
her there alone in the mountains. She might even shut her
up in a convent for life!—Then she should die!

No, she would say nothing.

CHAPTER VI.

THE marchesa was, as I have said, in a very bad humor. She had by no means recovered from what she conceived to be the affront put upon her by the brilliant display made by Count Nobili, at the festival of the Holy Countenance, nor, indeed, from the festival itself.

She had had the satisfaction of shutting up her palace, it is true; but she was not quite sure if this had impressed the public mind of Lucca as she had intended. She felt painful doubts as to whether the splendors opposite had not so entirely engrossed public attention that no eye was left to observe any thing else—at least, in that street. It was possible, she thought, that another year it might be wiser not to shut up her palace at all, but so far to over-come her feelings as to exhibit the superb hangings, the banners, the damask, and cloth of gold, used in the mediæ-val festivals and processions, and thus outdo the modern tinsel of Count Nobili.

Besides the festival, and Count Nobili's audacity, the marchesa had a further cause for ill-humor. No one had come on that evening to play her usual game of whist. Even Trenta had deserted her. She had said to herself that when she—the Marchesa Guinigi — "received," no other company, no other engagement whatever, ought to

3

interfere with the honor that her company conferred. These
were valid causes of ill-humor to any lady of the marchesa's
humor.

She was seated now in the sitting-room of her own particular suite, one of three small and rather stuffy rooms, on
the second floor. These rooms consisted of an anteroom,
covered with a cretonne paper of blue and brown, a carpet-
less floor, a table, and some common, straw chairs placed
against the wall. From the anteroom two doors led into
two bedrooms, one on either side. Another door, opposite
the entrance, opened into the sitting-room.

All the windows this way faced toward the garden, the
wall of which ran parallel to the palace and to the street.
The marchesa's room had flaunting green walls with a red
border; the ceiling was gaudily painted with angels, flowers,
and festoons. Some colored prints hung on the walls—a
portrait of the Empress Eugénie on horseback, in a Spanish
dress, and four glaring views of Vesuvius in full eruption.
A divan, covered with well-worn chintz, ran round two
sides of the room. Between the ranges of the graceful
casements stood a marble console-table, with a mirror in a
black frame. An open card-table was placed near the marchesa. On the table there was a pack of not over-clean
cards, some markers, and a pair of candles (the candles
still unlighted, for the days are long, and it is only six
o'clock). There was not a single ornament in the whole
room, nor any object whatever on which the eye could rest
with pleasure. White-cotton curtains concealed the delicate tracery and the interlacing columns of the Venetian
windows. Beneath lay the Moorish garden, entered from
the street by an arched gate-way, over which long trails of
ivy hung. Beautiful in itself, the Moorish garden was an
incongruous appendage to a Gothic palace. One of the
Guinigi, commanding for the Emperor Charles V., in Spain,
saw Granada and the Alhambra. On his return to Lucca,

he built this architectural plaisance on a bare plot of ground, used for jousts and tilting. That is its history. There it has been since. It is small—a city garden—belted inside by a pointed arcade of black-and-white marble.

In the centre is a fountain. The glistening waters shoot upward refreshingly in the warm evening air, to fall back on the heads of four marble lions, supporting a marble basin. Fine white gravel covers the ground, broken by statues and vases, and tufts of flowering shrubs growing luxuriantly under the shelter of the arcade—many-colored altheas, flaming pomegranates, graceful pepper-trees with bright, beady seeds, and magnolias, as stalwart as oaks, hanging over the fountain.

The strong perfume of the magnolia-blossoms, still white upon the boughs, is wafted upward to the open window of the marchesa's sitting-room; the sun is low, and the shadows of the pointed arches double themselves upon the ground. Shadows, too, high up the horizon, penetrate into the room, and strike across the variegated scagliola floor, and upon a table in the centre, on which a silver tray is placed, with glasses of lemonade. Round the table are ranged chairs of tarnished gilding, and a small settee with spindle-legs.

In her present phase of life, the squalor of these rooms is congenial to the marchesa. Hitherto reckless of expense, especially in law, she has all at once grown parsimonious to excess. As to the effect this change may produce on others, and whether this mode of life is in keeping with the stately palace she inhabits, the marchesa does not care in the least; it pleases her, that is enough. All her life she has been quite clear on two points—her belief in herself, and her belief in the name she bears.

The marchesa leans back on a high-backed chair and frowns. To frown is so habitual to her that the wrinkles on her forehead and between her eyebrows are prematurely deepened. She has a long, sallow face, a straight nose, keen black eyes, a high forehead, and a thin-lipped mouth. She is upright, and well made; and the folds of her plain black dress hang about her tall figure with a certain dig-nity. Her dark hair, now sprinkled with white, is fully dressed, the bands combed low on her forehead. She wears no ornament, except the golden cross of a *chanoi-nesse.*

As she leans back on her high-backed chair she silently observes her niece, seated near the open window, knitting.

"If she had been my child!" was the marchesa's thought. "Why was I denied a child?" And she sighed.

The rays of the setting sun dance among the ripples of Enrica's blond hair, and light up the dazzling whiteness of her skin. Seen thus in profile, although her features are regular, and her expression full of sweetness, it is rather the promise than the perfection of actual beauty—the rose-bud—by-and-by to expand into the perfect flower.

There was a knock at the door, and a ruddy old face looked in. It is the Cavaliere Trenta, in his official blue coat and gold buttons, nankeen inexpressibles, a broad-brimmed white hat and a gold-headed cane in his hand. Whatever speck of dust might have had the audacity to venture to settle itself upon any part of the cavaliere's official blue coat, must at once have hidden its diminished head after peeping at the cavaliere's beaming countenance, so scrubbed and shiny, the white hair so symmetrically arranged upon his forehead in little curls—his whole ap-pearance so neat and trim.

"Is it permitted to enter?" he asked, smiling blandly at the marchesa, as, leaning upon his stick, he made her a ceremonious bow.

"Yes, Cesarino, yes, you may enter," she replied, stiff-ly. "I cannot very well send you away now—but you deserve it."

"Why, most distinguished lady?" again asked Trenta, submissively, closing the door, and advancing to where she sat. He bent down his head and kissed her hand, then smiled at Enrica. "What have I done?"

"Done? You know you never came last night at all. I missed my game of whist. I do not sleep well without it."

"But, marchesa," pleaded Trenta, in the gentlest voice, "I am desolated, as you can conceive—desolated; but what could I do? Yesterday was the festival of the Holy Countenance, that solemn anniversary that brings prosperity to our dear city!" And the cavaliere cast up his mild blue eyes, and crossed himself upon the breast. "I was most of the day in the cathedral. Such a service! Better music than last year. In the evening I had promised to arrange the cotillon at Countess Orsetti's ball. As chamberlain to his late highness the Duke of Lucca, it is expected of me to organize every thing. One can leave nothing to that animal Baldassare—he has no head, no system; he dances well, but like a machine. The ball was magnificent—a great success," he continued, speaking rapidly, for he saw that a storm was gathering on the marchesa's brow, by the deepening of the wrinkles between her eyes. "A great success. I took a few turns myself with Teresa Ottolini—tra la la la la," and he swayed his head and shoulders to and fro as he hummed a waltz-tune.

"*You!*" exclaimed the marchesa, staring at him with a look of contempt—"*you!*"

"Yes. Why not? I am as young as ever, dear marchesa—eighty, the prime of life!"

"The festival of the Holy Countenance and the cotillon!" cried the marchesa, with great indignation. "Tell me nothing about the Orsetti ball. I won't listen to it. Good Heavens!" she continued, reddening, "I am thirty years younger than you are, but I left off dancing fifteen.

years ago. You ought to be ashamed of yourself, Cesarino!"

Cesarino only. smiled at her benignantly in reply. She
had called him a fool so often! He seated himself beside
her without speaking. He had come prepared to entertain
her with an account of every detail of the ball; but seeing
the temper she was in, he deemed it more prudent to be
silent—to be silent specially about Count Nobili. The
mention of his name would, he knew, put her in a fury, so,
being a prudent man, and a courtier, he entirely dropped
the subject of the ball. Yet Trenta was a privileged person. He never voluntarily contradicted the marchesa, but
when occasion arose he always spoke his mind, fearless of
consequences. As he and the marchesa disagreed on almost every possible subject, disputes often arose between
them; but, thanks to Trenta's pliant temper and perfect
good-breeding, they were always amicably settled.

"Count Marescotti and Baldassare are outside," continued Trenta, looking at her inquiringly, as the marchesa
had not spoken. "They are waiting to know if the illustrious lady receives this evening, and if she will permit
them to join her usual whist-party."

"Marescotti!—where may he come from?—the clouds,
perhaps—or the last balloon?" asked the marchesa, looking up.

"From Rome; he arrived two days ago. He is no longer so erratic. Will you allow him to join us?"

"I shall certainly play my rubber if I am permitted,"
answered the marchesa, drawing herself up.

This was intended as a sarcastic reminder of the disregard shown to her by the cavaliere the evening before;
but the sarcasm was quite thrown away upon Trenta; he
was very simple and straightforward.

"The marchesa has only to command me," was his polite reply. "I wonder Marescotti and Baldassare are not

here already," he added, looking toward the door. "I left them both in the street; they were to follow me up-stairs immediately."

" Ah!" said the marchesa, smiling sarcastically, "Count Marescotti is not to be trusted. He is a genius—he may be back on his way to Rome by this time."

"No, no," answered Trenta, rising and walking toward the door, which he opened and held in his hand, while he kept his eyes fixed on the staircase; "Marescotti is disgusted with Rome—with the Parliament, with the Government—with every thing. He abuses the municipality because a secret republican committee which he headed, in correspondence with Paris, has been discovered by the police and denounced. He had to escape in disguise."

" Well, well, I rejoice to hear it!" broke in the marchesa. "It is a good Government; let him find a better. Why has he come to Lucca? We want no *sans-culottes* here."

"Marescotti declares," continued the cavaliere, "that even now Rome is still in bondage, and sunk in superstition. He calls it superstition. He would like to shut up all the churches. He believes in nothing but poetry and Red republicans. Any kind of Christian belief he calls superstition."

"Marescotti is quite right," said the marchesa, angrily; she was determined to contradict the cavaliere. "You are a bigot, Trenta—an old bigot. You believe every thing a priest tells you. A fine exhibition we had yesterday of what that comes to! The Holy Countenance! Do you think any educated person in Lucca belives in the Holy Countenance? I do not. It is only an excuse for idleness —for idleness, I say. Priests love idleness; they go into the Church because they are too idle to work." She raised her voice, and looked defiantly at Trenta, who stood before her the picture of meek endurance—holding the door-

handle. "I hope I shall live to see all festivals abolished.
Why didn't the Government do it altogether when they
were about it?—no convents, no monks, no holidays, except on Sunday! Make the people work—work for their
bread! We should have fewer taxes, and no beggars."

Trenta's benignant face had gradually assumed as
severe an aspect as it was capable of bearing. He pointed
to Enrica, of whom he had up to this time taken no notice
beyond a friendly smile—the marchesa did not like Enrica
to be noticed—now he pointed to her, and shook his head
deprecatingly. Could he have read Enrica's thoughts, he
need have feared no contamination to her from the marchesa; her thoughts were far away—she had not listened
to a single word.

"Dio Santo!" he exclaimed at last, clasping his hands
together and speaking low, so as not to be overheard by
Enrica—"that I should live to hear a Guinigi talk so!
Do you forget, marchesa, that it was under the banner of
the blessed Holy Countenance (*Vulturum di Lucca*),
miraculously cast on the shores of the Ligurian Sea, that
your great ancestor Castruccio Castracani degli Antimelli
overcame the Florentines at Alto Passo?"

"The banner didn't help him, nor St. Nicodemus either
—I affirm that," answered she, angrily. Her temper was
rising. "I will not be contradicted, cavaliere—don't attempt it. I never allow it. Even my husband never contradicted me—and he was a Guinigi. Is the city to go
mad, eat, drink, and hang out old curtains because the
priests bid them? Did you see Nobili's house?" She
asked this question so eagerly, she suddenly forgot her
anger in the desire she felt to relate her injuries. "A
Guinigi palace dressed out like a booth at a fair!—What
a scandal! This comes of usury and banking. He will be
a deputy soon. Will no one tell him he is a presumptuous
young idiot?" she cried, with a burst of sudden rage, re-

membering the crowds that filled the streets, and the admiration and display excited. Then, turning round and looking Trenta full in the face, she added spitefully, "You may worship painted dolls, and kiss black crucifixes, if you like : I would not give them house-room."

"Mercy !" cried poor Trenta, putting his hands to his ears. "For pity's sake—the palace will fall about your ears ! Remember your niece is present."

And again he pointed to Enrica, whose head was bent down over her work.

"Ha! ha !" was all the reply vouchsafed by the marchesa, followed by a scornful laugh. "I shall say what I please in my own house. Poor Cesarino! You are very ignorant. I pity you !"

But Trenta was not there—he had rushed down-stairs as quickly as his old legs and his stick would carry him, and was out of hearing. At the mention of Nobili's name Enrica looked stealthily from under her long eyelashes, and turned very white. The sharp eyes of her aunt might have detected it had she been less engrossed by her passage of arms with the cavaliere.

"Ha! ha !" she repeated, grimly laughing to herself. "He is gone ! Poor old soul ! But I am going to have my rubber for all that.—Ring the bell, Enrica. He must come back. Trenta takes too much upon himself; he is always interfering."

As Enrica rose to obey her aunt, the sound of feet was heard in the anteroom. The marchesa made a sign to her to reseat herself, which she did in the same place as before, behind the thick cotton curtains of the Venetian casement.

CHAPTER VII.

COUNT MARESCOTTI, the Red count (the marchesa had said *sans-culotte;* Trenta had spoken of him as an atheist), was, unhappily, something of all this, but he was much more. He was a poet, an orator, and a patriot. Nature had gifted him with qualities for each vocation. He had a rich, melodious voice, with soft inflections; large dark eyes, that kindled with the impress of every emotion; finely-cut features, and a pale, bloodless face, that tells of a passionate nature. His manners were gracious, and he had a commanding presence. He was born to be a leader among men. Not only did he converse with ease and readiness on every conceivable topic—not only did strophe after strophe of musical verse flow from his lips with the facility of an *improvisatore,* but he possessed the supreme art of moving the multitude by an eloquence born of his own impassioned soul. While that suave voice rung in men's ears, it was impossible not to be convinced by his arguments. As a patriot, he worshiped Italy. His fervid imagination reveled in her natural beauties—art, music, history, poetry. He worshiped Italy, and he devoted his whole life to what he conceived to be her good.

Marescotti was no atheist; he was a religious reformer, sincerely and profoundly pious, and conscientious to the point of honor. Indeed, his conscience was so sensitive, that he had been known to confess two and three times on the same day. The cavaliere called him an atheist because he was a believer in Savonarola, and because he positively refused to bind himself to any priestly dogma, or special form of worship whatever. But he had never renounced the creed of his ancestors. The precepts of Savonarola did, indeed, afford him infinite consolation; they were to him a *via media* between Protestant latitude and dogmatic belief.

The republican simplicity, stern morals, and sweeping reforms both in Church and state preached by Savonarola (reforms, indeed, as radical as were consistent with Catholicism), were the objects of his special reverence. Savonarola had died at the stake for practising and for teaching them; Marescotti declared, with characteristic enthusiasm, that he was ready to do likewise. Wrong or right, he believed that, if Savonarola had lived in the nineteenth century, he would have acted as he himself had done. In the same manner, although an avowed republican, he was no *sans-culotte*. His strong sense of personal independence and of freedom, political and religious, caused him to revolt against what he conceived tyranny or coercion of any kind. Even constitutional monarchy was not sufficiently free for him. A king and a court, the royal prerogative of ministers, patent places, pensions, favors, the unacknowledged influence of a reigning house—represented to his mind a modified system of tyranny—therefore of corruption. Constant appeals to the sovereign people, a form of government where the few yielded to the many, and the rich divided their riches voluntarily with the poor—was in theory what he advocated.

Yet with these lofty views, these grand aspirations, with unbounded faith, and unbounded energy and generosity, Marescotti achieved nothing. He wanted the power of concentration, of bringing his energies to bear on any one particular object. His mind was like an old cabinet, crowded with artistic rubbish—gems and rarities, jewels of price and pearls of the purest water, hidden among faded flowers; old letters, locks of hair, daggers, tinsel reliquaries, crosses, and modern grimcracks—all that was incongruous, piled together pell-mell in hopeless confusion.

His countrymen, singularly timid and conventional, and always unwilling to admit new ideas upon any subject unless imperatively forced upon them, did not understand him. They did not appreciate either his originality or the real strength of his character. He differed from them and their mediæval usages—therefore he must be wrong. He was called eccentric by his friends, a lunatic by his enemies. He was neither. But he lived much alone; he had dreamed rather than reflected, and he had planned instead of acting.

"Count Marescotti," said the marchesa, holding out her hand, "I salute you.—Baldassare, you are welcome."

The intonation of her voice, the change in her manner, gave the exact degree of consideration proper to accord to the head of an ancient Roman family, and the dandy son of a Lucca chemist. And, lest it should be thought strange that the Marchesa Guinigi should admit Baldassare at all to her presence, I must explain that Baldassare was a *protégé*, almost a double, of the cavaliere, who insisted upon taking him wherever he went. If you received the cavaliere, you must, perforce, receive Baldassare also. No one could explain why this was so. They were continually quarreling, yet they were always together. Their intimacy had been the subject of many jokes and some gossip; but the character of the cavaliere was immaculate, and Baldassare's mother (now dead) had never lived at Lucca. Trenta, when spoken to on the subject of his partiality, said he was "educating him" to fill his place as master of the ceremo-

nies in Lucchese society. Except when specially bullied
by the cavaliere—who greatly enjoyed tormenting him in
public—Baldassare was inoffensive and useful.

Now he pressed forward to the front.

"Signora Marchesa," he said, eagerly, " allow me to
make my excuses to you."

· The marchesa turned a surprised and distant gaze upon
him ; but Baldassare was not to be discouraged. He had
that tough skin of true vulgarity which is impervious to
any thing but downright hard blows.

" Allow me to make my excuses," he continued. " The
cavaliere here has. been scolding me all the way up-stairs
for not bringing Count Marescotti sooner to you. I could
not."

Marescotti bowed an acquiescence.

" While we were standing in the street, waiting to
know if the noble lady received, an old beggar, known in
Lucca as the Hermit of Pizzorna, come down from the
mountains for the festival, passed by."

" Yes, it was a providence," broke in the count—" a
real hermit, not one of those fat friars, with shaven crowns,
we have in Rome, but a genuine recluse, a man whose life
is one long act of practical piety."

When Marescotti had entered, he seemed only the calm,
high-bred gentleman ; now, as he spoke, his eye sparkled,
and his pale cheeks flushed.

" Yes, I addressed the hermit," he continued, and he
raised his fine head and crossed his hands on his breast as
if he were still before him. " I kissed his bare feet, road-
stained with errands of charity. 'My father,' I said to him,
' bless me '—"

" Not only so," interrupted Baldassare, " but, would
you believe it, madame, the count cast himself down on
the dusty street to receive his blessing ! "

" And why not ? " asked the count, looking at him severely. "It came to me like a voice from heaven. The hermit is a holy man. Would I were like him! I have heard of him for thirty years past. Winter after winter, among those savage mountains, in roaring winds, in sweeping storms, in frost and snow, and water-floods, he has assisted hundreds, who, but for him, must infallibly have perished. What courage! what devotion! It is a poem." Marescotti spoke hurriedly and in a low voice. "Yes, I craved his blessing. I kissed his hands, his feet. I would have kissed the ground on which he stood." As he proceeded, Marescotti grew more and more abstracted. All that he described was passing like a vision before him. "Those venerable hands—yes, I kissed them.

"How much money did you leave in them, count?" asked the marchesa, with a sneer.

"Great is the mercy of God!" ejaculated the count, earnestly, not heeding her. "Sinner as I am, the touch of those hands—that blessing—purified me. I feel it."

"Incredible! Well," cried Baldassare, "the price of that blessing will keep the good man in bread and meat for a year. Let the old beggar go to the devil, count, his own way. He must soon appear there, anyhow. A good-for-nothing old cheat! His blessing, indeed! I can get you a dozen begging friars who will bless you all day for a few farthings."

The count's brow darkened.

"Baldassare," said he, very gravely, "you are young, and, like your age, inconsiderate. I request that, in my presence, you speak with becoming respect of this holy man."

"Per Bacco!" exclaimed the cavaliere, advancing from where he had been standing behind the marchesa's chair, and patting Baldassare patronizingly on the shoulder, "I never heard you talk so much before at one time, Baldassare. Now, you had better have held your tongue, and

listened to Count Marescotti. Leading the cotillon last
night has turned your head. Take my advice, however—
an old man's advice—stick to your dancing. You understand that. Every man has his *forte*—yours is the ballroom."

Baldassare smiled complaisantly at this allusion to the
swiftness of his heels.

"Out of the ballroom," continued Trenta, eying him
with quiet scorn, "I advise caution—great caution. Out
of the ballroom you are capable of any imbecility."

"Cavaliere!" cried Baldassare, turning very red and
looking at him reproachfully.

"You have deserved this reproof, young man," said the
marchesa, harshly. "Learn your place in addressing the
Count Marescotti."

That the son of a shopkeeper should presume to dispute
in her presence with a Roman noble, was a thing so un-
suitable that, even in her own house, she must put it down
authoritatively. She had never liked Baldassare—never
wanted to receive him, now she resolved never to see him
again; but, as she feared that Trenta would continue to
bring him, under pretext of making up her whist-table, she
did not say so.

The medical Adonis was forced to swallow his rage, but
his cheeks tingled. He dared not quarrel either with the
marchesa, Trenta, or the count, by whose joint support
alone he could hope to plant himself firmly in the realms
of Lucchese fashionable life—a life which he felt was his
element. Utterly disconcerted, however, he turned down
his eyes, and stared at his boots, which were highly glazed,
then glanced up at his own face (as faultless and impassive
as a Greek mask) in a mirror opposite, hastily arranged his
hair, and finally collapsed into silence and a corner.

At this moment Count Marescotti became suddenly
aware of Enrica's presence. She was, as I have said, sit-

ting in the same place by the casement, concealed by the
curtain, her head bent down over her knitting. She had
only looked up once when Nobili's name had been mentioned. No one had noticed her. It was not the usage
of Casa Guinigi to notice Enrica. Enrica was not the
marchesa's daughter; therefore, except in marriage, she
was not entitled to enjoy the honors of the house. She
was never permitted to take part in conversation.

Marescotti, who had not seen her since she was fourteen,
now bounded across the room to where she sat, overshad-
owed by the curtain, bowed to her formally, then touched
the tips of her fingers with his lips.

Enrica raised her eyes. And what eyes they were!—
large, melancholy, brooding, of no certain color, changing
as she spoke, as the summer sky changes the color of the
sea. They were more gray than blue, yet they were blue,
with long, dark eyelashes that swept upon her checks. As
she looked up and smiled, there was an expression of the
most perfect innocence in her face. It was like a flower
that opens its bosom frankly to the sun.

Marescotti's artistic nature was deeply stirred. He
gazed at her in silence for some minutes; he was seeking
in his own mind in what type of womanhood he should
place her. Suddenly an idea struck him.—She was the
living image of the young Madonna—the young Madonna
before the visit of the archangel—pale, meditative, pathetic, but with no shadow of the future upon her face. Marescotti was so engrossed by this idea that he remained motionless before her. Each one present observed his emotion,
the marchesa specially; she frowned her disapproval.

Trenta laughed quietly to himself, then stroked his well-
shaved chin.

"Signorina," said the count, at length breaking silence,
"permit me to offer my excuses for not having sooner perceived you. Will you forgive me?"

"Mio Dio!" muttered the marchesa to herself, "he will turn the child's head with his fine phrases."

"I have nothing to forgive, count," answered Enrica simply. She spoke low. Her voice matched the expression of her face; there was a natural tone of plaintiveness in it.

"When I last saw you," continued the count, standing as if spellbound before her, "you were only a child. Now," and his kindling eyes riveted themselves upon her, "you are a woman. Like the magic rose that was the guerdon of the Troubadours, you have passed in an hour from leaf to bud, from bud to fairest flower. You were, of course, at the Orsetti ball last night?" He asked this question, trying to rouse himself. "What ball in Lucca would be complete without you?"

"I was not there," answered Enrica, blushing deeply and glancing timidly at the marchesa, who, with a scowl on her face, was fanning herself violently.

"Not there!" ejaculated Marescotti, with wonder.—"Why, marchesa, is it not barbarous to shut up your beautiful niece? Is it because you deem her too precious to be gazed upon? If so, you are right."

And again his eyes, full of ardent admiration, were bent on Enrica.

Enrica dropped her head to hide her confusion, and resumed her knitting.

It was a golden sunset. The sun was sinking behind the delicate arcades of the Moorish garden, and spreading broad patches of rosy light upon the marble. The shrubs, with their bright flowers, were set against a tawny orange sky. The air was full of light—the last gleams of parting day. The splash of the fountain upon the lions' heads was heard in the silence, the heavy perfume of the magnolia-flowers stole in wafts through the sculptured casements, creeping upward in the soft evening air.

Still, motionless before Enrica, Marescotti was rapidly falling into a poetic rapture. The marchesa broke the awkward silence.

"Enrica is a child," she said, dryly. "She knows nothing about balls. She has never been to one. Pray do not put such ideas into her head, count," she added, looking at him angrily.

"But, marchesa, your niece is no child—she is a lovely woman," insisted the count, his eyes still riveted upon her. The marchesa did not consider it necessary to answer him.

Meanwhile the cavaliere, who had returned to his seat near her, had watched the moment when no one was looking that way, had given her a significant glance, and placed his finger warningly upon his lip.

Not understanding what he meant by this action, the marchesa was at first inclined to resent it as a liberty, and to rebuke him; but she thought better of it, and only glanced at him haughtily.

It was not the first time she had found it to her advantage to accept Trenta's hints. Trenta was a man of the world, and he had his eyes open. What he meant, however, she could not even guess.

Meanwhile the count had drawn a chair beside Enrica.

"Yes, yes, the Orsetti ball," he said, absently, passing his hand through the masses of black curls that rested upon his forehead.

He was following out, in his own mind, the notion of addressing an ode to her in the character of the young Madonna—the uninstructed Madonna—without that look of pensive suffering painters put into her eyes.

The Madonna figured prominently in Marescotti's creed, spite of his belief in the stern precepts of Savonarola—the plastic creed of an artist, made up of heavenly eyes, ravishing forms, melodious sounds, rich color, sweeping rhythms, moonlight, and violent emotions.

"I was not there myself—no, or I should have been aware you had not honored the Countess Orsetti with your presence. But in the morning—that glorious mass in the old cathedral—you were there?"

Enrica answered that she had not left the house all day, at which the count raised his eyebrows in astonishment.

"That mass," he continued, "in celebration of a local miracle (respectable from its antiquity), has haunted me ever since. The gloomy splendor of the venerable cathedral overwhelmed me; the happy faces that met me on every side, the spontaneous rejoicing of the whole population, touched me deeply. I longed to make them free. They deserve freedom; they shall have it!" A dark fire glistened in his eye. "I have been lost in day-dreams ever since; I must give them utterance." And he gazed steadfastly at Enrica.—"I have not left my room, marchesa, ever since"—at last Marescotti left Enrica's side, and approached the marchesa—"until an hour ago, when Baldassare"—and the count bowed to Adonis, still seated sulky in a corner—"came and carried me off in the hope that you would permit me to join your rubber. Had I known—" he added, in a lower voice, bending his head toward Enrica. Then he stopped, suddenly aware that every one was listening to all he said (a fact which he had been far too much absorbed to notice previously), colored, and retreated to the sofa with the spindle-legs.

"Per Bacco!" whispered the cavaliere to the marchesa, sitting near her on the other side; "I am convinced poor Marescotti has never touched a morsel of food since that mass—I am certain of it. He always lives upon a poetical diet, poor devil!—rose-leaves and the beauties of Nature, with a warm dish now and then in the way of a *ragoût* of conspiracy. God help him! he's a greater lunatic than ever." This was spoken aside into the marchesa's ear. "If you have a soul of pity, marchesa, order him a chicken

before we begin playing, or he will faint upon the floor."
The marchesa smiled.

"I don't like impressionable people at all," she responded, in the same tone of voice. "In my opinion, feelings should be concealed, not exhibited." And she sighed,
recalling her own silent vigils on the floor beneath, unknown
to all save the cavaliere.

"But—a thousand pardons!" cried Marescotti, gradually waking up to some social energy, "I have been talking
only of myself! Talking of myself in your presence, ladies!
—What can we do to amuse your niece, marchesa? Lucca
is horribly dull. If she is to go neither to festivals nor to
balls, it will not be possible for her to exist here."

"It will be quite possible," answered the marchesa,
greatly displeased at the turn the conversation was taking.
"Quite possible, if I choose it. Enrica will exist where I
please. You forget she has lived here for seventeen years.
You see she has not died of it. She stays at home by my
order, count."

Enrica cast a pleading look at her aunt, as if to say,
"Can I help all this?" As for Count Marescotti, he was
far too much engrossed with his own thoughts to be aware
that he was treading on delicate ground.

"But, marchesa," he urged, "you can't really keep your
niece any longer shut up like the fairy princess in the tower.
Let me be permitted to act the part of the fairy prince and
liberate her."

Again he had turned, and again his glowing eyes fixed
themselves on Enrica, who had withdrawn as much as possible behind the curtains. Her cheeks were dyed with
blushes. She shrank from the count's too ardent glances,
as though those glances were an involuntary treason to
Nobili.

"Something must be done," muttered the count, medi-
tating.

" Will you trust your niece with Cavaliere Trenta, and permit me to accompany them on some little excursion in the city, to make up for the loss of the cathedral and the ball ? "

The marchesa, who found the count decidedly troublesome, not to say impertinent, had opened her lips to give an unqualified negative, but another glance from Trenta checked her.

" An excellent idea," put in the cavaliere, before she could speak. " With *me*, marchesa—with *me*," he added, looking at her deprecatingly.

Trenta loved Enrica better than any thing in the world, but carefully concealed it, the better to serve her with her aunt.

" As for me, I am ready for any thing." And, to show his agility, he rose, and, with the help of his stick, made a *glissade* on the floor.

Baldassare laughed out loud from the corner. It gratified his wounded vanity to see his elder ridiculous.

Marescotti, greatly alarmed, started forward and offered his arm, in order to lead the cavaliere back to his seat, but Trenta indignantly refused his assistance. The marchesa shook her head.

" Calm yourself," she said, looking at him compassionately. " Calm yourself, Cesarino, I should not like you to have a fit in my house."

" Fit !—chè chè ? " cried Trenta, angrily. " Not while I am in the presence of the young and fair," he added, recovering himself. " It is that which has kept me alive all this time. No, marchesa, I refuse to sit down again. I refuse to sit down, or to take a hand at your rubber, until something is settled."

This was addressed to the marchesa, who had caught him by the tails of his immaculate blue coat and forced him into a seat beside her.

" *Vive la bagatelle!* Where shall we go? You cannot refuse the count," he added, giving the marchesa a
meaning look. " What shall we do? Let us all propose
something. Let me see. I propose to improve Enrica's
mind. She is young—the young have need of improve-
ment. I propose to take her to the church of San Frediano
and to show her the ancient fresco representing the discovery of the Holy Countenance; also the Trenta chapel,
containing the tombs of my family. I will try to explain
to her their names and history.—What do you say to this,
my child?"

And the cavaliere turned to Enrica, who, little accustomed to be noticed at all, much less to occupy the
whole conversation, looked supplicatingly at her aunt.
She would gladly have run out of the room if she had
dared.

" No, no," exclaimed the irrepressible Baldassare, from
the corner. " Never! What a ghastly idea! Tombs
and a mouldy old church! You may find satisfaction,
Signore Trenta, in the contemplation of your tomb, but the
signorina is not eighty, nor am I, nor is the count. I propose that after being shut up so many years the Guinigi
Palace be thrown open, and a ball given on the first floor
in honor of the signorina. There should be a band from
Florence and presents from Paris for the cotillon. What
do you say to *that*, Signora Marchesa?" asked the mis-
guided young man, with unconscious self-satisfaction.

If a mine had sprung under the marchesa's feet, she
could not have been more horrified. What she would have
said to Baldassare is difficult to guess, but fortunately for
him, while she was struggling for words in which she could
suitably express her sense of his presumption, Trenta, seeing what was coming, was beforehand.

" Be silent, Baldassare," he exclaimed, " or, per Dio, I
will never bring you here again."

Before Baldassare could offer his apologies, the count burst in—

"I propose that we shall show the signorina something that will amuse her." He thought for a moment. "Have you ever ascended the old tower of this palace?" he asked.

Enrica shook her head.

"Then I propose the Guinigi Tower—the stairs are rather rickety, but they are not unsafe. I was there the last time I visited Lucca. The view over the Apennines is superb. Will you trust yourself to us, signorina?"

Enrica raised her head and looked at him hesitatingly, glanced at her aunt, then looked at him again. Until the marchesa had spoken she dared not reply. She longed to go. If she ascended the tower, might she not see Nobili? She had not set her eyes on him for a whole week.

Marescotti saw her hesitation, but he misunderstood the cause. He returned her look with an ardent glance. Where was the young Madonna leading him? He did not stop to inquire, but surrendered himself to the enchantment of her presence.

"Is my proposal accepted?" Count Marescotti inquired, anxiously turning toward the marchesa, who sat listening to them with a deeply-offended air.

"And mine too?" put in the cavaliere. "Both can be combined. I should so much like to show Enrica the tombs of the Trenta. We have been a famous family in our time. Do not refuse us, marchesa."

All this was entirely out of the habits of Casa Guinigi. Hitherto Enrica had been kept in absolute subjection. If she were present no one spoke to her, or noticed her. Now all this was to be changed, because Count Marescotti had come up from Rome. Enrica was not only to be gazed at and flattered, but to engross attention.

The marchesa showed evident tokens of serious displeasure. Had Count Marescotti not been present, she would assuredly have expressed this displeasure in very strong language. In all matters connected with her niece, with her household, and with the management of her own affairs, she could not tolerate remark, much less interference. Every kind of interference was offensive to her. She believed in herself, as I have said, blindly: never, up to that time, had that belief been shaken. All this discussion was, to her mind, worse than interference—it was absolute revolution. She inwardly resolved to shut up her house and go into the country, rather than submit to it. She eyed the count, who stood waiting for an answer, as if he were an enemy, and scowled at the excellent Trenta.

Enrica, too, had fixed her eyes upon her beseechingly; Enrica evidently wanted to go. The marchesa had already opened her lips to give an abrupt refusal, when she felt a warning hand laid upon her arm. Again she was shaken in her purpose of refusal. She rose, and approached the card-table.

"I shall take time to consider," she replied to the inquiring eyes awaiting her reply.

The marchesa took up the pack of cards and examined the markers. She was debating with herself what Trenta could possibly mean by his extraordinary conduct, *twice* repeated.

"You had better retire now," she said to Enrica, with an expression of hostility her niece knew too well. "You have listened to quite enough· folly for one night. Men are flatterers."

"Not I! not I!" cried Marescotti. "I never say any thing but what I mean."

And he flew toward the door in order to open it before Enrica could reach it.

"All good angels guard you!" he whispered, with a tender voice, into her ear, as, greatly confused, she passed by him, into the anteroom. "May you find all men as true as I! Per Dio! she is the living image of the young Madonna!" he added, half aloud, gazing after her. "Countenance, manner, air—it is perfect!"

A match was now produced out of Trenta's pocket. The candles were lighted, and the casements closed. The party then sat down to whist.

The marchesa was always specially irritable when at cards. The previous conversation had not improved her temper. Moreover, the count was her partner, and a worse one could hardly be conceived. Twice he did not even take up the cards dealt to him, but sat immovable, staring at the print of the Empress Eugénie in the Spanish dress on the green wall opposite. Called to order peremptorily by the marchesa, he took up his cards, shuffled them, then laid them down again on the table, his eyes wandering off to the chair hitherto occupied by Enrica.

This was intolerable. The marchesa showed him that she thought so. He apologized. He did take up his cards, and for a few deals attended to the game. Again becoming abstracted, he forgot what were trumps, losing thereby several tricks. Finally, he revoked. Both the marchesa and the cavaliere rebuked him very sharply. Again he apologized, tried to collect his thoughts, but still played abominably.

Meanwhile, Trenta and Baldassare kept up a perpetual wrangle. The cavaliere was cool, sardonic, smiling, and provoking—Baldassare hot and flushed with a concentration of rage he dared not express. The cavaliere, thanks to his court education, was an admirable whist-player. His frequent observations to his young friend were excellent as instruction, but were conveyed in somewhat contemptuous language. Baldassare, having been told by the cavaliere that playing a good hand at whist was as necessary to his future social success as dancing, was much chagrined.

4

Poor Baldassare!—his life was a continual conflict—a sacrifice to his love of fine company. It might be doubted if he would not have been infinitely happier in the atmosphere of the paternal establishment, weighing out drugs, in shabby clothes, behind the counter, than he was now, snubbed and affronted, and barely tolerated.

After this the marchesa and Trenta became partners; but matters did not improve. A violent altercation ensued as to who led a certain crucial card, which decided the game. Once seated at the whist-table, the cavaliere was a real autocrat. *There* he did not affect even to submit to the marchesa. Now, provoked beyond endurance, he plainly told her "she never had played a good game, and, what was more, that she never would—she was too impetuous." Upon hearing this the marchesa threw down her cards in a rage, and rose from the table. Trenta rose also. With an imperturbable countenance he offered her his arm, to lead her back to her seat.

The marchesa, extremely irate at what he had said, pushed him rudely to one side and reseated herself.

Baldassare and Marescotti rose also. The count, having continued persistently absent up to the last, was utterly unconscious of the little fracas that had taken place between the marchesa and the cavaliere, and the consequent sudden conclusion of the game. He had seen her rise, and it was a great relief to him. He had been debating in his own mind whether he should adopt the Dante rhyme for his ode to the young Madonna, or make it in strophes. He inclined to the latter treatment as more picturesque, and therefore more suitable to the subject.

"May I," said he, suddenly roused to what was passing about him, and advancing with a gracious smile upon his mobile face, lit up by the pleasant musings of the whist-table—pleasant to him, but assuredly not pleasant to his partner—"may I hope, marchesa, that you will acquiesce in our little plan for to-morrow?"

The marchesa had come by this time to look on the count as a bore, of whom she was anxious to rid herself. She was so anxious, indeed, to rid herself of him that she actually assented.

"My niece, Signore Conte," she said, stiffly, "shall be ready with her gouvernante and the Cavaliere Trenta, at eleven o'clock to-morrow. Now—good-night!"

Marescotti took the hint, bowed, and departed arm-in-arm with Baldassare.

CHAPTER VIII.

WHEN the count and Baldassare had left the room, Cavaliere Trenta made no motion to follow them. On the contrary, he leaned back in the chair on which he was seated, and nursed his leg with the nankeen trouser meditatively. The expression of his face showed that his thoughts were busy with some project he desired to communicate. Until he had done so in his own way, and at his own time, he would continue to sit where he was. It was this imperturbable self-possession and good-humor combined which gave him so much influence over the irascible marchesa. They were as iron to fire, only the iron was never heated.

The marchesa, deeply resenting his remarks upon her whist-playing, tapped her foot impatiently on the floor, fanned herself, and glowered at him out of the darkness which the single pair of candles did not dispel. As he still made no motion to go, she took out her watch, looked at it, and, with an exclamation of surprise, rose. Quite useless. Trenta did not stir.

"Marchesa," he said at last, abruptly, raising his head and looking at her, "do me the favor to sit down. Spare me a few moments before you retire."

"I want to go to bed," she answered, rudely. "It is already past my usual hour."

"Marchesa—one moment. I permitted myself the liberty of an old friend just now—to check your speech to Count Marescotti."

"Yes," said she, drawing up her long throat, and throwing back her head, an action habitual to her when displeased, "you did so. I did not understand it. We have been acquainted quite long enough for you to know I do not like interference."

"Pardon me, noble lady "—(Trenta spoke very meekly —to soothe her now was absolutely necessary)—"pardon me, for the sake of my good intentions."

"And pray what *were* your good intentions, cavaliere ?" she asked, in a mocking tone, reseating herself. Her curiosity was rapidly getting the better of her resentment.

As she asked the question, the cavaliere left off nursing his leg with the nankeen trouser, rose, drew his chair closer to hers, then sat down again. The light from the single pair of candles was very dim, and scarcely extended beyond the card-table. Both their heads were therefore in shadow, but the marchesa's eyes gleamed nevertheless, as she waited for Trenta's explanation.

"Did you observe nothing this evening, my friend ?" he asked—"*nothing ?* " His manner was unusually excited

"No," she answered, thoughtfully. She had been so exclusively occupied·with the slights put upon herself that every thing else had escaped her. "I observed nothing except the impertinence of Count Marescotti, and the audacity—the—"

"Stop, marchesa," interrupted Trenta, holding up his hand. "We will talk of all that another time. If Count Marescotti and Baldassare have offended you, you can decline to receive them. You observed nothing, you say ? I did." He leaned forward, and spoke with emphasis —"Marescotti is in love with Enrica."

The marchesa started violently and raised herself bolt upright.

"The Red count in love with a child like Enrica!"

"Only a child in your eyes, Signora Marchesa," rejoined Trenta, warmly. (He had warmed with his own convictions, his benevolent heart was deeply interested in Enrica. He had known her since she had first come to Casa Guinigi, a baby; from his soul he pitied her.) "In the eyes of the world Enrica is not only a woman, but promises to be a very lovely one. She is seventeen years old, and marriageable. Young ladies of her name and position must have fortunes, or they do not marry well. If they do, it is a chance—quite a chance. Under these circumstances, it would be cruel to deprive her of so suitable an alliance as Count Marescotti. Now, allow me to ask you, seriously, how would this marriage suit you?"

"Not at all," replied the marchesa, curtly. "The count is a republican. I hate republicans. The Guinigi have always been Ghibelline, and loyal. I dislike him, too, personally. I was about to desire you never to bring him here again. Contact with low people has spoiled him. His manners are detestable."

"But, marchesa, che vuole?" Trenta shrugged his shoulders. "He belongs to one of the oldest families in Rome; he is well off, handsome (he reminds me of your ancestor, Castruccio Castracani); a wife might improve him." The marchesa shook her head.

"He like the great Castruccio!—I do not see it."

"Permit me," resumed Trenta, "without entering into details which, as a friend, you have confided to me, I must remind you that your affairs are seriously embarrassed."

The marchesa winced; she guessed what was coming. She knew that she could not deny it.

"You are embarrassed by lawsuits. Unfortunately, all have gone against you."

"I fought for the ancient privileges of the Guinigi!" burst out the marchesa, imperiously. "I would do it again."

"I do not in the least doubt you would do it again, exalted lady," responded Trenta, with a quiet smile. "Indeed, I feel assured of it. I merely state the fact. You have sacrificed large sums of money. You have lost every suit. The costs have been enormous. Your income is greatly reduced. Enrica is therefore portionless."

"No, no, not altogether." The marchesa moved nervously in her chair, carefully avoiding meeting Trenta's steely blue eyes. "I have saved money, Cesarino—I have indeed," she repeated. The marchesa was becoming quite affable. "I cannot touch the heirlooms. But Enrica will have a small portion."

"Well, well," replied Trenta. "But it is impossible you can have saved much since the termination of that last long suit with the chapter about your right to the second bench in the nave of the cathedral, the bench awarded to Count Nobili when he bought the palace. The expense was too great, and the trial too recent."

She made no reply.

"Then there was that other affair with the municipality about the right of flying the flag from the Guinigi Tower. I do not mention small affairs, such as disputes with your late steward at Corellia, trials at Barga, nor litigation here at Lucca on a small scale. My dear marchesa, you have found the law an expensive pastime." The cavaliere's round eyes twinkled as he said this. "Enrica is therefore virtually portionless. The choice lies between a husband who will wed her for herself, or a convent. If I understand your views, a convent would not suit you. Besides, you would not surely voluntarily condemn a girl, without vocation, and brought up beside you, to the seclusion of a convent?"

"But Enrica is a child—I tell you she is too young to think about marriage, cavaliere."

The marchesa spoke with anger. She would stave off as long as possible the principal question—that of marriage. Sudden proposals, too, emanating from others, always nettled her; it narrowed her prerogative.

"Besides," objected the marchesa, still fencing with the real question, "who can answer for Count Marescotti? He is so capricious! Supposing he likes Enrica to-day, he may change before to-morrow. Do you really think he can care enough about Enrica to marry her? Her name would be nothing to him."

"I think he does care for her," replied Trenta, reflectively; "but that can be ascertained. Enrica is a fit consort for a far greater man than Count Marescotti. Not that he, as you say, would care about her name. Remember, she will be your heiress—that is something."

"Yes, yes, my heiress," answered the marchesa, vaguely; for the dreadful question rose up in her mind, "What would Enrica have to inherit?"

That very day she had received a most insolent letter from a creditor. Under the influence of the painful thoughts, she turned her head aside and said nothing. One of her hands was raised over her eyes to shade them from the candles; the other rested on her dark dress.

If a marriage were really in question, what could be more serious? Was not Enrica's marriage to raise up heirs to the Guinigi—heirs to inherit the palace and the heirlooms? If—the marchesa banished the thought, but it would return, and haunt her like a spectre—if not the palace, then at least the name—the historic name, revered throughout Italy? Nothing could deprive Enrica of the name—that name was in itself a dower. That Enrica should possess both name and palace, with a husband of her—the marchesa's—own choosing, had been her dream, but it had been a far-off dream—a dream to be realized in the course of years.

Taken thus aback, the proposal made by Trenta appeared to her hurried and premature—totally wanting in the dignified and well-considered action that should mark the conduct of the great. Besides, if an immediate marriage were arranged between Count Marescotti and Enrica, only a part of her plan could be realized. Enrica was, indeed, now almost portionless; there would be no time to pile up those gold-pieces, or to swell those rustling sheaves of notes that she had—in imagination—accumulated.

"Portionless!" the marchesa repeated to herself, half aloud. "What a humiliation!—my own niece!"

It will be observed that all this time the marchesa had never considered what Enrica's feeling might be. She was to obey her—that was all.

But in this the marchesa was not to blame. She undoubtedly carried her idea of Enrica's subserviency too far; but custom was on her side. Marriages among persons of high rank are "arranged" in Italy—arranged by families or by priests, acting as go-betweens. The lady leaves the convent, and her marriage is arranged. She is unconscious that she has a heart—she only discovers that unruly member afterward. To love a husband is unnecessary; there are so many "golden youths" to choose from. And the husband has his pastime too. Così fan tutti! It is a round game!

All this time the cavaliere had never taken his eyes off his friend. To a certain extent he understood what was passing in her mind. A portionless niece would reveal her poverty.

"A good marriage is a good thing," he suggested, as a safe general remark, after having waited in vain for some response.

"In all I do," the marchesa answered, loftily, "I must

first consider what is due to the dignity of my position."
Trenta bowed.

"Decidedly, marchesa; that is your duty. But what
then?"

"No feeling *whatever* but that will influence me *now*,
or hereafter—nothing." She dwelt upon the last word defiantly, as the final expression of her mind. Spite of this
defiance, there was, however, a certain hesitation in her
manner which did not escape the cavaliere. As she spoke,
she looked hard at him, and touched his arm to arouse his
attention.

Trenta, who knew her so well, perfectly interpreted her
meaning. His ruddy cheeks flushed crimson; his kindly
eyes kindled; he felt sure that his advice would be accepted. She was yielding, but he must be most cautious not
to let his satisfaction appear. So strangely contradictory
was the marchesa that, although nothing could possibly be
more advantageous to her own schemes than this marriage,
she might, if indiscreetly pressed, veer round, and, in spite
of her interest, refuse to listen to another syllable on the
subject.

All this kept the cavaliere silent. Receiving no answer, she looked suspiciously at him, then grasped his arm
tightly.

"And you, cavaliere—how long have you been so deeply interested in Enrica? What is she to you? Her future
can only signify to you as far as it affects myself."

She waited for a reply. What was the cavaliere to
answer? He loved Enrica dearly, but he dared not say so,
lest he should offend the marchesa. He feared that if he
spoke he should assuredly say too much. Well as he knew
her, the marchesa's egotism horrified him.

"Poor Enrica!" he muttered, involuntarily, half aloud.

The marchesa caught at the name.

"Enrica?—yes. From the time of my husband's death

I have sacrificed my life to the duties imposed on me by my position. So must Enrica. No personal feeling for her shall bias me in the least."

Her eyes were fixed on those of Trenta. She paused again, and passed her white hand slowly one over the other. The cavaliere looked down; he durst not meet her glance, lest she should read his thoughts. Thinking of Enrica at that moment, he absolutely hated her!

"What would you advise me to do?" she asked, at last. Her voice fell as she put the question.

Trenta had been waiting for this direct appeal. Now his tongue was unloosed.

"I will tell you, Signora Marchesa, plainly what I would advise you to do," was his answer. "Let Enrica marry Marescotti. Put the whole matter into my hands, if you have sufficient confidence in me."

"Remember, Trenta, the humiliation!"

"What humiliation?" asked the cavaliere, with surprise.

"The humiliation involved in the confession that my niece is almost portionless." The words seemed to choke her. "She will inherit all I have to leave, and she glanced significantly at the cavaliere; "but that is—you understand me?—uncertain."

"Bagatella!—that will be all right," he rejoined, with alacrity. "The idea of money will not sway Marescotti in the least. He is wealthy—a fine fellow. Have no fear of that. Leave it all to me, Enrica, and Marescotti. I am an old courtier. Many a royal marriage has passed through my hands. Per Bacco—though no one but the duke knew it—through my hands! You may trust me, marchesa."

There was a proud consciousness of the past in the old man's face. He showed such perfect confidence in himself that he imparted the same confidence to the marchesa.

"I would trust no one else, Cesarino," she said, rising

from her chair. "But be cautious; bind me to nothing until we meet again. I must hear all that passes between you and the count, then judge for myself."

"I will obey you in all things, noble lady," replied Trenta, submissively.

How he dreaded betraying his secret exultation! To emancipate Enrica from her miserable life by an honorable marriage, was, to his benevolent heart, infinite happiness!

"Good-night, marchesa. May you repose well!"

"Good-night, Cesarino—a rivederci!"

So they parted.

CHAPTER IX.

THE ball at Casa Orsetti was much canvassed in Lucca. Hospitality is by no means a cardinal virtue in Italy. Even in the greatest houses, the bread and salt of the Arab is not offered to you—or, if offered at all, appears in the shape of such dangerously acid lemonade or such weak tea, it is best avoided. Every year there are dances at the Casino dei Nobili, during the Carnival, and there are veglioni, or balls, at the theatre, where ladies go masked and in dominoes, but do not dance; but these annual dissipations are paid for by ticket. A general reception, therefore, including dancing, supper, and champagne, *gratis*, was an event.

The Orsetti Palace, a huge square edifice of reddish-gray stone, with overtopping roof, four tiers of lofty windows, and a broad arched entrance, or portone, with dark-green doors, stands in the street of San Michele. You pass it, going from the railway-station to the city-gate (where the Lucchese lions keep guard), and the road leads onward to the peaked mountains over Spezia.

On the evening of the ball the entire street of San Michele was hung with Chinese lanterns, arranged in festoons. Opposite the entrance shone a gigantic star of gas. The palace itself was a blaze of light. As the night was warm, every window was thrown open; chandeliers—scintillating like jeweled fountains—hung from the ceilings; wax-lights innumerable, in gilded sconces, were grouped upon the walls; crimson-silk curtains cast a ruddy glare across the street, and the sound of harps and violins floated through the night air. The crowd of beggars and idlers, generally gathered in the street, saw so much that they might be considered to "assist," in an independent but festive capacity, at the entertainment from outside. Matches were hawked about for the convenience of the male portion of this extempore assembly, and fruit in baskets was on sale for the women. "Cigars—cigars of quality!"—"Good fruit—ripe fruit!" were cries audible even in the ballroom; and a fine aroma of coarse tobacco mounted rapidly upward to the illuminated windows.

Within the archway groups of servants were ranged in the Orsetti livery. Also a magnificent personage, not to be classed with any of the other domestics, wearing a silver chain with a key passed across his breast. The personage called a major-domo, in the discharge of his duty, divested the ladies of their shawls, and arranged their draperies.

All this was witnessed with much glee by the plebs outside—the men smoking, the women eating and talking. As the guests arrived in rapid succession, the plebs pressed more and more forward, until at last some of the boldest stood within the threshold. The giants in livery not only tolerated this, but might be said to observe them individually with favor—seeing how much of their admiration was bestowed on themselves and their fine clothes. The major-domo also, with amiable condescension, affected not to notice them—no, not even when one tall fellow, a butcher, with eyes as black as sloes, a pipe in his mouth, and a coarse cloak wrapped round him, took off his hat to the Princess Cardeneff, as she passed by him glittering with diamonds, and cried in her face, "Oh! bella, bella!"

When the major-domo had-performed those mysteries
intrusted to him, attendant giants threw open folding
doors at the farther end of the court, and the bright visions
disappeared into a long gallery on the ground-floor, painted
in brilliant frescoes, to the reception-room. The suite of
rooms on the ground-floor are the summer apartments,
specially arranged for air and coolness. Rustic chairs stand
against walls painted with fruit and flowers, the stems and
leaves represented as growing out of the floor, as at Pom-
peii. The whole saloon is like a *parterre*. Settees, sofas,
and cozy Paris chairs covered with rich satins, are placed
under arbors of light-gilt trellis-work, wreathed with exquisite creepers in full flower. Palms, orange and lemon
trees, flowering cacti, and large-leaved cane-plants, are
grouped about; consoles and marble tables, covered with
the loveliest cut flowers.

Near the door, in the first of these floral saloons where
sweet scents made the air heavy, stands the Countess
Orsetti. Although she had certainly passed that great
female climacteric, forty, a stately presence, white skin,
abundant hair, and good features treated artistically, gave
her still a certain claim to matronly beauty. She greets
each guest with compliments and phrases which would
have been deemed excessive out of Italy. Here in Lucca,
where she met most of her guests every day, these compliments and phrases were not only excessive, but wearisome
and out of place. Yet such is the custom of the country,
and to such fulsome flattery do the language and common
usage lend themselves. Countess Orsetti, therefore, is not
responsible for this absurdity.

Her son is beside her. He is short, stout, and smiling,
with a hesitating manner, and a habit of referring every
thing to his magnificent mamma. Away from his mamma,
he is frank, talkative, and amusing. It is to be hoped that
he will marry soon, and escape from the leading-strings.

If he marries Teresa Ottoltni—and it is said such a result
is certain—no palace in Lucca would be big enough to hold
Teresa and the countess-mother at one time.

Group after group enters, bows to the countess, and
passes on among the flowers : the Countess Navascoes
(with her lord), pale, statuesque, dark-eyed, raven-haired—
a type of Italian womanhood ; Marchesa Manzi—born of
the noble house of Buoncampagni—looking as if she had
walked out of a picture by Titian ; the Da Gia, separated
from her husband—a little habit, this, of Italian ladies, consequent upon intimacy with the *jeunesse dorée*, who prefer
the wives of their best friends to all other women—it saves
trouble, and a "golden youth" is essentially idle. This
little habit, moreover, of separation from husbands does not
damage the lady in the least; no one inquires what has
happened, or who is in the wrong. Society receives and
pets her just the same, and, quite impartial, receives and
pets the husband also.—Luisa Bernardini, a glowing little
countess, as plump as an ortolan, dimpling with smiles, an
ugly old husband at her side—comes next. It is whispered,
unless the ugly old husband is blind as well as deaf, they
will be separated, too, very shortly. Young Civilla, a
"golden youth," is so very pressing. He could live with
Luisa at Naples—a cheap place. They might have gone
on for years as a triangular household—but for Civilla's
carelessness. Civilla would always put out old Bernardini
about the dinner. (Civilla dined at Bernardini's house
every day, as he would at a *café.*) Now, old Bernardini
did not care a button that his little wife had a lover ; it
would not have been *en règle* if she had not—nor did he
care that his wife's lover should dine with him every day—
not a bit—but old Bernardini is a gourmand, and he does
care to be kept waiting for his dinner. He has lately confided to a friend, that he should be sorry to cause a scandal,
but that he must separate from his wife if Civilla will not

reform in the matter of the dinner-hour. "He is getting old," Bernardini says, "and his digestion suffers." No man keeps a French cook to be kept waiting for his dinner.

Luisa, who looks the picture of innocence, wears an unexceptionable pink dress, with a train that bodes ill-luck, and many apologies, to her partners. A long train is Luisa's little game. (Spite of Civilla, she has many other little games.) Fragments of the train fly about the room all the evening, and admirers take care that she shall see these picked up, fervently kissed, and stowed away as relics in breast-pockets. One enthusiast pinned his fragment to his shoulder, like an order—a knight of San Luisa, he called himself.

Teresa Ottolini, with her mother, has just arrived. Being single, Teresa either is, or affects to be, excessively steady ; no one would marry her if she were not—not even the good-natured Orsetti. Your Italian husband *in futuro* will pardon nothing in his wife that may be—not even that her dress should be conspicuous, much less her manners. Neither is it expedient that she should be seen much in society. That dangerous phalanx of "golden youth" are ever on the watch, "gentlemen sportsmen," to a man ; their sport, woman. If she goes out much these "golden youth" might compromise her. Less than a breath upon a maiden's name is social death. That name must not be coupled with any man's—not coupled even in lightest parlance. So the lady waits, waits until she has a husband— it is more piquant to be a naughty wife than a fast miss— then she makes her choice—one, or a dozen—it is a matter of taste. Danger is added to vice ; and that element of intrigue dear to the Italian soul, both male and female. The *jeunesse dorée* delight in mild danger—a duel with swords, not pistols, with a foolish husband. Why cannot he grin and bear it ?—others do.

But to return to Teresa. She is courtesying very low

to the Countess Orsetti. Although it is well known that
these ladies hate each other, Countess Orsetti receives Teresa with a special welcome, kisses her on both cheeks,
addresses more compliments to her, and makes her more
courtesies than to any one else. How beautiful she is, the
Ottolini, with those white flowers twisted into the braids
of her chestnut hair!—those large, lazy eyes, too—like
sleeping volcanoes!—Count Orsetti thinks her beautiful,
clearly; for, under the full battery of his mother's glances,
he advances to meet her, blushing like a girl. He presses
Teresa's hand, and whispers in her ear that "she must not
forget her promise about the cotillon. He has lived upon
it ever since." Her reply has apparently satisfied him, for
the honest fellow breaks out all over into smiles and bows
and amorous glances. Then she passes on, the fair Teresa,
like a queen, followed by looks of unmistakable admiration
—much more unmistakable looks of admiration than would
be permitted elsewhere; but we are in Italy, where men
are born artists and have artistic feelings.

The men, as a rule, are neither as distinguished looking
nor as well dressed as the women. The type of the Lucchese nobleman is dark, short, and commonplace—rustic is
the word.

There is the usual crowding in doorways, and appro-
priation of seats whence arrivals can be seen and criti-
cised. But there is no line of melancholy young girls
wanting partners. The gentlemen decidedly predominate,
and all the ladies, except Teresa Ottolini and the Boccarini,
are married.

The Marchesa Boccarini had already arrived, accompanied by her three daughters. They are seated near the
door leading from the first saloon, where Countess Orsetti
is stationed. In front of them is a group of flowering plants
and palm-trees. Madame Boccarini peers through the
leaves, glass in eye. As a general scans the advance of

the enemy's troops from behind an ambush, calculates what their probable movements will be, and how he can foil them —either by open attack or feigned retreat, skirmish or manœuvre—so Madame Boccarini scans the various arrivals between the dark-green foliage.

To her every young and pretty woman is a rival to her daughters; if a rival, an enemy—if an enemy, to be annihilated if possible, or at least disabled, and driven ignominiously from the field.

It is well known that the Boccarini girls are poor. They will have no portions—every one understands that. The Boccarini girls must marry as they can; no priest will interest himself in their espousals. It was this that made Nera so attractive. She was perfectly natural and unconventionally bold—"like an English mees," it was said—with looks of horror. (The Americans have much to answer for; they have emancipated young ladies; all their sins, and our own to boot, we have to answer for abroad.)

The Boccarini were in reality so poor that it was no uncommon thing for them to remain at home because they could not afford to buy new dresses in which to display themselves. (Poor Madame Boccarini felt this far more than the girls did themselves.) To be seen more than thrice in the same dress is impossible. Lucca is so small, every one's clothes are known. There was no throwing dust in the eyes of dear female friends in this particular.

On the present occasion the Boccarini girls had made great efforts to produce a brilliant result. Madame Boccarini had told her daughters that they must expect no fresh dresses for six months at least, so great had been the outlay. Nera, on hearing this, had tossed her stately head, and had inwardly resolved that before six months she would marry—and that, dress or no dress, she would go wherever she had a chance of meeting Count Nobili.

Her mother tacitly concurred in these views, as far as
Count Nobili was concerned, but said nothing.

A Belgravian mother who frankly drills her daughter
and points out, *viva voce*, when to advance and when to
retreat, and to whom the honors of war are to be accorded
—is an article not yet imported into classic Italy with the
current Anglomania.

Beside Nera sat Prince Ruspoli, a young Roman of
great wealth. Ruspoli aspired to lead the fashion, but not
even Poole could well tailor him. (Ruspoli was called
poule mouillée.) Nature had not intended it. His tall,
gaunt figure, long arms, and thin legs, rendered him artistically unavailable. The music has just sounded from a
large saloon at the end of the suite, and Prince Ruspoli has
offered his arm to Nera for the first waltz. If Count Nobili had arrived, she would have refused Ruspoli, even on
the chance of losing the dance; but he had not come. Her
sisters, who are older, and less attractive than herself, had
as yet found no partners; but they were habitually resigned
and amiable, and submitted with perfect meekness to be
obliterated by Nera.

A knot of young men have now formed near the door
of the dancing-saloon. They are eagerly discussing the
cotillon, the final dance of the evening. Count Orsetti
had left his mother's side and joined them.

The cotillon is a matter of grave consideration—the
very gravest. Indeed it was very seldom these young
heads considered any thing so grave. On the success of
the cotillon depends the success of the evening. All the
"presents" had come from Paris. Some of the figures
were new and required consultation.

"I mean to dance with Teresa Ottolini," announced
Count Orsetti, timidly — he could not name Teresa
without reddening. "We arranged it together a month
ago."

" And I am engaged to Countess Navascoes," said Count
Malatesta.

This engagement was said to have begun some years
back, and to be very enthralling. No one objected, least
of all the husband, who worshiped at the shrine of the
blooming Bernardini when she quarreled with Civilla. A
lady of fashion has a choice of lovers, as she has a choice
of dresses—for all emergencies.

" But how about these new figures ? " asked Orsetti.

" Per Bacco—hear the music ! " cried Malatesta. " What
a delicious .waltz ! I want to dance. Let's settle it at
once. Who's to lead ? "

" Oh ! Baldassare; of course," replied Franchi, a sallow,
languid young man, who looked as if he had been raised
in a hot-house, and had lost all his color. "Nobody else
would take the trouble. Who is he to dance with ? "

" Let him see who will have him. I shall not interfere.
He'll dance for both, anyhow," answered Orsetti, laughing.
" No one competes with Adonis."

" Where is he ? "

" Oh ! dancing, of course," returned Orsetti. " Don't
you see him twirling round like a teetotum, with Marchesa
Amici 'of the swan-neck ? ' " And he pointed to a pair
who were waltzing with such precision that they never by
a single step broke the circle—Baldassare gallantly receiving the charge of any free lancers who flung themselves in
their path.

Baldassare is much elated at being permitted to dance
with " the swan-neck," a little faded now, but once a noted
beauty. The swan-neck is a famous lady. Ill-natured
persons might have added an awkward syllable to *famous*.
She had been very dear to a great Russian magnate who
lived in a villa lined with malachite, and loaded her with
gifts. But as the marquis, her husband, was always with
her and invariably spoke of his wife as an angel, where

was the harm? Now the Russian magnate was dead, and
the Marchesa Amici had retired to Lucca, to enjoy the
spoils along with her discreet and complaisant marquis.

"How that young fellow does push himself!" observes
the cynical Franchi. "Dancing with the Amici—such a
great lady! Nothing is sacred to him."

"I wish Nobili were come." It was Orsetti who spoke
now. "I should have liked him to lead instead of Baldassare. Adonis is getting forward. He wants keeping in
order. Will no one else lead? I cannot, in my own house."

"Oh! but you would mortally offend poor Trenta if
you did not let Baldassare lead. The women will keep
him in order," was the immediate reply of a young man
who had not yet spoken. "The cavaliere must marshal
the dancers, and Baldassare must lead, or the old man
would break his heart."

"I wish Nobili were here all the same," replied Orsetti.
"If he does not come soon, we must select his partner for
him. Whom is he to have?"

"Oh! Nera Boccarini, of course," responded two or
three voices, amid a general titter.

"I don't think Nobili cares a straw about Nera," put in
the languid Franchi, drawling out his words. "I have
heard quite another story about Nobili. Give Nera to
Ruspoli. He seems about to take her for life. I wish him
joy!" with a sneer. "Ruspoli likes English manners.
Nera won't get Nobili, my word upon *that*—there are too
many stories about her."

But these remarks at the moment passed unnoticed.
No one asked what Franchi had heard, all being intent
about the cotillon and the choice of partners.

"Well," burst out Orsetti, no longer able to resist the
music (the waltz had been turned into a galop), "I am
sure I don't care if Nobili or Ruspoli likes Nera: I shall
not try to cut them out."

"No, no, not you, Orsetti! We know your taste does not lie in that quarter. Yours is the domestic style, chaste and frigid!" cried Malatesta, with a sardonic smile. There was a laugh. Malatesta was so bad, even according to the code of the "golden youths," that he compromised any lady by his attentions. Orsetti blushed crimson.

"Pardon me," he replied, much confused, "I must go; my partner is looking daggers at me. Call up old Trenta and tell him what he has to do." Orsetti rushes off to the next room, where Teresa Ottolini is waiting for him, with a look of gentle reproach in her sleepy eyes, where lies the hidden fire.

Meanwhile Cavaliere Trenta's white head, immaculate blue coat and gold buttons—to which coat were attached several orders—had been seen hovering about from chair to chair through the rooms. He attached himself specially to elderly ladies, his contemporaries. To these he repeated the identical high-flown compliments he had addressed to them thirty years before, in the court circle of the Duke of Lucca—compliments such as elderly ladies love, though conscious all the time of their absurd inappropriateness.

Like the dried-up rose-bud of one's youth, religiously preserved as a relic, there is a faint flavor of youth and pleasure about them, sweet still, as a remembrance of the past. "Always beautiful, always amiable!" murmured the cavaliere, like a rhyme, a placid smile upon his rosy face.

Summoned to the cabinet council held near the door, Trenta becomes intensely interested. He weighs each detail, he decides every point with the gravity of a judge: how the new figures are to be danced, and with whom Baldassare is to lead—no one else could do it. He himself would marshal the dances.

The double orchestra now play as if they were trying to drown each other. Half a dozen rooms are full of dancers. The matrons, and older men, have subsided into whist up-stairs. All the ladies have found partners; there is not a single wall-flower.

Nothing could exceed the stately propriety of the ball. It was a grand and stately gathering. Nobody but Nera Boccarini was natural. "To save appearances" is the social law. "Do what you like, but save appearances." A dignified hypocrisy none disobey. These men and women, with the historic names, dare not show each other what they are. There was no flirting, no romping, no loud laughter; not a loud word—no telltale glances, no sitting in corners. It was a pose throughout. Men bowed ceremoniously, and addressed as strangers ladies with whom they spent every evening. Husbands devoted themselves to wives whom they never saw but in public. Innocence *may* betray itself, *seems* to betray itself—guilt never. Guilt is cautious.

At this moment Count Nobili entered. He was received with lofty courtesy by the countess. Her manner implied a gentle protest. Count Nobili was a banker's son; his mother was not—*née*—any thing. Still he was welcome. She graciously bent her head, on which a tiara of diamonds glittered—in acknowledgment of his compliments on the brilliancy of her ball.

Nobili's address was frank and manly. There was an ease and freedom about him that contrasted favorably with the effeminate appearance and affected manners of the *jeunesse dorée.* His voice, too, was a pleasant voice, and gave a value to all he said. A sunny smile lighted up his fair-complexioned face, the face old Carlotta had called " lucky."

"You are very late," the countess had said, with the slightest tone of annoyance in her voice—fanning herself languidly as she spoke. "My son has been looking for you."

"It has been my loss, Signora Contessa," replied Nobili,

bowing. "Pardon me. I was delayed. With your permission, I will find your son." He bowed again, then walked on into the dancing-rooms beyond.

Nobili had come late. "Why should he go at all?" he had asked himself, sighing, as he sat at home, smoking a solitary cigar. "What was the Orsetti ball, or any other ball, to him, when Enrica was not there?"

Nevertheless, he did dress, and he did go, telling himself, however, that he was simply fulfilling a social duty by so doing. Now that he is here, standing in the ballroom, the incense of the flowers in his nostrils, the music thrilling in his ear—now that flashing eyes, flushed cheeks, graceful forms palpitating with the fury of the dance—and hands with clasping fingers, are turned toward him—does he still feel regretful—sad? Not in the least.

No sooner had he arrived than he found himself the object of a species of ovation. This put him into the highest possible spirits. It was most gratifying. He could not possibly do less than return these salutations with the same warmth with which they were offered.

Not that Count Nobili acknowledged any inferiority to those among whom he moved as an equal. Count Nobili held that, in New Italy, every man is a gentleman who is well educated and well mannered. As to the language the Marchesa Guinigi used about him, he shook with laughter whenever it was mentioned.

So it fell out that, before he had arrived many minutes, the remembrance of Enrica died out, and Nobili flung himself into the spirit of the ball with all the ardor of his nature.

"Why did you come so late, Nobili?" asked Orsetti, turning his head, and speaking in the pause of a waltz with Luisa Bernardini. "You must go at once and talk to Trenta about the cotillon."

"Well, Nobili, you gave us a splendid entertainment

5

for the festival," said Franchi. "Per Dio! there were no women to trouble us."

"No women!" exclaimed Civilla—"that was the only fault. Divine woman!—Otherwise it was superb. Who has been ill-treating you, Franchi, to make you so savage ? "

Franchi put up his eye-glass and stared at him.

"When there is good wine, I prefer to drink it without women. They distract me."

"Never saw such a reception in Lucca," said Count Malatesta; " never drank such wine. Go on, caro mio, go on, and prosper. We will all support you, but we cannot imitate you."

Nobili, passing on quickly, nearly ran over Cavaliere Trenta. He was in the act of making a profound obeisance, as he handed an ice to one of his contemporaries.

"Ah, youth! youth!" exclaimed poor Trenta, softly, with difficulty recovering his equilibrium by the help of his stick.—" Never mind, Count Nobili, don't apologize; I can bear any thing from a young man who celebrates the festival of the Holy Countenance with such magnificence. Per Bacco! you are the best Lucchese in Lucca. I have seen nothing like it since the duke left. My son, it was worthy of the palace you inhabit."

Ah! could the marchesa have heard this, she would never have spoken to Trenta again!

" You gratify me exceedingly, cavaliere," replied Nobili, really pleased at the old man's praise. "I desire, as far as I can, to become Lucchese at heart. Why should not the festivals of New Italy exceed those of the old days? At least, I shall do my best that it be so."

"Eh? eh?" replied Trenta, rubbing his nose with a doubtful expression; " difficult—very difficult. In the old days, my young friend, society was a system. Each sovereign was the centre of a permanent court circle. There

were many sovereigns and many circles—many purses, too,
to pay the expenses of each circle. Now it is all hap-haz-
ard; no money, no court, no king."

" No king ?" exclaimed Nobili, with surprise.

" I beg pardon, count," answered the urbane Trenta,
remembering Nobili's liberal politics—" I mean no society.
Society, as a system, has ceased to exist in Italy. But we
must think of the cotillon. It it now twelve o'clock.
There will be supper. Then we must soon begin. You,
count, are to dance with Nera Boccarini. You came so
late we were obliged to arrange it for you."

Nobili colored crimson.,

" Does the lady—does Nera Boccarini know this ?" he
asked, and as he asked his color heightened.

" Well, I cannot tell you, but I presume she does.
Count Orsetti will have told her. The cotillon was settled
early. You have no objection to dance with her, I presume ?"

" None—none in the world. Why should I ?" replied
Nobili, hastily (now the color of his cheeks had grown
crimson). " Only—only I might not have selected her."
The cavaliere looked up at him with evident surprise. " Am
I obliged to dance the cotillon at all, cavaliere ?" added
Nobili, more and more confused. " Can't I sit out ?"

" Oh, impossible—simply impossible !" cried Trenta,
authoritatively. " Every couple is arranged. Not a man
could fill your place; the whole thing would be a failure."

" I am sorry," answered Nobili, in a low voice—" sorry
all the same."

" Now go, and find your partner," said Trenta, not heeding this little speech. " I am about to have the chairs arranged. Go and find your partner."

" Now what could make Nobili object to dance with
Nera Boccarini ?" Trenta asked himself, when Nobili was

gone, striking his stick loudly on the floor, as a sign for the music to cease.

There was an instant silence. The gentlemen handed the ladies to a long gallery, the last of the suite of the rooms on the ground-floor. Here a buffet was arranged. The musicians also were refreshed with good wine and liquors, before the arduous labors of the cotillon commenced. No brilliant cotillon ends before 8 A. M.; then there is breakfast and driving home by daylight at ten o'clock.

Nobili, his cheeks still tingling, felt that the moment had come when he must seek his partner. It would be difficult to define the contending feelings that made him reluctant to do so. Nera Boccarini had taken no pains to conceal how much she liked him. This was flattering; perhaps he felt it was too flattering. There was a determination about Nera, a power of eye and tongue, an exuberance of sensuous youth, that repelled while it allured him. It was like new wine, luscious to the taste, but strong and heavy. New wine is very intoxicating. Nobili loved Enrica. At that moment every woman that did not in some subtle way remind him of her, was distasteful to him. Now, it was not possible to find two women more utterly different, more perfect contrasts, than the dreamy, reserved, tender Enrica—so seldom seen, so little known—and the joyous, outspoken Nera—to be met with at every mass, every *fête*, in the shops, on the Corso, on the ramparts.

Now, Nera, who had been dancing much with Prince Ruspoli, had heard from him that Nobili was selected as her partner in the cotillon.

"Another of your victims," Prince Ruspoli had said, with a kindling eye.

Nera had laughed gayly.

"My victims?" she retorted. "I wish you would tell me who they are."

This question was accompanied by a most inviting

glance. Prince Ruspoli met her glance, but said nothing. (Nera greatly preferred Nobili, but it is well to have two strings to one's bow, and Ruspoli was a prince with a princely revenue.)

When Nobili appeared, Prince Ruspoli, who had handed Nera to a seat near a window, bowed to her and retired.

"To the devil with Nobili!" was Prince Ruspoli's thought, as he resigned her. "I do like that girl—she is so English!" and Ruspoli glanced at Poole's dress-clothes, which fitted him so badly, and remembered with satisfaction certain balls in London, and certain water-parties at Maidenhead (Ruspoli had been much in England), where he had committed the most awful solecisms, according to Italian etiquette, with frank, merry-hearted girls, whose buoyant spirits were contagious.

Nobili's eyes fell instinctively to the ground as he approached Nera. The rosy shadow of the red-silk curtains behind her fell upon her face, bosom, and arms, with a ruddy glow.

"I am to have the honor of dancing the cotillon with you, I believe?" he said, still looking down.

"Yes, I believe so," she responded—"at least so I am told; but you have not asked me yet. Perhaps you would prefer some one else. I confess *I* am satisfied."

As she spoke, Nera riveted her full black eyes upon Nobili. If he only would look up, she would read his thoughts, and tell him her own thoughts also. But Nobili did not look up; he felt her gaze, nevertheless; it thrilled him through and through.

At this moment, the melody of a voluptuous waltz, the opening of the cotillon, burst from the orchestra with an *entrain* that might have moved an anchorite. As the sounds struck upon his ear, Nobili grew dizzy under the magnetism of those unseen eyes. His cheeks flushed suddenly, and the blood stirred itself tumultuously in his veins.

" Why should I repulse this girl because she loves me ? "
he asked himself.

This question came to him, wafted, as it were, upon the
wings of the music.

" Count Nobili, you have not answered me," insisted
Nera.· She had not moved. " You are very absent this
evening. Do you *wish* to dance with me ? Tell me."

She dwelt upon the words. Her voice was low and
very pleading. Nobili had not yet spoken.

"I ask you again," she said.

This time her voice sounded most enticing. She touched
his arm, too, laying her soft fingers upon it, and gazed up
into his face. Still no answer. ·

" Will you not speak to me, Nobili ? " She leaned forward, and grasped his arm convulsively. " Nobili, tell me,
I implore you, what have I done to offend you ? " ·

Tears gathered in her eyes. Nobili felt her hand tremble.

He looked up; their eyes met. There was a fire in hers
that was contagious. His heart gave a great bound. Pressing within his own the hand that still rested so lovingly
upon his arm, Nobili gave a rapid glance round. The room
was empty; they were standing alone near the window,
concealed by the ample curtains. Now the red shadow fell
upon them both—

" This shall be my answer, Nera—siren," whispered
Nobili.

As he speaks he clasps her in his arms ; a passionate
kiss is imprinted upon her lips.

Hours have passed ; one intoxicating waltz-measure has
been exchanged for another, that falls upon the ear as enthralling as the last. Not an instant had the dances ceased.
The Cavaliere Trenta, his round face beaming with smiles, is
seated in an arm-chair at the top of the largest ballroom.

He keeps time with his foot. Now and then he raps loudly with his stick on the floor and calls out the changes of
the figures. Baldassare and Luisa Bernardini lead with the
grace and precision of practised dancers.

"Brava! brava! a thousand times! Brava!" calls out
the cavaliere from his arm-chair, clapping his hands. "You
did that beautifully, marchesa!"—This was addressed to
the swan's-neck, who had circled round, conducted by her
partner, selecting such gentlemen as she pleased, and group-
ing them in one spot, in order to form a *bouquet*. "You
couldn't have done it better if you had been taught in
Paris.—Forward! forward!" to a timid couple, to whom
the intricacies of the figure were evidently distracting.
Belle donne! belle donne! Victory to the brave! Fear
nothing.—Orsetti, keep the circle down there; you are out
of your place. You will never form the *bouquet* if you
don't— Louder! louder!" to the musicians, holding up
his stick at them like a marshal's bâton—"loud as they
advance—then piano—diminuendo—pia-nis-si-mo—as they
retreat. That sort of thing gives picturesqueness—light
and shade, like a picture. Hi! hi! Malatesta! The
devil! You are spoiling every thing! Didn't I tell you
to present the flowers to your partner? So—so. The
flowers—they are there." Trenta pointed to a table. He
struggled to rise to fetch the bouquets himself. Malatesta
was too quick for him, however.

"Now bring up all the ladies and place them in chairs;
bow to them," etc., etc.

Thanks to the energy of the cavaliere, and the agility
of Baldassare—who, it is admitted on all hands, had never
distinguished himself so much as on this occasion—all the
difficulties of the new figures have been triumphantly surmounted. Gentlemen had become spokes of a gigantic
wheel that whirled round a lady seated on a chair in the
centre of the room. They had been named as roots, trees,

and even vegetables ; they had answered to such names, seeking corresponding weeds as their partners. At a clap of the cavaliere's hands they had dashed off wildly, waltzing. Gentlemen had worn paper nightcaps, put on masks, and been led about blindfold. They had crept under chairs, waved flags from tables, thrown up colored balls, and unraveled puzzles—all to the rhythm of the waltz-measure babbling on like a summer brooklet under the sun, through emerald meadows.

And now the exciting moment of the ribbons is come —the moment when the best presents are to be produced —the ribbons—a sheaf of rainbow-colors, fastened into a strong golden ring, which ring is to be held by a single lady, each gentleman grasping (as best he can) a single ribbon. As long as the lady seated on the chair in the centre pleases, the gentlemen are to gyrate round her. When she drops the ring holding the sheaf of ribbons, the Cavaliere Trenta is to clap his hands, and each gentleman is instantly to select that lady who wears a rosette corresponding in color to his ribbon—the lady in the chair being claimed by her partner.

Nobili has placed Nera Boccarini on the chair in the centre. (Ever since the flavor of that fervid kiss has rested on his lips, Nobili has been lost in a delicious dream. "Why should not he and Nera dance on—on—on—forever ?—Into indefinite space, if possible—only together ? " He asks himself this question vaguely, as she rests within his arms—as he drinks in the subtile perfume of the red roses bound in her glossy hair.)

Nera is triumphant. Nobili is her own ! As she sits in that chair when he has placed her, she is positively radiant. Love has given an unknown tenderness to her eyes, a more delicate brilliancy to her cheeks, a softness, almost a languor, to her movements. (Look out, acknowledged *belle* of Lucca—look out, Teresa Ottolini—here is a daugerous rival to your supremacy! If Nobili loves Nera as Nera believes he does—Nera will ripen quickly into yet more transcendent beauty.)

Now Nobili has left Nera, seated in the chair. He is distributing the various ribbons among the dancers. As there are over a hundred couples, and there is some murmuring and struggling to secure certain ladies, who match certain ribbons, this is difficult, and takes time. See—it is done; again Nobili retires behind Nera's chair, to wait the moment when he shall claim her himself.

How the men drag at the ribbons, whirling round and round, hand-in-hand!—Nera's small hand can scarcely hold them—the men whirling round every instant faster—tumbling over each other, indeed; each moment the ribbons are dragged harder. Nera laughs; she sways from side to side, her arms extended. Faster and more furiously the men whirl round—like runaway horses now, bearing dead upon the reins. The strain is too great, Nera lets fall the ring. The cavaliere claps his hands. Each gentleman rushes toward the lady wearing a rosette matching his ribbon. Nera rises. Already she is encircled by Nobili's arm. He draws her to him; she makes one step forward. Nera is a bold, firm dancer, but, unknown to her, the ribbons in falling have become entangled about her feet; she is bound, she cannot stir; she gives a little scream. Nobili, startled, suddenly loosens his hold upon her waist. Nera totters, extends her arms, then falls heavily backward, her head striking on the *parquet* floor. There is a cry of horror. Every dancer stops. They gather round her where she lies. Her face is turned upward, her eyes are set and glassy, her cheeks are ashen.

"Holy Virgin!" cries Nobili, in a voice of anguish, "I have killed her!" He casts himself on the floor beside her—he raises her in his strong arms. "Air, air!—give her air, or she will die!" he cries.

Putting every one aside, he carries Nera to the nearest window, he lays her tenderly on a sofa. It is the very spot where he had kissed her—under the fiery shadow of the red curtain. Alas! Nobili is sobered now from the passion of that moment. The glamour has departed with the light of Nera's eyes. He is ashamed of himself; but there is a swelling at his heart, nevertheless—an impulse of infinite compassion toward the girl who lies senseless before him—her beauty, her undisguised love for him, plead powerfully for her. Does he love her?

The Countess Boccarini and Nera's sisters are by her side. The poor mother at first is speechless; she can only chafe her child's cold hands, and kiss her white lips.

"Nera, Nera," at last she whispers, "Nera, speak to me—speak to me—one word—only one word!"

"But, alas! there is no sign of animation—to all appearance Nera is dead. Nobili, convinced that he alone is responsible, and too much agitated to care what he does, kneels beside her, and places his hand upon her heart.

"She lives! she lives!" he cries—"her heart beats! Thank God, I have not killed her!"

This leap from death to life is too much for him; he staggers to his feet, falls into a chair, and sobs aloud. Nera's eyelids tremble; she opens her eyes, her lips move.

"Nera, my child, my darling, speak to me!" cries Madame Boccarini. "Tell me that you can hear me."

Nera tries to raise her head, but in vain. It falls back upon the cushion.

"Home, mamma—home!" her lips feebly whisper.

At the sound of her voice Nobili starts up; he brushes away the tears that still roll down his cheeks. Again he lifts Nera tenderly in his arms. For that night Nera belongs to him; no one else shall touch her. He bears her down-stairs to a carriage. Then he disappears into the darkness of the night.

No one will leave the ball until there is some report of Nera's condition from the doctor who has been summoned. The gay groups sit around the glittering ballroom, and whisper to each other. The "golden youth" offer bets as to Nera's recovery; the ladies, who are jealous, back freely against it. In half an hour, however, Countess Orsetti is able to announce that "Nera Boccarini is better, and that, beyond the shock, it is hoped that she is not seriously hurt."

"You see, Malatesta, I was right," drawls out the languid Franchi as he descends the stairs. "You will believe me another time. You know I told you and Orsetti that Nera Boccarini and Nobili understood each other. He's desperately in love with her."

"I don't believe it, all the same," answers Malatesta, shaking his head. "A man can't half kill a girl and show no compunction—specially not Nobili—the best-hearted fellow breathing. Nobili is just the man to feel such an accident as that dreadfully. How splendid Nera looked to-night! She quite cut out the Ottolini." Malatesta spoke with enthusiasm; he had a practised eye for woman's fine points. "Here, Adonis—I beg your pardon—Baldassare, I mean—where are you going?"

"Home," replies the Greek mask.

"Never mind home; we are all obliged to you. You lead the cotillon admirably."

Baldassare smiles, and shows two rows of faultless teeth.

"Come and have some supper with us at the Universo. Franchi is coming, and all our set."

"With the greatest pleasure," replies Baldassare, smiling.

PART II.

CHAPTER I.

CALUMNY.

BALDASSARE was, of course, invited by the cavaliere to join the proposed expedition to the tombs of the Trenta and to the Guinigi Tower. Half an hour before the time appointed he appeared at the Palazzo Trenta. The cavaliere was ready, and they went out into the street together.

"If you have not been asleep since the ball, Baldassare—which is probable—perhaps you can tell me how Nera Boccarini is this morning?"

"She is quite well, I understand," answered Adonis, with an air of great mystery, as he smoothed his scented beard. "She is only a little shaken."

"By Jove!" exclaimed the cavaliere. "Never was I present at any thing like that! A love-scene in public! Once, indeed, I remember, on one occasion, when her highness Paulina threw herself into the arms of his serene highness—"

"Have you heard the news?" asked Baldassare, interrupting him.

He dreaded a long tirade from the old chamberlain on the subject of his court reminiscences; besides, Baldassare was bursting with a startling piece of intelligence as yet evidently unknown to Trenta.

" News !—no," answered the cavaliere, contemptuously.
" I dare say it is some lie. You have, I am sorry to say,
Baldassare, all the faults of a person new to society; you
believe every thing."

Baldassare eyed the cavaliere defiantly; but he pulled
at his curled mustache in silence.

The cavaliere stopped short, raised his head, and scanned
him attentively.

" Out with it, my boy, out with it, or it will choke you!
I see you are dying to tell me ! "

" Not at all, cavaliere," replied Baldassare, with assumed indifference; " only I must say that I believe you
are the only person in Lucca who has not heard it."

" Heard what ? " demanded Trenta, angrily.

Baldassare knew the cavaliere's weak point; he delighted to tease him. Trenta considered himself, and was
generally considered by others, as a universal news-monger;
it was a habit that had remained to him from his former
life at court. From the time of Polonius downward a
court-chamberlain has always been a news-monger.

" Heard ? · Why, the news—the great news," Baldassare spoke in the same jeering tone. He drew himself up,
affecting to look over the cavaliere's head as he bent on
his stick before him.

" Go on," retorted the cavaliere, doggedly.

" How strange you have not heard any thing ! " Trenta
now looked so enraged, Baldassare thought it was time to
leave off bantering him. " Well, then, cavaliere, since you
really appear to be ignorant, I will tell you. After you
left the Orsetti ball, Malatesta asked me and the other
young men of their set to supper at the Universo Hotel."

" Mercy on us ! " ejaculated the cavaliere, who was now
thoroughly irritated, " you consider yourself one of *their
set*, do you? I congratulate you, young man. This is
news to me."

"Certainly, cavaliere, if you ask me, I do consider myself one of their set."

The cavaliere shrugged his shoulders contemptuously.

"We talked of the accident," continued Baldassare, affecting not to notice his sneers, "and we talked of Nobili. Many said, as you do, that Nobili is in love with Nera Boccarini, and that he would certainly marry her. Malatesta laughed, as is his way, then he swore a little. Nobili would do no such thing, he declared, he would answer for it. He had it on the best authority, he said, that of an eye-witness." (Ah, cruel old Carlotta, you have made good your threat of vengeance!) "An eye-witness had said that Nobili was in love with some one else—some one who wrote to him; that they had been watched—that he met some one secretly, and that by-and-by all the city would know it, and that there would be a great scandal."

"And who may the lady be?" asked the cavaliere carelessly, raising his head as he put the question, with a sardonic glance at Baldassare. "Not that I believe one word Malatesta says. He is a young coxcomb, and you, Baldassare, are a parrot, and repeat what you hear. Per Bacco! if there had been any thing serious, I should have known it long ago. Who is the lady?" Spite of himself, however, his blue eyes sparkled with curiosity.

"The marchesa's niece, Enrica Guinigi."

"What!" roared out the cavaliere, striking his stick so violently on the ground that the sound echoed through the solitary street. "Enrica Guinigi, whom I see every day! What a lie!—what a base lie! How dare Malatesta—the beast—say so? I will chastise him myself!—with my own hand, old as I am, I will chastise him! Enrica Guinigi!"

Baldassare shrugged his shoulders and made a grimace. This incensed the cavaliere more violently.

"Now, listen to me, Baldassare Lena," shouted the

cavaliere, advancing, and putting his fist almost into his face. "Your father is a chemist, and keeps a shop. He is not a doctor, though you call him so. If ever you presume again to repeat scandals such as this—scandals, I say, involving the reputation of noble ladies, my friends—ladies into whose houses I have introduced you, there shall be no more question of your being of their ' set.' I will take care that you never enter one of their doors again. By the body of my holy ancestor, San Riccardo, I will disgrace you— publicly disgrace you ! "

Trenta's rosy face had grown purple, his lips worked convulsively. He raised his stick, and flourished it in the air, as if about to make it descend like a truncheon on Baldassare's shoulders. Adonis drew back a step or two, following with his eyes the cavaliere's movements. He was quite unmoved by his threats. Not a day passed that Trenta did not threaten him with his eternal displeasure. Adonis was used to it, and bore it patiently. He bore it because he could not help it. Although by no means overburdened with brains, he was conscious that as yet he was not sufficiently established in society to stand alone. Still, he had too high an opinion of his personal beauty, fine clothes, and general merits, to believe that the ladies of Lucca would permit of his banishment by any arbitrary decree of the cavaliere.

"You had better find out the truth, cavaliere," he muttered, keeping well out of the range of Trenta's stick, "before you put yourself in such a passion."

"Domine Dio ! that they should dare to utter such abominations ! " ejaculated the cavaliere. "Why, Enrica lives the life of a nun ! I doubt if she has ever seen Nobili—certainly she has never spoken to him. Let Malatesta, and the young scoundrels at the club, attack the married women. They can defend themselves. But, to calumniate an innocent girl !—it is horrible !—it is unman-

ly! His highness the Duke of Lucca would have banished
the wretch forthwith. Ah! Italy is going to the devil!
—Now, Baldassare," he continued, turning round and glaring upon Adonis, who still retreated cautiously before him,
"I have a great mind to send you home. We are about
to meet the young lady herself. You are not worthy to
be in her company."

"I only repeated what Malatesta told me," urged Baldassare, plaintively, looking very blank. "I am not answerable for him. Go and quarrel with Malatesta, if you
like, but leave me alone. You asked me a question, and I
answered you. That is all."

Baldassare had dressed himself with great care; his
hair was exquisitely curled for the occasion. He had nothing to do all day, and the prospect of returning home was
most depressing.

"You are not answerable for being born a fool!" was
the rejoinder. "I grant that. Who told Malatesta?"
asked the cavaliere, turning sharply toward Baldassare.

"He said he had heard it in many quarters. He insisted on having heard it from one who had seen them together."

(Old Carlotta, sitting in her shop-door at the corner of
the street of San Simone, like an evil spider in its web,
could have answered that question.)

The cavaliere was still standing on the same spot, in
the centre of the street.

"Baldassare," he said, addressing him more calmly,
"this is a wicked calumny. The marchesa must not hear
it. Upon reflection, I shall not notice it. Malatesta is a
chattering fool—an ape! I dare say he was tipsy when
he said it. But, as you value my protection, swear to me
not to repeat one word of all this. If you hear it mentioned, contradict it—flatly contradict it, on my authority—
the authority of the Marchesa Guinigi's oldest friend. No-

bili will marry Nera Boccarini, and there will be an end of
it; and Enrica—yes, Baldassare," cóntinued the cavaliere,
with an air of immense dignity—" yes, to prove to you how
ridiculous this report is, Enrica is about to marry also. I
am at this very time authorized by the family to arrange
an alliance with—"

" I guess !" burst out Baldassare, reddening with delight at being intrusted with so choice a piece of news—
" with Count Marescotti !" Trenta gave a conscious smile,
and nodded. This was done with a certain reserve, but
still graciously. " To be sure; it was easy to see how
much he admired her, but I did not know that the lady—"

" Oh, yes, the lady is all right—she will agree," rejoined
Trenta. " She knows no one else; she will obey her aunt's
commands and my wishes."

" I am delighted !" cried Baldassare. " Why, there
will be a ball at Palazzo Guinigi—a ball, after all ! "

" But the marchesa must never hear this scandal about
Nobili," added Trenta, suddenly relapsing into gravity.
" She hates him so much, it might give her a fit. Have a
care, Baldassare—have a care, or you may yet incur my
severest displeasure."

" I am sure I don't want the marchesa or any one else
to know it," replied Baldassare, greatly reassured as to the
manner in which he would pass his day by the change in
Trenta's manner. " I would not annoy her or injure the
signorina for all the world. I am sure you know that,
cavaliere. No word shall pass my lips, I promise you."

" Good ! good !" responded Trenta, now quite pacified
(it was not in Trenta's nature to be angry long). Now he
moved forward, and as he did so he took Baldassare's arm,
in token of forgiveness. " No names must be mentioned,"
he continued, tripping along—" mind, no names; but I
authorize you, on my authority, if you hear this abominable
nonsense repeated—I authorize you to say that you have

it from me—that Enrica Guinigi is to be married, *and not to .Nobili.* He! he! That will surprise them — those chattering young blackguards at the club."

Thus, once more on the most amiable terms, the cavaliere and Baldassare proceeded leisurely arm-in-arm toward the street of San Simone.

CHAPTER II.

COUNT MARESCOTTI was walking rapidly up and down in the shade before the Guinigi Palace when the cavaliere and Baldassare appeared. He was so absorbed in his own thoughts that he did not perceive them.

"I must speak to him as soon as possible about Enrica," was Trenta's thought on seeing him. "With this report going about, there is not an hour to lose."

"You have kept your appointment punctually, count," he said, laying his hand on Marescotti's shoulder.

"Punctual, my dear cavaliere? I never missed an appointment in my life when made with a lady. I was up long before daylight, looking over some books I have with me, in order to be able the better to describe any object of interest to the Signorina Enrica."

"An opportunity for you, my boy," said Trenta, nodding his head roguishly at Baldassare. "You will have a lesson in Lucchese history. Of course, you know nothing about it."

"Every man has his forte," observed the count, good-naturedly, seeing Baldassare's embarrassment at having his ignorance exposed. (The cavaliere never could leave poor Adonis alone.) "We all know your forte is the ball-room; there you beat us all."

"Taught by me, taught by me," muttered the cavaliere; "he owes it all to me."

Leaving the count and Baldassare standing together in the street, the cavaliere knocked at the door of the Guinigi Palace. When it was opened he entered the gloomy court. Within he found Enrica and Teresa awaiting his arrival.

At the sight of her whom he so much loved, and of whom he had just heard what he conceived to be such an atrocious calumny, the cavaliere was quite overcome. Tears gathered in his eyes; he could hardly reply to her when she addressed him.

"My Enrica," he said at last, taking her by the hand and imprinting a kiss upon her forehead, "you are a good child. Heaven bless you, and keep you always as you are!" A conscious blush overspread Enrica's face.

"If he knew all, would he say this?" she asked herself; and her pretty head with the soft curls dropped involuntarily.

Enrica was very simply attired, but the flowing lines of her graceful figure were not to be disguised by any mere accident of dress. A black veil, fastened upon her hair like a mantilla (a style much affected by the Lucca ladies), fell in thick folds upon her shoulders, and partially shaded her face.

Teresa stood by her young mistress, prepared to follow her. Trenta perceived this. He did not like Teresa. If she went with them, the whole conversation might be repeated in Casa Guinigi. This, with Count Marescotti in the company, would be—to say the least of it—inconvenient.

"You may retire," he said to Teresa. "I will take charge of the signorina."

"But—Signore Cavaliere"—and Teresa, feeling the affront, colored scarlet—"the marchesa's positive orders were, I was not to leave the signorina."

"Never mind," answered the cavaliere, authoritatively, "I will take that on myself. You can retire."

Teresa, swelling with anger, remained in the court. The cavaliere offered his arm to Enrica. She turned and addressed a few words to the exasperated Teresa; then, led by Trenta, she passed into the street. Upon the threshold, Count Marescotti met them.

"This is indeed an honor," he said, addressing Enrica —his face beamed, and he bowed to the ground. "I trembled lest the marchesa should have forbidden your coming."

"So did I," answered Enrica, frankly. "I am so glad. I fear that my aunt is not altogether pleased; but she has said nothing, and I came."

She spoke with such eagerness, she saw that the count was surprised. This made her blush. At any other time such an expedition as that they were about to make would have been delightful to her for its own sake, Enrica was so shut up within the palace, except on the rare occasions when she accompanied Teresa to mass, or took a formal drive on the ramparts at sundown with her aunt. But now she was full of anxiety about Nobili. They had not met for a week—he had not written to her even. Should she see him in the street? Should she see him from the top of the tower? Perhaps he was at home at that very moment watching her. She gave a furtive glance upward at the stern old palace before her. The thick walls of sun-dried bricks looked cruel; the massive Venetian casements mocked her. The outer blinds shut out all hope. Alas! there was not a chink anywhere. Even the great doors were closed.

"Ah! if Teresa could have warned him that I was coming!"—and she gave a great sigh. "If he only knew that I was here, standing in the very street! Oh, for one glimpse of his dear, bright face!"

Again Enrica sighed, and again she gazed up wistfully at the closed façade.

Meanwhile the cavaliere and Baldassare were engaged in a violent altercation. Baldassare had proposed walking to the church of San Frediano, which, in consideration of the cavaliere's wishes, they were to visit first. "No one would think of driving such a short distance," he insisted. "The sun was not hot, and the streets were all in shade." The cavaliere retorted that "it was too hot for any lady to walk," swung his stick menacingly in the air, called Baldassare "an imbecile," and peremptorily ordered him to call a *fiacre*. Baldassare turned scarlet in the face, and rudely refused to move.

"He was not a servant," he said. "He would do nothing unless treated like a gentleman."

This was spoken as he hurled what he intended to be a tremendous glance of indignation at the cavaliere. It produced no effect whatever. With an exasperating smile, the cavaliere again desired Baldassare to do as he was bid, or else to go home. The count interposed, a *fiacre* was called, in which they all seated themselves.

. . . .

San Frediano, a basilica in the Lombard style, is the most ancient church in Lucca. The mid-day sun now flashed full upon the front, and lighted up the wondrous colors of a mosaic on a gold ground, over the entrance. At one corner of the building a marble campanile, formed by successive tiers of delicate arcades, springs upward into the azure sky. Flocks of gray pigeons circled about the upper gallery (where hang the bells), or rested, cooing softly in the warm air, upon the sculptured cornice bordering the white arches. It was a quiet scene of tranquil beauty, significant of repose in life and of peace in death— the church, with its wide portals, offering an everlasting home to all who sought shelter within its walls.

The cavaliere was so impatient to do the honors that he actually jumped unaided from the carriage.

"This, dear Enrica, is my parish church," he said, as he handed her out, pointing upward to the richly-tinted pile, which the suns of many centuries had dyed of a golden hue. "I know every stone in the building. From a child I have played in this piazza, under these venerable walls. My earliest prayers were said at the altar of the Sacrament within. Here I confessed my youthful sins. Here I received my first communion. Here I hope to lay my bones, when it shall please God to call me."

Trenta spoke with a tranquil smile. It was clear neither life nor death had any terrors for him. "The very pigeons know me," he added, placidly. He looked up to the campanile, gave a peculiar whistle, and, putting his hand into his pocket, threw down some grains of corn upon the pavement. The pigeons, whirling round in many circles (the sunlight flashing upon their burnished breasts, and upon the soft gray and purple feathers of their wings), gradually—in little groups of twos and threes—flew down, and finally settled themselves in a knot upon the pavement, to peck up the corn.

"Good, pious old man, how I honor you!" ejaculated Count Marescotti, fervently, as he watched the timid gray-coated pigeons gathering round the cavaliere's feet, as he stood apart from the rest, serenely smiling as he fed them. "May thy placid spirit be unruffled in time and in eternity!"

The interior of the church, in the Longobardic style, is bare almost to plainness. On entering, the eye ranges through a long broad nave with rounded arches, the arches surmounted by narrow windows; these dividing arches, supported on single columns with monumental capitals, forming two dark and rather narrow aisles. The high altar is raised on three broad steps. Here burn a few lights, dimmed into solitary specks by the brightness of the sun. The walls on either side of the aisles are broken by various chapels. These lie in deep shadow. The roof, formed of open rafters, bearing marks of having once been elaborately gilded, is now but a mass of blackened timbers. The floor is of brick, save where oft-recurring sepulchral slabs are cut into the surface. These slabs, of black-and-white marble, or of alabaster stained and worn from its native whiteness into a dingy brown, are almost obliterated by the many footsteps which have come and gone upon them for so many centuries. Not a single name remains to record whom they commemorate. ˉ Dimly seen under a covering of dirt and dust deposited by the living, lie the records of these unknown dead: here a black lion rampant on a white shield; there a coat-of-arms on an escutcheon, with the fragment of a princely coronet; beyond, a life-sized monk, his shadowy head resting on a cushion—a matron with her robes soberly gathered about her feet, her hands crossed on her bosom—a bishop, under a painted canopy, mitre on head and staff in hand—a warrior, grimly helmeted, carrying his drawn sword in his hand. Who are these? Whence came they? None can tell.

Beside one of the most worn and defaced of these slabs the cavaliere stopped.

"On this stone," he said, his smiling countenance suddenly grown solemn—"on this very stone, where you see the remains of a mosaic"—and he pointed to some morsels of color still visible, crossing himself as he did so—"a notable miracle was performed. Before I relate it, let us adore the goodness of the Blessed Virgin, from whom all good gifts come."

Cavaliere Trenta was on his knees before he had done speaking; again he fervently crossed himself, reciting the "Maria Santissima." Enrica bowed her head, and timidly knelt beside him; Baldassare bent his knees, but, remem-

bering that his trousers were new, and that they might
take an adverse crease that could never be ironed out,
he did not allow himself to touch the floor; then, with
open eyes and ears, he rose and stood waiting for the cavaliere to proceed. Baldassare was uneducated and superstitious. The latter quality recommended him strongly to
Trenta. He was always ready to believe every word the
cavaliere uttered with unquestioning faith. At the mention of a church legend Count Marescotti turned away with
an expression of disgust, and leaned against a pillar, his
eyes fixed on Enrica.

The cavaliere, having risen from his knees, and carefully
dusted himself with a snowy pocket-handkerchief, took
Enrica by the hand, and placed her in such a position that
the sunshine, striking through the windows of the nave,
fell full upon the monumental stone before them.

"My Enrica," he said, in a subdued voice, "and you,
Baldassare"—he motioned to him to approach nearer—
"you are both young. Listen to me. Lay to heart what
an old man tells you. Such a miracle as I am about to relate must touch even the count's hard heart."

He glanced round at Marescotti, but it was evident he
was chagrined by what he saw. Marescotti neither heard
him, nor even affected to do so. Trenta's voice in the great
church was weak and piping—indistinct even to those beside him. Finding the count unavailable either for instruction or reproof, the cavaliere shook his head, and his countenance fell. Then he turned his mild blue eyes upon Enrica,
leaned upon his stick, and commenced:

"In the sixth century, the flag-stones in this portion of
the nave were raised for the burial of a distinguished lady,
a member of the Manzi family; but oh! stupendous prodigy!"—the cavaliere cast up his eyes to heaven, and clasped
his dimpled hands—"no sooner had the coffin been lowered
into the vault prepared for it, than the corpse of the lady

6

of the Manzi family sat upright in the open Bier, put aside the flowers and wreaths piled upon her, and uttered these memorable and never-to-be-forgotten words: ' Bury me elsewhere; here lies the body of San Frediano.' "

Baldassare, who had grown very pale, now shuddered visibly, and contemplated the cavaliere with awe.

"Stupendous!" he muttered — " prodigious ! — Indeed!"

Enrica did not speak; her eyes were fixed on the ground.

"Yes, yes, you may well say prodigious," responded Trenta, bowing his white head; then, looking round triumphantly: "It was prodigious, but a prodigy, remember, vouched for by the chronicles of the Church. (Chronicles of the Church are much more to be trusted than any thing else, much more than Evangelists, who were not bishops, and therefore had no authority—we all know that.) No sooner, my friends, had the corpse of the lady of the Manzi family spoken, as I have said, than diligent search was made by those assembled in the church, when lo !—within the open vault the remains of the adorable San Frediano were discovered in excellent preservation. I need not say that, having died in the odor of sanctity, the most fragrant perfume filled the church, and penetrated even to the adjacent streets. Several sick persons were healed by merely inhaling it. One man, whose arm had been shot off at the shoulder-joint many years before, found his limb come again in an instant, by merely touching the blessed relic." The cavaliere paused to take breath. No one had spoken.— "Have you heard the miracle of the glorious San Frediano?" asked Trenta, a little timidly, raising his voice to its utmost pitch as he addressed Count Marescotti.

" No, I have not, cavaliere; but, if I had, it would not alter my opinion. I do not believe in mediæval miracles." As he spoke, Count Marescotti turned round from the steps of a side-altar, whither he had wandered to look at a picture. " I did not hear one word you said, my dear cavaliere, but I am acquainted with the supposed miracles of San Frediano. They are entirely without evidence, and in no way shake my conclusions as to the utter worthlessness of such legends. In this I agree with the Protestants," he continued, " rather than with that inspired teacher, Savonarola. The Protestants, spite of so-called 'ecclesiastical authority,' persist in denying them. With the Protestants, I hold that the entire machinery of modern miracles is false and unprofitable. With the Apostles miraculous power ended."

" Marescotti ! " ejaculated the poor cavaliere, aghast at the effect his appeal had produced, " for God's sake, don't, don't! before Enrica—and in a church, too ! "

" I believe with Savonarola in other miracles," continued the count, in a louder tone, addressing himself directly to Enrica, on whom he gazed with a tender expression—he was far too much engrossed with her and with the subject to heed Trenta's feeble remonstrance—" I believe in the mystic essence of soul to soul—I believe in the reappearance of the disembodied spirit to its kindred affinity still on earth—still clothed with a fleshly garment. I believe in those magnetic influences that circle like an atmosphere about certain purified and special natures, binding them together in a closely-locked embrace, an embrace that neither time, distance, nor even death itself, can weaken or sever ! "

He paused for an instant; a dark fire lit up his eyes, which were still bent on Enrica.

" All this I believe—life would be intolerable to me without such convictions. At the same time, I am ready to grant that all cannot accept my views. These are mysteries to be approached without prejudice—mysteries that must be received absolutely without prejudice of religion, country, or race ; received as the æsthetic in-

stinct within us teaches. Who," he added, and as he spoke
he stood erect on the steps of the altar, his arms outstretched in the eagerness of argument, his grand face all
aglow with enthusiasm—"who can decide? It is faith
that convinces—faith that vivifies—faith that transforms—
faith that links us to the hierarchy of angels! To believe
—to act on our belief, even if that belief be false—that is true
religion. A merciful Deity will accept our imperfect sacrifice. Are we not all believers in Christ? Away with
creeds and churches, with formularies and doctrines, with
painted walls and golden altars, with stoled priests, infallible popes, and temporal hierarchies! What are these vain
distinctions, if we love God? Let the whole world unite
to believe in the Redeemer. Then we shall all be brothers.
—you, I—all, brothers—joined within the holy circle of
one universal family—of one universal worship!"

Count Marescotti ceased speaking, but his impassioned
words still echoed through the empty aisles. His eyes had
wandered from Enrica; they were now fixed on high. His
countenance glowed with rapture. Wrapped in the visions
his imagination had called forth, he descended from the
altar, and slowly approached the silent group gathered beside the monumental stone.

Enrica had eagerly drunk in every word the count had
uttered. He seemed to speak the language of her secret
musings; to interpret the hidden mysteries of her young
heart. She, at least, believed in the affinity of kindred
spirits. What but that had linked her to Nobili? Oh, to
live in such a union!

Trenta had become very grave.

"You are a visionary," he said, addressing the count,
who now stood beside them. "I am sorry for you. Such a
consummation as you desire is impossible. Your faith has
no foundation. It is a creation of the brain. The Catholic
Church stands upon a rock. It permits no change, it ac-

cepts no compromise,.it-admits no errors. The authority given to St. Peter by Jesus Christ himself, with the spiritual keys, can alone open the gates of heaven. All without are damned. Good intentions are nothing. Private interpretation, believe me, is of the devil. Obedience to the Holy Father, and the intercession of the saints, can alone save your soul. Submit yourself to the teaching of our mother Church, my dear count. Submit yourself—you have my prayers." Trenta watched Marescotti with a fixed gaze of such solemn earnestness, it seemed as though he anticipated that the blessed San Frediano himself might appear, and then and there miraculously convert him. "Submit yourself," he repeated, raising his arm and pointing to the altar, "then you will be blest."

No miraculous interposition, however, was destined to crown the poor cavaliere's strenuous efforts to convert the heretical count; but, long before he had finished, the sound of his voice had recalled Count Marescotti to himself. He remembered that the old chamberlain belonged, in years at least, if not in belief, to the past. He blamed himself for his thoughtlessness in having said a syllable that could give him pain. The mystic disciple of Savonarola became in an instant the polished gentleman.

"A thousand pardons, my dear Trenta," he said, passing his hand over his forehead, and putting back the dark, disordered hair that hung upon his brow—"a thousand pardons!—I am quite ashamed of myself. We are here, as I now remember, to examine the tombs of your ancestors in the chapel of the Trenta. I have delayed you too long. Shall we proceed?"

Trenta, glad to escape from the possibility of any further discussion with the count, whose religious views were to him nothing but the ravings of a mischievous maniac, at once turned into the side-aisle, and, with ceremonious politeness, conducted Enrica toward the chapel of the Trenta.

The chapel, divided by gates of gilt bronze from the line of the other altars bordering the aisles, forms a deep recess near the high altar. The walls are inlaid by what had once been brilliantly-colored marbles, in squares of red, green, and yellow; but time and damp had dulled them into a sombre hue. Above, a heavy circular cornice joins a dome-shaped roof, clothed with frescoes, through which the light descends through a central lantern. Painted figures of prophets stand erect within the four spandrils, and beneath, breaking the marble walls, four snow-white statues of the Evangelists fill lofty niches of gray-tinted stone. Opposite the gilded gates of entrance which Trenta had unlocked, a black sarcophagus projects from the wall. This sarcophagus is surmounted by a carved head. Many other monuments break the marble walls; some very ancient, others of more recent shape and construction. The floor, too, is almost entirely overlaid by tombstones, but, like those in the nave, they are greatly defaced, and the inscriptions are for the most part illegible. Over the altar a blackened painting represents " San Riccardo of the Trenta " battling with the infidels before Jerusalem.

"Here," said the cavaliere, standing in the centre under the dome, "is the chapel of the Trenta. Here I, Cesare Trenta, fourteenth in succession from Gualtiero Trenta—who commanded a regiment at the battle of Marignano against the French under Francis I.—hope to lay my bones. The altar, as you see, is sanctified by the possession of an ancestral picture, deemed miraculous." He bowed to the earth as he spoke, in which example he was followed by Enrica and Baldassare. " San Riccardo was the companion-in-arms of Godfrey de Bouillon. His bones lie under the altar. Upon his return from the crusades he died in our palace. We still show the very room. His body is quite entire within that tomb. I have seen it myself when ·a boy."

Even the count did not venture to raise any doubt as to the authenticity of the patron saint of the Trenta family. The cavaliere himself was on his knees; rosary in hand, he was devoutly offering up his innocent prayers to the ashes of an imaginary saint. After many crossings, bowings, and touchings of the tomb (always kissing the fingers that had been in contact with the sanctified stone), he arose, smiling.

"And now," said the count, turning toward Enrica, "I will ask leave to show you another tomb, which may, possibly, interest you more than the sepulchre of the respected Trenta." As he spoke he led her to the opposite aisle, toward a sarcophagus of black marble placed under an arch, on which was inscribed, in gilt letters, the name "Castruccio Castracani degli Antimelli," and the date "1328." "Had our Castruccio moved in a larger sphere," said the count, addressing the little group that had now gathered about him, "he would have won a name as great as that of Alexander of Macedon. Like Alexander, he died in the flower of his age, in the height of his fame. Had he lived, he would have been King of Italy, and Lucca would have become the capital of the peninsula. Chaste, sober, and merciful—brave without rashness, and prudent without fear —Castruccio won all hearts. Lucca at least appreciated her hero. Proud alike of his personal qualities, and of those warlike exploits with which Italy already rang, she unanimously elected him dictator. When this signal honor was conferred upon him," continued the count, addressing himself again specially to Enrica, who listened, her large dreamy eyes fixed upon him, "Castruccio was absent, engaged in one of those perpetual campaigns against Florence which occupied so large a portion of his short life. At that very moment he was encamped on the heights of San Miniato, preparing to besiege the hated rival of our city— broken and reduced by the recent victory he had gained

over her at 'Altopasso. At Altopasso he had defeated and
humiliated Florence. Now he had planted our flag under
her very walls. Upon the arrival of the embassadors sent
by the Lucchese Republic—one of whom was a Guinigi—" •

"There was a Trenta, too, among them; Antonio Trenta,
a knight of St. John," put in the cavaliere, gently, unwilling
to interrupt the count, but finding it impossible to resist
the temptation of identifying his family with his country's
triumphs. The count acknowledged the omission with a
courteous bow.

"Upon the arrival of the embassadors," he resumed,
" announcing the honor conferred upon him, Castruccio instantly left his camp, and returned with all haste to Lucca.
The dignity accorded to Castruccio exalted him above all
external demonstration, but he understood that his native
city longed to behold, and to surround with personal applause, the person of her idol. In the piazza without this
church, the very centre of Lucca, the heart, as it were,
whence all the veins and arteries of our municipal body
flow, Castruccio was received with all the pomp of a Roman
triumph. Ah! cavaliere"—and the count's lustrous eyes
rested on Trenta, who was devouring every word he uttered
with silent delight—" those were proud days for Lucca!"

"Recall them—recall them, O Count!" cried Trenta.
"It does me good to listen."

"Thirty thousand Florentine prisoners followed Castruccio to Lucca. His soldiers were laden with booty.
They drove before them innumerable herds of cattle;
strings of wagons, filled with the spoils of a victorious cam-
paign, blocked the causeways. Last of all appeared, rumbling on its ancient wheels, the carroccio, or state-car of the
Florentine Republic, bearing their captured flags lowered,
and trailing in the dust. Castruccio—whose sole representatives are the Marchesa Guinigi and yourself, signorina—
Castruccio followed. He was seated in a triumphal chariot,

drawn by eight milk-white horses. Banners fluttered around him. A golden crown of victory was suspended above his head. He was arrayed in a flowing mantle of purple, over a suit of burnished armor. His brows were bound by a wreath of golden laurel. In his right hand he carried a jeweled sceptre. Upon his knees lay his victorious sword unsheathed. Never was manly beauty more transcendent. His lofty stature and majestic bearing fulfilled the expectation of a hero. How can I describe his features ? They are known to all of you by that famous picture (the only likeness of him extant) belonging to the Marchesa Guinigi, placed in the presence-chamber of her palace."

" Yes, yes," burst forth Trenta, no longer able to control his enthusiasm. " Old as I am, when I think of those days, it makes me young again. Alas! what a change! Now we have lost not only our independence, but our very indentity. Our sovereign is gone—banished—our state broken up. We are but the slaves of a monster called the kingdom of Italy, ruled by Piedmontese barbarians ! "

" Hush !—hush ! " whispered the irrepressible Baldassare. " Pray do not interrupt the count." Even the stolid Adonis was moved.

" The daughters of the noblest houses of Lucca," continued Marescotti, " strewed flowers in Castruccio's path. The magistrates and nobles received him on their knees. Young as he was, with one voice they saluted him ' Father of his Country !' "

The count paused. He bowed his head toward the sarcophagus before which they were gathered, in a mute tribute of reverence. After a few minutes of rapt silence he resumed :

" When the multitude heard that name, ten thousand thousand voices echoed it. ' Father of his Country !' resounded to the summits of the surrounding Apennines.

The mountain-tops tossed it to and fro—the caves thundered it—the very heavens bore it aloft to distant hemispheres! Our great soldier, overcome by such overwhelming marks of affection, expressed in every look and gesture how deeply he was moved. Before leaving the piazza, Castruccio was joined by his relative, young Paolo Guinigi!—after his decease to become dictator, and Lord of Lucca. Amid the clash of arms, the brayings of trumpets, and the applause of thousands, they cordially embraced. They were fast friends as well as cousins. Our Castruccio was of a type incapable of jealousy. Paolo was a patriot—that was enough. Together they proceeded to the cathedral of San Martino. At the porch Castruccio was received by the archbishop and the assembled clergy. He was placed in a chair of carved ivory, and carried in triumph up the nave to the chapel of the Holy Countenance. Here he descended, and, while he prostrated himself before the miraculous image, hymns and songs of praise burst from the choir.

"Such, Signorina Enrica," said the count, turning toward her, "is a brief outline of the scene that passed within this city of Lucca, before that tomb held the illustrious dust it now contains."

"Bravo, bravo, count!" exclaimed the mercurial Trenta, in a delighted tone. (He was ready to forgive all the count's transgressions, in the fervor of the moment.) "That is how I love to hear you talk. Now you do yourself justice. Gesù mio! how seldom it is given to a man to be so eloquent! How can he bring himself to employ such gifts against the infallible Church?" This last remark was addressed to Enrica in a tone too low to be overheard.

"And now," said the old chamberlain, always on the lookout to marshal every one as he had marshaled every one at court—"now we will leave the church, and proceed to the Guinigi Tower."

CHAPTER III.

COUNT MARESCOTTI, by reason of too much imagination, and Baldassare, by reason of too little, were both oblivious; consequently the key and the porter were neither of them forthcoming when the party arrived at the door of the tower, which opened from a side-street behind and apart from the palace. Both the count and Baldassare ran off to find the man, leaving Trenta alone with Enrica.

"Ahi!" exclaimed the cavaliere, looking after them with a comical smile, "this youth of New Italy! They have no more brains than a pin. When I was young, and every city had its own ruler and its own court, I should not have escorted a lady and kept her waiting outside in the sun. Bah! those were not the manners of my day. At the court of the Duke of Lucca ladies were treated like divinities, but now the young men don't know how to kiss a woman's hand."

Receiving no answer, Trenta looked hard at Enrica. He was struck by her absent expression. There was a far-away look on her face he had never noticed on it before.

"Enrica," he said, taking both her hands within his own, "I fear you are not amused. These subjects are too grave to interest you. What are you thinking about?"

An anxious look came into her eyes, and she glanced hastily round, as if to assure, herself that no one was near.

"Oh! I am thinking of such strange things!" She stopped and hesitated, seeing the cavaliere's glance of surprise. "I should like to tell you all, dear cavaliere—I would give the world to tell you—"

Again she stopped.

"Speak—speak, my child," he answered; "tell me all that is in your mind."

Before she could reply, the count and Baldassare reappeared, accompanied by the porter of the Guinigi Palace and the keys.

"Are you sure you would rather not return home again, Enrica? You have only to turn the corner, remember," asked Trenta, looking at her with anxious affection.

"No, no," she answered, greatly confused; "please say nothing—not now—another time. I should like to ascend the tower; let us go on."

The cavaliere was greatly puzzled. It was plain there was something on her mind. What could it be? How fortunate, he told himself, if she had taken a liking to Marescotti, and desired to confess it! This would make all easy. When he had spoken to the count, he would contrive to see her alone, and insist upon knowing if it were so.

The door was now opened, and the porter led the way, followed by the count and Baldassare. Trenta came next, Enrica last. They ascended stair after stair almost in darkness. After having mounted a considerable height, the porter unlocked a small door that barred their farther advance. Above appeared the blackened walls of the hollow tower, broken by the loop-holes already mentioned, through which the ardent sunshine slanted. Before them was a wooden stair, crossing from angle to angle up to a dizzy height, with no other support but a frail banister;

this even was broken in places. The count and Enrica both entreated the cavaliere to remain below. Marescotti ventured to allude to his great age—a subject he himself continually, as has been seen, mentioned, but which he generally much resented when alluded to by others.

Trenta listened with perfect gravity and politeness, but, when the count had done speaking, he placed his foot firmly on the first stair, and began to ascend after the porter. The others were obliged to follow. At the last flight several loose planks shook ominously under their feet; but Trenta, assisted by his stick, stepped on perseveringly. He also insisted on helping Enrica, who was next to him, and who by this time was both giddy and frightened. At length a trap-door, at the top of the tower, was reached and unbarred by the attendant. Without, covered with grass, is a square platform, protected by a machicolated parapet of turreted stone-work. In the centre rises a cluster of ancient bay-trees, fresh and luxuriant, spite of the wind and storms of centuries.

The count leaped out upon the greensward and rushed to the parapet.

"How beautiful!" he exclaimed, throwing back his head and drawing in the warm air. "See how the sun of New Italy lights up the old city! Cathedral, palace, church, gallery, roof, tower, all ablaze at our feet! Speak, tell me, is it not wonderful?" and he turned to Enrica, who, anxiously turning from side to side, was trying to discover where she could best overlook the street of San Simone and Nobili's palace.

Addressed by Marescotti, she started and stopped short.

"Never, never," he continued, becoming greatly excited, "shall I forget this meeting!—here with you—the golden-haired daughter of this ancient house!"

"I!" exclaimed Enrica. "O count, what a mistake!

I have no house, no home. I live on the charity of my aunt."

"That makes no difference in your descent, fair Guinigi. Charity! charity! Who would not shower down oceans of charity to possess such a treasure?" He leaned his back against the parapet, and bent his eyes with fervent admiration on her. "It is only in verse that I can celebrate her," he muttered, "prose is too cold for her warm coloring. The Madonna — the uninstructed Madonna — before the archangel's visit—"

"But, count," said Enrica timidly (his vehemence and strange glances made her feel very shy), "will you tell me the names of the beautiful mountains around? I have seen so little—I am so ignorant."

"I will, I will," replied Marescotti, speaking rapidly, his glowing eyes raising themselves from her face to look out over the distance; "but, in mercy, grant me a few moments to collect myself. Remember I am a poet; imagination is my world; the unreal my home; the Muses my sisters. I live there above, in the golden clouds"—and he turned and pointed to a crest of glittering vapor sailing across the intense blue of the sky. Then, with his hand pressed on his brow, he began to pace rapidly up and down the narrow platform.

The cavaliere and Baldassare were watching him from the farther end of the tower.

"He! he!" said Trenta, and he gave a little laugh and nudged Baldassare. "Do you see the count? He is fairly off. Marescotti is too poetical for this world. Unpractical, poor fellow—very unpractical. The fit is on him now. Look at him, Baldassare; see how he stares about, and clinches his fist. I hope he will not leap over the parapet in his ecstasy."

"Ha! ha!" responded Baldassare, who with eyes wide open, and hands thrust into his pockets, leaned back beside

Trenta against the wall. "Ha, ha!—I must laugh," Baldassare whispered into his ear—" I cannot help it—look how the count's lips are moving. He is in the most extraordinary excitement."

"It's all very fine," rejoined Trenta, " but I wonder he does not frighten Enrica. There she stands, quite still. I can't see her face, but she seems to like it. It's all very fine," he repeated, nodding his white head reflectively. " Republicans, communists, orators, poets, heretics — all the plagues of hell! Dio buono! give me a little plain common-sense—plain common-sense, and a paternal government. As to Marescotti, these new-fangled notions will turn his brain; he'll end in a mad-house. I don't believe he is quite in his senses at this very minute. Look! look! What strides he is taking up and down! For the love of Heaven, my boy, run and fasten the trap-door tight! He may fall through! He's not safe! I swear it, by all the saints!" Baldassare, shaking with suppressed laughter, secured the trap-door.

"I must say you are a little hard on the count," Baldassare said. " Why, he's only composing. I know his way. Trust me, it's a sonnet. He is composing a sonnet addressed perhaps to the signorina. He admires her very much."

Trenta smiled, and mentally determined, for the second time, to take the earliest opportunity of speaking to Count Marescotti before the ridiculous reports circulating in Lucca reached him,

" Per Bacco !" he replied, " when the count is as old as I am, he will have learned that quiet is the greatest luxury a man can enjoy—especially in Italy, where the climate is hot and fevers frequent."

How long the count would have continued in the clouds, it is impossible to say, had he not been suddenly brought down to earth—or, at least, the earth on the top of the tower—by something that suddenly struck his gaze.

Enrica, who had strained her eyes in vain to discover some trace of Nobili in the narrow street below, or in the garden behind his palace, had now thrown herself on the grass under the overhanging branches of the glossy bay-trees. These inclosed her as in a bower. Her colorless face rested upon her hand, her eyes were turned toward the ground, and her long blond hair fell in a tangled mass below the folds of her veil, upon her white dress. The count stood transfixed before her.

"Move not, sweet vision!" he cried. "Be ever so! That innocent face shaded by the classic bay; that white robe rustling with the thrill of womanly affinities; those fair locks floating like an aureole in the breeze thy breath has softly perfumed! Rest there enthroned—the world thy backguard, the sky thy canopy! Stay, let me crown thee!"

As he spoke he hastily plucked some sprays of bay, which he twisted into a wreath. He approached Enrica, who had remained quite still, and, kneeling at her feet, placed the wreath upon her head.

"Enrica Guinigi"—the count spoke so softly that neither Trenta nor Baldassare could catch the words—"there is something in your beauty too ethereal for this world."

Enrica, covered with blushes, tried to rise, but he held out his hands imploringly for her to remain.

"Suffer me to speak to you. Yours is a face of one easily moved to love—to love and to suffer," he added, strange lights coming into his eyes as he gazed at her.

Enrica listened to him in painful silence; his words sounded prophetic.

"To love and to suffer; but, loving once"—again the count was speaking, and his voice enchained her by its sweetness—"to love forever. Where shall the man be found pure enough to dare to accept such love as you can bestow ? By Heavens !" he added, and his voice fell to a whisper, and his black eyes seemed to penetrate into her very soul, " you love already. I read it in the depths of those heavenly eyes, in the shadow that already darkens that soft brow, in the dreamy, languid air that robs you of your youth. You love—is it possible that you love—? "

He stopped before the question was finished—before the name was uttered. A spasm, as if wrung from him by sharp bodily pain, passed over his features as he asked this question, never destined to be answered. No one but Enrica had heard it. An indescribable terror seized her ; from pale she grew deadly white ; her eyelids dropped, her lips trembled. Tears gathered in Marescotti's eyes as he gazed at her, but he dared not complete the question.

" If you have guessed my secret, do not—oh ! do not betray me ! "

She said this so faintly that the sound came to him like a whisper from the rustling bay-leaves.

" Never ! " he responded in a low, earnest tone— " never ! "

She believed him implicitly. With that look, that voice, who could doubt him ?

" I have cause to suffer," she replied with a sigh, not venturing to meet his eyes—" to suffer and to wait. But my aunt—"

She said no more ; her head fell on her bosom, her arms dropped to her side, she sighed deeply.

" May I be at hand to shield you ! " was his answer.

After this, he, too, was silent. Rising from his knees, he leaned against the trunk of the bay-tree and contemplated her steadfastly. There was a strange mixture of passion and of curiosity in his mobile face. If she would not tell him, could he not rend her secret from her ?

Trenta, seated at the opposite side of the platform, observed them as they stood side by side, half concealed by

the foliage—observed them with benign satisfaction. It
was all as it should be; his mission would be easy. It was
clear they understood each other. He believed at that
very moment Enrica was receiving the confession of Marescotti's love; the confusion of her looks was conclusive.
The cavaliere's whole endeavor was, at that moment, to
keep Baldassare quiet; he rejoiced to see that he was gently
yielding to the influence of the heat, and nodding at his
side

"Count," said Enrica, looking up and endeavoring to
break a silence which had become painful, "if I have inspired you with any interest—"

She hesitated.

"*If* you have inspired me?" ejaculated Marescotti, reproachfully, not moving his eyes off her.

"I can hardly believe it," she added; "but, if it be
so, speak to me in the voice of poetry. Tell me your
thoughts."

"Yes," exclaimed the count, clasping his hands; "I
have been longing to do so ever since I first saw you. Will
you permit it? If so, give me paper and pencil, that I may
write."

Enrica had neither. Rising from the ground, she
crossed over to where Trenta sat, apparently absorbed in
the contemplation of the roofs of his native city. Fortunately, after diving into various pockets, he found a pencil
and the fly-leaf of a letter. Marescotti took them and retreated to the farther end of the tower; Enrica leaned
against the wall beside the cavaliere.

In a few minutes the count joined them; he returned
the pencil with a bow to the cavaliere. The sonnet was
already written on the fly-leaf of the letter.

"Oh!" cried Enrica, "give me that paper, I know it
will tell me my fate. Give it to me. Count, do not refuse
me." Her look, her manner, was eager—imploring. As

the count drew back, she endeavored to seize the paper from his hand. But Marescotti, holding the paper above his head, in one moment had crushed it in his fingers, and, rushing forward, he flung it over the battlements.

"It is not worthy of you!" he exclaimed, with excitement; "it is worthy neither of you nor of me! No, no," and he leaned over the tower, and watched the paper as it floated downward in the still air. "Let it perish."

"Oh! why have you destroyed it?" cried Enrica, greatly distressed. "That paper would have told me all I want to know. How cruel! how unkind!"

But there was no help for it. No lamentation could bring the paper back again. The sonnet was gone. Marescotti had sacrificed the man to the poet. His artistic sense had conquered.

"Excuse me, dear signorina," he pleaded, "the composition was imperfect. It was too hurried. With your permission, on my return, I will address some other verses to you, more appropriate—more polished."

"Ah! they will not be like those. They will not tell me what I want to know. They cannot come from your very soul like those. The power to divine is gone from you." Enrica could hardly restrain her tears.

"I am very sorry," answered the count, "but I could not help it; I did it unconsciously."

"Indeed, count, you did very wrong," put in the cavaliere; "one understands you wrote *in furore*—so much the better," and Trenta gave a sly wink, which was entirely lost on Marescotti. "But time is getting on. When are we to have that oration on the history and beauties of Lucca that we came up to hear? Had you not better begin?"

The count was engaged at that moment in plucking a sprig of bay for himself and for the cavaliere to wear, as he said, "in memoriam." "I am ready," he replied. "It is a subject that I love."

"Let us begin with the mountains; they are the nearest to God." As he pronounced that name, the count raised his eyes reverently, and uncovered his head. Enrica had placed herself on his right hand, but all interest had died out of her face. She only listened mechanically.

(Yes, the mountains, the glorious mountains! There they were—before, behind, in front; range upon range—peak upon peak, like breakers on a restless sea! Mountains of every shade, of every shape, of every height. Already their mighty tops were flecked with the glow of the western sunbeams; already pink and purple mists had gathered upon their sides, filling the valleys with mystery!)

"There," said the count, pointing in the direction of the winding river Serchio, "is La Panga, the loftiest Apennine in Central Italy. The peaked summits of those other mountains more to the right are the marble-bosomed range of Carrara. One might believe them at this time covered with a mantle of snow, but for the ardent sun, the deep green of the belting plains, and the luxuriance of the forests. Yonder steep-chestnut-clothed height that terminates the valley opening before us is Bargilio, a mountain fortress of the Panciatici over the Baths of Lucca."

Marescotti paused to take breath. Enrica's eyes languidly followed the direction of his hand. The cavaliere, standing on his other side, was adjusting his spectacles, the better to distinguish the distance.

"To the south," continued the count, pointing with his finger—"in the centre of that rich vine-trellised Campagna, lies Pescia, a garden of luscious fruits. Beyond, nestling in the hollows of the Apennines, shutting in the plain of that side, is ancient Lombard-walled Pistoja—the key to the passes of Northern Italy. Farther on, nearer Florence, rise the heights of Monte Catni, crowned as with a diadem by a small burgh untouched since the middle ages. Nearer

at hand, glittering like steel in the sunshine, is the lake
of Bientina. You can see its low, marshy shores fringed
by beauteous woodlands, but without a single dwelling."

Enrica, in a fit of abstraction, leaned over the parapet.
Her eyes were riveted upon the city beneath. Marescotti
followed her eyes.

"Yes," said he, "there is Lucca;" and as he spoke he
glanced inquiringly at her, and the tones of his clear, melodious voice grew soft and tender. "Lucca the Industrious,
bound within her line of ancient walls and fortifications.
Great names and great deeds are connected with Lucca.
Here, tradition says, Julius Cæsar ruled as proconsul.
How often may the sandals of his feet have trod these narrow streets—his purple robes swept the dust of our piazza!
Here he may have officiated as high-priest at our altars—
dictated laws from our palaces! It was after the conquest
of the Nervii (most savage among the Gaulish tribes) that
Julius Cæsar is said to have first come to Lucca. Pompey
and Crassus met him here. It was at this time that Domi-
tius—Cæsar's enemy, then a candidate for the consulship
—boasted that he would ruin him. But Cæsar, seizing the
opportune moment of his recent victories over the Gauls,
and his meeting with Pompey—formed the bold plan of
grasping universal power by means of his deadliest enemies.
These enemies, rather than see the supreme power vested
in each other, united to advance him. The first triumvirate
was the consequence of the meeting. Ages pass by. The
Roman Empire dissolves. Barbarians invade Italy. Lucca
is an independent state—not long to remain so, however,
for the Countess Matilda, daughter of Duke Bonifazio, is
born within her walls. At Lucca Countess Matilda holds
her court. By her counsels, assistance, and the rich legacy
of her patrimonial dominions, she founds the temporal
power of the papacy. To Lucca came, in the fifteenth century, Charles VIII. of France, presumptuous enough to at-

tempt the conquest of Naples; also that mighty dissembler, Charles V., to meet the reigning pontiff Paul III. in
our cathedral of San Martino. But more precious far to
me than the traditions of the shadowy pomp of defunct
tyrants is the remembrance that Lucca was the Geneva of
Italy—that these streets beneath us resounded to the public teaching of the Reformation! Such progress, indeed,
had the reformers made, that it was publicly debated in
the city council, 'If Lucca should declare herself Protestant—'"

"Per Bacco! a disgraceful fact in our history!" burst
out Trenta, a look of horror in his round blue eyes. "Hide
it, hide it, count! For the love of Heaven! You do not
expect me to rejoice at this? Pray, when you mention it,
add that the Protestants were obliged to flee for their lives,
and that Lucca purified itself by abject submission to the
Holy Father."

"Yes; and what came of that?" cried the count, raising his voice, a sudden flush of anger mounting over his
face. "The Church—your Catholic and Apostolic Church
—established the Inquisition. The Inquisition condemned
to the flames the greatest prophet and teacher since the
apostles—Savonarola!"

Trenta, knowing how deeply Marescotti's feelings were
engaged in the subject of Savonarola, was too courteous to
desire any further discussion. But at the same time he
was determined, if possible, to hear no more of what was
to him neither more nor less than blasphemy.

"Do you know how long we have been up here,
count?" he asked, taking out his watch. "Enrica must
return. I hope you won't detain us," he said, with a pitiful look at the count, who seemed preparing for an oration
in honor of the mediæval martyr. "I have already got a
violent rheumatism in my shoulder.—Here, Baldassare,
open the trap-door, and let us go down.—Where is Bal-

dassare?—Baldassare! Where are you, imbecile? Baldassare, I say! Why, diamine! Where can the boy be? He's not been privately practising his last new step behind the bay-trees, and taken a false one over the parapet?"

The small space was easily searched. Baldassare was discovered stretched at full length and fast asleep under a bench on the other side of the bay-trees.

"Ah, wretch!" grumbled the old chamberlain, "if you sleep like this you will outlive me, who mean to flourish for the next hundred years. He's always asleep, except when dancing," he added indignantly appealing to Marescotti. "Look at him. There's beauty without expression. Doesn't he inspire you? Endymion who has overslept himself and missed Diana—Narcissus overcome by the sight of his own beauty."

After being called, pushed, and pinched, by the cavaliere, Baldassare at last opened his eyes in great bewilderment—stretched himself, yawned, then, suddenly clapping his hand to his side, looked fiercely at Trenta. Trenta was shaking with laughter.

"Mille diavoli!" cried Baldassare, rubbing himself vigorously, "how dare you pinch me so, cavaliere? I shall be black and blue. Why should not I sleep? Nobody spoke to me."

"I fear you have heard little of the history of Lucca," said the count, smiling.

"Dio buono! what is history to me? I hate it!—I tell you what, cavaliere, you have hurt me very much." And Baldassare passed his hand carefully down his side. "The next time I go to sleep in your company, I'll trouble you to keep your fingers to yourself. .You have rapped me like a drum."

Trenta watched the various phases of Baldassare's wrath with the greatest amusement. The descent having been safely accomplished, the whole party landed in the street.

Count Marescotti, who came last, advanced to take leave of Enrica. At this moment an olive-skinned, black-eyed girl rose out of the shadow of a neighboring wall, and, lowering a basket from her head, filled with fruit—tawny figs, ruddy peaches, purple grapes, and russet-skinned medlars, shielded from the heat by a covering of freshly-picked vine-leaves—offered it to Enrica. Our Adonis, still sulky and sore from the pinches inflicted by the mischievous fingers of the cavaliere, waved the girl rudely away.

"Fruit! Chè! Begone! our servants have better. Such fruit as that is not good enough for us; it is full of worms."

The girl looked up at him timidly, tears gathered in her dark eyes.

"It is for my mother," she answered, humbly; "she is ill."

As she bent her head to replace the basket, Marescotti, who had listened to Baldassare with evident disgust, raised the basket in his arms, and with the utmost care poised it on the coil of her dark hair.

"Beautiful peasant," he said, "I salute you. This is for your mother," and he placed some notes in her hand.

The girl thanked him, coloring as red as the peaches in her basket, then, hastily turning the corner of the street, disappeared.

"A perfect Pomona! I make a point of honoring beauty whenever I find it," exclaimed the count, looking after her. He cast a reproving glance at Baldassare, who stood with his eyes wide open. "The Greeks worshiped beauty—I agree with them. Beauty is divine. What say you? Were not the Greeks right?"

The words were addressed to Baldassare—the sense and the direction of his eyes pointed to Enrica.

"Yes; beauty," replied Baldassare, smoothing his glossy mustache, and trying to look very wise (he was not in the least conscious of the covert rebuke administered by Mare-scotti)—"beauty is very refreshing, but I must say I prefer it in the upper classes. For my part, I like beauty that can dance—wooden shoes are not to my taste."

"Ah ! canaglia ! " muttered the cavaliere, "there is no teaching you. You will never be a gentleman."

Baldassare was dumfounded. He had not a word to reply.

"Count "—and the old chamberlain, utterly disregarding the dismay of poor Adonis, who never clearly understood what he had done to deserve such severity, now addressed himself to Marescotti—"will you be visible to-morrow after breakfast ? If so, I shall have the honor of calling on you."

"With pleasure," was the count's reply.

Enrica stood apart. She had not spoken one word since the disappearance of the sonnet—that sonnet which would have told her of her future ; for had not Marescotti, by some occult power, read her secret ? Alas ! too, was she not about to reënter her gloomy home without catching so much as a glimpse of Nobili ? Count Marescotti had no opportunity of saying a word to Enrica that was not audible to all. He did venture to ask her if she would be present next evening, if he joined the marchesa's rubber ? Before she could reply, Trenta had hastily answered for her, that "he would settle all that with the count when they met in the morning." So, standing in the street, they parted. Count Marescotti sought in vain for one last glance from Enrica. When he turned round to look for Baldassare, Baldassare had disappeared.

7

CHAPTER IV.

WHEN Nobili rushed home through the dark streets from the Countess Orsetti's ball, he shut himself up in his own particular room, threw himself on a divan, and tried to collect his thoughts. At first he was only conscious of one overwhelming feeling—a feeling of intense joy that Nera Boccarina was alive. The unspeakable horror he had felt, as she lay stretched out on the floor before him, had stupefied him. If she had died?—As the horrible question rose up within him, his blood froze in his veins. But she was not dead—nay, if the report of Madame Orsetti was to be trusted, she was in no danger of dying.

"Thank God!—thank God!" Then, as the quiet of the night and the solitude of his own room gradually restored his scattered senses, Nobili recalled her, not only in the moment of danger, as she lay death-like, motionless, but as she stood before him lit up by the rosy shadow of the silken curtains. Was it an enchantment? Had he been under a spell? Was Nera fiend or angel? As he asked himself these questions, again her wondrous eyes shone upon him like stars; again the rhythm of that fatal waltz struck upon his ears soft and liquid as the fall of oars upon the smooth bosom of an inland lake, bathed in the mellow light of sunset.

What had he done ? He had kissed her—her lips had clung to his; her fingers had linked themselves in his grasp; her eyes—ah!—those eyes had told him that she loved him. Loved him!—why not?

And Enrica!—the thought of Enrica pierced through him like the stab of a knife. Nobili sprang to his feet, pressed both hands to his bosom, then sank down again, utterly bewildered. Enrica!—He had forgotten her! He, Nobili, was it possible? Forgotten her!—A pale plaintive face rose up before him, with soft, pleading eyes. There was the little head, with its tangled meshes of yellow curls, the slight girlish figure, the little feet. "Enrica! my Enrica!" he cried aloud, so palpable did her presence seem — "I love you, I love you only!" He dashed, as it were, Nera's image from him. She had tempted him—tempted him with all the fullness of her beauty, tempted him—and he had yielded! On a sudden it came over him. Yes, she had tempted him. She had followed him—pursued him rather. Wherever he went, there Nera was before him. He recalled it all. And how he had avoided her with the avoidance of an instinct! He clinched his fists as he thought of it. What devil had possessed him to fall headlong into the snare? What was Nera—or any other woman—to him now? If he had been obliged to dance with her, why had he yielded to her?

"I will never speak to her again," was his instant resolve. But the next moment he remembered that he had been indirectly the cause of an accident which might have been fatal. He must see her once more if she were visible —or, if not, he must see her mother. Common humanity demanded this. Then he would set eyes on her no more. He had almost come to hate her, for the spell she had thrown over him.

But for Enrica he would have left Lucca altogether for

a time. What had passed that evening would be the subject of general gossip. He remembered with shame—and
as he did so the blood rushed over his face and brow—how
openly he had displayed his admiration. He remembered
the hot glances he had cast upon Nera. He remembered
how he had leaned entranced over her chair; how he had
pressed her to him in the fury of that wild waltz, her white
arms entwined round him—the fragrance of the red roses
she wore in her hair mounting to his brain! At the moment he had been too much entranced to observe what was
passing about him. Now he recalled glances and muttered
words. The savage look Ruspoli had cast on him, when he
led her up to him in one of the figures of the cotillon; how
Malatesta had grinned at him—how Orsetti had whispered
."Bravo!" in his ear. Might not some rumor of all this
reach Enrica?—through Trenta, perhaps, or that chattering fool, Baldassare? If they spoke of the accident, they
would surely connect his name with that of Nera. Would
they say he was in love with her? He grew cold as he
thought of it.

Neither could Nobili conceal from himself how probable
it was that the Marchesa Guinigi should come to some
knowledge of his clandestine interviews with her niece.
It had been necessary to trust many persons. Spite of
heavy bribes, one of these might at any moment betray
them. He might be followed and watched, spite of his
precautions. Their letters might be intercepted. Should
any thing happen, what a situation for Enrica! She was
too trusting and too inexperienced fully to appreciate the
danger; but Nobili understood it, and trembled for her.
Something must, he felt, be done at once. Enrica must be
prepared for any thing that might happen. He must write
to her—write this very night to her.

And then came the question—what should he say to
her? Then Nobili felt, and felt keenly, how much he had

compromised himself. Hitherto his love for Enrica, and Enrica's love for him, had been so full, so entire, that every thought was hers. Now there was a name he must hide from her, an hour of his life she must never know.

Nobili rose from the divan on which he had been lying, lighted some candles, and, sitting down at a table, took a pen in his hand. But the pen did not help him. He tore it between his teeth, he leaned his head upon his hand, he stared at the blank paper before him. What should he say to her? was the question he asked himself. After all, should he confess all his weakness, and implore her forgiveness? or should he take the chance of her hearing nothing?

After much thought and many struggles with his pen, he decided he would say nothing. But write he would; write he must. Full of remorse for what had passed, he longed to assure her of his love. He yearned to cast himself for pardon at her feet; to feast his eyes upon the sweetness of her fair face; to fill his ears with the sound of her soft voice; to watch her heavenly eyes gathering upon him with the gleam of incipient passion.

How pure she was! How peerless, how different from all other women! How different from Nera! dark-eyed, flashing, tempting Nera!—Nera, so sensual in her ripe and dazzling beauty. At that moment of remorse and repentance he would have likened her to an alluring fiend, Enrica to an angel! Yes, he would write; he would say something decisive. This point settled, Nobili put down the pen, struck a match, and lit a cigar. A cigar would calm him, and help him to think.

His position, even as he understood it, was sufficiently difficult. How much more, had he known all that lay behind! He had entered life a mere boy at his father's death, with some true friends; his wealth had created him a host of followers. His frank, loyal disposition, his generosity, his lavish hospitality, his winning manners, had insured

him general popularity. Not one, even of those who envied
him, could deny that he was the best fellow in Lucca.
Women adored him, or said so, which came to the same
thing, for he believed them. Many had proved, with more
than words, that they did so. In a word, he had been *fêted*,
followed, and caressed, as long as he could remember.
Now the incense of flattery floating continually in the
air which he breathed had done its work. He was not
actually spoiled, but he had grown arrogant; vain of his person and of his wealth. He was vain, but not yet frivolous;
he was insolent, but not yet heartless. At his age, impres-
sions come from without, rather than from within. Nobili
was extremely impressionable; he also, as has been seen,
wanted resolution to resist temptation. As yet, he had not
developed the firmness and steadfastness that really belonged to his character.

But spite of foibles, spite of weakness — foibles and
weakness were but part of the young blood within him—
Nobili possessed, especially toward women, that rare union
of courage, tenderness, and fortitude, we call chivalry; he
forgot himself in others. He did this as the most natural
thing in the world—he did it because he could not help it.
He was capable of doing a great wrong—he was also capable of a great repentance. His great wealth had hitherto
enabled him to indulge every fancy. With this power of
wealth, unknown almost to himself, a spirit of conquest had
grown upon him. He resolved to overcome whatever opposed itself to him. Nobili was constantly assured by those
ready flatterers who lived upon him—those toadies who, like
a mildew, dim and deface the virtues of the rich—that "he
could do what he pleased."

With the presumption of youth he believed this, and he
acted on it, especially in regard to women. He was of an
age and temperament to feel his pulse quicken at the sight
of every pretty woman he met, even if he should meet a

dozen in the day. Until lately, however, he had cared for
no one. . He had trifled, dangled, ogled. He had plucked
the fair fruit where it hung freely on the branch, and he had
turned away heart-whole. He knew that there was not a
young lady in Lucca who would not accept him as her suitor
—joyfully accept him, if he asked her. Not a father, let
his name be as old as the Crusades, his escutcheon decorated with " the golden rose," or the heraldic ermine of the
emperors, who would not welcome him as a son-in-law.

The Marchesa Guinigi alone had persistently repulsed
him. He had heard and laughed at the outrageous words
she had spoken. He knew what a struggle it had cost her
to sell the second Guinigi Palace at all. He knew that of
all men she had least desired to sell it to him. For that
special reason he had resolved to possess it. He had bought
it, so to say, in spite of her, at the price of gold.

Yet, although Nobili laughed with his friends at the
marchesa's outrageous words, in reality they greatly nettled
him. By constant repetition they came even to rankle.
At last he grew—unconfessed, of course—so aggravated by
them that a secret longing for revenge rose up within him.
She had thrown down the gauntlet, why should he not pick
it up? The marchesa, he knew, had a niece, why should
he not marry the niece, in defiance of the aunt ?

No sooner was this idea conceived than he determined,
if he married at all (marriage to a young man leading his
dissipated life is a serious step), that, of all living women,
the marchesa's niece should be his wife. All this time he
had never seen Enrica. Yes, he would marry the niece, to
spite the marchesa. Marry—she, the marchesa, should see
a Guinigi head his board ; a Guinigi seated at his hearth;
worse than all, a Guinigi mother of his children !

All this he kept closely locked within his own breast.
As the marchesa had intimated to him, at the time he
bought the palace, that she would never permit him to cross

her threshold, he was debarred from taking the usual social steps to accomplish his resolve. Not that he in the least desired to see her, save for that overbearing disposition which impelled him to combat all opposition. With great difficulty, and after having expended various sums in bribes among the ill-paid servants of the marchesa, he had learned the habits of her household.

Enrica, he found, had a servant, formerly her nurse, who never left her. Teresa, this servant, was cautiously approached. She was informed that Count Nobili was distractedly in love with the signorina, and addressed himself to her for help. Teresa, ignorant, well-meaning, and brimming over with that mere animal fondness for her foster-child uneducated women share with brute creatures, was proud of becoming the medium of what she considered an advantageous marriage for Enrica. The secluded life she led, the selfish indifference with which her aunt treated her, had long moved Teresa's passionate southern nature to a high pitch of indignation. Up to this time no man had been permitted to enter Casa Guinigi, save those who formed the marchesa's whist-party.

"How, then," reasoned Teresa, shrewdly, "was the signorina to marry at all ? Surely it was right to help her to a husband. Here was one, rich, handsome, and devoted, one who would give the eyes out of his head for the signorina." Was such an opportunity to be lost? Certainly not.

So Teresa took Nobili's bribes (bribes are as common in Italy as in the East), putting them to fructify in the National Bank with an easy conscience. Was she not emancipating her foster-child from that old devil, her aunt? Had she not seen Nobili himself when he sent for her ?— seen him, face to face, inside his palace glittering like paradise ? And had he not given her his word, with his hand upon his heart (also given her a pair of solid gold ear-rings, which she wore on Sundays), that to marry Enrica was the one hope of his life ? Seeing all this, Teresa was, as I have said, perfectly satisfied.

When Nobili had done all this, impelled by mixed feelings of wounded pride, obstinacy, and defiance, he had never, let it be noted, seen Enrica. But after a meeting had been arranged by Teresa one morning at early mass in the cathedral, near a dark and unfrequented altar in the transept—an arrangement, be it observed, unknown to Enrica—all his feelings changed. From the moment he saw her he loved her with all the fervor of his ardent nature; from that moment he knew that he had never loved before. The mystery of their stolen meetings, the sweet flavor of this forbidden fruit—and what man does not love forbidden fruit better than labeled pleasures ?—the innocent frankness with which Enrica confessed her love, her unbounded faith in him—all served to heighten his passion. He gloried—he reveled in her confidence. Never, never, he swore a thousand times, should she have cause to repent it. In the possession of Enrica's love, all other desires, aims, ambitions, had—up to the night of the Orsetti ball—vanished. Up to that night, for her sake, he had grown solitary, silent—nay, even patient and subtle. He had clean forgotten his feud with the Marchesa Guinigi, or only remembered it as a possible obstacle to his union with Enrica; otherwise the marchesa was absolutely indifferent to him. Up to the night of the Orsetti ball the whole world was indifferent to him. But now !—

Nobili, sitting very still, his face shaded by his hand, had finished his cigar. While smoking it he had decided what he would say to Enrica. Again he took up his pen. This time he dropped it in the ink, and wrote as follows:

"AMORE: I have treasured all the love you gave me when last we met. I know that love witnesses for me also

in your own heart. Beyond all earthly things you are dear
to me. Come to me, O my Enrica—come to me; never
let us part. I must have you, you only. I must gaze
upon you hour by hour; I must hang upon that dear voice.
I must feel that angel-presence ever beside me. When
will you meet me? I implore you to answer. After our
next meeting I am resolved to claim you, by force or by
free-will, to be my wife. To wait longer, O my Enrica,
is good neither for you nor for me. My love! my love!
you must be mine—mine—mine! Come to me—come
quickly. '   Your adoring

"MARIO NOBILI."

CHAPTER V.

CESARE TRENTA is dressed with unusual care. His linen is spotless; his white hair, as fine as silk, is carefully· combed; his chin is well shaven. He wears a glossy white hat, and carries his gold-headed cane in his hand. Not that he condescends to use that cane as he mounts the marble staircase of the Universo Hotel (once the Palazzo Buffero) a little stiffly, on his way to keep his appointment with Count Marescotti; oh, no—although the cavaliere is well past eighty, he intends to live much longer; he reserves that cane, therefore, to assist him in his old age. Now he does not want it.

It is quite clear that Trenta is come on a mission of great importance; his sleek air, and the solemnly official expression of his plump rosy face, say so. His glassy blue eyes are without their pleasant twinkle, and his lips, tightly drawn over his teeth, lack their usual benignant smile. Even his fat white hand dimples itself on the top of his cane, so tightly does he clutch it. He has learned below that Count Marescotti lives at No. 4 on the second story; at the door of No. 4 he raps softly. A voice from within asks, " Who is there ? "

" I," replies Trenta, and he enters.

The count, who is seated at a table near the window,

rises. His tall figure is enveloped in a dark dressing-gown, that folds about him like a toga. He has all the aspect of a man roused out of deep thought; his black hair stands straight up in disordered curls all over his head—he had evidently been digging both his hands into it—his eyes are wild and abstracted. Taken as he is now, unawares, that expression of mingled sternness and sweetness in which he so much resembles Castruccio Castracani is very striking. From the manner he fixes his eyes upon Trenta it is clear he does not at once recognize him. The cavaliere returns his stare with a look of blank dismay.

"Oh, carissimo!" the count exclaims at last, his countenance changing to its usual expression—he holds out both hands to grasp those of the cavaliere—"how I rejoice to see you! Excuse my absence; I had forgotten our appointment at the moment. That book"—and he points to an open volume lying on a table covered with letters, manuscripts, and piles of printed sheets tossed together in wild confusion—"that book must plead my excuse; it has riveted me. The wrongs of persecuted Italy are so eloquently pleaded! Have you read it, my dear cavaliere? If not, allow me to present you with a copy."

Trenta made a motion with his hand, as if putting both the book and the subject from him with a certain disgust: he shakes his head.

"I have not read it, and I do not wish to read it," he replies, curtly.

The poor cavaliere feels that this is a bad beginning; but he quickly consoles himself—he was of a hopeful temperament, and saw life serenely and altogether in rose-color—by remembering that the count is habitually absent, also that he habitually uses strong language, and that he had probably not been so absorbed by the wrongs of Italy as he pretends.

"I fear you have forgotten our appointment, count,"

recommences the cavaliere, finding that Marescotti is silent, and that his eyes have wandered off to the pages of the open book.

"Not at all, not at all, my dear Trenta. On the contrary, had you not come, I was about to send for you. I have a very important matter to communicate to you."

The cavaliere's face now breaks out all over into smiles. "Send for me," he repeats to himself. "Good, good! I understand." He seats himself with great deliberation in a large, well-stuffed arm-chair, near the table, at which Marescotti still continues standing. He places his cane across his knees, folds his hands together, then looks up in the other's face.

"Yes, yes, my dear count," he answers aloud, "we have much to say to each other—much to say on a most interesting subject." And he gives the count what he intends to be a very meaning glance.

"Interesting!" exclaims the count, his whole countenance lighting up—"enthralling, overwhelming!—a matter to me of life or death!"

As he speaks he turns aside, and begins to stride up and down the room, as was his wont when much moved.

"He! he! my dear count, pray be calm." And Trenta gives a little laugh, and feebly winks. "We hope it is a matter of *life*, not of *death*—no—not of *death*, surely."

"Of death," replied the count, solemnly, and his mobile eyes flash out, and a dark frown gathers on his brow—"of death, I repeat. Do you take me for a trifler? I stake my life on the die."

Trenta felt considerably puzzled. Before he begins, he is anxious to assure himself that the nature of his errand had at least distinctly dawned upon the count's mind, if it had not (as he hoped) been fully understood by him. Should he let Marescotti speak first; or should he, Trenta, address him formally? In order to decide, he again scans

the count's face closely. But, after doing so, he is obliged
to confess that Marescotti is impenetrable. Now he no
longer strode up and down the room, but he has seated
himself opposite the cavaliere, and again his speaking eyes
have wandered off toward the book which he has been
reading. It is evident he is mentally resuming the same
train of thought Trenta's entrance had interrupted. Trenta
feels therefore that he must begin. He has prepared himself for some transcendentalism on the subject of marriage;
but with a man who is so much in love as Count Marescotti,
and who was about to send for him and to tell him so, there
can be no great difficulty; nor can it matter much who
opens the conversation. The cavaliere takes a spotless handkerchief from his pocket, uses it, replaces it, then coughs.

"Count," he begins, in a tone of conscious importance,
"when I proposed this meeting, it was to make you a
proposal calculated to exercise the utmost influence over
your future life, and—the life of another," he adds, in a
lower tone. "You appear to have anticipated me by desiring to send for me. You are, of course, aware of my
errand ? "

As he asks this question, there is, spite of himself, a
slight tremor in his voice, and the usual ruddiness of his
cheeks pales a little.

"How very mysterious ! " exclaims the count, throwing
himself back in his chair. "You look like a benevolent
conspirator, cavaliere ! Surely, my dear old friend, you are
not about to change your opinions, and to become a disciple of freedom ? "

"Change my opinions ! At my age, count !—Chè, chè ! "
—Trenta waves his hand impatiently. "When a man ar-
rives at my age, he does not change his opinions—no,
count, no; it is, if you will permit me to say so, it is yourself in whom the change is to be wrought—yourself
only—"

The count, who is still leaning back in his chair in an attitude of polite attention, starts violently, sits straight upright, and fixes his eyes upon Trenta.

"What do you mean, cavaliere? After a life devoted to my country, you cannot imagine I should change? The very idea is offensive to me."

"No, no, my dear count, you misapprehend me," rejoins Trenta, soothingly. (He perceived the mistake into which the word "change" had led Count Marescotti, and dreaded exciting his too susceptible feelings.) "It is no change of that kind I allude to; the change I mean is in the nature of a reward for the life of sacrifice you have led—a reward, a consolation to your fervid spirit. It is to bring you into an atmosphere of peace, happiness, and love. To reconcile you perhaps, as a son, erring, but repentant, with that Holy Mother Church to which you still belong. This is the change I am come to offer you."

As the cavaliere proceeds, the count's expressive eyes follow every word he utters with a look of amazement. He is about to reply, but Trenta places his finger on his lips.

"Let me continue," he says, smiling blandly. "When I have done, you shall answer. In one word, count, it is marriage I am come to propose to you."

The count suddenly rises from his seat, then he hurriedly reseats himself. A look of pain comes into his face.

"Permit me to proceed," urges the cavaliere, watching him anxiously. "I presume you mean to marry?"

Marescotti was silent. Trenta's naturally piping voice grows shriller as he proceeds, from a certain sense of agitation.

"As the common friend of both parties, I am come to propose a marriage to you, Count Marescotti."

"And who may the lady be?" asks the count, drawing back with a sudden air of reserve. "Who is it that would consent to leave home and friends, perhaps country, to share the lot of a fugitive patriot?"

"Come, come, count, this will not do," answers Trenta, smiling, a certain twinkle returning to his blue eyes. "You are a perfectly free agent. If you are a fugitive, it is because you like change. You bear a great name—you are rich, singularly handsome—an ardent admirer of beauty in art and Nature. Now, ardor on one side excites ardor on the other,"

While he is speaking, Trenta had mentally decided that Marescotti was the most impracticable man he had ever encountered in the various phases of his court career.

"A fugitive," he repeats, almost with a sneer. "No, no, count, this will not do with me." The cavaliere pauses and clears his throat.

· "You have not yet answered me," says the count, speaking low, a certain suppressed eagerness penetrating the assumed indifference of his manner. "Who is the lady?"

"Who is the lady?" echoes the cavaliere. "Did you not tell me just now you were about to send for me?" Trenta speaks fast, a flush overspreads his cheeks. "Who is the lady?—You astonish me! Per Bacco! There can be but one lady in question between you and me—that lady is Enrica Guinigi." His voice drops. There is a dead silence.

"That the marriage is suitable in all respects," Trenta continues, reassured by the silence—"I need not tell you; else I, Cesare Trenta, would not be here as the embassador."

Again the stout little cavaliere stops to take breath, under evident agitation; then he draws himself up, and turns his face toward the count. As Trenta proceeds, Marescotti's brow is overclouded with thought—a haggard expression now spreads over his features. His eyes are turned downward on the floor, else the cavaliere might have seen that their brilliancy is dimmed by rising tears. With his elbow resting on the arm of the chair on which he sits, the count passes his other hand from time to time slowly to and fro across his forehead, pushing back the disordered curls that fall upon it.

"To restore and to continue an illustrious race—to unite yourself with a lovely girl just bursting into womanhood." Trenta's voice quivers as he says this. "Ah! lovely indeed, in mind as well as body," he adds, half aloud. "This is a privilege you, Count Marescotti, can appreciate above all other men. That you do appreciate it you have already made evident. There is no need for me to speak about Enrica herself; you have already judged her. You have, before my eyes, approached her with the looks and the language of passionate admiration. It is not given to all men to be so fascinating. I have seen it with delight. I love her'—his voice broke and shook with emotion—"I love her as if she were my own child."

All the enthusiasm of which the old chamberlain is capable passes into his face as he speaks of Enrica. At that moment he really did look as young as he was continually telling every one that he felt.

"Count Marescotti," he continues, a solemn tone in his voice as he slowly pronounces the words, raising his head at the same time, and gazing fixedly into the other's face— "Count Marescotti, I am come here to propose a marriage between you and Enrica Guinigi. The marchesa empowers me to say that she constitutes Enrica her sole heiress, not only of the great Guinigi name, but of the remaining Guinigi palace, with the portrait of our Castruccio, the heirlooms, the castle of Corellia, and lands of—"

"Stop, stop, my dear Trenta!" cries the count, holding up both his hands in remonstrance; "you overwhelm me. I require no such inducements; they horrify me. Enrica

Guinigi is sufficient in herself—so bright a jewel requires no golden settings."

At these words the cavaliere beams all over. He rubs his fat hands together, then gently claps them.

"Bravo!—bravo, count! I see you appreciate her. Per Dio! you make me feel young again! I never was so happy in my life! I should like to dance! I will dance by-and-by at the wedding. We will open the state-rooms. There is not a grander suite in all Italy. It is superb. I will dance a quadrille with the marchesa. Bagatella! I shall insist on it. I will execute a solo in the figure of the *pastorelle*. I will show Baldassare and all the young men the finish of the old style. People did steps then—they did not jump like wild horses—nor knock each other down. No—then dancing was practised as a fine art."

Suddenly the brisk old cavaliere stops. The expression of Marescotti's large, earnest eyes, fixed on him wonderingly, recalls him to himself.

"Excuse me, my dear friend; when you are my age, you will better understand an old man's feelings. We are losing time. Now get your hat, and come with me at once to Casa Guinigi; the marchesa expects you. We will settle the day of the betrothal.—My sweet Enrica, how I long to see you!"

While he is speaking Trenta rises and strikes his cane on the ground with a triumphant air; then he holds out both his hands toward the count.

"Shake hands with me, my dear Marescotti. I congratulate you—with my whole soul I congratulate you! She will be your salvation, the dear, blue-eyed little angel?"

In the tumult of his excitement Trenta had taken every thing for granted. His thoughts had flown off to Enrica. His benevolent heart throbbed with joy at the thought of her emancipation from the thralldom of her home. A vision of the dark-haired, pale-faced Marescotti, and the little blond head, with its shower of golden curls, kneeling together before the altar in the sunshine, danced before his eyes. Marescotti would become a Christian—a firm pillar of the Church; he would rear up children who would worship God and the Holy Father; he would restore the glory of the Guinigi!

From this roseate dream the poor cavaliere was abruptly roused. His outstretched hand had not been taken by Marescotti. It dropped to his side. Trenta looked up sharply. His countenance suddenly fell; a purple flush covered it from chin to forehead, penetrating even the very roots of his snowy hair. His cane dropped with a loud thud, and rolled away along the uncarpeted floor. He thrust both his hands into his pockets, and stood motionless, with his eyes wide open, like a man stunned.

"Dio buono!—Dio buono!" he muttered, "the man is mad!—the man is mad!" Then, after a few minutes of absolute silence, he asked, in a husky voice, "Marescotti, what does this mean?"

The count had turned away toward the window. At the sound of the cavaliere's husky voice, he moved and faced him. In the space of a few moments he had greatly changed. Suddenly he had grown worn and weary-looking. His eyes were sunk into his head; dark circles had formed round them. His bloodless cheeks, transparent with the pallor of perfect health, were blanched; the corners of his mouth worked convulsively.

"Does the lady—does Enrica Guinigi know of this proposal?" he asked, in a voice so sad that the cavaliere's indignation against him cooled considerably.

"Good God!" exclaimed Trenta, "such a question is an insult to me and to my errand. Can you imagine that I, all my life chamberlain to his highness the Duke of Lucca, am capable of compromising a lady?"

"Thank God!" ejaculated the count, emphatically, clasping his hands together, and raising his eyes—"thank God! Forgive me for asking." His whole voice and manner had changed as rapidly as his aspect. There was a sense of suffering, a quiet resignation about him, so utterly unlike his usual excitable manner that Trenta was puzzled beyond expression—so puzzled, indeed, that he was speechless. Besides, a veteran in etiquette, he felt that it was to himself an explanation was due. Marescotti had been about to send for him. Now he was there, Marescotti had heard his proposal, it was for Marescotti to answer.

That the count felt this also was apparent. There was something solemn in his manner as he turned away from the window and slowly advanced toward the cavaliere. Trenta was still standing immovable on the same spot where he had muttered in the first moment of amazement, "He is mad!"

"My dear old friend," said the count, speaking with evident effort in a dull, sad voice, "there is some mistake. It was not to speak about any lady that I was about to send for you."

"Not about a lady!" cried Trenta, aghast. "Mercy of God!—"

"Let that pass," interrupted the count, waving his hand. "You have asked me for an explanation—an explanation you shall have." He sighed deeply, then proceeded—the crvaliere following every word he uttered with open mouth and wildly-staring eyes: "Of the lady I can say no more than that, on my honor as a gentleman, to me she approaches nearer the divine than any woman I have ever seen—nay, than any woman I have ever dreamed of."

A flash of fire lit up the depths of the count's dark eyes, and there was a tone of melting tenderness in his rich voice as he spoke of Enrica. Then he relapsed into his former weary manner—the manner of a man pronouncing his own death-warrant.

"Of the unspeakable honor you have done me, as has also the excellent Marchesa Guinigi—it does not become me to speak. Believe me, I feel it profoundly." And the count laid his hand upon his heart and bent his grand head. Trenta, with formal politeness, returned the silent salute.

"But"—and here the count's voice faltered, and there was a dimness in his eyes; round which the black circles had deepened—"but it is an honor I must decline."

Trenta, still rooted to the same spot, listened to each word that fell from the count's lips with a look of anguish.

"Sit down, cavaliere—sit down," continued Marescotti, seeing his distress. He put his arm round Trenta's burly, well-filled figure, and drew him down gently into the depths of the arm-chair. "Listen, cavaliere—listen to what I have to say before you altogether condemn me. The sacrifice I am making costs me more than I can express. You hold before my eyes what is to me more precious than life; you tempt me with what every sense within me—heart, soul, manliness—urges me to clutch; yet I dare not accept it."

He paused; so profound a sigh escaped him that it almost formed itself into a groan.

"I don't understand all this," said Trenta, reddening with indignation. He had been by degrees collecting his scattered senses. "I don't understand it at all. You have, count, placed me in a most awkward position; I feel it very much. You speak of a mistake—a misapprehension. I beg to say there has been none on my part; I am not in the habit of making mistakes."—It will be seen that the cavaliere's temper was rising with the sense of the intolerable injury Count Marescotti was inflicting on himself and all concerned.—"I have undertaken a very serious responsibility; I have failed, you tell me. What am I to say to the marchesa?"

His shrill voice rose into an angry cry. Altogether, it was more than he could bear. For a moment, the injury to Enrica was forgotten in his own personal sense of wrong. It was too galling to fail in an official embassy Trenta, who always acted upon mature reflection, abhorred failure.

"Tell her," answered the count, raising his voice, his eyes kindling as he spoke—"tell her I am here in Lucca on a sacred mission. I confide it to her honor. A man sworn to a mission cannot marry. As in the kingdom of heaven they neither marry nor are given in marriage, so I, the anointed priest of the people, dare not marry; it would be sacrilege." His powerful voice rang through the room; he raised his hands aloft, as if invoking some unseen power to whom he belonged. "When you, cavaliere, entered this room, I was about to confide my position to you. I am at Lucca—Lucca, once the foster-mother of progress, and, I pray Heaven, to become so again!—I am at Lucca to found a mission of freedom." A sudden gesture told him how much Trenta was taken aback at this announcement. "We differ in our opinions as widely as the poles," continued the count, warming to his subject, "but you are my old friend—I felt you would not betray me. Now, after what has passed, as a man of honor, I am bound to confide in you. O Italy! my country!" exclaimed the count, clasping his hands, and throwing back his head in a frenzy of enthusiasm, "what sacrifice is too great for thee? Youth, hope, love—nay, life itself—all—all I devote to thee!"

As he was speaking, a ray of sunlight penetrated through the closed windows. It struck like a fiery arrow across the darkened room, and fell full upon the count's up-turned face, lighting up every line of his noble countenance. There was a solemn passion in his eyes, a rapt fervor in his gaze, that silenced even the justly-irritated Trenta.

Nevertheless the cavaliere was not a man to be put off by mere words, however imposing they might be. He returned, therefore, to the charge perseveringly.

"You speak of a mission, Count Marescotti; what is the nature of this mission? Nothing political, I hope?"

He stopped abruptly. The count's eyelids dropped over his eyes as he met Trenta's inquiring glance. Then he bowed his head in acquiescence.

"Another revolution may do much for Italy," he answered, in a low tone.

"For the love of God," ejaculated Trenta, stung to the quick by what he looked upon at that particular moment as in itself an aggravation of his wrongs, "don't remind me of your politics, or I shall instantly leave the room. Domine Dio! it is too much. You have just escaped by the veriest good luck (good luck, by-the-way, you did not in the least deserve) a life-long imprisonment at Rome. You had a mission there, too, I believe."

This was spoken in as bitter a sneer as the cavaliere's kindly nature permitted.

"Now pray be satisfied. If you and I are not to part this very instant, don't let me realize you as the 'Red count.' That is a character I cannot tolerate."

Trenta, so seldom roused to anger, shook all over with rage. "I believe sincerely that it is such so-called patriots as yourself, with their devilish missions, that will ruin us all."

"It is because you are ignorant of the grandeur of our cause, it is because you do not understand our principles, that you misjudge us," responded the count, raising his eyes upon Trenta, and speaking with a lofty disregard of his hot words. "Permit me to unfold to you something of our philosophy, a philosophy which will resuscitate our country, and place her again in her ancient position, as intellectual monitress of Europe. You must not, cavaliere,

judge either of my mission or of my creed by the yelping
of the miserable curs that dog the heels of all great enter-
prises.   There is the penetralia, the esoteric belief, in all
great systems of national belief."

The count spoke with emphasis, yet in grave and measured accents; but his lustrous eyes, and the wild confusion
of those black locks, that waved, as it were, sympathetic to
his humor, showed that his mind was engrossed with
thoughts of overwhelming interest.

The cavaliere, after his last indignant outburst, had subsided into the depths of the arm-chair in which Marescotti
had placed him; it was so large as almost to swallow up
the whole of his stout little person.   With his hands joined,
his dimpled fingers interlaced and pointing upward, he
patiently awaited what the count might say.   He felt painfully conscious that he had failed in his errand.   This irritated him exceedingly.   He had not entered that room—
No. 4, at the Universo Hotel—in order to listen to the
elaboration of Count Marescotti's mission, but in order to
set certain marriage-bells ringing.   These marriage-bells
were, it seemed, to be forever mute.   Still, having demanded an explanation of what he conceived to be the
count's most incomprehensible conduct, he was bound, he
felt, in common courtesy, to listen to all he had to say.

Now Trenta never in his life was wanting in the very
flower of courtesy; he would much sooner have shot himself than be guilty of an ill-bred word.   So, under protest,
therefore—a protest more distinctly written in the general
puckering up of his round, plump face, and a certain sulky
swell about his usually smiling mouth—it was clear he
meant to listen, cost him what it might.   Besides, when
he had heard what the count had to say, it was clearly his
duty to reason with him.   Who could tell that he might
not yield to such a process?   He avowed that he was deeply
enamored of Enrica—a man in love is already half van-

quished. Why should Marescotti throw away his chance of happiness for a phantasy—a mere dream? There was no real obstacle. He was versatile and visionary, but the very soul of honor. How, if he—Trenta—could bring Marescotti to see how much it would be to Enrica's advantage that he should transplant her from a dreary home, to become a wife beside him?

Decidedly it was still possible that he, Cesare Trenta, who had arranged satisfactorily so many most difficult royal complications, might yet bring Marescotti to reason. Who could tell that he might not yet be spared the humiliation of returning to impart his failure to the marchesa? A return, be it said, the good Trenta dreaded not a little, remembering the characteristics of his dear friend, and the responsibility of success which he had so confidently taken upon himself before he started.

8

CHAPTER VI.

A NEW PHILOSOPHY.

THERE had been an interval of silence, during which the count paced up and down the spacious room meditatively, each step sounding distinctly on the stone floor. The rugged look of conscious power upon his face, the far-away glance in his sombre eyes, showed that his mind was working upon what he was about to say. Presently he ceased to walk, reseated himself opposite the cavaliere, and fixed a half-absent gaze upon him.

Trenta, who would cheerfully have undergone any amount of suffering rather than listen to the abominations he felt were coming, sat with half-closed eyes, gathered into the corner of the arm-chair, the very picture of patient martyrdom.

The count contemplated him for a moment. As he did so an expression, half cynical, half melancholy, passed over his countenance, and a faint smile lurked about the corners of his mouth. Then in a voice so full and sweet that the ear eagerly drank in the sound, like the harmony of a cadence, he began:

"The Roman Catholic Church," he said, "styles itself divinely constituted. It claims to be supreme arbiter in religion and morals; supreme even in measuring intellectual progress; absolute in its jurisdiction over the state, and solely responsible to itself as to what the limit of that jurisdiction shall be. It calls itself supreme and absolute, because infallible—infallible because divine. Thus the vicious circle is complete. Now entire obedience necessarily comes into collision with every species of freedom—nay, it is in itself antagonistic to freedom—freedom of thought, freedom of action—specially antagonistic to national freedom."

"The supremacy of the pope (the Holy Father)," put in Trenta, meekly; he crossed himself several times in rapid succession, looking afterward as if it had been a great consolation to him.

"The supremacy of the pope," repeated the count, firmly, the shadow of a smile parting his lips, "is eternal. It is based as firmly in the next world as it is in this. It constitutes a condition of complete tyranny both in time and in eternity. Now I," and the count's voice rose, and his eyes glowed, "I—both in my public and private capacity—(call me Antichrist if you please)." A visible shudder passed over the poor cavaliere; his eyes closed altogether, and his lips moved. (He was repeating an Ave Maria Sanctissima). "I abhor, I renounce this slavery!—I rebel against it!—I will have none of it. Who shall control the immortality of thought?—a Pius, a Gregory? Ignorant dreamers, perjured priests!—never!"

As he spoke, the count raised his right arm, and circled it in the air. In imagination he was waving the flag of liberty over a prostrate world.

"But, alas! this slavery is riveted by the grasp of centuries; it requires measures as firm and uncompromising as its own to dislodge it. Now the pope"—Trenta did not this time attempt to correct Marescotti—"the pope is theoretically of no nation, but in reality he is of all nations; and he is surrounded by a court of celibate priests, also

without nation. Observe, cavaliere—this absolute domin-
ion is attained by celibates only—men with no family ties
—no household influences." (This was spoken, as it
were, *en parenthèse*, as a comment on the earlier portion
of the conversation that had taken place between them.)
" Each of these celibate priests is the pope's courtier—his
courtier and his slave ; his slave because he is subject to a
higher law than the law of his own conscience, and the
law of his own country. Without home or family, nation-
ality or worldly interest, the priest is a living machine, to
be used in whatever direction his tyrant dictates. Every
priest, therefore, be he cardinal or deacon, moves and acts
the slave of an abstract idea; an idea incompatible with
patriotism, humanity, or freedom."

An audible and deep groan escaped from the suffering
cavaliere as the count's voice ceased.

" Now, Cavaliere Trenta, mark the application." As
the count proceeded with his argument, his dark eyes, lit
up with the enthusiasm of his own oratory, riveted themselves on the arm-chair. (It could not properly be said
that his eyes riveted themselves on Trenta, for he was
stooping down, his face covered with his hands, altogether
insensible to any possible appeal that might be addressed
to him.) "I, Manfredi Marescotti, consecrated priest of
the people "—and the count drew himself up to the full
height of his lofty figure—" I am as devoted to my cause—
God is my witness "—and he raised his right hand as
though to seal a solemn pledge of truth—" as that consecrated renegade, the pope ! My followers—and their name
is legion—believe in me as implicitly as do the tonsured
dastards of the Vatican."

Another ill-suppressed groan escaped from Trenta, and
for a moment interrupted the count's oration. The miserable cavaliere ! He had, indeed, invoked an explanation,
and, cost him what it might, he must abide it. But he be-

gan to think that the explanation had gone too far. He was sitting there listening to blasphemies. He was actually imperiling his own soul. He was horrified as he reflected that he might not obtain absolution when he confessed the awful language which was addressed to him. Such a risk was really greater than his submission to etiquette exacted. There were bound seven to that, the aged chamberlain told himself.

Gracious heavens!—for him, an unquestioning papalino, a sincere believer in papal infallibility and the temporal power—to hear the Holy Father called a renegade, and his faithful servants stigmatized as dastards! It was monstrous!

He secretly resolved that, once escaped from No. 4 at the Universo Hotel—and he wondered that a thunderbolt had not already struck the count dead where he stood —he would never allow himself to have any further intercourse whatever with him.

"I have been elected," continued the count, speaking in the same emphatic manner, and in the same distinct and harmonious voice, utterly careless or unobservant of the conflict of feelings under which the cavaliere was struggling —"head pope, if you please, cavaliere, so to call me."— ("God forbid!" muttered Trenta.)—"It makes my analogy the clearer—I have been elected by thousands of devoted followers. But my followers are not slaves, nor am I a tyrant. I have accepted the glorious title of Priest of the People, and nothing—*nothing*," the count repeated, vehemently, "shall tempt me from my duty. I am here at Lucca to establish a mission—to plant in this fertile soil the sacred banner of freedom—red as the first streaks of light that lace the eastern heavens; red as the life-blood from which we draw our being. I am here, under the protection of this glorious banner, to combat the tyranny upon which the church and the throne are based. Instead of the

fetters of the past, binding mankind in loathsome trammels
of ignorance—instead of the darkness that broods over a
subjugated world—of terrors that rend agonized souls with
horrible tortures—I bring peace, freedom, light, progress.
To the base ideal of perpetual tyranny—both here and
hereafter—I oppose the pure ideal of absolute freedom—
freedom to each separate soul to work out for itself its own
innate convictions—freedom to form its independent des-
tiny. Freedom in state, freedom in church, freedom iu religion, literature, commerce, government—freedom as boundless as the sunshine that fructifies the teeming earth! Freedom of thought necessitates freedom in government. As
the soul wings itself toward the light of simple truth, so
should the body politic aspire to perfect freedom. This
can only be found in a pure republic; a republic where
all men are equal—where each man lives for the other in living for himself—where brother cleaves to brother as his own
flesh—family is knit to family—one, yet many—one, yet of
all nations!"

"Communism, in fact!" burst forth the cavaliere. His
piping voice, now hoarse with rage, quivered. "You are
here to form a communistic association! God help us!"

"I care not what you call it," cried the count, with a
rising passion. "My faith, my hope, is the ideal of freedom as opposed to the abstraction of hierarchical superstition and monarchic tyranny. What are popes, kings,
princes, and potentates, to me who deem all men equal?
It is by a republic alone that we can regenerate our beloved, our unfortunate Italy, now tossed between a de-
bauched monarch—a traitor, who yielded Savoy—an effete
Parliament—a pack of lawyers who represent nothing but
their own interests, and a pope—the recreant of Gaeta!
The sooner our ideas are circulated, the sooner they will
permeate among the masses. Already the harvest has been
great elsewhere. I am here to sow, to reap, and to gather.

For this end—mark me, cavaliere, I entreat you—I am
here, for none other."

Here the triumphant patriot became suddenly embarrassed. He stopped, hesitated, stopped again, took breath,
and sighed; then turned full upon Trenta, in order to obtain some response to the appeal he had addressed to him.
But again Trenta, sullenly silent, had buried himself in the
depths of the arm-chair, and was, so to say, invisible.

"For this end" (a mournful cadence came into the
count's voice when he at length proceeded) "I am ready
to sacrifice my life. My life!—what is that? I am ready
to sacrifice my love—ay, my love—the love of the only
woman who fulfills the longings of my poetic soul."

The count ceased speaking. The fair Enrica, with her
tender smile, and patient, chastened loveliness—Enrica, as
he had imagined her, the type of the young Madonna, was
before him. No, Enrica could never be his; no child of
his would ever be encircled by those soft, womanly arms!
With a strong effort to shake off the feeling which so
deeply moved him, the count continued:

"In the boundless realms of ideal philosophy"—his
noble features were at this moment lit up into the living
image of that hero he so much resembled—"man grapples
hand to hand with the unseen. There are no limits to his
glorious aspirations. He is as God himself. He, too, becomes a Creator; and a new and purer world forms beneath
his hand."

"Have you done?" asked Trenta, looking up out of
the arm-chair. He was so thoroughly overcome, so subdued, he could have wept. From the very commencement
of the count's explanation, he had felt that it was not
given to him to combat his opinions. If he could, he was
not sure that he would have ventured to do so. "Let
pitch alone," says the proverb.

Now Trenta, of a most cleanly nature, morally and

physically—abhorred pitch, especially such pitch as this. He had long looked upon Count Marescotti as an atheist, a visionary—but he had never conceived him capable of establishing an organized system of rebellion and communism. At Lucca, too! It was horrible! By some means such an incendiary must be got rid of. Next to the foul Fiend himself established in the city, he could conceive nothing more awful! It was a Providence that Marescotti could not marry Enrica! He should tell the marchesa so. Such sophistry might have perverted Enrica also. It was more than probable that, instead of reforming him, she might have fallen a victim to his wickedness. This reflection was infinitely comforting to the much-enduring cavaliere. It lightened also much of his apprehension in approaching the marchesa, as the bearer of the count's refusal.

To Trenta's question as to "whether he had done," Marescotti had promptly replied with easy courtesy, "Certainly, if you desire it. But, my dear cavaliere," he went on to say, speaking in his usual manner, "you will now understand why, cost me what it may, I cannot marry. Never, never, I confess, have I been so fiercely tempted! But the pang is past!" And he swept his hand over his brow. "Marriage with me is impossible. You will understand this."

"Yes, yes, I quite agree with you, count," put in Trenta—sideways, as it were. He was rejoiced to find he had any common standing-point left with Marescotti. "I agree with you—marriage is quite impossible. I hope, too," he added, recovering himself a little, with a faint twinkle in his eye, "you will find your mission at Lucca equally impossible. San Riccardo grant it!" And the old man crossed himself, and secretly fingered an image of the Virgin he wore about his neck.

"Putting aside the sacred office with which I am invested," resumed the count, without noticing Trenta's observation, "no wife could sympathize with me. It would be a case of Byron over again. What agony it would be to me to see the exquisite Enrica unable to understand me! A poet, a mystic, I am only fit to live alone. My path "—and a far-away look came into his eyes—"my path lies alone upon the mountains—alone! alone!" he added sorrowfully, and a tear trembled on his eyelid.

"Then why, may I ask you," retorted Trenta, with energy, raising himself upright in the arm-chair, "why did you mislead me by such passionate language to Enrica? Recall the Guinigi Tower, your attitude—your glances—I must say, Count Marescotti, I consider your conduct unpardonable—quite unpardonable."

Trenta's face and forehead were scarlet, his steely blue eyes were rounded to their utmost width, and, as far as such mild eyes could, they glared at the count.

"You have entirely misled me. As to your political opinions, I have, thank God, nothing to do with them; that is your affair. But in this matter of Enrica you have unjustifiably misled me. I shall not forgive you in a hurry, I can tell you." There was a rustling of anger all over the cavaliere, as the leaves of the forest-trees rustle before the breath of the coming tempest.

"My admiration for women," replied the count, "has hitherto been purely æsthetic. You, cavaliere, cannot understand the discrepancies of an artistic nature. Women have been to me heretofore as beautiful abstractions. I have adored them as I adore the works of the great masters. I would as soon have thought of plucking a virgin from the canvas—a Venus from her pedestal, as of appropriating one of them. Enrica Guinigi "—there was a tender inflection in Count Marescotti's voice whenever he named her, an involuntary bending of the head that was infinitely touching —"Enrica Guinigi is an exception. I could have loved her

—ah! she is worthy of all love! Her soul is as rare as
her person. I read in the depths of her plaintive eyes the
trust of a child and the fortitude of a heroine. If I dared
to give these thoughts utterance, it was because I knew *she
loved another!*"

"Loved another?" screamed Trenta, losing all self-control and tottering to his feet. "Loved another?" he repeated, every feature working convulsively. "What do
you mean?"

Marescotti rose also. Was it possible that Trenta could
be in ignorance, he asked himself, hurriedly, as he stared
at the aged chamberlain, trembling from head to foot.

"Loved another? You are mad, Count Marescotti, I
always said so—mad! mad!" Trenta gasped for breath.
He was hardly able to articulate.

The count bowed to him ironically.

"Calm yourself, cavaliere," he said, haughtily, measuring from head to foot the plump little cavaliere, who stood
before him literally panting with rage. "There is no need
for violence. You and the marchesa must have known of
this. I shuddered, when I thought that Enrica might have
been driven into acquiescence with your proposal against
her will. I love her too much to have permitted it."

The cavaliere could with difficulty bring himself to allow
Marescotti to finish. He was too furious to take in the full
sense of what he said. His throat was parched.

"You must answer to me for this!" Trenta could barely
articulate. His voice was dry and hoarse. "You must—
you shall. You have refused Enrica, now you insult her.
I demand—I demand satisfaction. No excuse—no excuse!"
he shouted. And seeing that Marescotti drew back toward
the window, the cavaliere pressed closer upon him, stamped
his foot upon the floor, and raised his clinched fist as near
to the count's face as his height permitted.

Had the official sword hung at Trenta's side, he would

undoubtedly have drawn it at that moment and attacked him. In the defense of Enrica he forgot his age—he forgot every thing. His very voice had changed into a manly barytone. In the absence of his sword, Trenta was evidently about to strike Marescotti. As he advanced, the other retreated.

A hot flush overspread the count's face for an instant, then it faded out, and grew pale and rigid. He remembered the cavaliere's great age, and checked himself. To avoid him, the count retreated to the farthest limit of the room, hastily seized a chair, and barricaded himself behind it. "I will not fight you, Cavaliere Trenta," he answered, speaking with calmness.

"Ah, coward!" screamed Trenta, "would you dishonor me?"

"Cavaliere Trenta, this is folly," said the count, crossing his arms on his breast. "Strike me if you please," he added, seeing that Trenta still threatened him. "Strike me; I shall not return it. On my honor as a gentleman, what I have said is true. Had you, cavaliere, been a younger man, you must have heard it in the city, at the club, the theatre; it is known everywhere."

"What is known?" asked Trenta, hoarsely, standing suddenly motionless, the flush of rage dying out of his countenance, and a look of helpless suffering taking its place.

"That Count Nobili loves Enrica Guinigi," answered Marescotti, abruptly.

Like a shot Baldassare's words rose to Trenta's remembrance. The poor old chamberlain turned very white. He quivered like a leaf, and clung to the table for support.

"Pardon me, oh! pardon me a thousand times, if I have pained you," exclaimed the count; he left the place where he was standing, threw his arms round Trenta, and placed him with careful tenderness on a seat. His generous heart upbraided him bitterly for having allowed himself for an instant to be heated by the cavaliere's reproaches. "How could I possibly imagine you did not know all this?" he asked, in the gentlest voice.

Trenta groaned.

"Take me home, take me home," he murmured, faintly. "Gran Dio! the marchesa! the marchesa!" He clasped his hands, then let them fall upon his knees.

"But what real obstacle can there be to a marriage with Count Nobili?"

"I cannot speak," answered the cavaliere, almost inaudibly, trying to rise. "Every obstacle." And he sank back helplessly on the chair.

Count Marescotti took a silver flask from a drawer, and offered him a cordial. Trenta swallowed it with the submissiveness of a child. The count picked up his cane, and placed it in his hand. The cavaliere mechanically grasped it, rose, and moved feebly toward the door.

"Let me go," he said, faintly, addressing Marescotti, who urged him to remain. "Let me go. I must inform the marchesa. I must see Enrica. Ah! if you knew all!" he whispered, looking piteously at the count. "My poor Enrica!—my pretty lamb! Who can have led her astray? How can it have happened? I must go—go at once. I am better now. Yes—give me your arm, count, I am a little weak. I thank you—it supports me."

The door of No. 4 was at last opened. The cavaliere descended the stairs very slowly, supported by Marescotti, whose looks expressed the deepest compassion. A *fiacre* was called from the piazza.

"The Palazzo Trenta," said Count Marescotti to the driver, handing in the cavaliere.

"No, no," he faintly interrupted, "not there. To Casa Guinigi. I must instantly see the marchesa," whispered Trenta in the count's ear.

The *fiacre* containing the unhappy chamberlain drove from the door, and plunged into a dark street toward the cathedral.

Count Marescotti stood for some minutes in the doorway, gazing after it. The full blaze of a hot September sun played round his uncovered head, lighting it up as with a glory. Then he turned, and, slowly reascending the stairs to No. 4, opened his door, and locked it behind him.

CHAPTER VII.

THE Marchesa Guinigi dined early. She had just finished when a knock at the door of her squalid sitting-room
on the second story, with the pea-green walls and shabby
furniture, aroused her from what was the nearest approach
to a nap in which she ever indulged. In direct opposition
to Italian habits, she maintained that sleeping in the day
was not only lazy, but pernicious to health. As the marchesa did not permit herself to be lulled by the morphitic
influences of those long, dreary days of an Italian summer,
which must perforce be passed in closed and darkened
chambers, and in a stifling atmosphere, she resolutely set
her face against any one in her palace enjoying this national
luxury.

At the hottest moment of the twenty-four hours, and in
the dog-days, when the rays of a scalding sun pour down
upon roof and wall and tower like molten lead, searching
out each crack and cranny with cruel persistence, the marchesa was wont stealthily to descend into the very bowels,
as it were, of that great body corporate, the Guinigi Palace
—to see with her own eyes if her orders were obeyed.
With hard words, and threats of instant dismissal, she
aroused her sleeping household. No refuge could hide an

offender—no hole, however dark, could conceal so much as a kitchen-boy.

The marchesa's eye penetrated everywhere. From garret to cellar she knew the dimensions of every cupboard —the capacity of each nook—the measure of the very walls. Woe to the unlucky sleeper! his slumbers from that hour were numbered; she watched him as if he had committed a crime.

When the marchesa, as I have said, was aroused by a knock, she sat up stiffly, and rubbed her eyes before she would say, "Enter." When she spoke the word, the door slowly opened, and Cavaliere Trenta stood before her. Never had he presented himself in such an abject condition; he was panting for breath; he leaned heavily on his gold-headed cane; his snowy hair hung in disorder about his forehead, deep wrinkles had gathered on his face; his eyes were sunk in their sockets, and his white lips twitched nervously, showing his teeth.

"Cristo!" exclaimed the marchesa, fixing her keen eyes upon him, "you are going to have a fit!"

Trenta shook his head slowly.

The marchesa pulled a chair to her side. The cavaliere sank into it with a sigh of exhaustion, put his hand into his pocket, drew out his handkerchief, placed it before his eyes, and sobbed aloud.

"Trenta—Cesarino!"—and the marchesa rose, laid her long, white fingers on his shoulder—it was a cruel hand, spite of its symmetry and aristocratic whiteness—"what does this mean? Speak, speak! I hate mystification. I order you to speak!" she added, imperiously. "Have you seen Count Marescotti?"

Trenta nodded.

"What does he say? Is the marriage arranged?"

Trenta shook his head. If his life had depended upon it he could not have uttered a single word at that moment.

His sobs choked him. Tears ran down his aged cheeks, moistening the wrinkles and furrows now so apparent. He was in such a piteous condition that even the marchesa was softened as she looked at him.

"If all this is because the marriage with Count Mare. scotti has failed, you are a fool, Trenta! a fool, do you hear?" And she leaned over him, tightened her hand upon his shoulder, and actually shook him.

Trenta submitted passively.

"On the whole, I am very glad of it. Do you hear? You talked me over, Cesarino; I have repented it ever since. Count Marescotti is not the man I should have selected for raising up heirs to the Guinigi. Now don't irritate me," she continued, with a disdainful glance at the cavaliere. "Have done with this folly. Do you hear?"

"Enrica, Enrica!" groaned Trenta, who, always accustomed to obey her, began wiping his eyes—they would, however, keep overflowing—"O marchesa! how can I tell you?"

"Tell me what?" demanded the marchesa, sternly.

Her breath came short and quick, her thin face grew set and rigid. Like a veteran war-horse, she scented the battle from afar!

"Ah! if you only knew all!" And a great spasm passed over the cavaliere's frame. "You must prepare yourself for the worst."

The marchesa laughed—a short, contemptuous laugh— and shrugged her shoulders.

"Enrica, Enrica—what can she do?—a child! She cannot compromise me, or my name."

"Enrica has compromised both," cried Trenta, roused at last from his paroxysm of grief. "Enrica has more than compromised it; she has compromised all the Guinigi that ever lived—you, the palace, herself—every one. Enrica has a lover!" The marchesa bounded from her chair; her face turned livid in the waning light.

"Who told you this?" she asked, in a strange, hollow voice, without turning her eyes or moving a muscle of her face.

"Count Marescotti," answered Trenta, meekly.

He positively cowered beneath the pent-up wrath of the marchesa.

"Who is the man?"

"Nobili."

"What!—Count Nobili?"

"Yes, Count Nobili."

With a great effort she commanded herself, and continued interrogating Trenta.

"How did Marescotti hear it?"

"From common report. It is known all over Lucca."

"Was this the reason that Count Marescotti declined to marry my niece?"

The marchesa spoke in the same strange tone, but she fixed her eyes savagely on Trenta, so as to be able to convince herself how far he might dare to equivocate.

"That was a principal reason," replied the cavaliere, in a faltering voice; "but there were others."

"What are the others to me? The dishonor of my niece is sufficient."

There was a desperate composure about the marchesa, more terrible than passion.

"Her dishonor! God and all the saints forbid!" retorted Trenta, clasping his hands. "Marescotti did not speak of dishonor."

"But I speak of dishonor!" shrieked the marchesa, and the pent-up rage within her flashed out over her face like a tongue of fire. "Dishonor!—the vilest, basest dishonor! What do I care"—and she stamped her foot loudly on the brick floor—"what do I care what Nobili has done to her? By that one fact of loving him she has soiled this sacred roof." The marchesa's eyes wandered wildly round the room. "She has soiled the name I bear. I will cast her forth into the street to beg—to starve !"

And as the words fell from her lips she stretched out her long arm and bony finger as in a withering curse.

"But, ha! ha!"—and her terrible voice echoed through the empty room—"I forgot. Count Nobili loves her; he will keep her—in luxury, too—and in a Guinigi palace !" She hissed out these last words. "She has learned her way there already. Let her go—go instantly," the marchesa's hand was on the bell. "Let her go, the soft-voiced viper !"

The transport of fury which possessed the marchesa had had the effect of completely recalling Trenta to himself. For his great age, Trenta possessed extraordinary recuperative powers, both of body and mind. Not only had he so far recovered while the marchesa had been speaking as to arrange his hair and his features, and to smoothe the creases of his official coat into something of their habitual punctilious neatness, but he had had time to reflect. Unless he could turn the marchesa from her dreadful purpose, Enrica (still under all circumstances his beloved child) would infallibly be turned into the street by her remorseless aunt.

At the moment that the marchesa had laid her hand upon the bell, Trenta darted forward and tore it from her hand.

"For the love of the Virgin, pause before you commit so horrible an act !"

So sudden had been his movement, so unwonted his energy, that the marchesa was checked in the very climax of her passion.

"If you have no mercy on a child that you have reared at your side," exclaimed Trenta, laying his hand on hers, "spare yourself, your name, your house, such a scandal! Is it for this that you cherish the name of the great Paolo Guinigi, whose acts were acts of clemency and wisdom? Is it for this you honor the memory of Castruccio Castracani, who was called the 'father of the people?' Bethink you, marchesa, that they lived under this very roof. You dare not—no, not even you—dare not tarnish their memories! Call Enrica here. It is the barest justice that the accused should be heard. Ask her what she has done? Ask her what has passed? How she has met Count Nobili? Until an hour ago I could have sworn she did not even know him."

"Ay, ay," burst out the marchesa, "so could I. How did she come to know him?"

"That is precisely what we must learn," continued Trenta, eagerly seizing on the slightest abatement of the marchesa's wrath. "That is what we must ask her. Marchesa, in common decency, you cannot put your own niece out of your house without seeing her and hearing her explanation."

"You may call her, if you please," answered the marchesa, with a look of dogged rage; "but I warn you, Cesare Trenta, if she avows her love for Nobili in my presence, I shall esteem that in itself the foulest crime she can commit. If she avows it, she leaves my house to-night. Let her die!—I care not what becomes of her!"

CHAPTER VIII.

THE Cavaliere Trenta, without an instant's delay, seized the bell and rang it. The broken-down retainer, in his suit of well-worn livery, shuffled in through the ante-room.

"What did the excellency command?" he asked in a dreary voice, as the marchesa did not address him.

"Tell the signorina that the Marchesa Guinigi desires her presence immediately," answered the cavaliere, promptly. He would not give her an opportunity of speaking.

"Her excellency shall be obeyed," replied the servant, still addressing himself to the marchesa. He bowed, then glided noiselessly from the room.

. A door is heard to open, then to shut; a bell is rung; there is a muttered conversation in the anteroom, and the sound of receding footsteps; then a side-door in the corner of the sitting-room near the window opens; there is the slight rustle of a summer dress, and Enrica stands before them.

It is the same hour of sunset as when she had sat there three days before, knitting beside the open casement, with the twisted marble colonnettes and delicate tracery. The same subtile fragrance of the magnolia rises upward from the waxy leaves of the tall flowering trees growing beneath in the Moorish garden. The low rays of the setting sun flit upon her flaxen hair, defining each delicate curl, and sharply marking the outline of her slight girlish figure; the slender waist, the small hands. Even the little foot is visible under the folds of her light dress.

Enrica's face is in shadow, but, as she raises it and sees the cavaliere seated beside her aunt, a quiet smile plays about her mouth, and a gleam of pleasure rises in her eyes.

What is it that makes youth in Italy so fresh and beautiful—so lithe, erect, and strong? What gives that lustre to the eye, that ripple to the hair, that faultless mould to the features, that mellowness to the skin—like the ruddy rind of the pomegranate—those rounded limbs that move with sovereign ease—that step, as of gods treading the earth? Is it the color of the golden skies? Is it a philter brewed by the burning sunshine? or is it found in the deep shadows that brood in the radiance of the starry night? Is it in those sounds of music ever floating in the air? or in the solemn silence of the primeval chestnut-woods? Does it come in the crackling of the mountain-storm—in the terror of the earthquake? Does it breathe from the azure seas that belt the classic land—or in the rippling cadence of untrodden streams amid lonely mountains? Whence comes it?—how?—where? I cannot tell.

The marchesa is seated on her accustomed seat; her face is shaded by her hand. So stern, so solemn, is her attitude that her chair seems suddenly turned into a judgment-seat.

The cavaliere has risen at Enrica's entrance. Not daring to display his feelings in the presence of the marchesa, he thrusts his hands into his pockets, and stands behind her, his head partly turned away, leaning against the edge of the marble mantel-piece. There is such absolute silence in the room that the ticking of a clock is distinctly heard. It is the deadly pause before the slaughter of the battle.

"You sent for me, my aunt?" Enrica speaks in a timid voice, not moving from the spot where she has entered, near the open window. "What is your pleasure?"

"My pleasure!" the marchesa catches up and echoes the words with a horrible jeer. (She had been collecting her forces for attack; she had lashed herself into a transport of fury. Her smooth, snake-like head was reared erect; her upright figure, too thin to be majestic, stiffened. Thunder and lightning were in her eyes as she turned them on Enrica.) "You dare to ask me my pleasure! You shall hear it, lost, miserable girl! Leave this house—go to your lover! Let it be the motto of his low-born race that a Nobili dishonored a Guinigi. Go—I wish you were dead!" and she points with her finger toward the door.

Every word that fell from the marchesa sounded like a curse. As she speaks, the smiles fade out of Enrica's face as the lurid sunlight fades before the rising tempest. She grasps a chair for support. Her bosom heaves under the folds of her thin white dress. Her eyes, which had fixed themselves on her aunt, fall with an agonized expression on the floor. Thus she stands, speechless, motionless, passive; stunned, as it were, by the shock of the words.

Then a low cry of pain escapes her, a cry like the complaint of a dumb animal—the bleat of a lamb under the butcher's knife.

"Have I not reared you as my own child?" cries the marchesa—too excited to remain silent in the presence of her victim. "Have you ever left my side? Yet under my ancestral roof you have dared to degrade yourself. Out upon you!—Go, go—or with my own hand I shall drive you into the street!"

She starts up, and is rushing upon Enrica, who stands motionless before her, when Trenta steps forward, puts his hand firmly on the marchesa's arm, and draws her back.

"You have called Enrica here," he whispers, "to question her. Do so—do so. Look, she is so overcome she cannot speak," and he points to Enrica, who is now trembling like an aspen-leaf, her fair head bowed upon her bosom, the big tears trickling down her white cheeks.

When the marchesa, checked by Trenta, has ceased speaking, Enrica raises her heavy eyelids and turns her eyes, swimming in tears, upon her aunt. Then she clasps her hands—the small fingers knitting themselves together with a grasp of agony—and wrings them. Her lips move, but no sound comes from them. Something there is so pitiful in this mute appeal—she looks so slight and frail in the background of the fading sunlight—there is such a depth of unspoken pathos in every line of her young face—that the marchesa pauses ; she pauses ere putting into execution her resolve of turning Enrica herself, with her own hands, from the palace.

A new sentiment has also within the last few minutes arisen within her—a sentiment of curiosity. The marchesa is a woman; in many respects a thorough woman. The first flash of fury once passed, she feels an intense longing to know how all this had come about. What had passed ? How had Enrica met Nobili ? Whether any of her household had betrayed her ? On whom her just vengeance shall fall ?

Each moment that passes as the quick thoughts rattle through her brain, it seems to her more and more imperative that she should inform herself what had really happened under her roof !

At this moment Enrica speaks in a low voice.

" O my aunt ! I have done nothing ! Indeed, indeed," —and a great sob breaks in and cuts her speech. " I have done nothing."

" What ! " cries the marchesa, her fury again roused by such a daring assertion. " What do you call nothing ? Do you deny that you love Nobili ? "

"No, my aunt. I love him—I love him."

The mention of Nobili's name gave Enrica courage. With that name the sunlit days of meeting came back again. A gleam of their divine refraction swam before her. Nobili—is he not strong, and brave, and true? Is he not near at hand? Oh, if he only knew her need!—oh, if he could only rush to her—bear her in his arms away —away to untrodden lands of love and bliss where she could hide her head upon his breast and be at peace!

All this gave her courage. She passes her hand over her face and brushes the tears away. Her blue eyes, that shine out now like a rent in a cloudy sky, are meekly but fearlessly cast upon her aunt.

"You dare to tell me you love him—you dare to avow it in my presence, degraded girl! have you no pride—no decency?"

"I have done nothing," Enrica answers in the same voice, "of which I am ashamed. From the first moment I saw him I loved him. I loved—him—oh! how I loved him!" She repeats this softly, as if speaking to herself. An inner light shines over her whole countenance. "And Nobili loves me. I know it." Her voice sounds sweet and firm. "He is mine!"

"Fool, you think so; you are but one of many!" The marchesa, incensed beyond endurance at her firmness, raises her head with the action of a snake about to spring upon its prey. "Dare you deny that you are his mistress?"

(Could the marchesa have seen the cavaliere standing behind her, at that moment, and how those eyes of his were riveted on Enrica with a look in which hope, thankfulness, pity, and joy, crossed and combated together— mercy on us! she would have turned and struck him!)

The shock of the words overcame Enrica. She fixes her eyes on her aunt as if not understanding their meaning. Then a deep blush covers her from head to foot; she trembles and presses both her hands to her bosom as if in pain.

"Spare her, spare her!" is heard in less audible sounds from Trenta to the marchesa. The marchesa tosses her head defiantly.

"I am to be Count Nobili's wife," Enrica says at last, in a faltering voice. "The Holy Mother is my witness, I have done nothing wrong. I have met him in the cathedral, and at the door of the Moorish garden. He has written to me, and I have answered."

"Doubtless; and you have met him alone?" asked the marchesa, with a savage sneer.

"Never, my aunt; Teresa was always with me."

"Teresa, curse her! She shall leave the house as naked as she came into it. How many other of my servants did you corrupt?"

"Not one; it was known to her and to me only."

"And why not to me, your guardian? why not to me?" And the marchesa advances step by step toward Enrica, as the bitter consciousness of having been hoodwinked by such a child fills her with fresh rage. "You have deceived me—I who have fed and clothed and nourished you —I who, but for this, would have endowed you with all I have, bequeathed to you a name greater than that of kings! Answer me this, Enrica. Leave off wringing your hands and turning up your eyes. Answer me!"

"My aunt, I was afraid."

"Afraid!" and the marchesa laughs a loud and scornful laugh; "you were not afraid to meet this man in secret."

"No. Fear him! what had I to fear? Nobili loves me."

The word was spoken. Now she had courage to meet the marchesa's gaze unmoved, spite of the menace of her look and attitude. Enrica's conscience acquitted her of any wrong save the wrong of concealment. "Had you asked

9

me," she adds, more timidly, "I should have spoken. You have asked me now, and I have told you."

The very spirit of truth spoke in Enrica. Not even the marchesa could doubt her. Enrica had not disgraced the name she bore. She believed her; but there was a sting behind sharper to her than death. That sting remained. Enrica had confessed her love for the man she hated!

As to the cavaliere, the difficulty he experienced at this moment in controlling his feelings amounted to positive agony. His Enrica is safe! San Riccardo be thanked! She is safe—she is pure! Except his eyes, which glowed with the secret ecstasy he felt, he appeared outwardly as impassive as a stone. The marchesa turned and reseated herself. There is, spite of her violence, an indescribable majesty about her as she sits erect and firm upon her chair in judgment on her niece. Right or wrong, the marchesa is a woman born to command.

"It is not for me," she says, with lofty composure, "to reason with a love-sick girl, whose mind runs to the tune of her lover's name. Of all living men I abhor Count Nobili. To love him, in my eyes, is a crime—yes, a crime," she repeats, raising her voice, seeing that Enrica is about to speak. "I know him—he is a vain, purse-proud reprobate. He has come and planted himself like a mushroom within our ancient walls. Nor did this content him—he has had the presumption to lodge himself in a Guinigi palace. The blood in his veins is as mud. That he cannot help, nor do I reproach him for it; but he has forced himself into our class—he has mingled his name with the old names of the city; he has dared to speak—live—act—as if he were one of us. You, Enrica, are the last of the Guinigi. I had hoped that a child I had reared at my side would have learned and reflected my will—would have repaid me for years of care by her obedience."

"O my aunt!" exclaims Enrica, sinking on her knees, "forgive me—forgive me! I am ungrateful."

"Rise," cries the marchesa, sternly, not in the least touched by this outburst of natural feeling. "I care not for words—your acts show you have defied me. The project which for years I have silently nursed in my bosom, waiting for the fitting time to disclose it to you—the project of building up through you the great Guinigi name."

The marchesa pauses; she gasps, as if for breath. A quick flush steals over her white face, and for a moment she leans back in her chair, unable to proceed. Then she presses her hand to her forehead, on which the perspiration had risen in beads.

"Alas! I did not know it!" Enrica is now sobbing bitterly. "Why—oh! why, did you not trust me?"

In a strange, weary-sounding voice the marchesa continues:

"Let us not speak of it. Enrica"—she turns her gray eyes full upon her, as she stands motionless in front of the pillared casement—"Enrica, you must choose. Renounce Nobili, or prepare to enter a convent. His wife you can never be."

As a shot that strikes a brightly-plumaged bird full in its softly-feathered breast, so did these dreadful words strike Enrica. There is a faint, low cry, she has fallen upon the floor!

The marchesa did not move, but, looking at her where she lay, she slowly shook her head. Not so the cavaliere. He rushed forward, and raised her tenderly in his arms. The tears streamed down his aged cheeks.

"Take her away!" cried the marchesa; "take her away! She has broken my heart!"

CHAPTER IX.

WHEN Cavaliere Trenta returned, after he had led away Enrica, and consigned her to Teresa, he was very grave. As he crossed the room toward the marchesa, he moved feebly, and leaned heavily on his stick. Then he drew a chair opposite to her, sat down, heaved a deep sigh, and raised his eyes to her face.

The marchesa had not moved. She did not move now, but sat the picture of hard, haughty despair—a despair that would gnaw body and soul, yet give no sigh. But the cavaliere was now too much absorbed by Enrica's sufferings to affect even to take much heed of the marchesa.

"This is a very serious business," he began, abruptly. "You may have to answer for that girl's life. I shall be the first to witness against you."

Never in her life had the marchesa heard Cesare Trenta deliver himself of such a decided censure upon her conduct. His wheedling, coaxing manner was all gone. He was neither the courtier nor the counselor. He neither insinuated nor suggested, but spoke bluntly out bold words, and those upon a subject she esteemed essentially her own. Even in the depth of her despondency it made a certain impression upon her.

She roused herself and glared at him, but there was no

shrinking in his face. Trenta's clear round eyes, so honest and loyal in their expression, seemed to pierce her through and through. She fancied, too, that he contemplated her with a sort of horror.

"You have accused Enrica," he continued; "she has cleared herself. You cannot doubt her. Why do you continue to torture her?"

"That is my affair," answered the marchesa, doggedly. "She has deceived me, and defied me. She has outraged the usages of society. Is not that enough?"

"You have brought her up to fear you," interrupted Trenta. "Had she not feared you, she would never have deceived you."

"What is that to you? How dare you question me?" cried the marchesa, the glitter of passion lighting up her eyes. "Is it not enough that by this deception she has foiled me in the whole purpose of my life? I have given her the choice. Resign Nobili, or a convent."

Saying this, she closed her lips tightly. Trenta, in the heat of his enthusiasm for Enrica, had gone too far. He felt it; he hastened to rectify his error.

"Every thing that concerns you and your family, Marchesa Guinigi, is a subject of overwhelming interest to me."

Now the cavaliere spoke in his blandest manner. The smoothness of the courtier seemed to unknit the wrinkles on his face. The look of displeasure melted out of his eyes, the roughness fled from his voice.

"Remember, marchesa, I am your oldest friend. A crisis has arrived; a scandal may ensue. You must now decide."

"I have decided," returned the marchesa; "that decision you have heard." And again her lips closed hermetically.

"But permit me. There are many considerations that

will doubtless present themselves to· you as necessary in-
gredients of this decision.   If Enrica goes into religion, the
Guinigi race is doomed.   Why should you, with your own
hand, destroy the work of your life ?   If Enrica will not
consent to renounce her engagement to Count Nobili, why
should she not marry him ?   There is no real obstacle other
than your will."

No sooner were these daring words uttered, than the
cavaliere positively trembled.   The marchesa listened to
them in ominous silence.   Such a possibility had never presented itself for a instant to her imagination.   She turned
slowly round, pressed her hands tightly on her knees, and
darkly eyed him.

" You think that I should consent to such a marriage ? "
she asked in a deep voice, a mocking smile upon her lips.

" I think, marchesa, that you should sacrifice every
thing—yes—every thing."   And Trenta, feeling himself
on safe ground, repeated the word with an audacity that
would have surprised those who only knew him in the
polite details of ordinary life.   " I think that you should
sacrifice every thing to the interests of your house."

This was hitting the marchesa home.   She felt it and
winced; but her resolution was unshaken.

" Did I not know that you are descended from a line as
ancient, though not so illustrious as my own, I should
think I was listening to a Jew peddler of Leghorn," she replied, with insolent cynicism.

The cavaliere felt deeply offended, but had the presence of mind to affect a smile, as though what she had said
was an excellent joke.

" Nobili shall never mix his blood with the Guinigi—I
swear it !   Rather let our name die out from the land."

She raised both her hands in the twilight to ratify the
imprecation she had hurled upon her race.   Her voice died
away into the corner of the darkening room; her thoughts

wandered. She sat in spirit upon the seigneurial throne, below, in the presence-chamber. Should Nobili sit there, on that hallowed seat of her ancestors?—the old Lombard palace call him master, living—gather his bones with their ashes, dead?—Never! Better far moulder into ruin as they had mouldered. Had she not already permitted herself to be too much influenced? She had offered Enrica in marriage to Count Marescotti, and he had refused her—refused her niece!

Suddenly she shook off the incubus of these thoughts and turned toward Trenta. He had been watching her anxiously.

"I can never forgive Enrica," she said. "She may not have disgraced herself—that matters little—but she has disgraced me. She must enter a convent; until then I will allow her to remain in my house."

"Exactly," burst in Trenta, again betrayed into undue warmth by this concession.

The cavaliere was old; he had seen that life revolves itself strangely in a circle, from which we may diverge, but from which we seldom disentangle ourselves. Desperate resolves are taken, tragedies are planned, but Fate or Providence intervenes. The old balance pendulates again—the foot falls into the familiar step. Death comes to cut the Gordian knot. The grave-sod covers all that is left, and the worm feeds on the busy brain.

As a man of the world, Trenta was a profound believer in the chapter of accidents.

"I will not put Enrica out of my house," resumed the marchesa, gazing at him suspiciously. (Trenta seemed, she thought, wonderfully interested in Enrica's fate. She had noticed this interest once before. She did not like it. What was Enrica to him? Trenta was *her* friend.) "But she shall remain on one condition only — Nobili's name must never be mentioned. You can inform her of this,

as you have taken already so much upon yourself. Do you
hear ? "

" Certainly, certainly," answered the chamberlain with
alacrity. "You shall be obeyed. I will answer for it—
excellent marchesa, you are right, always right"—and he
stooped down and gently took her thin fingers in his fat
hands, and touched them with his lips.

" I will cause no scandal," she continued, withdrawing
her hand. " Once in a convent, Enrica can harm no one."

" No, certainly not," responded Trenta, " and the family will become extinct. This palace and its precious heirlooms will be sold."

The marchesa put out her hand with silent horror.

" It is the case with so many of our great families," continued the impassable Trenta. " Now, on the other hand,
Enrica may possibly change her mind ; Nobili may change
his mind. Circumstances quite unforeseen may occur—who
can answer for circumstances ? "

The marchesa listened silently. This was always a
good sign; she was too obstinate to confess herself convinced. But, spite of her prejudices, her natural shrewd-
ness forbade her to reject absolutely the voice of reason.

" I shall not treat Enrica cruelly," was her reply, " nor
will I cause a scandal, but I can never forgive her. By
this act of loving Nobili she has separated herself from me
irrevocably. Let her renounce him ; she has her choice—
mine is already made."

The cavaliere listened in silence. Much had been
gained, in his opinion, by this partial concession. The
subject had been broached, the hated name mentioned,
the possibility of the marriage mooted. He rose with a
cheerful smile to take his leave.

" Marchesa, it is late—permit me to salute you; you
must require repose."

" Yes," she answered, sighing deeply. " It seems to

me a year since I entered this room. I must leave Lucca. Enrica cannot, after what has passed, remain here. Thanks to her, I, in the solitude of my own palace, am become the common town-talk. Cesare, I shall leave Lucca to-morrow for my villa of Corellia. Good-night."

The cavaliere again kissed her hand and departed.

"If that weathercock of a thousand colors, that idiot, Marescotti," muttered the cavaliere, as he descended the stairs, "could only be got to give up his impious mission, and marry the dear child, all might yet be right. He has an eye and a tongue that would charm a woman into anything. Alas! alas! what a pasticcio!—made by herself— made by herself and her lawsuits about the defunct Guinigi —damn them!"

It was seldom that the cavaliere used bad words—excuse him.

PART III.

CHAPTER I.

THE road from Lucca to Corellia lies at the foot of lofty mountains, over-mantled by chestnut-forests, and cleft asunder by the river Serchio—the broad, willful Serchio, sprung from the flanks of virgin fastnesses. In its course a thousand valleys open up, scoring the banks. Each valley has its tributary stream, down which, even in the dogdays, cool breezes rustle. The lower hills lying warm toward the south, and the broad glassy lands by the river, are trellised with vines. Some fling their branches in wild festoons on mulberry or aspen trees. Some trained in long arbors are held up by pillars of unbarked wood; others trail upon the earth in delicious luxuriance. The white and purple grapes peep from the already shriveled leaves, or hang in rich masses on the brown earth.

It is the vintage. The peasants, busy as bees, swarm on the hill-sides; the women pluck the fruit; the men bear it away in wooden measures. While they work, they sing those wild Tuscan melodies that linger in the air like longdrawn sighs. The donkeys, too, climb up and down, saddled with wooden panniers, crammed with grapes. These grapes are shot into large tubs, and placed in a shady outhouse. Some black-eyed boy will dance merrily on these tubs, by-and-by, with his naked feet, and squeeze out the juice. This juice is then covered and left to ferment, then bottled into flasks, covered with wicker-work, corked with tow, and finally stowed away in caves among the rocks.

The marchesa's lumbering coach, drawn by three horses harnessed abreast (another horse, smaller than the rest, put in tandem in front), creaks along the road by the river-side, on its high wheels. She sits within, a stony look upon her hard white face. Enrica, pale and silent, is beside her. No word has passed between them since they left Lucca two hours ago. They pass groups of peasants, their labors over for the day—turning out of the vineyards upon the high-road. The donkeys are driven on in front. They are braying for joy; their faces are turned homeward. Boys run at their heels, and spur them on with sticks and stones. The women lag behind talking—their white head-gear and gold ear-rings catching the low sunshine that strikes through rents of parting mountains. Every man takes off his hat to the marchesa; every woman wishes her good-day.

It is only the boys who do not fear her. They have no caps to raise; when the carriage has passed, they leave the donkeys and hang on behind like a swarm of bees. The driver is quite aware of this, and his long whip, which he has cracked at intervals all the way from Lucca—would reach the grinning, white-toothed little vagabonds well; but he—the driver—grins too, and spares them.

Together they all mount the zigzag mountain-pass, that turns short off from the right bank of the valley of the Serchio, toward Corellia. The peasants sing choruses as they trudge upward, taking short cuts among the trees at the angles of the zigzag. The evening lights come and go among the chestnut-trees and on the soft, short grass. Here a fierce flick of sunshine shoots across the road; there deep gloom darkens an angle into which the coach plunges, the peasants, grouped on the top of a bank overhead, standing out darkly in the yellow glow.

It is a lonely pass in the very bosom of the Apennines, midway between Lucca and Modena. In winter the road is clogged with snow; nothing can pass. Now, there is no sound but the singing of water-falls, and the trickle of water-courses, the chirrup of the *cicala*, not yet gone to its rest—and the murmur of the hot breezes rustling in the distant forest.

No sound—save when sudden thunder-pelts wake awful echoes among the great brotherhood of mountain-tops— when torrents burst forth, pouring downward, flooding the narrow garden ledges, and tearing away the patches of corn and vineyard, the people's food. Before—behind— around—arise peaks of purple Apennines, cresting up- ward into the blue sky—an earthen sea dashed into sudden breakers, then struck motionless. In front, in solitary state, rises the lofty summit of La Pagna, casting off its giant mountain-fellows right and left, which fade away into a golden haze toward Modena.

High up overhead, crowning a precipitous rock, stands Corellia, a knot of browned, sun-baked houses, flat-roofed, open-galleried, many-storied, nestling round a ruined cas- tle, athwart whose rents the ardent sunshine darts. This ruined castle and the tower of an ancient Lombard church, heavily arched and galleried with stone, gleaming out upon a surface of faded brickwork, form the outline of the lit- tle town. It is inclosed by solid walls, and entered by an archway so low that the marchesa's driver has to dismount as he passes through. The heavy old carriage rumbles in with a hollow noise; the horses' hoofs strike upon the rough stones with a harsh, loud sound.

The whole town of Corellia belongs to the marchesa. It is an ancient fief of the Guinigi. Legend says that

Castruccio Castracani was born here. This is enough for the marchesa. As in the palace of Lucca, she still—even at lonely Corellia—lives as it were under the shadow of that great ancestral name.

Lonely Corellia! Yes, it is lonely! The church bells, high up in the Lombard tower sound loudly the matins and the eventide. They sound louder still on the saints' days and festivals. With the festivals pass summer and winter, both dreary to the poor. Children are born, and marriage-flutes wake the echoes of the mountain solitudes —and mothers weep, hearing them, remembering their young days and present pinching want. The aged groan, for joy to them comes like a fresh pang!

The marchesa's carriage passes through Corellia at a foot's pace. The driver has no choice. It is most difficult to drive at all—the street is so narrow, and the door-steps of the houses jut out so into the narrow space. The horses, too, hired at Lucca, twenty miles away, are tired, poor beasts, and reeking with the heat. They can hardly keep their feet upon the rugged, slippery stones that pave the dirty alley. As the marchesa passes slowly by, wan-faced women—colored handkerchiefs gathered in folds upon their heads, knitting or spinning flax cut from the little field without upon the mountain-side—put down the black, curly-headed urchins that cling to their laps—rise from where they are resting on the door-step, and salute the marchesa with an awe-struck stare. She, in no mood for condescension, answers them with a frown. Why have these wan-faced mothers, with scarcely bread to eat, children between their knees? Why has God given her none? Again the impious thought rises within her which tempted her when standing before the marriage-bed in the nuptial chamber. "God is my enemy." "He has smitten me with a curse." "Why have I no child?" "No child, nothing but her"—and she flashes a savage glance at En-

rica, who has sunk backward, covering her tear-stained
face with a black veil, to avoid the peering eyes of the
Corellia townsfolk—"nothing but her. Born to disgrace
me. Would she were dead! Then all would end, and I
should go down—the last Guinigi—to an honored grave."

The sick, too, are sitting at the doorways as the marchesa passes by. The mark of fever is on many an ashy
cheek. These sick have been carried from their beds to
breathe such air as evening brings. Air! There is no air
from heaven in these foul streets. No sweet breath circu-
lates; no summer scents of grasses and flowers reach the
lonely town hung up so high. The summer sun scorches.
The icy winds of winter, sweeping down from Alpine ridges,
whistle round the walls. Within are chilly, desolate
hearths, on which no fire is kindled. These sick, as the
carriage passes, turn their weary eyes, and lift up their
wasted hands in mute salutations to that dreaded mistress
who is lord of all—the great marchesa. Will they not lie
in the marchesa's ground when their hour comes? Alas!
how soon—their weakness tells them very soon! Will
they not be carried in an open bier up those long flights of
steps—all hers—cut in the rocky sides of overlapping rocks,
to the cemetery, darkly shaded by waving cypresses? The
ground is hers, the rocks, the steps, the stones, the very
flowers that brown, skinny hands will sprinkle on their bier
—all hers. From birth to bridal, and the marriage-bed (so
fruitful to the poor), from bridal to death, all hers. The
land they live on, and the graves they fill, all—but a
shadow of her greatness!

At the corner of the squalid, ill-smelling street through
which she is now passing, is the town fountain. This fountain, once a willful mountain-torrent, now cruelly captured
and borne hither by municipal force, splashes downward
through a sculptured circle cut in a marble slab, into a covered trough below. Here bold-eyed maidens are gathered,

who poise copper vessels on their dark heads—maidens who
can chat, and laugh, and romp, on holidays, and with flushed
faces dance wild tarantellas (fingers for castanets), where
the old tale of love is told in many a subtile step, and shuf-
fle, rush, escape, and feint, ending in certain capture! Beside the maidens linger some mountain lads. Now their
work is over, they loll against the wall, pipe in mouth, or
lie stretched on a plot of grass that grows green under the
spray of the fountain. In a dark angle, a little behind from
these, there is a shrine hollowed out of the city wall.
Within the shrine an image of the Holy Mother of the
Seven Sorrows stands, her arms outstretched, her bosom
pierced by seven gilded arrows. The shrine is protected
by an iron grating. Bunches of pale hill-side blossoms,
ferns, and a few blades of corn, are thrust in between the
bars. Some lie at the Virgin's feet—offerings from those
who have nothing else to give. A little group (but these
are old, and bowed by grief and want) kneel beside the
shrine in the quiet evening-tide.

The rumble of a carriage, so strange a sound in lonely
Corellia, rouses all. From year to year, no wheels pass
through the town save the marchesa's. Ere she appears,
all know who it must be. The kneelers at the shrine start
up and hobble forward to stare and wonder at that strange
world whence she comes, so far away at Lucca. The
maidens courtesy and smile; the lads jump up, and range
themselves respectfully against the wall; yet in their hearts
neither care for her—neither the maidens nor the lads—no
one cares for the marchesa. They are all looking out for
Enrica. Why does the signorina lie back in the carriage a
mass of clothes? The maidens would like to see how those
clothes are made, to cut their poor garments something like
them. The lads would like to let their eyes rest on her
golden hair. Why does the Signorina Enrica not nod and
smile to those she knows, as is her wont? Has that old

tyrant, her aunt—these young ones are bold, and dare to whisper what others think; they have no care, and, like the lilies of the field, live in the wild, free air—has that old tyrant, her aunt, bewitched her?

Now the carriage has emerged from the dark alley, and entered the dirty but somewhat less dark piazza—the market-place of Corellia. The old Lombard church of Santa Barbara, with its big bells in the arched tower, hanging plainly to be seen, opens into the piazza by a flight of steps and a sculptured doorway. The Municipio, too, calling itself a *palace* (heaven save the mark!), with its list of births, deaths, and marriages, posted on a black-board outside the door, to be seen of all, adorns it. The Café of the Tricolor, and such shops as Corellia boasts of, are there opposite. Men, smoking, and drinking native wine, are lounging about. Ser Giacomo, the notary, spectacles on nose, sits at a table in a corner, reading aloud to a select audience a weekly broad-sheet published at Lucca, news of men and things not of the mountain-tops. Every soul starts up as they hear wheels approaching. If a bomb had burst in the piazza the panic could not be greater. They know it is the marchesa. They know that now the marchesa is come she will grind and harry them, and seize her share of grapes, and corn, and olives, to the uttermost farthing. Silvestro, her steward, a timid, pitiful man, can be got over by soft words, and the sight of want and misery. Not so the marchesa. They know that now she is come she will call the Town Council, fine them, pursue them for rent, cite them to the High Court of Barga, imprison them if they cannot pay. They know her, and they curse her. The ill-news of her arrival runs from lip to lip. Checco, the butcher, who sells his meat cut into dark, indescribably-shaped scraps, more fit for dogs than men, first sees the carriage turn into the piazza. He passes the word on to Oreste, the barber round the corner. Oreste, who, with his brother Pilade, both wearing snow-white aprons, are squaring themselves at their open doorway, over which hangs a copper basin, shaped like Manbrino's helmet, looking for customers— Oreste and Pilade turn pale. Then Oreste tells the baker, Pietro, who, naked as Nature made him, has run out from his oven to the open door, for a breath of air. The bewildered clerk at the Municipio, who sits and writes, and sleeps by turns, all day, in a low room beside a desk, taking notes for the sindaco (mayor) from all who come (he is so tired, that clerk, he would hear the last trumpet sound unmoved), even he hears the news, and starts up.

Now the carriage stops. It has drawn up in the centre of the piazza. It is the marchesa's custom. She puts her head out of the window, and takes a long, grave look all round. These are her vassals. They fear her. She knows it, and she glories in it. Every head is uncovered, every eye turned upon her. It is obviously some one's duty to salute her and to welcome her to her domain. She has stopped for this purpose. It is always done. No one, however, stirs. Ser Giacomo, the notary, bows low beside the table where he has been caught reading the Lucca broad-sheet; but Ser Giacomo does not stir. How he wishes he had staid at home !

He has not the courage to move one step toward her. Something must be done, so Ser Giacomo he runs and fetches the sindaco from inside the recesses of the *café*, where he is playing dominoes under a lighted lamp. The sindaco must give the marchesa a formal welcome. The sindaco, a saddler by trade—a snuffy little man, with a face drawn and yellow as parchment, wearing his working-clothes —advances to the carriage with a step as cautious as a cat.

" I trust the illustrious lady is well," he says timidly, bowing low and trying to smile. Mr. Sindaco is frightened, but he can be proud enough to his fellow-townsfolk, and he is downright cruel to that poor lad his clerk, at the Municipal Palace.

The marchesa, with a cold, distant air, that would instantly check any approach to familiarity—if any one were bold enough to be familiar—answers gravely, " That she is thankful to say she is in her usual health."

The sindaco—although better off than many, painfully conscious of long arrears of unpaid rent—waxing a little bolder at the sound of his own voice and his well-chosen phrases, continues:

" I am glad to hear it, Signora Marchesa." The sindaco further observes, " That he hopes for the illustrious lady's indulgence and good-will."

His smile has faded now; his voice trembles. If his skin were not so yellow, he would be white all over, for the marchesa's looks are not encouraging. The sindaco dreads a summons to the High Court of Barga, where the provincial prisons are—with which he may be soon better acquainted, he fears.

In reply, the marchesa—who perfectly understands all this in a general way—scowls, and fixes her rigid eyes upon him.

" Signore Sindaco, I cannot stop to listen to any grievance now; I will promise no indulgence. I must pay my bills. You must pay me, Signore Sindaco; that is but fair."

The poor little snuffy mayor bows a dolorous acquiescence. He is hopeless, but polite—like a true Italian, who would thank the hangman as he fastens the rope round his neck. But the marchesa's words strike , terror into all who hear them. All owe her long arrears of rent, and much besides. Why—oh! why—did the cruel lady come to Corellia ?

Having announced her intentions in a clear, metallic voice, the marchesa draws her head back into the coach.

" Send Silvestro to me," she adds, addressing the sin-

daco. " Silvestro will inform me of all I want to know."
(Silvestro is her steward.)

" Is the noble young Lady Enrica unwell?" asks the
perservering sindaco, gazing earnestly through the window.

He knows his doom. He has nothing to hope from the
marchesa's clemency, so he may as well gratify his burning
curiosity by a question about the much-beloved Enrica,
who must certainly have been ill-used by her aunt to keep
so much out of sight.

" The people of Corellia would also offer their respectful homage to her," bravely adds Mr. Sindaco, tempting
his fate. " The Lady Enrica is much esteemed here in the
town."

As he speaks the sindaco gazes in wonder at the muffled
figure in the corner. Can this be·she? Why does she not
move forward and answer?—and show her pretty face,
and approve the people's greeting?

"My niece has a headache; leave her alone," answers
the marchesa, curtly. " Do not speak to her, Mr. Sindaco.
She will visit Corellia another day; meanwhile, adieu."

The marchesa waves her hand majestically, and signs
for him to retire. This the sindaco does with an inward
groan at the thought of what is coming on him.

Poor Enrica, feeling as if a curse were on her, cutting
her off from all her former life, shrinks back deeper into the
corner of the carriage, draws the black veil closer about her
face, and sobs aloud. The marchesa turns her head away.
The driver cracks his long whip over the steaming horses,
which move feebly forward with a jerk. Thus the coach
slowly traverses the whole length of the piazza, the wheels
rumbling themselves into silence out in a long street leading to another gate on the farther side of the town.

Not another word more is said that night among the
townsfolk; but there is not a man at Corellia who does
not curse the marchesa in his heart. Ser Giacomo, the

notary, folds up his newspaper in dead silence, puts it into his pocket, and departs. The lights in the dark *café*, which burn sometimes all day when it is cloudy, are extinguished. The domino-players disappear. Oreste and Pilade shut up their shop despondingly. The baker Pietro comes out no more to cool at the door. Anyway, there must be bakers, he reflects, to bake the bread; so Pietro retreats, comforted, to his oven, and works frantically all night. He is safe, Pietro hopes, though he has paid no rent for two whole years, and has sold some of the corn which ought to have gone to the marchesa.

Meanwhile the heavy carriage, with its huge leather hood and double rumble, swaying dangerously to and fro, descends a steep and rugged road embowered in forest, leading to a narrow ledge upon the summit of a line of cliffs. On the very edge of these cliffs, formed of a dark-red basaltic stone, the marchesa's villa stands. A deep, dark precipice drops down beneath. Opposite is a range of mountains, fair and forest-spread on the lower flanks, rising above into wild crags, and broken, blackened peaks, that mock the soft blue radiance of the evening sky.

CHAPTER II.

SILVESTRO, the steward, is a man "full of conscience," as people say, deeply sensible of his responsibilities, and more in dread of the marchesa than of the Church. It is this dread that makes him so emaciated—hesitate when he speaks, and bend his back and shoulders into a constant cringe. But for this dread, Silvestro would forgive the poor people more. He sees such pinching misery every day—lives in it—suffers from it; how can he ask those for money who have none? It is like forcing blood out of a stone. He is not the man to do it. Silvestro lives at hand; he hears the rattle of the hail that burns the grapes up to a cinder—the terrible din of the thunder before the forked lightning strikes the cattle; he sees with his own eyes the griping want of bread in the savage winter-time; his own eyes behold the little lambs, dead of hunger, lying by the road-side. Worse still, he sees other lambs—human lambs with Christian souls—fade and pine and shrink into a little grave, from failing of mother's milk, dried up for want of proper food. He sees, too, the aged die before God calls them, failing through lack of nourishment—a little wine, perhaps, or a mouthful of soup; the young and strong grow old with ceaseless striving. Poor Silvestro! he sees too much. He cannot be severe. He is born

merciful. Silvestro is honest as the day, but he hides
things from the marchesa; he is honest, but he cannot—
no, he cannot—grind and vex the poor, as she would have
him do. Yet she has no one to take his place in that God-
forgotten town—so they pull on, man and mistress—a
truly ill-matched pair—pull on, year after year. It is a
weary life for him when the great lady comes up for her
villeggiatura—Silvestro, divided, cleft in twain, so to say,
as he is, between his awe and respect for the marchesa and
her will, and his terrible sympathy for all suffering creatures, man or beast.

As to the marchesa, she despises Silvestro too profoundly to notice his changing moods. It is not her habit
to look for any thing but obedience—absolute obedience
—from those beneath her. A thousand times she has told
herself such a fool would ruin her; but, up to this present time, she has borne with him, partly from convenience,
and partly because she fears to get a rogue in his place.
She does not guess how carefully Silvestro has hid the
truth from her; she would not give him credit for the
power of concealing any thing.

The sindaco having sent a boy up to Silvestro's house
with the marchesa's message, "that he is to attend her,"
the steward comes hurrying down through the terraces
cut in the steep ground behind the villa—broad, stately
terraces, with balustrades, and big empty vases, and statues,
and grand old lemon-trees set about. Great flights of
marble steps cross and recross, rest on a marble stage,
and then recross again. Here and there a pointed cypress-
tree towers upward like a green pyramid in a desert of
azure sky. Bright-leaved autumn flowers lie in masses on
the rich brown earth, and dainty streamlets come rushing
downward in little sculptured troughs.

What a dismal sigh Silvestro gave when he got the
marchesa's message, and knew that she had arrived! How

he wrung his hands and looked hopelessly upward to heaven with vacant, colorless eyes, the big heat-drops gathering on his bald, wrinkled forehead! He has so much to tell her!—It must be told too; he can hide the truth no longer. She will be sure to ask to see the accounts. Alas! alas! what will his mistress say? For a moment Silvestro gazes wistfully at the mountains all around with a vacant stare. Oh, that the mountains would cover him! Anyway, there are caves and holes, he thinks, where the marchesa's wrath would never reach him; caves and holes where he might live hidden for years, cared for by those who love him. Shall he flee, and never see his mistress's dark, dreadful eyes again? Folly!

Silvestro rouses himself. He resolves to meet his fate like a man, whatever that may be. He will not forsake his duty.—So Silvestro comes hurrying down by the terraces, upon which the shadows fall, to the house—a gray mediæval tower, machicolated and turreted—the only remains of a strong fortress that in feudal times guarded these passes from Modena into Tuscany. To this gray tower is attached a large modern dwelling—a villa—painted of a dull-yellow color, with an overlapping roof, the walls pierced full of windows. The tower, villa, and the line of cliffs on which they stand, face east and west; on one side the forest and Corellia crowning a rocky height, on the other side mountains, with a deep abyss at the foot of the cliffs, yawning between. It is the marchesa's pleasure to inhabit the old tower rather than the pleasant villa, with its big windows and large, cheerful rooms.

Being tall and spare, Silvestro stoops under the low, arched doorway, heavily clamped with iron and nails, leading into the tower; then he mounts very slowly a winding stair of stone to the second story. The sound of his footsteps brings a whole pack of dogs rushing out upon the gravel.

(On the gravel before the house there is a fountain
springing up out of a marble basin full of gold-fish. Pots
are set round the edge with the sweetest-smelling flowers
—tuberoses, heliotropes, and gardenias.) The dogs, barking loudly, run round the basin and upset some of the
pots. One noble mastiff, with long white hair and strong
straight limbs—the leader of the pack—pursues Silvestro
up the dark, tiring stairs. When the mastiff has reached
him and smelt at him he stands still, wags his tail, and
thrusts his nose into Silvestro's hand.

" Poor Argo ! " says the steward, meekly. " Don't bark
at me; I cannot bear it now."

Argo gives a friendly sniff, and leaves him.

At a door on the right, Silvestro stops short, to collect
his thoughts and his breath. He has not seen his mistress
for a year. His soul sinks at the thought of what he must
tell her now. " Can she punish me ? " he asks himself,
vaguely. Perhaps. He must bear it if she does. He has
done all he can. Consoled by this reflection, he knocks.
A well-known voice answers, " Come in." Silvestro's clam-
my hand is on the lock—a worm-eaten door creaks on its
hinges—he enters.

The marchesa nods to Silvestro without speaking. She
is seated before a high desk of carved walnut-wood, facing
the door. The desk is covered with papers. A file of papers is in her hand; others lie upon her lap. All round
there are cupboards, shelves, and drawers, piled with papers
and documents, most of them yellow with age. These con-
sist of old leases, contracts, copies of various lawsuits with
her tenants, appeals to Barga, mortgages, accounts. The
room is low, and rounded to the shape of the tower. Naked joists and rafters of black wood support the ceiling.
The light comes in through some loop-holes, high up, cut in
the thickness of the wall. Some tall, high-backed chairs,
covered with strips of faded satin, stand near the chimney.

A wooden bedstead, without curtains, is partly concealed behind a painted screen, covered with gods and goddesses, much consumed and discolored from the damp. As the room had felt a little chilly from want of use, a large fire of unbarked wood had been kindled. The fire blazes fiercely on the flat stones within an open hearth, unguarded by a grate.

Having nodded to Silvestro, the marchesa takes no further notice of him. From time to time she flings a loose paper from those lying before her—over her shoulder toward the fire, which is at her back. Of these papers some reach the fire; others, but half consumed, fall back upon the floor. The flames of the wood-fire leap out and seize the papers—now one by one—now as they lie in little heaps. The flames leap up; the burning papers crumple along the floor, in little streaks of fire, catching others that lie, still farther on in the room, still unconsumed. Ere these papers have sunk into ashes, a fresh supply, thrown over her shoulder by the marchesa, have caught the flames. All the space behind her chair is covered with smouldering papers. A stack of wood, placed near to replenish the fire, has caught, and is smouldering also. The fire, too, on the hearth is burning fiercely; it crackles up the wide open chimney in a mass of smoke and sparks.

The marchesa is far too much absorbed to notice this. Silvestro, standing near the door—the high desk and the marchesa's tall figure between him and the hearth—does not perceive it either. Still the marchesa bends over her papers, reading some and throwing others over her shoulders into the flames behind.

Silvestro, who had grown hot and cold twenty times in a minute, standing before her, his book under his arm—thinking she had forgotten him—addresses her at last.

"How does madama feel?" Silvestro asks most humbly, turning his lack-lustre eyes upon her.

10

"Well," is the marchesa's brief reply. She signs to him to lay his book upon her desk. She takes it in her hand. She turns over the pages, following line after line with the tip of her long, white forefinger.

"There seems very little, Silvestro," she says, running her eyes up and down each page as she turns it slowly over. Her brow knits until her dark eyebrows almost meet—"very little. Has the corn brought in so small a sum, and the olives, and the grapes?"

"Madama," begins Silvestro, and he bends his head and shoulders, and squeezes his skinny hands together, in a desperate effort to obliterate himself altogether, if possible, in the face of such mishaps—"madama will condescend to remember the late spring frosts. There is no corn anywhere. Upon the lowlands the frost was most severe; in April, too, when the grain was forward. The olives bore a little last season, but Corellia is a cold place—too cold for olives; the trees, too, are very old. This year there will be no crop at all. As for the grapes—"

"*Accidente* to the grapes!" interrupts the marchesa, reddening. "The grapes always fail. Every thing fails under you."

Silvestro shrinks back in terror at the sound of her harsh voice. Oh, that those purple mountains around would cover him! The moment of her wrath is come. What will she say to him?

"I wish I had not an acre of vineyard," the marchesa continues. "Disease, or hail, or drought, or rain, it is always the same—the grapes always fail."

"The peasants are starving, madama," Silvestro takes courage to say, but his voice is low and muffled.

"They have chestnuts," she answers quickly, "let them live on chestnuts."

Silvestro starts violently. He draws back a step or two nearer the door.

"Let the gracious madama consider, many have not even a patch of chestnuts. There is great misery, madama —indeed, there is great misery," Silvestro goes on to say. He must speak now or never. "Madama"—and he holds up his bony hands—"you will have no rent at all from the peasants. They must be kept all the winter."

"Silvestro, you are a fool," cries the marchesa, eying him contemptuously, as she would do a troublesome child —"a fool; pray how am I to keep the peasants, and pay the taxes? I must live."

"Doubtless, excellent madama." Silvestro was infinitely relieved at the calmness with which the marchesa received his announcement. He could not have believed it. He feels most grateful to her. "But, if madama will speak to Fra Pacifico, he will tell her how bitter the distress must be this winter. The Town Council"—Silvestro, deceived by her apparent calmness, has made a mistake in naming the Town Council. It is too late. The words have been spoken. Knowing his mistress's temper, Silvestro imperceptibly glides toward the door as he mentions that body—"The Town Council has decreed—" His words die away in his throat at her aspect.

"Santo dei Santi!" she screams, boiling over with rage, "I forbid you to talk to me of the Town Council!"

Silvestro's hand is upon the lock to insure escape.

"Madama—consider," pleads Silvestro, wellnigh desperate. "The Town Council might appeal to Barga," Silvestro almost whispers now.

"Let them—let them; it is just what I should like. Let them appeal. I will fight them at law, and beat them in full court—the ruffians!" She gives a short, scornful laugh. "Yes, we will fight it out at Barga."

Suddenly the marchesa stops. Her eyes have now reached the balance-sheet on the last page. She draws a long breath.

"Why, there is nothing!" she exclaims, placing her forefinger on the total, then raising her head and fixing her eyes on Silvestro—"nothing!"

Silvestro shrinks, as it were, into himself. He silently bows his head in terrified acquiescence.

"A thousand francs! How am I to live on a thousand francs!"

Silvestro shakes from head to foot. One hand slides from the lock; he joins it to the other, clasps them both together, and sways himself to and fro as a man in bodily anguish.

At the sight of the balance-sheet a kind of horror has come over the marchesa. So intense is this feeling, she absolutely forgets to abuse Silvestro. All she desires is to get rid of him before she has betrayed her alarm.

"I shall call a council," she says, collecting herself; "I shall take the chair. I shall find funds to meet these wants. Give the sindaco and Ser Giacomo notice of this, Silvestro, immediately."

The steward stares at his mistress in mute amazement. He inclines his head, and turns to go; better ask her no questions and escape.

"Silvestro!"—the marchesa calls after him imperiously—"come here." (She is resolved that he, a menial, shall see no change in her.) "At this season the woods are full of game. I will have no poachers, mind. Let notices be posted up at the town-gate and at the church-door—do you hear? No one shall carry a gun within my woods."

Silvestro's lips form to two single words, and these come very faint: "The poor!" Then he holds himself together, terrified.

"The poor!" retorts the marchesa, defiantly—"the poor! For shame, Silvestro! They shall not overrun my woods and break through my vineyards—they shall not! You hear?" Her shrill voice rings round the low room.

"No poachers—no trespassers, remember that; I shall tell Adamo the same. Now go, and, as you pass, tell Fra Pacifico I want him to-morrow." ("He must help me with Enrica," was her thought.)

When Silvestro was gone, a haggard look came over the marchesa's pale face. One by one she turned over the leaves of the rental lying before her, glanced at them, then laid the book down upon the desk. She leaned back in her chair, crossed her arms, and fell into a fit of museing— the burning papers on the hearth, and those also smouldering on the floor, lighting up every grain in the wood-work of the cupboards at her back.

This was ruin—absolute ruin! The broad lands that spread wellnigh for forty miles in the mountains and along the river Serchio—the feudal tower in which she sat, over which still floated, on festivals, the banner of the Guinigi (crosses of gold on a red field—borne at the Crusades); the stately palace at Lucca — its precious heirlooms — strangers must have it all!

She had so fortified herself against all signs of outward emotion, other than she chose to show, that even in solitude she was composed; but the veins swelled in her forehead, and she turned very white. Yet there had been a way. "Enrica"—her name escaped the marchesa's thin lips unwittingly. "Enrica."—The sound of her own voice startled her. (Enrica was now alone, shut up by her aunt's order in her little chamber on the third floor over her own. On their arrival, the marchesa had sternly dismissed her without a word.)

"Enrica."—With that name rose up within her a thousand conflicting thoughts. She had severed herself from Enrica. But for Cavaliere Trenta she would have driven her from the palace. She had not cared whether Enrica lived or died—indeed, she had wished her dead. Yet Enrica could save the land—the palace—make the great name live! Had she but known all this at Lucca! Was it too late? Trenta had urged the marriage with Count Nobili. But Trenta urged every marriage. Could she consent to such a marriage? Own herself ruined—wrong?—Feel Nobili's foot upon her neck?—Impossible! Her obstinacy was so great, that she could not bring herself to yield, though all that made life dear was slipping from her grasp.

Yes—yes, it was too late.—The thing was done. She must stand to her own words. Tortures would not have wrung it from her—but in the solitude of that bare room the marchesa felt she had gone too far. The landmark of her life, her pride, broke down; her stout heart failed— tears stood in her dark eyes.

At this moment the report of a gun was heard ringing out from the mountains opposite. It echoed along the cliffs and died away into the abyss below. The marchesa was instanty leaning out of the lowest loop-hole, and calling in a loud voice, "Adamo—Adamo—Angelo, where are you?" (Adamo and Pipa his wife, and Angelo their son, were her attendants.)

Adamo, a stout, big-limbed man, bull-necked—with large lazy eyes and a black beard as thick as horse-hair, a rifle slung by a leather strap across his chest, answered out of the shrubs—now blackening in the twilight: "I am here, padrona, command me."

"Adamo, who is shooting on my land?"

"Padrona, I do not know."

"Where is Angelo?"

"Here am I," answered a childish voice, and a ragged, loose-limbed lad—a shock of chestnut hair, out of which the sun had taken all the color, hanging over his face, from which his merry eyes twinkle—leaped out on the gravel.

"You do not know, Adamo? What does this mean? You ought to know. I am but just come back, and there are strangers about already with guns. Is this the way you serve me, Adamo?—and I pay you a crown a month. You idle vagabond!"

"Padrona," spoke Adamo in a deep voice—"I am here alone—this boy helps me but little."

"Alone, Adamo! you dare to say alone, and you have the dogs? Hear how they bark—they have heard the shot too—good dogs, good dogs, they are left me—alone.— Why, Argo is stronger than three men; Argo knocks over any one, and he is trained to follow on the scent like a bloodhound. Adamo, you are an idiot!" Adamo hung his head, either in shame or rage, but he dared not reply.

"Now take the dogs out with you instantly—you hear, Adamo? Argo, and Ponto the bull-dog, and Tuzzi and the others. Take them and go down at once to the bottom of the cliffs. Search among the rocks everywhere. Creep along the vines-terraces, and through the olive-grounds. Be sure when you go down below the cliffs to search the mouth of the chasm. Go at once. Set the dogs on all you find. Argo will pin them. He is a brave dog. With Argo you are stronger than any one you will meet. If you catch any men, take them at once to the municipality. Wretches, they deserve it!—poaching in my woods! Listen—before you go, tell Pipa to come to me soon."

Pipa's footsteps came clattering up the stairs to the marchesa's room. The light of the lamp she carried—for it was already dark within the tower—caught the spray of the fountain outside as she passed the narrow slits that served for windows.

"Pipa," said the marchesa, as she stood before her in the doorway, a broad smile on her merry brown face, "set that lamp on the desk here before me. So—that will do. Now go up-stairs and tell the Signorina Enrica that I bid her 'Good-night,' and that I will see her to-morrow morning after breakfast. Then you may go to bed, Pipa. I am busy, and shall sit up late." Pipa curtesied in silence, and closed the marchesa's door.

CHAPTER III.

WHAT CAME OF BURNING THE MARCHESA'S PAPERS.

MIDNIGHT had struck from the church-clock at Corellia. The strokes seemed to come slower by night than day, and sounded hollower. Hours ago the last light had gone out. The moon had set behind the cleft summits of La Pagna. Distant thunder had died away among the rocks. The night was close and still. The villa lay in deep shadow, but the outline of the turrets of the tower were clearly marked against the starry sky. All slept, or seemed to sleep.

A thin blue vapor curls out from the marchesa's casement. This vapor, at first light as a fog-drift, winds itself upward, and settles into a cloud, that hovers in the air. Each moment the cloud rises higher and higher. Now it has grown into a lurid canopy, that overhangs the tower. A sudden glow from an arched loop-hole on the second story shows every bar of iron across it. This is caught up below in a broad flash across the basin of the fountain. Within there is a crackling as of dry leaves—a clinging, heavy smell of heated air. Another and another flame curls round the narrow loop-hole, twisting upward on the solid wall.

At this instant there is a low growl, as from a kicked dog. A door below is banged-to and locked. Then steps are heard upon the gravel. It is Adamo. He had returned, as the marchesa bade him, and has come to tell her he has searched everywhere—down even to the reeds by the river Serchio (where he had discharged his gun at a water-hen), but had found no one, though all the way the dogs had sniffed and whined.

Adamo catches sight of the crimson glare reflected upon the fountain. He looks up at the tower—he sees the flames. A look of horror comes into his round black eyes. Then, with a twitch, settling his gun firmly upon his shoulder, he rushes to the unlocked door and flings it wide open.

"Pipa! Wife! Angelo!" Adamo shouts down the stone passage connecting the tower with the villa where they slept. "Wake up! The tower is on fire! Fire! Fire!"

As Adam opened his mouth, the rush of hot air, pent upon the winding stair, drawn downward by the draught from the open door, catches his breath. He staggers against the wall. Then the strong man shook himself together—again he shouts, "Pipa! Pipa! rise!"

Without waiting for an answer, putting his hand over his mouth, Adamo charges up the stone stairs—up to the marchesa's door. Her room is on fire.

"I must save her! I must save her! I will think of Pipa and the children afterward."

Each step Adamo takes upward, the heat grows fiercer, the smoke that pours down denser. Twice he had slipped and almost fallen, but he battles bravely with the heat and blinding smoke, and keeps his footing.

Now Adamo is on the landing of the first floor—Adamo blinded, his head reeling—but lifting his strong limbs, and firm broad feet, he struggles upward. He has reached the marchesa's door. The place is marked by a chink of fire underneath. Adamo passes his hand over the panel; it is unconsumed, the fire drawing the other way out by the window.

"O God! if the door is bolted! I shall drop if I am not quick." Adamo's fingers were on the lock. "The door is bolted! Blessed Virgin, help me!"

He unslings his unloaded gun—he had forgotten it till then—and, tightly seizing it in his strong hands, he flings the butt end against the lock. The wood is old, the bolt is loose.

"Holy Jesus! It yields! It opens!"

Overcome by the rush of fiery air, again Adamo staggers. As he lifts his hands to raise the hair, which, moist from heat, clings to his forehead, his fingers strike against a medal of the Virgin he wore round his naked throat.

"Mother of God, help me!" A desperate courage seizes him; he rushes in—all before him swims in a red mist. "Help me, Madonna!" comes to his parched lips. "O God, where is the marchesa?"

A puff of wind from the open door for an instant raised the smoke and sparks; in that instant Adamo sees a dark heap lying on the floor close to the door. It is the marchesa. "Is she dead or alive?" He cannot stop to tell. He raises her. She lay within his arms. Her dark dress, though not consumed, strikes hot against his chest. Not an instant is to be lost. The fresh rush of air up the stairs has fanned the flames. Every moment they are rising higher. They redden on the dark rafters of the ceiling. The sparks fly about in dazzling clouds. Adamo is on the threshold. Outside it is now so dark that, spite of danger, he has to pause and feel his way downward, or he might dash his precious burden against the walls. In that pause a piercing cry from above strikes upon his ear, but in the crackling of the increasing flames and a fresh torrent of smoke and burning sparks that burst out from the room, Adamo's brain—always of the dullest—is deadened. He forgets that cry. All his thought is to save his mistress. Even Pipa and Angelo and little Gigi are forgotten.

Ere he reaches the level of the first story, the alarm-bell over his head clangs out a goodly peal. A bound of joy within his honest heart gives him fresh courage.

"It is the Madonna! When I touched her image, I knew that she would help me. Pipa has heard me. Pipa has pulled the bell. She is safe! And Angelo—and little Gigi, safe! safe! Brave Pipa! How I love her!"

Before a watch could tick twenty seconds, and while Adamo's foot was still on the last round of the winding stair, the church-bells of Corellia clash out in answer to the alarm-bell

Now Adamo has reached the outer door. He stands beneath the stars. His face and hands are black, his hair is singed; his woolen clothes are hot and burn upon him. The cool night air makes his skin smart with pain. Already Pipa's arms are round him. Angelo, too, has caught him by the legs, then leaps into the air with a wild hoot. Bewildered Pipa cannot speak. No more can Adamo; but Pipa's clinging arms say more than words. Tenderly Adamo lays the marchesa down beside the fountain. He totters on a step or two, feeling suddenly giddy and strangely weak. He stands still. The strain had been too much for the simple soul, who led a quiet life with Pipa and the children. Tears rise in his big black eyes. Greatly ashamed, and wondering what has come to him, he sinks upon the ground. Pipa, watching him, again flings her arms about him; but Adamo gave her a glance so fierce, as he points to the marchesa lying helpless upon the ground, it sent her quickly from him. With a smothered sob Pipa turns away to help her.

(Ah! cruel Pipa, and is your heart so full that you have forgotten Enrica, left helpless in the tower?—Yet so it was. Enrica is forgotten. Cruel, cruel Pipa! And stupid Adamo, whose head turns round so fast he must hold on by a tree not to fall again.)

Silvestro and Fra Pacifico now rushed out of the darkness; Fra Pacifico aroused out of his first sleep. He had
not seen the marchesa since her arrival. He did not know
whether Enrica had come with her from Lucca or not.
Seeing Pipa busy about the fountain, the women, thought
Fra Pacifico, were safe; so Fra Pacifico strode off on his
strong legs to see what could be done to quench the fire,
and save, if possible, the more combustible villa. Surely
the villa must be consumed! The smoke now darkened
the heavens. The flames belted the thick tower-walls
as with a burning girdle. Showers of sparks and flames
rose out from each aperture with sudden bursts, revealing
every detail on the gray old walls; moss and lichen, a trail
of ivy that had forced itself upward, long grass that floated
in the hot air; a crevice under the battlements where a
bird had built its nest. Then a swirl of smoke swooped
down and smothered all, while overhead the mighty company of constellations looked calmly down in their cold
brightness!

A crowd of men now came running down from Corellia,
roused by the church-bells. Pietro, the baker, still hard at
work, was the first to hear the bell, to dash into the street,
and shout, "Help! help! Fire! fire! At the villa!"

Oreste and Pilade heard him. They came tumbling
out. Ser Giacomo roused the sindaco—who in his turn
woke his clerk; but when Mr. Sindaco was fairly off down
the hill, this much-injured and very weary youth turned
back and went to bed.

Some bore lighted torches, others copper buckets. Pietro, the butcher, brought the municipal ladder. These men
promptly formed a line down the hill, to carry the water
from the willful mountain-stream that fed the town fountain.
Fra Pacifico took the lead. (He had heard the alarm, and
had rung the church-bells himself.) No one cared for the
marchesa; but a burning house was a fine sight, and where

Fra Pacifico went all Corellia followed. Adamo, recovered now, was soon upon the ladder, receiving the buckets from below. Pipa beside the fountain watched the marchesa, sprinkling water on her face. "Surely her eyelids faintly quiver!" thinks Pipa.—Pipa watched the marchesa speechless—watched her as birth and death are only watched!

The marchesa's eyes had quivered; now they slowly unclose. Pipa, who, next to the Virgin and the saints, worshiped her mistress—laughed wildly—sobbed—then laughed again—kissed her hand, her forehead—then pressed her in her arms. Supported by Pipa, the marchesa sat up—she turned, and then she saw the mountains of smoke bursting from the tower, forming into great clouds that rose over the tree-tops, and shut out the stars. The marchesa glanced quickly round with her keen, black eyes—she glanced as one searching for some thing she cannot find; then her lips parted, and one word fell faintly from them: "Enrica!"

Pipa caught the half-uttered name, she echoed it with a scream.

"Ahi! The signorina! The Signorina Enrica!" Pipa shouted to Adamo on the ladder.

"Adamo! Adamo! where is the signorina?"

Adamo's heart sank at her voice. On the instant he recalled that cry he had heard upon the stairs.

"Where did you see her last?" Adamo shouted back to Pipa out of the din—his big stupid eyes looking down upon her face. "Up-stairs?"

Pipa nodded. She could not speak, it was too horrible.

"Santo Dio! I did not know it!" He struck upon his breast. "Assassin! I have killed her! Assassin! Beast! what have I done?"

Again the air rang with Pipa's shrill cries. The Corellia men, who with eager hands pass the buckets down the hill, stop, and stare, and wonder. Fra Pacifico, who had eyes and ears for every one, turned, and ran forward to where Pipa sat wringing her hands upon the ground, the marchesa leaning against her.

"Is Enrica in the tower?" asked Fra Pacifico.

"Yes, yes!" the marchesa answered feebly. "You must save her!"

"Then follow me!" shouted the priest, swinging his strong arms above his head.

Adamo leaped from the ladder. Others—they were among the very poorest—stepped out and joined him and the priest; but at the very entrance they were met and buffeted by such a gust of fiery wind, such sparks and choking smoke, that they all fell back aghast. Fra Pacifico alone stood unmoved, his tall, burly figure dark against the glare. At this instant a man wrapped in a cloak rushed out of the wood, crossed the red circle reflected from the fire, and dashed into the archway.

"Stop him! stop him!" shouted Adamo from behind.

"You go to certain death!" cried Fra Pacifico, laying his hand upon him.

"I am prepared to die," the other answered, and pushed by him.

Twice he essayed to mount the stairs. Twice he was driven back before them all. See! He has covered his head with his cloak. He has set his foot firmly upon the stone steps. Up, up he mounts—now he is gone! Without there was a breathless silence. "Who is he?—Can he save her?"—Words were not spoken, but every eye asked this question. The men without are brave, ready to face danger in dark alley—by stream or river—or on the mountain-side. Danger is pastime to them, but each one feels in his own heart he is glad not to go. Fra Pacifico stands motionless, a sad stern look upon his swarthy face. For the first time in his life he has not been foremost in danger!

By this time, Fra Pacifico thinks, unless choked, the stranger must be near the upper story.

The marchesa has now risen. She stands upright, her eyes riveted on the tower. She knows there is a door that opens from the top of the winding stair, on the highest story, next Enrica's room, a door out on the battlements. Will the stranger see it? O God! will he see it?—or is the smoke too thick?—or has he fainted ere he reached so high?—or, if he has reached her, is Enrica dead? How heavy the moments pass—weighted with life or death! Look, look! Surely something moves between the turrets of the tower! Yes, something moves. It rises—a muffled form between the turrets—the figure of a man wrapped in a cloak—on the near side out of the smoke and flames. Yes—it is the stranger—Enrica in his arms! All is clear-ly seen, cut as it were against a crimson background. A shout rises from every living man—a deep, full shout as out of bursting hearts that vent themselves. Out of the· shout the words ring out—" The steps!—the steps!—There —to the right—cut in the battlements! The steps!—the steps!—close by the flagstaff! Pass the steps down to the lower roof of the villa." (The wind set on the oth-er side, drawing the fire that way. The villa was not touched.)

The stranger heard and bowed his head. He has found the steps—he has reached the lower roof of the villa—he is safe!

No one below had moved. The hands by which the water was passed were now laid upon the ladder. It was shifted over to the other side against the villa walls. Adamo and Fra Pacifico stand upon the lower rungs, to steady it. The stranger throws his cloak below, the better to descend.

" Who is he?" That strong, well-knit frame, those square shoulders, that curly chestnut hair, the pleasant

smile upon his glowing face, proclaim him. It is Count
Nobili! He has lands along the Serchio, between Barga
and Corellia, and was well known as a keen sportsman.

"Bravo! bravo! Evviva! Count Nobili — evviva!"
Caps were tossed into the air, hands were wildly clapped,
friendly arms are stretched out to bear him up when he descends. Adamo is wildly excited; Adamo wants to mount
the ladder to help. The others pull him back. Fra Pacifico stands ready to receive Enrica, a baffled look on his
face. It is the first time Fra Pacifico has stood by and seen
another do his work.

See, Count Nobili is on the ladder, Enrica in his arms!
As his feet touch the ground, again the people shout:
"Bravo! Count Nobili! Evviva!" Their hot southern
blood is roused by the sight of such noble daring. The
people press upon him—they fold him in their arms—they
kiss his hands, his cheeks, even his very feet.

Nobili's eyes flash. He, too, forgets all else, and, with
a glance that thrills Enrica from head to foot, he kisses
her before them all. The men circle round him. They shout
louder than before.

As the crowd parted, the dark figure of the marchesa,
standing near the fountain, was disclosed. Before she had
time to stir, Count Nobili had led Enrica to her. He knelt
upon the ground, and, kissing Enrica's hand, placed it within her own. Then he rose, and, with that grace natural to
him, bowed and stood aside, waiting for her to speak.

The marchesa neither moved nor did she speak. When
she felt the warm touch of Enrica's hand within her own,
it seemed to rouse her. She drew her toward her and
kissed her with more love than she had ever shown before.

"I thank you, Count Nobili," she said, in a strange,
cold voice. Even at that moment she could not bring herself to look him in the face. "You have saved my niece's
life."

"Madame," replied Nobili, his sweet-toned voice trembling, "I have saved my own. Had Enrica perished, I should not have lived."

In these few words the chivalric nature of the man spoke out. The marchesa waved her hand. She was stately even now. Nobili understood her gesture, and, stung to the very soul, he drew back.

"Permit me," he said, haughtily, before he turned away, "to add my help to those who are laboring to save your house."

The marchesa bowed her head in acquiescence; then, with unsteady steps, she moved backward and seated herself upon the ground.

Pipa, meanwhile, had flung her arms about Enrica, with such an energy that she pinned her to the spot. Pipa pressed her hands about Enrica, feeling every limb; Pipa turned Enrica's white face upward to the blaze ; she stroked her long, fair hair that fell like a mantle round her.

"Blessed Mother!" she sobbed, drawing her coarse fingers through the matted curls, "not a hair singed! Oh, the noble count! Oh, how I love him—"

"No, dear Pipa," Enrica answered, softly, "I am not hurt—only frightened. The fire had but just reached the door when he came. He was just in time."

"To think we had forgotten her!" murmured Pipa, still holding her tightly.

"Who remembered me first?" asked Enrica, eagerly.

"The marchesa, signorina, the marchesa. She remembered you. The marchesa was brought down by Adamo. Your name was the first word she uttered."

Enrica's blue eyes glistened. In an instant she had disengaged herself from Pipa, and was kneeling at the marchesa's feet.

"Dear aunt, forgive me. Now that I am saved, forgive me! You must forgive me, and forgive him, too!"

.

These last words came faint and low. The marchesa put her finger on her lip.

" Not now, Enrica, not now. To-morrow we will speak."

Meanwhile Count Nobili, Fra Pacifico, and the Corellia men, strove what human strength could do to put the fire out. Even the sindaco, forgetting the threats about his rent, labored hard and willingly—only Silvestro did nothing. Silvestro seemed stunned; he sat upon the ground staring, and crying like a child.

To save the rooms within the tower was impossible. Every plank of wood was burning. The ceilings had fallen in; only the blackened walls and stone stairs remained. The villa was untouched—the wind, setting the other way, and the thick walls of the tower, had saved it.

Now every hand that could be spared was turned to bring beds from the steward's for the marchesa and Enrica. They had gone into Pipa's room until the villa was made ready. Pipa told Adamo, and he told the others, that the marchesa had not seen the burning papers, and the lighted pile of wood, until the flames rose high behind her back. She had rushed forward, and fallen.

When all was over, Count Nobili was carried up the hill back to Corellia, in triumph, on the shoulders of Pietro the baker, and Oreste, the strongest of the brothers. Every soul of the poor townsfolk—women as well as men who had not gone down to help—had risen, and was out. They had put lights into their windows. They crowded the doorways. The market-place was full, and the church-porch. The fame of Nobili's courage had already reached them. All bless him as he passes—bless him louder when Nobili, all aglow with happiness, empties his pockets of all the coin he has, and promises more to-morrow. At this the women lay hold of him, and dance round him. It was long before he was released. At last Fra Pacifico carried him off, almost by force, to sleep at the curato.

CHAPTER IV.

FRA PACIFICO was a dark, burly man, with a large, weather-beaten face, kind gray eyes under a pair of shaggy eyebrows, a resolute nose, large, full-lipped mouth, and a clean-shaven double chin, that rested comfortably upon his priestly stock. He was no longer young, but he had a frame like iron, and in his time he had possessed a force of arm and muscle enough to fell an ox. His strength and daring were acknowledged by all the mountain-folks from Corellia to Barga, hardy fellows, and judges of what a man can do. Moreover, Fra Pacifico was more than six feet high—and who does not respect a man of such inches? In fair fight he had killed his man—a brigand chief—who prowled about the mountains toward Carrara. His band had fled and never returned.

Fra Pacifico had stood with his strong feet planted on the earth, over the edge of a rocky precipice—by which the high-road passed—and seized a furious horse dragging a cart holding six poor souls below. Fra Pacifico had found a shepherd of Corellia—one of his flock—struck down by fever on a rocky peak some twenty miles distant, and he had carried him on his back, and laid him on his bed at home. Every one had some story to tell of his prowess, coolness, and manly daring. When he walked

along the streets, the ragged children—as black with sun
and dirt as unfledged ravens—sidled up to him, and, looking up into his gray eyes, ran between his firm-set legs,
plucked him by the cassock, and felt in his pockets for an
apple or a cake. Then the children held him tight until
he had raised them up and kissed them.

Spite of the labors of the previous night (no one had
worked harder), Fra Pacifico had risen with daybreak. His
office accustomed him to little sleep. There was no time
by day or night that he could call his own. If any one
was stricken with sickness in the night, or suddenly seized
for death in those pale hours when the day hovers, half-
born, over the slumbering earth, Fra Pacifico must rise
and wake his acolyte, the baker's boy, who, going late to
bed, was hard to rouse. Along with him he must grope
up and down slippery steps, and along dark alleys, bearing
the Host under a red umbrella, until he had placed it within
the dying lips. If a baby was weakly, or born before its
time, and, having given one look at this sorrowful world,
was about to lose its eyes on it forever, Fra Pacifico must
run out at any moment to christen it.

There was no doctor at Corellia, the people were too
poor; so Fra Pacifico was called upon to do a doctor's duty.
He must draw the teeth of such as needed it; bind up cuts
and sores; set limbs; and give such simple drugs as he
knew the nature of. He must draw up papers for those
who could not afford to pay the notary; write letters for
those who could only make a cross; hear and conceal every
secret that reached him in the confessional or on the death-
bed. He must be at hand at any hour in the twenty-four
—ready to counsel, soothe, command, and reprimand; to
bless, to curse, and, if need be, to strike, when his righteous anger rose; to fetch and carry for all, and, poor
himself, to give out of his scanty store. These were his
priestly duties.

Fra Pacifico lived at the back of the old Lombard church of Santa Barbara, in a house overlooking a damp square, overgrown with moss and weeds. Between the tower where the bells hung, and the body of the church, an open loggia (balcony), roofed with wood and tiles, rested on slender pillars. In the loggia, Fra Pacifico, when at leisure, would sit and rest and read his breviary; sometimes smoke a solitary pipe—stretching out his shapely legs in the luxury of doing nothing. Behind the loggia were the priest's four rooms, bare even for the bareness of that squalid place. He kept no servant, but it was counted an honor to serve him, and the mothers of Corellia came by turns to cook and wash for him.

Fra Pacifico, as I have said, had risen at daybreak. Now he is searching to find a messenger to send to Lucca, as the marchesa had desired, to summon Cavaliere Trenta. That done, he takes a key out of his pocket and unlocks the church-door. Here, kneeling at the altar, he celebrates a private mass of thanksgiving for the marchesa and Enrica. Then, with long strides, he descends the hill to see what is doing at the villa.

CHAPTER V.

"SAY NOT TOO MUCH."

THE sun was streaming on mountain and forest before Count Nobili woke from a deep sleep. As he cast his drowsy eyes around upon the homely little room, the coarsely-painted frescoes on the walls—the gaudy cups and plates arranged in a cupboard opposite the bed—and on a wax Gesù Bambino, placed in state upon the mantel-piece, surrounded by a flock of blue sheep, browsing on purple grass, he could not at first remember where he was. The noises from the square below—the clink of the donkeys' hoofs upon the pavement as they struggled up the steep alley laden with charcoal; the screams of children—the clamor of women's voices moving to and fro with their wooden shoes—and the boom of the church-bells sounding overhead for morning mass—came to him as in a dream.

As he raised his hand to push back the hair which fell over his eyes, a sharp twitch of pain—for his hands were scorched and blistered—brought all that had happened vividly before him. A warmth of joy and love glowed at his heart. He had saved Enrica's life. Henceforth that life was his. From that day they would never part. From that day, forgetting all others, he would live for her alone.

He must see her instantly—if possible, before his enemy, her aunt, had risen—see Enrica, and speak to her, alone. Oh, the luxury of that! How he longed to feast his eyes upon the softness of her beauty! To fill his ears with the music of her voice! To touch her little hand, and scent the fragrance of her breath upon his cheek! There was no thought within Nobili but love and loyalty. At that moment Enrica was the only woman in the world whom he loved, or ever could love!

He dressed himself in haste, opened the door, and stepped out into the loggia. Not finding Fra Pacifico there, or in the other rooms, he passed down the stone steps into the little square, threading his way beyond as he best could, through the tortuous little alleys toward the gate. Most of the men had already gone to work; but such as lingered, or whose business kept them at home, rose as he passed, and bared their heads to him. The mothers and the girls stared at him and smiled; troops of children followed at his heels through the town, until he reached the gate.

Without, the holiness of Nature was around. The morning air blew upon him crisp and clear. The sky, blue as a turquoise, was unbroken by a cloud. The trees were bathed in gold. The chain of Apennines rose up before him in lines of dreamy loveliness, like another world, midway toward heaven. A passing shower veiled the massive summits toward Massa and Carrara, but the broad valley of the Serchio, mapped out in smallest details, lay serenely luminous below. Beyond the gate there was no certain road. It broke into little tracts and rocky paths terracing downward. Following these, streams ran bubbling, sparkling like gems as they dashed against the stones. No shadows rested upon the grass, cooled by the dew and carpeted by flowers. The woods danced in the October sunshine. Painted butterflies and gnats circled in the warm air; green lizards gamboled among the rocks that cut the turf. Flocks of autumn birds swooped round in rapid flight.

Some freshly-shorn sheep, led by a ragged child, cropped the short herbage fragrant with strong herbs. A bristly pig carrying a bell about his neck, ran wildly up and down the grassy slope in search of chestnuts.

Through this sylvan wilderness Nobili came stepping downward by the little paths, like a young god full of strength and love!

The villa lay beneath him; the blackened ruins of the tower rose over the chestnut-tops. These blackened ruins showed him which way to go. As he set his foot upon the topmost terrace of the garden, his heart beat fast.

Enrica would be there, he knew it. Enrica would be waiting for him. Could Nobili yearn so fondly for Enrica and she not know it? Could the mystic bond that knit them together, from the first moment they had met, leave her unconscious of his presence? No; that subtile charm that draws lovers together, and breathes from heart to heart the sacred fire, had warned her. She was standing there—there, beneath him, under the shadow of a flowery thicket. Enrica was leaning against the trunk of a magnolia-tree, the shining leaves forming her in a rich canopy, through which a glint of sunshine pierced, falling upon her light hair and the white dress she wore.

Nobili paused to look at her. Miser-like, he would pause to gloat upon his treasure! How well a golden glory would become that sunny head! She only wanted wings, he thought, to make an angel of her. Enrica's face was bent. Her thoughts, far away, were lost in a delicious world, neither earth nor heaven—a world with Nobili! What mysteries were there, what unknown joys, or sharper pains perchance, she neither knew nor cared. She would share all with him! In a moment the place she stood on was darkened. Something stood between her and the sun. She looked up and gave a little cry, then stood motionless, the color going and coming upon her cheek. One bound,

chesa must own this. Last night the old life died out as
the smoke from that old tower. To-day you have waked
to a new life with me."

Again Nobili's arms stole round her; again he sealed
the sacrament of love with a fervid kiss.

Enrica trembled from head to foot—a scared look came
over her. The rush of passionate joy, coming upon the terrors of the past night, was more than she could bear. Nobili watched the change.

"Forgive me, love," he said, "I will be calmer. Lay
your dear head against me. We will sit together here—
under the trees."

"Yes," said Enrica in a faltering voice; "I have so much
to say." Then, suddenly recalling the blessing of his presence, a smile stole about her bloodless lips. She gave a
happy sigh. "Yes, Nobili—we can talk now without fear.
But I can talk only of you. I have no thought but you. I
never dreamed of such happiness as this! O Nobili!"
And she hid her face in the strong arm entwined about
her.

"Speak to me, Enrica; I will listen to you forever."

Enrica clasped his hand, looked at it, sighed, pressed
it between both of hers, sighed again, then raised it to her
lips.

"Dear hand," she said, "how it is burnt! But for this
hand, I should be nothing now but a little heap of ashes in
the tower. Nobili"—her tone suddenly changed—"Nobili, I will try to love life now that you have given it to
me." Her voice rang out like music, and her telltale eyes
caught his, with a glance as passionate as his own. "Count
Marescotti," she said, absently, as giving utterance to a passing thought—"Count Marescotti told me, only a week ago,
that I was born to be unhappy. He said he read it in my
eyes. I believed him then—not now—not now."

Why, she could not have explained, but, as the count's

name passed her lips, Enrica was sorry she had mentioned
it. Nobili noted this. He gave an imperceptible start, and
drew back a little from her.

"Do you know Count Marescotti?" Enrica asked him,
timidly.

"I know him by sight," was Nobili's reply. "He is a
mad fellow—a republican. Why does he come to Lucca?"

Enrica shook her head.

"I do not know," she answered, still confused.

"Where did you meet him, Enrica?"

She blushed, and dropped her eyes. As she gave him
no answer, he asked another question, gazing down upon
her earnestly:

"How did Count Marescotti come to know what your
eyes said?"

As Nobili spoke, his voice sounded changed. He waited
for an answer with a look as if he had been wronged. Enrica's answer did not come immediately. She felt frightened.

"Oh! why," she thought, "had she mentioned Marescotti's name?" Nobili was angry with her—she was sure
he was angry with her.

"I met him at my aunt's one evening," she said at last,
gathering courage as she stole her little hand into one of
his, and knit her fingers tightly within his own. "We
went up into the Guinigi Tower together. There were
dear old Trenta and Baldassare Lena with us."

"Indeed!" replied Nobili, coldly. "I did not know
that the Marchesa Guinigi ever received young men."

As Nobili said this he fixed his eyes upon Enrica's face.
What could he read there but assurance of the perfect innocence within? Yet the name of Count Marescotti had
grated upon his ear like a discord clashing among sweet
sounds. He shook the feeling off, however, for the time.
Again he was her gracious lover.

"Tell me, love," he said, drawing Enrica to him, "did you hear my signal last night?—the shot I fired below, out of the woods?"

"Yes, I heard a shot. Something told me it must be you. I thought I should have died when I heard my aunt order Adamo to unloose those dreadful dogs. How did you escape them?"

"The cunning beasts! They were upon my track. How I did it in the darkness I cannot tell, but I managed to scramble down the cliff and to reach the opposite mountain. The chasm was then between us. So the dogs lost the scent upon the rocks, and missed me. I left Lucca almost as soon as you. Trenta told me that the marchesa had brought you here because you would not give me up. Dear heart, how I grieved that I had brought suffering on you!"

He seized her hand and pressed it to his lips, then continued:

"As long as it was day, I prowled about under the cliffs in the shadow of the chasm. I watched the stars come out. There was one star that shone brightly above the tower; to me that star was you, Enrica. I could have knelt to it."

"Dear Nobili!" murmured Enrica, softly.

"As I waited there, I saw a great red vapor gather over the battlements. The alarm-bell sounded. I climbed up through the wood, where the rocks are lower, and watched among the shrubs. I saw the marchesa carried out in Adamo's arms. I heard your name, dear love, passed from mouth to mouth. I looked around—you were not there. I understood it all; I rushed to save you."

Again Nobili wound his arms round Enrica and drew her to him with passionate ardor. The thought of Count Marescotti had faded out like a bad dream at daylight.

Enrica's blue eyes dimmed with tears.

"Oh, do not weep, Enrica!" he cried. "Let the past

go, love. Did the marchesa think that bolts and bars, and Adamo, and watch-dogs, would keep Nobili from you?" He gave a merry laugh. "I shall not leave Corellia until we are affianced. Fra Pacifico knows it—I told him so last night. Cavaliere Trenta is expected to-day from Lucca. Both will speak to your aunt. One may have done so already, for what I know, for Fra Pacifico had left his house before I rose. He must be here. Is this a time to weep, Enrica?" he asked her tenderly. How comely Nobili looked! What life and joy sparkled in his bright eyes!

"I am very foolish—I hope you will forgive me," was Enrica's answer, spoken a little sadly. Her confidence in herself was shaken, since Count Marescotti's name had jarred between them. "Let us walk a little in the shade."

"Yes. Lean on me, dearest; the morning is delicious. But remember, Enrica, I will have smiles—nothing but smiles."

As Nobili bore her up on his strong arm, pacing up and down among the flowering trees that, bowing in the light breeze, shed gaudy petals at their feet—Nobili looked so strong, and resolute, and bold—his eyes had such a power in them as he gazed down proudly upon her—that the tears which trembled upon Enrica's eyelids disappeared. Nobili's strength came to her as her own strength. She, who had been so crushed and wounded, brought so near to death, needed this to raise her up to life. And now it came—came as she gazed at him.

Yes, she would live—live a new life with him. And Nobili had done it—done it unconsciously, as the sun unfolds the bosom of the rose, and from the delicate bud creates the perfect flower.

Something Nobili understood of what was passing within her, but not all. He had yet to learn the treasures of faith and love shut up in the bosom of that silent girl—to learn how much she loved him—only *him*. (A new lesson for one who had trifled with so many, and given and taken such facile oaths!)

Neither spoke, but wandered up and down in vague delight.

Why was it that at this moment Nobili's thoughts strayed to Lucca, and to Nera Boccarini?—Nera rose before him, glowing and velvet-eyed, as on that night she had so tempted him. He drove her image from him. Nera was dead to him. Dead?—Fool!—And did he think that any thing can die? Do not our very thoughts rise up and haunt us in some subtile consequence of after-life? Nothing dies—nothing is isolated. Each act of daily intercourse—the merest trifle, as the gravest issue—makes up the chain of life. Link by link that chain draws on, weighted with good or ill, and clings about us to the very grave.

Thinking of Nera, Nobili's color changed—a dark look clouded his ready smile. Enrica asked, "What pains you?"

"Nothing, love, nothing," Nobili answered vaguely, "only I fear I am not worthy of you."

Enrica raised her eyes to his. Such a depth of tenderness and purity beamed from them, that Nobili asked himself with shame, how he could have forgotten her With this blue-eyed angel by his side it seemed impossible, and yet—

Pressing Enrica's hand more tightly, he placed it fondly on his own. "So small, so true," he murmured, gazing at it as it lay on his broad palm.

"Yes, Nobili, true to death," she answered, with a sigh.

Still holding her hand, "Enrica," he said, solemnly, "I swear to love you and no other, while I live. God is my witness!"

As he lifted up his head in the earnestness with which

he spoke, the sunshine, streaming downward, shone full upon his face.

Enrica trembled. "Oh! do not say too much," she cried, gazing up at him entranced.

With that sun-ray upon his face, Nobili seemed to her, at that moment, more than mortal!

"Angel!" exclaimed Count Nobili, wrought up to sudden passion, "can you doubt me?"

Before Enrica could reply, a snake, warmed by the hot sun, curled upward from the terraced wall behind them, where it had basked, and glided swiftly between them. Nobili's heel was on it; in an instant he had crushed its head. But there between them lay the quivering reptile, its speckled scales catching the light. Enrica shrieked and started back.

"O God! what an evil omen!" She said no more, only her shifting color and uneasy eyes told what she felt.

"An evil omen, love!" and Nobili brushed away the snake with his foot into the underwood, and laughed. "Not so. It is an omen that I shall crush all who would part us. That is how I read it."

Enrica shook her head. That snake crawling between them was the first warning to her that she was still on earth. Till then it had seemed to her that Nobili's presence nust be like paradise. Now for a moment a terrible doubt crept over her. Could happiness be sad? It must be so, for now she could not tell whether she was sad or happy.

"Oh! do not say too much, dear Nobili," she repeated almost to herself, "or—" Her voice dropped. She looked toward the spot where the snake had fallen, and shuddered.

Nobili did not then reply, but, taking Enrica by the hand, he led her up a flight of steps to a higher terrace, where a cypress avenue threw long shadows across the marble pavement.

· "You are mine," he whispered, "mine—as by a miracle!"

There was such rapture in his voice that heaven came down into her heart, and every doubt was stilled.

At this moment Fra Pacifico's towering figure appeared ascending a lower flight of steps toward them, coming from the house. He trod with that firm, grand step churchmen have in common with actors—only the stage upon which each treads is different. Behind Fra Pacifico was the short, plump figure and the white hat of Cavaliere Trenta (a dwarf beside the priest), his rosy face rosier than ever from the rapid drive from Lucca. Trenta's kind eyes twinkled under his white eyebrows as he spied Enrica above, standing side by side with Nobili. How different the dear child looked from that last time he had seen her at Lucca!

Enrica flew down the steps to meet him. She threw her arms round his neck. Count Nobili followed her; he shook hands with the cavaliere and Fra Pacifico.

"His reverence and I thought we should find you two together," said Cavaliere Trenta, with a chuckle. "Count Nobili, I wish you joy."

His voice faltered a little, and a spotless handkerchief was drawn out and called into service. Nobili reddened, then bowed with formal courtesy.

"It is all come right, I see."—Trenta gave a sly glance from one to the other, though the tears were in his eyes.— "I shall live to open the marriage-ball on the first floor of the palace yet. Bagatella! I would have tried to give the dear child to you myself, had I known how much she loved you—but you have taken her. Well, well—possession is better than gift."

"She gave herself to me, cavaliere. Last night's work only made the gift public," was Nobili's reply.

There was a tone of triumph in Nobili's voice as he said

this. He stooped and pressed his lips to Enrica's hand. Enrica stood by with downcast eyes—a spray of pink oleander swaying from the terrace-wall in the light breeze above her head, for background.

The old cavaliere nodded his head, round which the little curls set faultlessly under his white hat.

"My dear Count Nobili, permit me to offer my advice. You must settle this matter at once—at once, I say;" and Trenta struck his stick upon the marble balustrade for greater emphasis.

"I quite agree with you," put in Fra Pacifico in his deep voice. "The impression made by your courage last night must not be lost by delay. I never saw an act of greater daring. Had you not come, I should have tried to save Enrica, but I am past my prime; I should have failed."

"You cannot count on the marchesa's gratitude," continued Trenta; "an excellent lady, and my oldest friend, but proud and capricious. You mnst take her like the wind when it blows—ha! ha! like the wind. I am come here to help you both."

"Cavaliere," said Nobili, turning toward him (his vagrant eyes had wandered off to Enrica, so charming, with the pink oleander and its dark-green leaves waving above her blond head), "do me the favor to ask the Marchesa Guinigi at what hour she will admit me to sign the marriage-contract. I have pressing business that calls me back to Lucca to-day."

"So soon, dear Nobili?" a soft voice whispered at his ear, "so soon?" And then there was a sigh. Surely her paradise was very brief! Enrica had thought in her simplicity that, once met, they two never should part again, but spend the live-long days together side by side among the woods, lingering by flowing streams; or in the rich shade of purple vine-bowers; or in mossy caves, shaded

by tall ferns, hid on the mountain-side, and let time and
the world roll by. This was the life she dreamed of. Could
any grief be there?

"Yes, love," Nobili answered to her question. "I
must return to Lucca to-night. I started on the instant,
as the cavaliere knows. Before I go, however, all must be
settled about our marriage, and the contract signed. I will
take no denial."

Nobili spoke with the determination that was in him.
Enrica's heart gave a bound. "The contract!" She had
never thought of that. "The contract and the marriage!"
—"Both close at hand!—Then the life she dreamed of
must come true in very earnest!"

The cavaliere looked doubtingly at Fra Pacifico. Fra
Pacifico shrugged his big shoulders, looked back again at
Cavaliere Trenta, and smiled rather grimly. There was
always a sense of suppressed power, moral and physical,
about Fra Pacifico. In conversation he had a way of leaving the burden of small talk to others, and of reserving
himself for special occasions; but when he spoke he must
be listened to.

"Quick work, my dear count," was all the priest said
to Nobili in answer. "Do you think you can insure the
marchesa's consent?" Now he addressed the cavaliere.

"Oh, my friend will be reasonable, no doubt. After
last night, she must consent." The cavaliere was always
ready to put the best construction upon every thing. "If
she raises any obstacles, I think I shall be able to remove
them."

"Consent!" cried Nobili, fiercely echoing back the
word, "she must consent—she will be mad to refuse."

"Well—well—we shall see.—You, Count Nobili, have
done all to make it sure. The terms of the contract (I have
heard of them from Fra Pacifico) are princely." A look
from Count Nobili stopped Trenta from saying more.

" Now, Enrica," and the cavaliere turned and took her arm, " come in and give me some breakfast. An old man of eighty must eat, if he means to dance at weddings."

" You, Nobili, must come with me," said Fra Pacifico, laying his hand on the count's shoulder. " We will wait the cavaliere's summons to return here over a bottle of the marchesa's best vintage, and a cutlet cooked by Maria. She is my best cook; I have one for every day in the week."

So they parted—Trenta with Enrica descending flight after flight of steps, leading from terrace to terrace, down to the villa ; Nobili mounting upward to the forest with Fra Pacifico toward Corellia, to await the marchesa's answer.

CHAPTER VI.

FRA PACIFICO, with Adamo and Pipa, had labored ever since daybreak to arrange the rooms at the villa before the marchesa rose. Pipa had freely used the broom and many pails of water. All the windows were thrown open, and clouds of invisible incense from the flowers without sweetened the fusty rooms.

The villa had not been inhabited for nearly fifty years. It was scantily provided with furniture, but there were chairs and tables and beds, and all the rough necessaries of life. To make all straight, whole generations of beetles had been swept away; and patriarchal spiders, which clung tenaciously to the damp spots on the walls. A scorpion or two had been found, which, firmly resisting to quit the chinks where they had grown and multiplied, had died by decapitation. Fra Pacifico would not have owned it, but he had discovered and killed a nest of black adders that lay concealed, curled up in a curtain.

He had with his own hands, in the early morning, carefully fashioned the spacious sala on the ground-floor to the marchesa's liking. A huge sofa, with a faded amber cover, had been drawn out of a recess, and so placed that the light should fall at her back.—She objected to the sunshine, with true Italian perverseness. Some arm-chairs, once gilt, and still bearing a coronet, were placed in a semicircle opposite. The windows of the sala, and two glass doors of the same size and make, looked east and west; toward the terraces and the garden on one side, and over the cliffs and the chasm to the opposite mountains on the other. The walls were broken by doors of varnished pine-wood. These doors led, on the right, to the chapel, Enrica's bedroom, and many empty apartments; on the left, to the marchesa's suite of rooms, the offices, and the stone corridor which communicated with the now ruined tower. High up on the walls of the sala, two large and roughly-painted frescoes decorated the empty spaces. A Dutch seaport on one side, with sloping roofs and tall gables, bordering a broad river, upon which ships sailed vaguely away into a yellow haze. (Not more vaguely sailing, perhaps, than many human ships, with life-sails set to catch the wind of fortune—ships which never make more way than these painted emblems !) Opposite, a hunting-party of the olden time picnicked in a forest-glade; a brown and red palace in the background, in front lords and ladies lounging on the grass—bundles of satin, velvet, powder, ribbons, feathers, shoulder-knots, ruffles, long-tailed coats, and trains.

A door to the left opened. There was a sound of voices talking.

"My honored marchesa," the cavaliere was heard to say in his most dulcet tones, "in the state of your affairs, you cannot refuse. Why then delay? The day is passing by; Count Nobili is impatient. Let me implore you to lose no more time."

While he was speaking the marchesa entered the sala, passing close under the fresco of the vaguely-sailing ships upon the wall.—Can the marchesa tell whither she is drifting more than these?—She glanced round approvingly, then seated herself upon the sofa. Trenta obsequiously placed a footstool at her feet, a cushion at her back. Even the tempered light, which had been carefully prepared for her by closing the outer wooden shutters, could not conceal how sallow and worn she looked, nor the black circles that had gathered round her eyes. Her dark dress hung about her as if she had suddenly grown thin; her white hands fell listlessly at her side. The marchesa knew that she must consent to Count Nobili's conditions. She knew she must consent this very day. But such a struggle as this knowledge cost her, coming so close upon the agitation of the previous night, was more than even her iron nerves could bear. As she leaned back upon the sofa, shading her eyes with her hand, as was her habit, she felt she could not frame the words with which to answer the cavaliere, were it to save her life.

As for the cavaliere, who had seated himself opposite, his plump little person was so engulfed in an arm-chair, that nothing but his snowy head was visible. This he waved up and down reflectively, rattled his stick upon the floor, and glanced indignantly from time to time at the marchesa. Why would she not answer him?

Meanwhile a little color had risen upon her cheeks. She forced herself to sit erect, arranged the folds of her dark dress, then, in a kind of stately silence, seemed to lend herself to listen to what Trenta might have to urge, as though it concerned her as little as that rose-leaf which comes floating in from the open door and drops at her feet.

" Well, marchesa, well—what is your answer? " asked Trenta, much nettled at her assumed indifference. " Remember that Count Nobili and Fra Pacifico have been waiting for some hours."

"Let Nobili wait," answered the marchesa, a sudden glare darting into her dark eyes; "he is born to wait for such as I."

" Still "—Trenta was both tired and angry, but he

dared not show it; only he rattled his stick louder on the floor, and from time to time aimed a savage blow with it against· the carved legs of a neighboring table—"still, why do the thing ungraciously? The count's offers are magnificent. Surely in the face of absolute ruin—Fra Pacifico assures me—"

"Let Fra Pacifico mind his own business," was the marchesa's answer.

"Nobili·saved Enrica's life last night; that cannot be denied."

"Yes—last night, last night; and I am to be forced and fettered because I set myself on fire! I wish I had perished, and Enrica too!"

A gesture of horror from the cavaliere recalled the marchesa to a sense of what she had uttered.

"And do you deem it nothing, Cesare Trenta, after a life spent in building up the ancient name I bear, that I should be brought to sign a marriage-contract with a peddler's son?" She trembled with passion.

"Yet it must be done," answered Trenta.

"Must be done! Must be done! I would rather die! Mark my words, Cesare. No good will come of this marriage. That young man is weak and dissolute. He is mad with wealth, and the vulgar influence that comes with wealth. As a man, he is unworthy of my niece, who, I must confess, has the temper of an angel."

"I believe that you are wrong, marchesa; Count Nobili is much beloved in Lucca. Fra Pacifico has known him from boyhood. He praises him greatly. I also like him."

"Like him!—Yes, Cesare, you are such an easy fool you like every one. First Marescotti, then Nobili. Marescotti was a gentleman, but this fellow—" She left the sentence incomplete. "Remember my words—you are deceived in him."

"At all events," retorted the cavaliere, "it is too late

to discuss these matters now. Time presses. Enrica loves him. He insists on marrying her. You have no money, and cannot give her a portion. My respected marchesa, I have often ventured to represent to you what those law-suits would entail! Per Bacco! There must be an end of all things—may I call them in?"

The poor old chamberlain was completely exhausted. He had spent four hours in reasoning with his friend. The marchesa turned her head away and shuddered; she could not bring herself to speak the word of bidding. The cavaliere accepted this silence for consent. He struggled out of the ponderous arm-chair, and went out into the garden. There (leaning over the balustrade of the lowest terrace, under the willful branchesof a big nonia-tree, weighted with fronds of scarlet trumpet-flowers, that hung out lazily from the wall, to which the stem was nailed) Cavaliere Trenta found Count Nobili and Fra Pacifico awaiting the marchesa's summons. Behind them, at a respectful distance, stood Ser Giacomo, the notary from Corellia. Streamlets pure as crystal ran bubbling down beside them in marble runnels; statues of gods and goddesses balanced each other, on pedestals, at the angles where the steps turned. In front, on the gravel, a pair of peacocks strutted, spreading their gaudy tails in the sunshine.

As the four men entered the sala, they seemed to bring the evening shadows with them. These suddenly slanted across the floor like pointed arrows, darkening the places where the sun had shone. Was it fancy, or did the sparkling fountain at the door, as it fell backward into the marble basin, murmur with a sound like human sighs?

Count Nobili walked first. He was grave and pale. Having made a formal obeisance to the marchesa, his quick eye traveled round in search of Enrica. Not finding her, it settled again upon her aunt. As Nobili entered, she raised her smooth, snake-like head, and met his gaze in silence. She had scarcely bowed, in recognition of his salute. Now, with the slightest possible inclination of her head, she signed to him to take his place on one of the chairs before her.

Fra Pacifico, his full, broad face perfectly unmoved, and Cavaliere Trenta, who watched the scene nervously with troubled, twinkling eyes, placed themselves on either side of Count Nobili. Ser Giacomo had already slipped round behind the sofa, and seated himself at a table placed against the wall, the marriage-contract spread out before him. There was an awkward pause. Then Count Nobili rose, and, in that sweet-toned voice which had fallen like a charm on many a woman's ear, addressed the marchesa.

"Marchesa Guinigi, hereditary Governess of Lucca, and Countess of the Garfagnana, I am come to ask in marriage the hand of your niece, Enrica Guinigi. I desire no portion with her. The lady herself is a portion more than enough for me."

As Nobili ceased speaking, the ruddy color shot across his brow and cheeks, and his eyes glistened. His generous nature spoke in those few words.

"Count Nobili," replied the marchesa, carefully avoiding his eye, which eagerly sought hers—"am I correct in addressing you as Count Nobili?—Pardon me if I am wrong." Here she paused, and affected to hesitate. "Do you bear any other name? I am really quite ignorant of the new titles."

This question was asked with outward courtesy, but there was such a twang of scorn in the marchesa's tone, such an expression of contempt upon her lip, that the old chamberlain trembled on his chair. Even at this last moment it was possible that her infernal pride might scatter every thing to the winds.

"Call me Mario Nobili—that will do," answered the count, reddening to the roots of his chestnut curls.

The marchesa inclined her head, and smiled a sarcastic smile, as if rejoicing to acquaint herself with a fact before unknown. Then she resumed:

"Mario Nobili—you saved my niece's life last night. I am advised that I cannot refuse you her hand in marriage, although—"

Such a black frown clouded Nobili's countenance under the sting of her covert insults that Trenta hastily interposed.

"Permit me to remind you, Marchesa Guinigi, that, subject to your approval, the conditions of the marriage have been already arranged by me and Fra Pacifico, before you consented to meet Count Nobili. The present interview is purely formal. We are met in order to sign the marriage-contract. The notary, I see, is ready. The contract lies before him. May I be permitted to call in the lady?"

"One moment, Cavaliere Trenta," interposed Nobili, who was still standing, holding up his hand to stop him— "one moment. I must request permission to repeat myself the terms of the contract to the Marchesa Guinigi before I presume to receive the honor of her assent."

It was now the marchesa's turn to be discomfited. This was the avowal of an open bargain between Count Nobili and herself. A common exchange of value for value; such as low creatures barter for with each other in the exchange. She felt this, and hated Nobili more keenly for having had the wit to wound her.

"I bind myself, immediately on the signing of the contract, to discharge every mortgage, debt, and incumbrance on these feudal lands of Corellia in the Garfagnana; also any debts in and about the Guinigi Palace and lands, within and without the walls of Lucca. I take upon myself every incumbrance," Nobili repeated emphatically, raising his voice. "My purpose is fully noted in that contract, hastily drawn up at my desire. I also bestow on the marchesa's niece the Guinigi Palace I bought at Lucca—to the marchesa's niece, Eurica Guinigi, and her heirs forever; also a dowry of fifty thousand francs a year, should she survive me."

What is it about gold that invests its possessor with such instant power? Is knowledge power?—or does gold weigh more than brains? I think so. Gold-pieces and Genius weighed in scales would send poor Genius kicking!

From the moment Count Nobili had made apparent the wealth which he possessed, he was master of the situation. The marchesa's quick perception told her so. While he was accepting all her debts, with the superb indifference of a millionaire, she grew cold all over.

"Tell the notary," she said, endeavoring to maintain her usual haughty manner, "to put down that, at my death, I bequeath to my niece all of which I die possessed—the palace at Lucca, and the heirlooms, plate, jewels, armor,· and the picture of my great ancestor Castruccio Castracani, to be kept hanging in the place where it now is, opposite the seigneurial throne in the presence-chamber."

Here she paused. The hasty scratch of Ser Giacomo's pen was heard upon the parchment. Spite of her efforts to control her feelings, an ashy pallor spread over the marchesa's face. She grasped her two hands together so tightly that the finger-tips grew crimson; a nervous quiver shook her from head to foot. Cavaliere Trenta, who read the marchesa like a book, watched her in perfect agony. What was going to happen? Would she faint?

"I also bequeath," continued the marchesa, rising from her seat with solemn action, and speaking in a low, hushed voice, her eyes fixed on the floor—"I also bequeath the great Guinigi name and our ancestral honors to my niece —to bear them after my death, together with her husband, then to pass to her eldest child. And may that great name be honored!"

The marchesa reseated herself, raised her thin white hands, and threw up her eyes to heaven. The sacrifice was made!

"May I call in the lady?" again asked the cavaliere, addressing no one in particular.

"I will fetch her in," replied Fra Pacifico, rising from his chair. "She is my spiritual daughter."

No one moved while Fra Pacifico was absent. Ser Giacomo, the notary, dressed in his Sunday suit of black, remained, pen in hand, staring at the wall. Never in his humble life had he formed one of such a distinguished company. All his life Ser Giacomo had heard of the Marchesa Guinigi as a most awful lady. If Fra Pacifico had not caught him within his little office near the *café*, rather than have faced her, Ser Giacomo would have run away.

The door opened, and Enrica stood upon the threshold. There was an air of innocent triumph about her. She had bound a blue ribbon in her golden curls, and placed a rose in the band that encircled her slight waist. Enrica was, in truth, but a common mortal, but she looked so fresh, and bright, and young, with such tender, trusting eyes—there was such an aureole of purity about her, she might have passed for a virgin saint.

As he caught sight of Enrica, the moody expression on Count Nobili's face changed, and broke into a smile. In her presence he forgot the marchesa. Was not such a prize worthy of any battle? What did it signify to him if Enrica were called Guinigi? And as to those tumble-down palaces and heirlooms—what of them? He could buy scores of old palaces any day if he chose. Quickly he stepped forward to meet her as she entered. Fra Pacifico rose, and with great solemnity signed them both with a thrice-repeated cross, then he placed Enrica's hand in Nobili's. The count raised it to his lips, and kissed it fervently.

"My Enrica," he whispered, "this is a glorious day!"

"Oh, it is heavenly!" she answered back, softly.

The marchesa's white face darkened as she looked at Enrica. How dared Enrica be so happy? But she repressed the reproaches that rose to her lips, though her heart swelled to bursting, and the veins in her forehead distended with rage.

"Can Enrica be of my flesh and blood?" exclaimed the marchesa in a low voice to the cavaliere who now stood at her side. "Fool! she believes in her lover! It is a horrible sacrifice! Mark my words—a horrible sacrifice!"

Nobili and Enrica had taken their places behind the notary. The slanting shadows from the open door struck upon them with deeper gloom, and the low murmur of the fountain seemed now to form itself into a moan.

"Do I sign here?" asked Count Nobili.

Ser Giacomo trembled like a leaf.

"Yes, excellency, you sign here," he stammered, pointing to the precise spot; but Ser Giacomo looked so terrified that Nobili, forgetting where he was, laughed out loud and turned to Enrica, who laughed also.

"Stop that unseemly mirth," called out the marchesa from the sofa; "it is most indecent. Let the act that buries a great name at least be conducted with decorum."

"That great name shall not die," spoke the deep voice of Fra Pacifico from the background; "I call a blessing upon it, and upon the present act. The name shall live. When we are dead and rotting in our graves, a race shall rise from them"—and he pointed to Nobili and Enrica— "that shall recall the great legends of the past among the citizens of Lucca."

Fearful of what the marchesa might be moved to reply (even the marchesa, however, had a certain dread of Fra

Pacifico when he assumed the dignity of his priestly office), Trenta hurried forward and offered his arm to lead her to the table. She rose slowly to her feet, and cast her eyes round at the group of happy faces about her; all happy save the poor notary, on whose forehead the big drops of sweat were standing.

"Come, my daughter," said Fra Pacifico, advancing, "fear not to sign the marriage-contract. Think of the blessings it will bring to hundreds of miserable peasants, who are suffering from your want of means to help them!"

"Fra Pacifico," exclaimed the marchesa, scarcely able to control herself, "I respect your office, but this is still my house, and I order you to be silent. Where am I to sign?"—she addressed herself to Ser Giacomo.

"Here, madame," answered the almost inaudible voice of the notary.

The marchesa took the pen, and in a large, firm hand wrote her full name and titles. She took a malicious pleasure in spreading them out over the page.

Enrica signed her name, in delicate little letters, after her aunt's. Count Nobili had already affixed his signature. Cavaliere Trenta and the priest were the witnesses.

"There is one request I would make, marchesa," Nobili said, addressing her. "I shall await in Lucca the exact day you may please to name; but, madame"—and with a lover's ardor strong within him, he advanced nearer to where the marchesa stood, and raised his hand as if to touch her—"I beg you not to keep me waiting long."

The marchesa drew back, and contemplated him with a haughty stare. His manner and his request were both alike offensive to her. She would have Count Nobili to understand that she would admit no shadow of familiarity; that her will had been forced, but that in all else she regarded him with the same animosity as before.

Nobili had understood her action and her meaning.

"Devil!" he muttered between his clinched teeth. He hated himself for having been betrayed into the smallest warmth. With a flashing eye he turned from the marchesa to Enrica, and whispered in her ear, "My only love, this is more than I can bear!"

Enrica had heard nothing. She had been lost in happy thoughts. In her mind a vision was passing. She was in the close street of San Simone, within its deep shadows that fell so early in the afternoon. Before her stood the two grim palaces, the cavernous doorways and the sculptured arms of the Guinigi displayed on both : one, her old home ; the other, that was to be her home. She saw herself go in here, cross the pillared court and mount upward. It was neither day nor night, but all shone with crystal brightness. Then Nobili's voice came to her, and she roused herself.

"My love," he repeated, "I must go—I must go! I cannot trust myself a moment longer with—"

What he had on his lips need not be written. "That lady," he added, hastily correcting himself, and he pointed to the marchesa, who, led by the cavaliere, had reseated herself upon the sofa, looking defiance at everybody.

"I have borne it all for your sake, Enrica." As Nobili spoke, he led her aside to one of the windows. "Now, good-by," and his eyes gathered upon her with passionate fondness ; "think of me day and night."

Enrica had not uttered a single word since she first entered, except to Nobili. When he spoke of parting, her head dropped on her breast. A dread—a horror came suddenly upon her. "O Nobili, why must we part?"

"Scarcely to part," he answered, pressing her hand— "only for a few days; then always to be together."

Enrica tried to withdraw her hand from his, but he held it firmly. Then she turned away her head, and big tears rolled down her cheeks. When at last Nobili tore himself

from her, Enrica followed him to the door, and, regardless of her aunt's furious glances, she kissed her hand, and waved it after him. There was a world of love in the action.

Spite of his indignation, Count Nobili did not fail duly to make his salutation to the marchesa.

The cavaliere and Fra Pacifico followed him out. Twilight now darkened the garden. The fragrance of the flowers was oppressive in the still air. A star or two had come out, and twinkled faintly on the broad expanse of deep-blue sky. The fountain murmured hollow in the silence of coming night.

"Good-by," said Cavaliere Trenta to Nobili, in his thin voice. "I deeply regret the marchesa's rudeness. She is unhinged—quite unhinged; but her heart is excellent, believe me, most excellent."

"Do not talk of the marchesa," exclaimed Nobili, as he rapidly ascended flight after flight of the terraces. "Let me forget her, or I shall never return to Corellia. Dio Sagrato!" and Nobili clinched his fist. "The marchesa is the most cursed thing God ever created!"

CHAPTER VII.

THE piazza at Lucca is surrounded by four avenues of plane-trees. In the centre stands the colossal statue of a Bourbon with disheveled hair, a cornucopia at her feet. Facing the west is the ducal palace, a spacious modern building, in which the sovereigns of Lucca kept a splendid court. Here Cesare Trenta had flourished. Opposite the palace is the Hotel of the Universo, where, as we know, Count Marescotti lodged at No. 4, on the second story. Midway in the piazza a deep and narrow street dives into the body of the city—a street of many colors, with houses red, gray, brown, and tawny, mellowed and tempered by the hand of Time into rich tints that melt into warm shadows. In the background rise domes, and towers, and mediæval church-fronts, galleried and fretted with arches, pillars, and statues. Here a golden mosaic blazes in the sun, yonder a brazen San Michele with outstretched arms rises against the sky; and, scattered up and down, many a grand old palace-roof uprears its venerable front, with open pillared belvedere, adorned with ancient frescoes. A dull, sleepy old city, Lucca, but full of beauty!

On the opposite side of the piazza, behind the plane-trees, stand two separate buildings, of no particular pretension, other than that both are of marble. One is the the-

12

Pacifico when he assumed the dignity of his priestly office),
Trenta hurried forward and offered his arm to lead her to
the table. She rose slowly to her feet, and cast her eyes
round at the group of happy faces about her; all happy
save the poor notary, on whose forehead the big drops of
sweat were standing.

"Come, my daughter," said Fra Pacifico, advancing,
"fear not to sign the marriage-contract. Think of the
blessings it will bring to hundreds of miserable peasants,
who are suffering from your want of means to help them!"

"Fra Pacifico," exclaimed the marchesa, scarcely able
to control herself, "I respect your office, but this is still
my house, and I order you to be silent. Where am I to
sign?"—she addressed herself to Ser Giacomo.

"Here, madame," answered the almost inaudible voice
of the notary.

The marchesa took the pen, and in a large, firm hand
wrote her full name and titles. She took a malicious pleasure in spreading them out over the page.

Enrica signed her name, in delicate little letters, after
her aunt's. Count Nobili had already affixed his signature.
Cavaliere Trenta and the priest were the witnesses.

"There is one request I would make, marchesa," Nobili
said, addressing her. "I shall await in Lucca the exact
day you may please to name; but, madame"—and with a
lover's ardor strong within him, he advanced nearer to
where the marchesa stood, and raised his hand as if to
touch her—"I beg you not to keep me waiting long."

The marchesa drew back, and contemplated him with
a haughty stare. His manner and his request were both
alike offensive to her. She would have Count Nobili to understand that she would admit no shadow of familiarity;
that her will had been forced, but that in all else she regarded him with the same animosity as before.

Nobili had understood her action and her meaning.

"Devil!" he muttered between his clinched teeth. He hated himself for having been betrayed into the smallest warmth. With a flashing eye he turned from the marchesa to Enrica, and whispered in her ear, "My only love, this is more than I can bear!"

Enrica had heard nothing. She had been lost in happy thoughts. In her mind a vision was passing. She was in the close street of San Simone, within its deep shadows that fell so early in the afternoon. Before her stood the two grim palaces, the cavernous doorways and the sculptured arms of the Guinigi displayed on both : one, her old home ; the other, that was to be her home. She saw herself go in here, cross the pillared court and mount upward. It was neither day nor night, but all shone with crystal brightness. Then Nobili's voice came to her, and she roused herself.

"My love," he repeated, "I must go—I must go! I cannot trust myself a moment longer with—"

What he had on his lips need not be written. "That lady," he added, hastily correcting himself, and he pointed to the marchesa, who, led by the cavaliere, had reseated herself upon the sofa, looking defiance at everybody.

"I have borne it all for your sake, Enrica." As Nobili spoke, he led her aside to one of the windows. "Now, good-by," and his eyes gathered upon her with passionate fondness; "think of me day and night."

Enrica had not uttered a single word since she first entered, except to Nobili. When he spoke of parting, her head dropped on her breast. A dread—a horror came suddenly upon her. "O Nobili, why must we part?"

"Scarcely to part," he answered, pressing her hand—"only for a few days; then always to be together."

Enrica tried to withdraw her hand from his, but he held it firmly. Then she turned away her head, and big tears rolled down her cheeks. When at last Nobili tore himself

Pacifico when he assumed the dignity of his priestly office), Trenta hurried forward and offered his arm to lead her to the table. She rose slowly to her feet, and cast her eyes round at the group of happy faces about her; all happy save the poor notary, on whose forehead the big drops of sweat were standing.

"Come, my daughter," said Fra Pacifico, advancing, "fear not to sign the marriage-contract. Think of the blessings it will bring to hundreds of miserable peasants, who are suffering from your want of means to help them!"

"Fra Pacifico," exclaimed the marchesa, scarcely able to control herself, "I respect your office, but this is still my house, and I order you to be silent. Where am I to sign?"—she addressed herself to Ser Giacomo.

"Here, madame," answered the almost inaudible voice of the notary.

The marchesa took the pen, and in a large, firm hand wrote her full name and titles. She took a malicious pleasure in spreading them out over the page.

Enrica signed her name, in delicate little letters, after her aunt's. Count Nobili had already affixed his signature. Cavaliere Trenta and the priest were the witnesses.

"There is one request I would make, marchesa," Nobili said, addressing her. "I shall await in Lucca the exact day you may please to name; but, madame "—and with a lover's ardor strong within him, he advanced nearer to where the marchesa stood, and raised his hand as if to touch her—"I beg you not to keep me waiting long."

The marchesa drew back, and contemplated him with a haughty stare. His manner and his request were both alike offensive to her. She would have Count Nobili to understand that she would admit no shadow of familiarity; that her will had been forced, but that in all else she regarded him with the same animosity as before.

Nobili had understood her action and her meaning.

"Devil!" he muttered between his clinched teeth. He hated himself for having been betrayed into the smallest warmth. With a flashing eye he turned from the marchesa to Enrica, and whispered in her ear, "My only love, this is more than I can bear!"

Enrica had heard nothing. She had been lost in happy thoughts. In her mind a vision was passing. She was in the close street of San Simone, within its deep shadows that fell so early in the afternoon. Before her stood the two grim palaces, the cavernous doorways and the sculptured arms of the Guinigi displayed on both: one, her old home; the other, that was to be her home. She saw herself go in here, cross the pillared court and mount upward. It was neither day nor night, but all shone with crystal brightness. Then Nobili's voice came to her, and she roused herself.

"My love," he repeated, "I must go—I must go! I cannot trust myself a moment longer with—"

What he had on his lips need not be written. "That lady," he added, hastily correcting himself, and he pointed to the marchesa, who, led by the cavaliere, had reseated herself upon the sofa, looking defiance at everybody.

"I have borne it all for your sake, Enrica." As Nobili spoke, he led her aside to one of the windows. "Now, good-by," and his eyes gathered upon her with passionate fondness; "think of me day and night."

Enrica had not uttered a single word since she first entered, except to Nobili. When he spoke of parting, her head dropped on her breast. A dread—a horror came suddenly upon her. "O Nobili, why must we part?"

"Scarcely to part," he answered, pressing her hand— "only for a few days; then always to be together."

Enrica tried to withdraw her hand from his, but he held it firmly. Then she turned away her head, and big tears rolled down her cheeks. When at last Nobili tore himself

Pacifico when he assumed the dignity of his priestly office), Trenta hurried forward and offered his arm to lead her to the table. She rose slowly to her feet, and cast her eyes round at the group of happy faces about her; all happy save the poor notary, on whose forehead the big drops of sweat were standing.

"Come, my daughter," said Fra Pacifico, advancing, "fear not to sign the marriage-contract. Think of the blessings it will bring to hundreds of miserable peasants, who are suffering from your want of means to help them!"

"Fra Pacifico," exclaimed the marchesa, scarcely able to control herself, "I respect your office, but this is still my house, and I order you to be silent. Where am I to sign?"—she addressed herself to Ser Giacomo.

"Here, madame," answered the almost inaudible voice of the notary.

The marchesa took the pen, and in a large, firm hand wrote her full name and titles. She took a malicious pleasure in spreading them out over the page.

Enrica signed her name, in delicate little letters, after her aunt's. Count Nobili had already affixed his signature. Cavaliere Trenta and the priest were the witnesses.

"There is one request I would make, marchesa," Nobili said, addressing her. "I shall await in Lucca the exact day you may please to name; but, madame "—and with a lover's ardor strong within him, he advanced nearer to where the marchesa stood, and raised his hand as if to touch her—"I beg you not to keep me waiting long."

The marchesa drew back, and contemplated him with a haughty stare. His manner and his request were both alike offensive to her. She would have Count Nobili to understand that she would admit no shadow of familiarity; that her will had been forced, but that in all else she regarded him with the same animosity as before.

Nobili had understood her action and her meaning.

"Devil!" he muttered between his clinched teeth. He hated himself for having been betrayed into the smallest warmth. With a flashing eye he turned from the marchesa to Enrica, and whispered in her ear, "My only love, this is more than I can bear!"

Enrica had heard nothing. She had been lost in happy thoughts. In her mind a vision was passing. She was in the close street of San Simone, within its deep shadows that fell so early in the afternoon. Before her stood the two grim palaces, the cavernous doorways and the sculptured arms of the Guinigi displayed on both : one, her old home ; the other, that was to be her home. She saw herself go in here, cross the pillared court and mount upward. It was neither day nor night, but all shone with crystal brightness. Then Nobili's voice came to her, and she roused herself.

"My love," he repeated, "I must go—I must go! I cannot trust myself a moment longer with—"

What he had on his lips need not be written. "That lady," he added, hastily correcting himself, and he pointed to the marchesa, who, led by the cavaliere, had reseated herself upon the sofa, looking defiance at everybody.

"I have borne it all for your sake, Enrica." As Nobili spoke, he led her aside to one of the windows. "Now, good-by," and his eyes gathered upon her with passionate fondness; "think of me day and night."

Enrica had not uttered a single word since she first entered, except to Nobili. When he spoke of parting, her head dropped on her breast. A dread—a horror came suddenly upon her. "O Nobili, why must we part?"

"Scarcely to part," he answered, pressing her hand— "only for a few days; then always to be together."

Enrica tried to withdraw her hand from his, but he held it firmly. Then she turned away her head, and big tears rolled down her cheeks. When at last Nobili tore himself

Pacifico when he assumed the dignity of his priestly office),
Trenta hurried forward and offered his arm to lead her to
the table. She rose slowly to her feet, and cast her eyes
round at the group of happy faces about her; all happy
save the poor notary, on whose forehead the big drops of
sweat were standing.

"Come, my daughter," said Fra Pacifico, advancing,
"fear not to sign the marriage-contract. Think of the
blessings it will bring to hundreds of miserable peasants,
who are suffering from your want of means to help them!"

"Fra Pacifico," exclaimed the marchesa, scarcely able
to control herself, "I respect your office, but this is still
my house, and I order you to be silent. Where am I to
sign?"—she addressed herself to Ser Giacomo.

"Here, madame," answered the almost inaudible voice
of the notary.

The marchesa took the pen, and in a large, firm hand
wrote her full name and titles. She took a malicious pleasure in spreading them out over the page.

Enrica signed her name, in delicate little letters, after
her aunt's. Count Nobili had already affixed his signature.
Cavaliere Trenta and the priest were the witnesses.

"There is one request I would make, marchesa," Nobili
said, addressing her. "I shall await in Lucca the exact
day you may please to name; but, madame "—and with a
lover's ardor strong within him, he advanced nearer to
where the marchesa stood, and raised his hand as if to
touch her—"I beg you not to keep me waiting long."

The marchesa drew back, and contemplated him with
a haughty stare. His manner and his request were both
alike offensive to her. She would have Count Nobili to understand that she would admit no shadow of familiarity;
that her will had been forced, but that in all else she regarded him with the same animosity as before.

Nobili had understood her action and her meaning.

"Devil!" he muttered between his clinched teeth. He hated himself for having been betrayed into the smallest warmth. With a flashing eye he turned from the marchesa to Enrica, and whispered in her ear, "My only love, this is more than I can bear!"

Enrica had heard nothing. She had been lost in happy thoughts. In her mind a vision was passing. She was in the close street of San Simone, within its deep shadows that fell so early in the afternoon. Before her stood the two grim palaces, the cavernous doorways and the sculptured arms of the Guinigi displayed on both: one, her old home; the other, that was to be her home. She saw herself go in here, cross the pillared court and mount upward. It was neither day nor night, but all shone with crystal brightness. Then Nobili's voice came to her, and she roused herself.

"My love," he repeated, "I must go—I must go! I cannot trust myself a moment longer with—"

What he had on his lips need not be written. "That lady," he added, hastily correcting himself, and he pointed to the marchesa, who, led by the cavaliere, had reseated herself upon the sofa, looking defiance at everybody.

"I have borne it all for your sake, Enrica." As Nobili spoke, he led her aside to one of the windows. "Now, good-by," and his eyes gathered upon her with passionate fondness; "think of me day and night."

Enrica had not uttered a single word since she first entered, except to Nobili. When he spoke of parting, her head dropped on her breast. A dread—a horror came suddenly upon her. "O Nobili, why must we part?"

"Scarcely to part," he answered, pressing her hand— "only for a few days; then always to be together."

Enrica tried to withdraw her hand from his, but he held it firmly. Then she turned away her head, and big tears rolled down her cheeks. When at last Nobili tore himself

are undetected in New Italy, where there is so much to learn). Prince Ruspoli swings round this whip as he mounts the steps of the club. The others, who are watching his approach, are secretly devoured with envy.

"Wall, Pietrino—wall, Beppo," said Ruspoli, shaking hands with Orsetti and Malatesta, and nodding to Orazio, out of whose sails he took the wind by force of stolid indifference (Baldassare he ignored, or mistook him for a waiter, if he saw him at all), "you are all discussing the news, of course. Lucca's lively to-day. You'll all do in time, even to steeple-chases. We must run one down on the low grounds in the spring. Dick, my English groom, is always plaguing me about it."

Then Prince Ruspoli pulled himself together with a jerk, as a man does stiff from the saddle, laid his hunting-whip upon a table, stuffed his hands into his pockets, and looked round.

"What news have you heard?" asked Beppo Malatesta. "There's such a lot."

"Wall, the news I have heard is, that Count Nobili is engaged to marry the Marchesa Guinigi's little niece. Dear little thing, they say—like an English ' mees '—fair, with red hair."

"Is that your style of beauty?" lisped Orazio, looking hard at him. But Ruspoli did not notice him.

"But that's not half," cried Malatesta. "You are an innocent, Ruspoli. Let me baptize you with scandal."

"Don't, don't, I hate scandal," said Ruspoli, taking one of his hands out of his pocket for a moment, and holding it up in remonstrance. "There is nothing but scandal in these small Italian towns. Take to hunting, that's the cure. Nobili is to marry the little girl, that's certain. He's to pay off all the marchesa's debts, that's certain too. He's rich, she's poor. He wants blood, she has got it."

"I do not believe in this marriage," said Orazio, measuring Prince Ruspoli as he stood erect, his slits of eyes without a shadow of expression. "You remember the ballroom, prince? And the Boccarini family grouped—and Nobili crying in a corner? Nobili will marry the Boccarini. She is a stunner."

After Orazio had ventured this observation about Nera Boccarini, Prince Ruspoli brought his small, steely eyes to bear upon him with a fixed stare.

Orazio affected total unconsciousness, but he quailed inwardly. The others silently watched Ruspoli. He took up his hunting-whip and whirled it in the air dangerously near Orazio's head, eying him all the while as a dog eyes a rat he means to crunch between his teeth.

"Whoever says that Count Nobili will marry the Boccarini, is a liar!" Prince Ruspoli spoke with perfect composure, still whirling his whip. "I shall be happy to explain my reason anywhere, out of the city, on the shortest notice."

Orazio started up. "Prince Ruspoli, do you call me a liar?"

"I beg your pardon," replied Ruspoli, quite unmoved, making Orazio a mock bow. "Did you say whom Count Nobili would marry? If you did, will you favor me by repeating it?"

"I only report town-talk," Franchi answered, sullenly. "I am not answerable for town-talk."

Ruspoli was a dead-shot; Orazio only fought with swords.

"Then I am satisfied," replied Ruspoli, quiet defiance in his look and tone. "I accuse you, Signore Orazio Franchi, of nothing. I only warn you."

"I don't see why we should quarrel about Nobili's marriage. He will be here himself presently, to explain which of the ladies he prefers," observed the peaceable Orsetti.

"I don't know which lady Count Nobili prefers," retorted Ruspoli, doggedly. "But I tell you the name of the lady he is to marry. It is Enrica Guinigi."

"Why, there is Count Nobili!" cried Baldassare, quite loud—"there, under the plane-trees."

"Bravo, Adonis!" cried Beppo; "your eyes are as sharp as your feet are swift."

Nobili crossed the square; he was coming toward the club. Every face was turned toward him. He had come down to Lucca like one maddened by the breath of love. All along the road he had felt drunk with happiness. To him love was everywhere—in the deep gloom of the mountain-forests, in the flowing river, diamonded with light under the pale moonbeams; in the splendor of the starry sky, in midnight dreams of bliss, and in the awakening of glorious morning. The two old palaces were full of love—the Moorish garden; the magnolias that overtopped the wall, and the soft, creamy perfume that wafted from them; the very street through which he should lead her home; every one he saw; all he said, thought, or did—it was all love and Enrica!

Now, having with lover's haste made good progress with all he had to do, Nobili has come down to the club to meet his friends, and to receive their congratulations. Every hand is stretched out toward him. Even Ruspoli, spite of obvious jealousy, liked him. Nobili's face is lit up with its sunniest smile. Having shaken hands with him, an ominous silence ensues. Orsetti and Malatesta suddenly find that their cigars want relighting, and turn aside. Orazio seats himself at a distance, and scowls at Prince Ruspoli. Nobili gives a quick glance round. An instant tells him that something is wrong.

Prince Ruspoli breaks the awkward silence. He walks up, looks at Nobili with immovable gravity, then slaps him on the shoulder.

"I congratulate you, Nobili. I hear you are to marry the Marchesa Guinigi's niece."

"Balduccio, I thank you. Within a week I hope to bring her home to Lucca. There will then be but one Guinigi home in the two palaces. The marchesa makes her heiress of all she possesses."

Prince Ruspoli is satisfied. Now he will back Count Nobili to any odds. He will name his next foal Mario Nobili.

Again Nobili glances round; this time there is the shadow of a frown upon his smooth brow. Orsetti feels that he must speak.

"Have you known the lady long?" Orsetti asks, with an embarrassment foreign to him.

"Yes, and no," answers Nobili, reddening, and scanning the veiled expression on Orsetti's face with intense curiosity. "But the matter has been brought to a crisis by the accidental burning of the marchesa's house at Corellia. I was present—I saved her niece."

"I thought it was rather sudden," says Orazio, from behind, in a tone full of suggestion. "We were in doubt, before you came, to whom the lady was engaged."

Nobili starts.

"What do you mean?" he asks, hastily.

The color has left his cheeks; his blue eyes grow dark.

"There has been some foolish gossip from persons who know nothing," Orsetti answers, advancing to the front. "About some engagement with another gentleman, whom she had accepted—"

"Nonsense! Don't listen to him, my good fellow," breaks in Ruspoli. "These lads have nothing to do but to breed scandal. They would slander the Virgin; not for wickedness, but for idleness. I mean to make them hunt. Hunting is the cure."

Nobili stands as if turned to stone.

"But I must listen," replies Nobili, fiercely, fire flaming in his eyes. "This lady's honor is my own. Who has

dared to couple her name with any other man? Orsetti—
Ruspoli "—and he turns to them in great excitement—
" you are my friends. What does this mean ? "

" Nothing," said Orsetti, trying to smile, but not suc-
ceeding. " I hear, Nobili, you have behaved with extraordinary generosity," he adds, fencing the question.

" Yes, by Jove ! " adds Prince Ruspoli. Ruspoli was
leaning up against a pillar, watching Orazio as he would a
mischievous cur. " A most suitable marriage. Not that
I care a button for blood, except in horses."

Nobili has not moved, but, as each speaks, his eye
shifts rapidly from one to the other. His face from pale
grows livid, and there is a throb about his temples that
sounds in his ears like a thousand hammers.

" Orsetti," Nobili says, sternly, " I address myself to
you. You are the oldest here. You are the first man I
knew after I came to Lucca. You are all concealing something from me. I entreat you, Orsetti, as man to man, tell
me whose name has been coupled with that of my affianced
wife? That it is a lie I know beforehand—a base and palpable lie ! She has been reared at home in perfect solitude."

  Nobili spoke with passionate vehemence. The hot
blood rushed over his face and neck, and tingled to his
very fingers. Now he glances from man to man in an appeal defiant, yet pleading, pitiful to behold. Every face
grows grave.

Orsetti is the first to reply.

" I feel deeply for you, Nobili. We all love you."

" Yes, all," responded Malatesta and Ruspoli, speaking
together.

" You must not attach too much importance to idle
gossip," says Orsetti.

" No, no," cried Ruspoli, " don't. I will stand by you,
Nobili. I know the lady by sight—a little English beauty."

"Scandal! Who is the man? By God, I'll have his blood within this very hour!"

Nobili is now wrought up beyond all endurance.

"You can't," says Orazio Franchi, tapping his heel upon the marble pavement. "He's gone."

"Gone! I'll follow him to hell!" roars Nobili "Who is he?"

"Possibly he may find his own way there in time," answers Orazio, with a sneer. He rises so as to increase the distance between himself and Prince Ruspoli. "But as yet the wretch crawls on mother earth."

"Silence, Orazio!" shouts Ruspoli, "or you may go there yourself quicker than Marescotti." -

"Marescotti! Is that the name?" cries Nobili, with a hungry eye, that seems to thirst for vengeance. "Who is Marescotti?"

"This is some horrid fiction," Nobili mutters to himself. Stay!—Where had he heard that name lately? He gnawed his fingers until the blood came, and a crimson drop fell upon the marble floor. Suddenly an icy chill rose at his heart. He could not breathe. He sank into a chair —then rose again, and stood before Orsetti with a face out of which ten years of youth had fled. Yes, Marescotti— that is the very man Enrica had mentioned to him under the trees at Corellia. Each letter of it blazes in fire before his eyes. Yes—she had said Marescotti had read her eyes. "O God!" and Nobili groans aloud, and buries his face within his hands.

"You take this too much to heart, my dear Mario," Count Orsetti said; "indeed you do, else I would not say so. Remember there is nothing proved. Be careful," Orsetti whispered in the other's ear, glancing round. Every eye was riveted on Nobili.

Orsetti felt that Nobili had forgotten the public place and the others present—such as Count Malatesta, Orazio

Franchi, and Baldassare, who, though they had not spoken, had devoured every word.

"It is nothing but a sonnet found among Marescotti's papers." Orsetti now was speaking. "Marescotti has fled from the police. Nothing but a sonnet addressed to the lady—a poet's day-dream—untrue of course."

"Will no one tell me what the sonnet said?" demanded Nobili. He had mastered himself for the moment.

"Stuff, stuff!" cried Ruspoli. "Every pretty woman has heaps of sonnets and admirers. It is a brevet of beauty. After all this row, it was only an offer of marriage made to Count Marescotti and refused by him. Probably the lady never knew it."

"Oh, yes, she did, she accepted him," sounded from behind. It was Baldassare, whose vanity was piqued because no one had referred to him for imformation.

"Accepted! Refused by Count Marescotti!" Nobili caught and repeated the words in a voice so strange, it sounded like the echo from a vault.

"Wall! by Jove! It's five o'clock!" exclaimed Prince Ruspoli, looking at his watch. "My dear fellow," he said, addressing Nobili, "I have an appointment on the ramparts; will you go with me?" He passed his arm through that of Nobili. It was a painful scene, which Ruspoli desired to end. Nobili shook his head. He was so stunned and dazed he could not speak.

"If it is five o'clock," said Malatesta, "I must go too."

Malatesta drew Nobili a little apart. "Don't think too much of this, Nobili. It will all blow over and be forgotten in a month. Take your wife a trip to Paris or London. We shall hear no more of it, believe me. Good-by."

"Count Nobili," called out Franchi, from the other end of the portico, making a languid bow, "after all that I have heard, I congratulate you on your marriage most sincerely."

Nobili did not hear him. All were gone. He was alone with Ruspoli. His head had dropped upon his breast. There was the shadow of a tear in Prince Ruspoli's steely eye. It was not enough to be brushed off, for it absorbed itself and came to nothing, but it was there nevertheless.

" Wall, Mario," he said, apparently unmoved, " it seems to me the club is made too hot to hold you. Come home."

Nobili nodded. He was so weak he had to hang heavily on Prince Ruspoli's arm as they crossed the piazza. Prince Ruspoli did not leave him until he saw him safe to his own door.

" You will judge what is right to do," were Ruspoli's last words. " But do not be guided by those young scamps. They live in mischief. If you love the girl, marry her— that is my advice."

CHAPTER VIII.

I HAVE seen a valley canopied by a sky of blue and opaline, girt in by wooded heights, on which the sun poured down in mid-day splendor. A broad river sparkled downward, giving back ray for ray. The forest glowed without a shadow. Each little detail of leaf or stone, even a blade of grass, was turned to flame. The corn lay smooth and golden. The grapes and olives hung safe upon the branch. The flax—a goodly crop—reached to the trees. The peasants labored in the rich brown soil, singing to the oxen. The women sat spinning beside their doors. A little maid led out her snowy lamb to graze among the woods, and children played at "morra" beside the river, which ran at peace, lapping the silver sand.

A cloud gathers behind the mountains—yonder, where they come interlacing down, narrowing the valley. It is a little cloud, no one observes it; yet it gathers and spreads and blackens, until the sky is veiled. The sun grows pale. A greenish light steals over the earth. In the still air there is a sudden freshness. The tall canes growing in the brakes among the vineyards rustle as if shaken by a spectral hand. The white-leaved aspens quiver. An icy wind sweeps down the mountain-sides. A flash of lightning shoots across the sky. Then the storm bursts. Thunder rolls, and cracks, and crashes; as if the brazen gates of heaven clashed to and fro. The peasants fly, driving their cattle before them. The pigs run grunting homeward. The helpless lamb is stricken where it stands, crouching in a deep gorge; the little maid sits weeping by. Down beats the hail like pebbles. It strikes upon the vines, scorches and blackens them. The wheat is leveled to the ground. The river suddenly swells into a raging torrent. Its turbid waters bear away the riches of the poor—the cow that served a little household and followed the children, lowing, to reedy meadows bathed by limpid streams—a horse caught browsing in a peaceful vale, thinking no ill —great trees hurling destruction with them. Rafters, roofs of houses, sometimes a battered corpse, float by.

The roads are broken up. The bridge is snapped. Years will not repair the fearful ravage. The evening sun sets on a desolate waste. Men sit along the road-side wringing their hands beside their ruined crops. Children creep out upon their naked feet, and look and wonder. Where is the little kid that ran before and licked their hands? Where is the gray-skinned, soft-eyed cow that hardly needed a cord to lead her? The shapely cob, so brave with its tinkling bells and crimson tassels? The cob that daddy drove to market, and many merry fairs? Gone with the storm! all gone!

.   .   .   .

Count Nobili was like the Italian climate—in extremes. Like his native soil, he must live in the sunshine. His was not a nature to endure a secret sorrow. He must be kissed, caressed, and smoothed by tender hands and loving voices. He must have applause, approval, be flattered, envied, and followed. Hitherto all this had come naturally to him. His gracious temper, generous heart, and great wealth, had made all bright about him. Now a sudden storm had swept over him and brought despair into his heart.

When Prince Ruspoli left him, Nobili felt as battered and sore as if a whirlwind had caught him, then let him go, and he had dropped to earth a broken man. Yet in the turmoil of his brain a pale, scared little face, with wild, beseeching eyes, was ever before him. It would not leave him. What was this horrible nightmare that had come over him in the heyday of his joy? It was so vague, yet so tangible if judged by its effect on others. Others held Enrica dishonored, that was clear. Was she dishonored? He was bound to her by every tie of honor. He loved her. She had a charm for him no other woman ever possessed, and she loved him. A woman's eye, he told himself, had never deceived him. Yes, she loved him. Yet if Enrica were as guileless as she seemed, how could she conceal from him she had another lover—less loved perhaps than he— but still a lover? And this lover had refused to marry her? That was the stab. That every one in Lucca should know his future bride had been scouted by another man who had turned a rhyme upon her, and left her! Could he bear this?

What were Enrica's relations with Marescotti? Some one had said she had accepted him. Nobili was sure he· had heard this. He, Marescotti, must have approached her nearly by her own confession. He had celebrated her in sonnets, amorous sonnets—damnable thought!—gone with her to the Guinigi Tower—then rejected her! A mist seemed to gather about Nobili as he thought of this. He grew stupid in long vistas of speculation. Had Enrica not dared to meet him—Nobili—clandestinely? Was not this very act unmaidenly? (Such are men: they urge the slip, the fall, then judge a woman by the force of their own urging!) Had Enrica met Marescotti in secret also? No —impossible! The scared, white face was before Nobili, now plainer than ever. No—he hated himself for the very thought. All the chivalry of his nature rose up to acquit her.

Still there was a mystery. How far was Enrica concerned in it? Would she have married Count Marescotti?
Trenta was away, or he would question him. *Had he
better ask? What might he hear?* Some one had deceived him grossly. The marchesa would stick at nothing;
yet what could the marchesa have done without Enrica?
Nobili was perplexed beyond expression. He buried his
head within his arms, and leaned upon a table in an agony
of doubt. Then he paced up and down the splendid room,
painted with frescoed walls, and hung with rose and silver
draperies from Paris (it was to have been Enrica's boudoir),
looking south into a delicious town-garden, with statues,
and flower-beds, and terraces of marble diamonded in brilliant colors. To be so cheated!—to be the laughing-stock
of Lucca! Good God! how could he bear it? To marry
a wife who would be pointed at with whispered words!
Of all earthly things this was the bitterest! Could he
bear it?—and Enrica—would she not suffer? And if she
did, what then? Why, she deserved it—she must deserve
it, else why was she accused? Enrica was treacherous—
the tool of her aunt. He could not doubt it. If she cared
for him at all, it was for the sake of his money—hateful
thought!—yet, having signed the contract, he supposed
he *must* give her the name of wife. But the future mother
of his children was branded.

Oh, the golden days at mountain-capped Corellia!—that
watching in the perfumed woods—that pleading with the
stars that shone over Enrica to bear her his lovesick sighs!
Oh, the triumph of saving her dear life!—the sweetness
of her lips in that first embrace under the magnolia-
tree! Fra Pacifico too, with his honest, sturdy ways—and
the white-haired cavaliere, so wise and courteous. Cheats,
cheats—all! It made him sick to think how they must
have laughed and jeered at him when he was gone. Oh,
it was damnable!

His teeth were set. He started up as if he had been stung, and stamped upon the floor. Then like a madman he rushed up and down the spacious floor. After a time, brushing the drops of perspiration from his forehead, Nobili grew calmer. He sat down to think.

Must he marry Enrica?—he asked himself (he had come to that)—marry the lady of the sonnet—Marescotti's love? He did not see how he could help it. The contract was signed, and nothing proved against her. Well—life was long, and the world wide, and full of pleasant things. Well—he must bear it—unless there had been sin! Nobili did not see it, nor did he hear it; but much that is never seen, nor heard, nor known, is yet true—horribly true. He did see it, but as he thought these cruel thoughts, and hardened himself in them, a pale, scared face, with wild, pleading eyes, vanished with a shriek of anguish.

Others had loved him well, Nobili reasoned—other women—"*Not so well as I,*" an inaudible voice would have whispered, but it was no longer there to answer—others that had not been rejected—others fairer than Enrica—Nera!

With that name there came a world of comfort to him. Nera loved him—she loved him! He had not seen Nera since that memorable night she lay like one dead before him. Before he took a final resolve (by-and-by he must investigate, inquire, know when, and how, and by whom, all this talk had come), would it not be well to see Nera? It was a duty, he told himself, he owed her; a duty delayed too long; only Enrica had so absorbed him. Nera would have heard the town-talk. How would she take it? Would she be glad, or sorry, he wondered? Then came a longing upon Nobili he could not resist, to know if Nera still loved him. If so, what constancy! It deserved reward. He had treated her shamefully. How sweet her company would be if she would see him! At all events, he could but try. At this point he rose and rang the bell.

When the servant came, Nobili ordered his dinner. He was hungry, he said, and would eat at once. His carriage he should require later.

CHAPTER IX.

CLOSE to the Church of San Michele, where a brazen archangel with outstretched wings flaunts in the blue sky, is the narrow, crypt-like street of San Salvador. Here stands the Boccarini Palace. It is an ancient structure, square and large, with an overhanging roof and open, pillared gallery. On the first floor there is a stone balcony. Four rows of windows divide the front. The lower ones, barred with iron, are dismal to the eye. Over the principal entrance are the Boccarini arms, carved on a stone escutcheon, supported by two angels, the whole so moss-eaten the details cannot be traced. Above is a marquis's coronet in which a swallow has built its nest. Both in and out it is a house where poverty has set its seal. The family is dying out. When Marchesa Boccarini dies, the palace will be sold, and the money divided among her daughters.

As dusk was settling into night a carriage rattled along the deserted street. The horses—a pair of splendid bays—struck sparks out of the granite pavement. With a bang they draw up at the entrance, under an archway, guarded by a *grille* of rusty iron. A bell is rung; it only echoes through the gloomy court. The bell was rung again, but no one came. At last steps were heard, and a dried-up old man, with a face like parchment, and little ferret eyes, appeared, hastily dragging his arms into a coat much too large for him.

He shuffled to the front and bowed. Taking a key from his pocket he unlocked the iron gates, then planted himself on the threshold, and turned his ear toward the well-appointed brougham, and Count Nobili seated within.

"Do the ladies receive?" Nobili called out. The old man nodded, bringing his best ear and ferret eyes to bear upon him.

"Yes, the ladies do receive. Will the excellency descend?"

Count Nobili jumped out and hurried through the archway into a court surrounded by a colonnade.

It is very dark. The palace rises upward four lofty stories. Above is a square patch of sky, on which a star trembles. The court is full of damp, unwholesome odors. The foot slips upon the slimy pavement. Nobili stopped. The old man came limping after, buttoning his coat together.

"Ah! poor me!—The excellency is young!" He spoke in the odd, muffled voice, peculiar to the deaf. "The excellency goes so fast he will fall if he does not mind. Our court-yard is very damp; the stairs are old."

"Which is the way up-stairs?" Nobili asked, impatiently. "It is so dark I have forgotten the turn."

"Here, excellency—here to the right. By the Madonna there, in the niche, with the light before it. A thousand excuses! The excellency will excuse me, but I have not yet lit the lamp on the stairs. I was resting. There are so many visitors to the Signora Marchesa. The excellency will not tell the Signora Marchesa that it was dark upon the stairs? Per pieta!"

The shriveled old man placed himself full in Nobili's path, and held out his hands like claws entreatingly.

13

"A thousand devils! no," was Nobili's irate reply, pushing him back. "Let me go up; I shall say nothing. Cospetto! What is it to me?"

"Thanks! thanks! The excellency is full of mercy to an old, overworked servant. There was a time when the Boccarini—"

Nobili did not wait to hear more, but strode through the darkness at hazard, to find the stairs.

"Stop! stop! the excellency will break his limbs against the wall!" the old man shouted.

He fumbled in his pocket, and drew out some matches. He struck one against the wall, held it above his head, and pointed with his bony finger to a broad stone stair under an inner arch.

Nobili ascended rapidly; he was in no mood for delay. The old man, standing at the foot, struck match after match to light him.

"Above, excellency, you will find our usual lamps. You must go on to the second story."

On the landing at the first floor there was still a little daylight from a window as big as if set in the tribune of a cathedral. Here a lamp was placed on an old painted table. Some moth-eaten tapestry hung from a mildewed wall. Here and there a rusty nail had given way, and the stuff fell in downward folds. Nobili paused. His head was hot and dizzy. He had dined well, and he had drunk freely. His eyes traveled upward to the old tapestry—(it was the daughter of Herodias dancing before Herod the cancan of the day). Something in the face and figure of the girl recalled Nera to him, or he fancied it—his mind being full of her. Nobili envied Herod in a dreamy way, who, with round, leaden eyes, a crown upon his head—watched the dancing girl as she flung about her lissome limbs. Nobili envied Herod—and the thought came across him, how pleasant it would be to sit royally enthroned,

and see Nera gambol so! From that—quicker than I can
write it—his thoughts traveled backward to that night when
he had danced with Nera at the Orsetti ball. Again the
refrain of that waltz buzzed in his ear. Again the measure rose and fell in floods of luscious sweetness—again
Nera lay within his arms—her breath was on his cheek—
the perfume of the flowers in her flossy hair was wafted in
the air—the blood stirred in his veins.

The old man said truly. All the way up the second
stair was lit by little lamps, fed by mouldy oil; and all the
way up that waltz rang in Nobili's ear. It mounted to his
brain like fumes of new wine tapped from the skin. A
green door of faded baize faced him on the upper landing,
and another bell—a red tassel fastened to a bit of whip-
cord. He rang it hastily. This time a servant came
promptly. He carried in his hand a lamp of brass.

"Did the ladies receive?"

"They did," was the answer; and the servant held the
lamp aloft to light Nobili into the anteroom.

This anteroom was as naked as a barrack. The walls
were painted in a Raphaelesque pattern, the coronet and
arms of the Boccarini in the centre.

Count Nobili and the servant passed through many
lofty rooms of faded splendor. Chandeliers hung from
vaulted ceilings, and reflected the light of the brass lamp
on a thousand crystal facets. The tall mirrors in the antique frames repeated it. In a cavern-like saloon, hung
with rows of dark pictures upon amber satin, Nobili and
the servant stopped before a door. The servant knocked.
A voice said, "Enter." It was the voice of Marchesa Boccarini. She was sitting with her three daughters. A lamp,
with a colored shade, stood in the centre of a small room,
bearing some aspect of life and comfort. The marchesa
and two of her daughters were working at some mysterious garments, which rapidly vanished out of sight. Nera

was leaning back on a sofa, superbly idle—staring idly at an opposite window, where the daylight still lingered. When Count Nobili was announced, they all rose and spoke together with the loud peacock voices, and the rapid utterance, which in Italy are supposed to mark a special welcome. Strange that in the land of song the talking voices of women should be so harsh and strident! Yet so it is.

"How long is it since we have seen you, Count Nobili?" It was the sad-faced marchesa who spoke, and tried to smile a welcome to him. "I have to thank you for many inquiries, and all sorts of luxuries sent to my dear child. But we expected you. You never came."

The two sisters echoed, "You never came."

Nera did not speak then, but when they had finished, she rose from the sofa and stood before Nobili drawn up to her full height, radiant in sovereign beauty. "I have to thank you most." As Nera spoke, her cheeks flushed, and she dropped her hand into his. It was a simple act, but full of purpose as Nera did it. Nera intended it should be so. She reseated herself. As his eye met hers, Nobili grew crimson. The twilight and the shaded lamp hid this in part, but Nera observed it, and noted it for future use.

Count Nobili placed himself beside the marchesa.

"I am overwhelmed with shame," he said. "What you say is too true. I had intended coming. Indeed, I waited until your daughter"—and he glanced at Nera—"could receive me, and satisfy me herself she was not hurt. I longed to make my penitent excuses for the accident."

"Oh! it was nothing," said Nera, with a smile, answering for her mother.

"What I suffered, no words can tell," continued Nobili. "Even now I shudder to think of it—to be the cause—"

"No, not the cause," answered Marchesa Boccarini.

The elder sisters echoed—

"Not the cause."

" It was the ribbon," continued the marchesa. " Nera was entangled with the ribbon when she rose; she did not know it."

" I ought to have held her up," returned Nobili with a glance at Nera, who, with a kind of queenly calm, looked him full in the face with her bold, black eyes.

" I assure you, marchesa, it was the horror of what I had done that kept me from calling on you."

This was not true, and Nera knew it was not true. Nobili had not come, because he dreaded his weakness and her power. Nobili had not come, because he doted on Enrica to that excess, a thought alien to her seemed then to him a crime. What folly ! Now he knew Enrica better ! All that was changed.

" We have felt very grateful," went on to say the marchesa, "I assure you, Count Nobili, very grateful."

The poor lady was much exercised in spirit as to how she could frame an available excuse for leaving the count alone with Nera. Had she only known beforehand, she would have arranged a little plan to do so, naturally. But it must be done, she knew. It must be done at any price, or Nera would never forgive her.

" You have been so agreeably occupied, too," Nera said, in a firm, full voice. " No wonder, Count Nobili, you had no time to visit us."

There was a mute reproach in these few words that made Nobili wince.

" I have been absent," he replied, much confused.

" Yes, absent in mind and body," and Nera laughed a cruel little laugh. " You have been at Corellia, I believe ?" she added, significantly, fixing him with her lustrous eyes.

" Yes, I have been at Corellia, shooting." Nobili shrank from shame at the lack of courtesy on his part which had made these social lies needful. How brilliant Nera was !

A type of perfect womanhood. Fresh, and strong, and healthy—a mother for heroes.

"We have heard of you," went on Nera, throwing her grand head backward, a quiet deliberation in each word, as if she were dropping them out, word by word, like poison. "A case of Perseus and Andromeda, only you rescued the lady from the flames. You half killed me, Count Nobili, and *en revanche* you have saved another lady. She must be very grateful."

"O Nera!" one of her sisters exclaimed, reproachfully. These innocent sisters never could accommodate themselves to Nera's caustic tongue.

Nera gave her sister a look. She rose at once; then the other sister rose also. They both slipped out of the room.

"Now," thought the marchesa, "I must go, too."

"May I be permitted," she said, rising, "before I leave the room to speak to my confessor, who is waiting for me, on a matter of business"—this was an excellent sham, and sounded decorous and natural—"may I be permitted, Count Nobili, to congratulate you on your approaching marriage? I do not know Enrica Guinigi, but I hear that she is lovely."

Nobili bowed with evident constraint.

"And I," said Nera, softly, directing a broadside upon him from her brilliant eyes—"allow me to congratulate you also."

"Thank you," murmured Nobili, scarcely able to form the words.

"Excuse me," the marchesa said. She courtesied to Nobili and left the room.

Nobili and Nera were now alone. Nobili watched her under his eyelids. Yes, she was splendid. A luxuriant form, a skin mellow and ruddy as a ripe peach, and such eyes!

Nera was silent. She guessed his thoughts. She knew men so well. Men had been her special study. Nera was only twenty-four, but she was clever, and would have excelled in any thing she pleased. To draw men to her, as the magnet draws the needle, was the passion of her life; whether she cared for them or not, to draw them. Not to succeed argued a want of skill. That maddened her. She was keen and hot upon the scent, knocking over her man as a sportsman does his bird, full in the breast. Her aim was marriage. Count Nobili would have suited her exactly. She had felt for him a warmth that rarely quickened her pulses. Nobili had evaded her. But revenge is sweet. Now his hour is come.

"Count Nobili"—Nera's tempting looks spoke more than words—"come and sit down by me." She signed to him to place himself upon the sofa.

Nobili rose as she bade him. He came upon his fate without a word. Seated so near to Nera, he gazed into her starry eyes, and felt it did him good.

"You look ill," Nera said, tuning her voice to a tone of tender pity; "you have grown older too since I last saw you. Is it love, or grief, or jealousy, or what?"

Nobili heaved a deep sigh. His hand, which rested near hers, slipped forward, and touched her fingers. Nera withdrew them to smooth the braids of her glossy hair. While she did so she scanned Nobili closely. "You are not a triumphant lover, certainly. What is the matter?"

"You are very good to care," answered Nobili, sighing again, gazing into her face; "once I thought that my fate did touch you."

"Yes, once," Nera rejoined. "Once—long ago." She gave an airy laugh that grated on Nobili's ears. "But we meet so seldom."

"True, true," he answered hurriedly, "too seldom."

His manner was most constrained. It was plain his mind was running upon some unspoken thought.

"Yes," Nera said. "Spite of your absence, however, you make yourself remembered. You give us so much to talk of! Such a succession of surprises!"

One by one Nera's phrases dropped out, suggesting so much behind.

Nobili, greatly excited, felt he must speak or flee.

"I must confess," she added, giving a stealthy glance out of the corners of her eyes, "you have surprised me. When do you bring your wife home, Count Nobili?" As Nera asked this question she bent over Nobili, so that her breath just swept his heated cheek.

"Never, perhaps!" cried Nobili, wildly. He could contain himself no longer. His heart beat almost to bursting. A desperate seduction was stealing over him. "Never, perhaps!" he repeated.

Nera gave a little start; then she drew back and leaned against the sofa, gazing at him.

"I am come to you, Nera"—Nobili spoke in a hoarse voice—his features worked with agitation—"I am come to tell you all; to ask you what I shall do. I am distracted, heart-broken, degraded! Nera, dear Nera, will you help me? In mercy say you will!"

He had grasped her hand—he was covering it with hot kisses. He was so heated with wine and beauty, and a sense of wrong, he had lost all self-command.

Nera did not withdraw her hand. Her eyelids dropped, and she replied, softly:

"Help you? Oh! so willingly. Could you see my heart you would understand me."

She stopped.

"You can make all right," urged Nobili, maddened by her seductions.

Again that waltz was buzzing in his ears. Nobili was

about to clasp her in his arms, and ask her he knew not what, when Nera rose, and seated herself upon a chair opposite to him.

"You leave me," cried Nobili, piteously, seizing her dress. "That is not helping me."

"I must know what you want," she answered, settling the folds of her dress about her. "Of course, in making this marriage, you have weighed all the consequences? I take that for granted."

As Nera spoke she leaned her head upon her hand; the rich beauty of her face was brought under the lamp's full light.

"I thought I had," was Nobili's reply, recalled by her movement to himself, and speaking with more composure— "I thought I had—but within the last three hours every thing is changed. I have been insulted at the club."

"Ah!—you must expect that sort of thing if you marry Enrica Guinigi. That is inevitable."

Nobili knit his brows. This was hard from her.

"What reason do you give for this?" he asked, trying to master his feelings. "I came to ask you this."

"Reason, my dear count?" and a smile parted Nera's lips. "A very obvious reason. Why force me to name it? No one can respect you if you make such a marriage. You will be always liked—you are so charming." She paused to fling an amorous glance upon him. "Why did you select the Guinigi girl?" The question was sharply put. "The marchesa would never receive you. Why choose her niece?"

"Because I liked her." Nobili was driven to bay. "A man chooses the woman he likes."

"How strange!" exclaimed Nera, throwing up her hands. "How strange!—A pale-faced school-girl! But —ha! ha!"—(that discordant laugh almost betrayed her) —"she is not so, it seems."

Nobili changed color. With every word Nera uttered, he grew hot or cold, soothed or wild, by turns. Nera watched it all. She read Nobili like a book.

"How cunning Enrica Guinigi must be!—very cunning!" Nera repeated as if the idea had just struck her. "The marchesa's tool!—They are so poor!—Her niece! Chè vuole!—The family blood! Anyhow, Enrica has caught you, Nobili."

Nera leaned back, drew out a fan from behind a cushion, and swayed it to and fro.

"Not yet," gasped Nobili—"not yet."

And Nobili had listened to Nera's cruel words, and had not risen up and torn out the lying tongue that uttered them! He had sat and heard Enrica torn to pieces as a panting dove is severed by a hawk limb by limb! Even now Nobili's better nature, spite of the glamour of this woman, told him he was a coward to listen to such words, but his good angel had veiled her wings and fled.

"I am glad you say 'not yet.' I hope you will take time to consider. If I can help you, you may command me, Count Nobili." And Nera paused and sighed.

"Help me, Nera!—You can save me!" He started to his feet. "I am so wretched—so wounded—so desperate!"

"Sit down," she answered, pointing to the sofa.

Mechanically he obeyed.

"You are nothing of all this if you do not marry Enrica Guinigi; if you do, you are all you say."

"What am I to do?" exclaimed Nobili. "I have signed the contract."

"Break it"—Nera spoke the words boldly out—"break it, or you will be dishonored. Do you think you can live in Lucca with a wife that you have bought?"

Nobili bounded from his chair.

"O God!" he said, and clinched his hands.

"You must be calm," she said, hastily, "or my mother will hear you." (All she can do, she thinks, is not worse than Nobili deserves, after that ball.) "Bought!—Yes. Will any one believe the marchesa would have given her niece to you otherwise?"

Nobili was pale and silent now. Nera's words had called up long trains of thought, opening out into horrible vistas. There was a dreadful logic about all she said that brought instant conviction with it. All the blood within him seemed whirling in his brain.

"But Nera, how can I—in honor—break this marriage?" he urged.

"Break it! well, by going away. No one can force you to marry a girl who allowed herself to be hawked about here and there—offered to Marescotti, and refused—to others probably."

"She may not have known it," said Nobili, roused by her bitter words.

"Oh, folly! Why come to me, Count Nobili? You are still in love with her."

At these words Nobili rose and approached Nera. Something in her expression checked him; he drew back. With all her allurements, there was a gulf between them Nobili dared not pass.

"O Nera! do not drive me mad! Help me, or banish me."

"I am helping you," she replied, with what seemed passionate earnestness. "Have you seen the sonnet?"

"No."

"If you mean to marry her, do not. Take advice. My mother has seen it," Nera added, with well-simulated horror. "She would not let me read it."

Now this was the sheerest malice. Madame Boccarini had never seen the sonnet. But if she had, there was not one word in the sonnet that might not have been addressed to the Blessed Virgin herself.

"No, I will not see the sonnet," said Nobili, firmly. "Not that I will marry her, but because I do not choose to see the woman I loved befouled. If it is what you say —and I believe you implicitly—let it lie like other dirt, I will not stir it."

"A generous fellow!" thought Nera. "How I could have loved him! But not now, not now."

"You have been the object of a base fraud," continued Nera. Nera would follow to the end artistically; not leave her work half done.

"She has deceived me. I know she has deceived me," cried Nobili, with a pang he could not hide. "She has deceived me, and I loved her!"

His voice sounded like the cry of a hunted animal.

Nera did not like this. Her work was not complete. Nobili's obstinate clinging to Enrica chafed her.

"Did Enrica ever speak to you of her engagement to Count Marescotti?" she asked. She grew impatient, and must probe the wound.

"Never," he answered, shrinking back.

"Heavens! What falseness! Why, she has passed days and days alone with him."

"No, not alone," interrupted Nobili, stung with a sense of his own shame.

"Oh, you excuse her!" Nera laughed bitterly. "Poor count, believe me. I tell you what others conceal."

Nobili shuddered. His face grew black as night.

"Do not see that sonnet if you persist in marriage. If not, your course is clear—fly. If Enrica Guinigi has the smallest sense of decency, she cannot urge the marriage."

And Nobili heard this in silence! Oh, shame, and weakness and passion of hot blood; and women's eyes, and cruel, bitter tongues; and jealousy, maddening jealousy, hideous, formless, vague, reaching he knew not whither! Oh, shame!

"Write to her, and say you have discovered that she was in league with her aunt, and had other lovers. Every one knows it."

"But, Nera, if I do, will you comfort me? I shall need it." Nobili opened both his arms. His eyes clung wildly to hers. She was his only hope.

Nera did not move; only she turned her head away to hide her face from him. She dared not let Nobili move her. Poor Nobili! She could have loved him dearly!

Seeing her thus, Nobili's arms dropped to his side hopelessly; a wan look came over his face.

"Forgive me! Oh, forgive me, Nera! I offer you a broken heart; have pity on me! Say, can you love me, Nera? Only a little. Speak! tell me!"

Nobili was on his knees before her; every feature of his bright young face formed into an agony of entreaty.

There was a flash of triumph in Nera's black eyes as she bent them on Nobili, that chilled him to the soul. Kneeling before her, he feels it. He doubts her love, doubts all. She has wrought upon him until he is desperate.

"Rise, dear Nobili," Nera whispered softly, touching his lips with hers, but so slightly. "To-morrow—come again to-morrow. I can say nothing now." Her manner was constrained. She spoke in little sentences. "It is late. Supper is ready. My mother waiting. To-morrow." She pressed the hand he had laid imploringly upon her knee. She touched the curls upon his brow with her light finger-tips; but those fixed, despairing eyes beneath she dared not meet.

"Not one word?" urged Nobili, in a faltering voice. "Send me away without one word of hope? I shall struggle with horrible thoughts all night. O Nera, speak one word—but one!" He clasped her hands, and looked up into her face. He dared do no more. "Love me a little, Nera," he pleaded, and he laid her warm, full hand upon his throbbing heart.

Nera trembled. She rose hastily from her chair, and raised Nobili up also.

"I—I—" (she hesitated, and avoided his passionate glance)—"I have given you good advice. To-morrow I will tell you more about myself."

"To-morrow, Nera! Why not to-night?"

Spite of himself Nobili was shocked at her reserve. She was so self-possessed. He had flung his all upon the die.

"You have advised me," he answered, stung by her coldness. "You have convinced me. I shall obey you. Now I must go, unless you bid me stay."

Again his eyes pleaded with hers; again found no response. Nera held out her hand to him.

"To-morrow," the full, ripe lips uttered—"to-morrow."

Seeing that he hesitated, Nera pointed with a gesture toward the door, and Nobili departed.

When the door had closed, and the sound of his retreating footsteps along the empty rooms had ceased, Nera raised her hand, then let it fall heavily upon the table.

"I have done it!" she exclaimed, triumphantly. "Now I can bear to think of that Orsetti ball. Poor Nobili! if he had spoken then! But he did not. It is his own fault."

After standing a minute or two thinking, Nora uncovered the lamp. Then she took it up in both her hands, stepped to a mirror that hung near, and, turning the light hither and thither, looked at her blooming face, in full and in profile. Then she replaced the lamp upon the table, yawned, and left the room.

Next morning a note was put into Count Nobili's hand

at breakfast. It bore the Boccarini arms and the initials of the marchesa. The contents were these:

"MOST ESTEEMED COUNT: As a friend of our family, I have the honor of informing you that the marriage of my dear daughter Nera with Prince Ruspoli is arranged, and will take place in a week. I hope you will be present. I have the honor to assure you of my most sincere and distinguished sentiments.

"MARCHESA AGNESA BOCCARINI."

In the night train from Lucca that evening, Count Nobili was seated. ".He was about to travel," he had informed his household. "Later he would send them his address." Before he left, he wrote a letter to Enrica, and sent it to Corellia.

PART IV.

CHAPTER I.

It was the morning of the fourth day since Count No-bili had left Corellia. All had been very quiet about the house. The marchesa herself took little heed of any thing. She sat much in her own room. She was silent and pre-occupied; but she was not displeased. The one dominant passion of her soul—the triumph of the Guinigi name—was now attained. Now she could bear to think of the grand old palace at Lucca, the seigneurial throne, the nuptial-chamber; now she could gaze in peace on the countenance of the great Castruccio. No spoiler would dare to tread these sacred floors. No irreverent hand would presume to handle her ancestral treasures; no vulgar eye would rest on the effigies of her race gathered on these walls. All would now be safe—safe under the protection of wealth, enormous wealth—wealth to guard, to preserve, to possess.

Enrica had been the agent by which all this had been effected, therefore she regarded Enrica at this time with more consideration than she had ever done before. As to any real sentiments of affection, the marchesa was inca-pable of them—a cold, hard woman from her youth, now vindictive, as well as cold.

The day after the signing of the contract she called Enrica to her. Enrica trod lightly across the stuccoed floor to where her aunt was standing; then she stopped and waited for her to address her. The marchesa took Enrica's hand within her own for some minutes, and silently stroked each rosy finger.

"My child Enrica, are you content?" This question was accompanied by an inquiring look, as if she would read Enrica through and through. A sweet smile of ineffable happiness stole over Enrica's soft face. The marchesa, still holding her hand, uttered something which might almost be called a sigh. "I hope this will last, else—" She broke off abruptly.

Enrica, resenting the implied doubt, disengaged her hand, and drew back from her. The marchesa, not appearing to observe this, continued:

"I had other views for you, Enrica; but, before you knew any thing, you chose a husband for yourself. What do you know about a husband? It is a bad choice."

Again Enrica drew back still farther from her aunt, and lifted up her head as if in remonstrance. But the marchesa was not to be stopped.

"I hate Count Nobili!" she burst out. "I have had my eye upon him ever since he came to Lucca. I know him—you do not. It is possible he may change, but if he does not—"

For the second time the marchesa did not finish the sentence.

"And do you think he loves you?"

As she asked this question she seated herself, and contemplated Enrica with a cynical smile.

"Yes, he loves me. It is you who do not know him!" exclaimed Enrica. "He is so good, so generous, so true; there is no one in the world like him."

How pure Enrica looked, pleading for her lover!—her

face thrown out in sharp profile against the dark wall; her short upper lip raised by her eager speech; the dazzling fairness of her complexion; and her soft hair hanging loose about her head and neck.

"I think I do—I think I know him better than you do," the marchesa answered, somewhat absently.

She was struck by Enrica's exceeding beauty, which seemed within the last few days to have suddenly developed and matured.

"The young man appreciates you, too, I do not doubt. I am told he is a lover of beauty."

This was added with a sneer. Enrica grew crimson.

"Well, well," the marchesa went on to say, "it is too late now—the thing is done. But remember I have warned you. You chose Count Nobili, not I. Enrica, I have done my duty to you and to my own name. Now go and tell the cavaliere I want him."

The marchesa was always wanting the cavaliere; she was closeted with him for hours at a time. These conferences all ended in one conclusion—that she was irretrievably ruined. No one knew this better than the marchesa herself; but her haughty reluctance either to accept Count Nobili's money, or to give up Enrica, was the cause of unknown distress to Trenta.

Meanwhile the prospect of the wedding had stirred up every one in the house to a sort of aimless activity. Adamo strode about, his sad, lazy eyes gazing nowhere in particular. Adamo affected to work hard, but in reality he did nothing but sweep the leaves away from the border of the fountain, and remove the *débris* caused by the fire. Then he would go down and feed the dogs, who, when at home, lived in a sort of cave cut out of the cliff under the tower —Argo, the long-haired mastiff, and Tootsey, the rat-terrier, and Juno, the lurcher, and the useless bull-dog, who grinned horribly—Adamo fed them, then let them out to run at will over the flowers, while he went to his mid-day meal.

Adamo had no soul for flowers, or he could not have done this; he could not have seen a bright, many-eyed balsam, or an amber-leaved zinnia with tufted yellow breast, die miserably on their earthy beds, trampled under the dogs' feet. Even the marchesa, who concerned herself so little with such things, had often chidden him for his carelessness ; but Adamo had a way of his own, and by that way he abided, slowly returning to it, spite of argument or remonstrance.

"Domine Dio orders the weather, not I," Adamo said in a grunt to Pipa when his mistress had specially upbraided him for not watering the lemon-trees ranged along the terraces. "Am I expected to give holy oil to the plants as Fra Pacifico does to the sick ? Chè! chè! what will be will be !"

So Adamo went to his dinner in all peace ; and Argo and his friends knocked down the flowers, and scratched deep holes in the gravel, barking wildly all the time.

The marchesa, sitting in grave confabulation with Cavaliere Trenta, rubbed her white hands as she listened.

There was neither portcullis, nor moat, nor drawbridge to her feudal stronghold at Corellia, but there was big, white Argo. Argo alone would pin any one to the earth.

"Let out the dogs, Adamo," the marchesa would say. "I like to hear them. They are my soldiers—they defend me."

"Yes, padrona," Adamo would reply, stolidly. "Surely the Signora Marchesa wants no other. Argo has the sense of a man when I discourse to him."

So Argo barked and yelped, and tore up and down undisturbed, followed by the pack in full chase after imaginary enemies. Woe betide the calves of any stranger arriving at that period of the day at the villa ! They might feel Argo's glistening teeth meeting in them, or be hurled

on the ground, for Argo had a nasty trick of clutching
stealthily from behind. Woe betide all but Fra Pacifico,
who had so often licked him in drawn battles, when the dog
had leaped upon him, that now Argo fled at sight of his
priestly garments with a howl!

Adamo, who, after his mid-day meal, required tobacco
and repose, would not move to save any one's soul, much
less his body.

"Argo is a lunatic without me," he would observe,
blandly, to Pipa, if roused by a special outburst of barking,
the smoke of his pipe curling round his bullet-head the
while. "Lunatics, either among men or beasts, are not
worth attending to. A sweating horse, a crying woman,
and a yelping cur, heed not."

Adamo added many more grave remarks between the
puffs of his pipe, turning to Pipa, who sat beside him, dis-
taff in hand, the silver pins, stuck into her glossy plaits,
glistening in the sun.

When Adamo ceased he nodded his head like an oracle
that had spoken, and dozed, leaning against the wall, until
the sun had sunk to rest into a bed of orange and saffron,
and the air was cooled by evening dews. Not till then did
Adamo rise up to work.

Pipa, who, next to Adamo and the marchesa, loved Enrica with all the strength of her warm heart, sings all day
those unwritten songs of Tuscany that rise and fall with
such spontaneous cadence among the vineyards, and in the
olive-grounds, that they seem bred in the air—Pipa sings
all day for gladness that the signorina is going to marry a
rich and handsome gentleman. Marriage, to Pipa's simple
mind—especially marriage with money—must bring certain
blessings, and crowds of children; she would as soon doubt
the seven wounds of the Madonna as doubt this. Pipa has
seen Count Nobili. She approves of him. His curly au-
burn hair, so short and crisp; his bold look and gracious

smile—not to speak of certain notes he slipped into her hand—have quite conquered her. Besides, had Count Nobili not come down, the noble gentleman, like San Michele, with golden wings behind him, and a terrible lance in his hand, as set forth in a dingy fresco in the church at Corellia—come down and rescued the dear signorina when—oh, horrible!—she had been forgotten in the burning tower? Pipa's joy develops itself in a vain endeavor to clean the entire villa. With characteristic discernment, she has begun her labors in the upper story, which, being unfurnished, no one ever enters. Pipa has set open all the windows, and thrown back all the blinds; Pipa sweeps and sprinkles, and sweeps again, combating with dust, and fleas and insects innumerable, grown bold by a quiet tenancy of nearly fifty years. While she sweeps, Pipa sings:

> "I'll build a house round, round,.quite round,
> For us to live at ease, all three;
> Father and mother there shall dwell,
> And my true love with me."

Poor Pipa! It is so pleasant to hear her clear voice caroling overhead like a bird from the open window, and to see her bright face looking out now and then, her gold ear-rings bobbing to and fro—her black rippling hair, and her merry eyes blinded with dust and flue—to swallow a breath of air. Adamo does not work, but Pipa does. If she goes on like this, Pipa may hope to clean the entire floor in a month; of the great sala below, and the other rooms where people live, Pipa does not think. It is not her way to think; she lives by happy, rosy instinct.

Pipa chatters much to Enrica about Count Nobili and her marriage when she is not sweeping or spinning. Enrica continually catches sight of her staring at her with open mouth and curious eyes, her head a little on one side the better to observe her.

"Sweet innocent! she knows nothing that is coming
on her," Pipa is thinking; and then Pipa winks, and laughs
outright—laughs to the empty walls, which echo the laugh
back with a hollow sound.

But if any thing lurks there that mocks Pipa's mirth, it
is not visible to Pipa's outward eye, so she continues addressing herself to Enrica, who is utterly bewildered by
her strange ways.

Pipa cannot bear to think that Enrica never dressed for
her betrothed. "Poverina!" she says to her, "not dress—
not dress! What degradation! Why, when the Gobbina
—a little starved hump-backed bastard—married the blind
beggar Gianni at Corellia, for the sake of the pence he got
sitting all day shaking his box by the *café*—even the Gobbina had a white dress and a wreath—and you, beloved
lady, not so much as to care to change your clothes! What
must the Signore Conte have thought? Misera mia! We
must all seem pagans to him!" And Pipa's heart smote
her sorely, remembering the notes. "Caro Gesù! When
you are to be married we must find you something to wear.
To be sure, the marchesa's luggage was chiefly burnt in
the fire, but one box is left. Out of that box something
will come," Pipa feels sure (miracles are nothing to Pipa,
who believes in pilgrimages and the evil-eye); she feels
sure that it will be so. After much talk with Enrica, who
only answers her with a smile, and says absently, looking
at the mountains which she does not see—

"Dear Pipa, we will look in the box, as you say."

"But when, signorina?" insists Pipa, and she kisses
Enrica's hand, and strokes her dress. "But when?"

"To-morrow," says Enrica, absently. "To-morrow,
dear Pipa, not to-day."

"Holy mother!" is Pipa's reply, "it has been 'to-morrow' for four days." "Always to-morrow," mutters Pipa to
herself, as she makes the dust fly with her broom; "and

the Signore Conte is to return in a week! Always to-morrow. What can I do? Such a disgrace was never known.
No bridal dress. No veil. The signorina is too young to
understand such things, and the marchesa is not like other
ladies, or one might venture to speak to her about it. She
would only give me 'accidenti' if I did, and that is so unlucky! To-morrow I must make the signorina search that
box. There will be a white dress and a veil. I dreamed
so. Good dreams come from heaven. I have had a candle
lighted for luck before the Santissima in the market-place,
and fresh flowers put into the pots. There will be sure to
be a white dress and a veil—the saints will send them to
the signorina."

Pipa sweeps and sings. Her children, Angelo and Gigi,
are roasting chestnuts under the window outside.

This time she sings a nursery rhyme:

> " Little Trot, that trots so gayly,
> And without legs can walk so bravely!
> Trottolin! Trottolino!—
> Via! via! "

Pipa, in her motherly heart looking out, blesses little Gigi
—a chubby child blackened by the sun—to see him sitting
so meek and good beside his brother. Angelo is a naughty
boy. Pipa does not love him so well as Gigi. Perhaps
this is the reason Angelo is so ill-furnished in point of
clothes. His patched and ragged trousers are hitched on
with a piece of string. Shirt he has none; only a little
dingy waistcoat buttoned over his chest, on which lies a
silver medal of the Madonna. Angelo's arms are bare, his
face mahogany-color, his head a hopeless tangle of colorless hair. But Angelo has a pair of eyes that dance, and a
broad, red-lipped mouth, out of which two rows of white
teeth shine like pearls. Angelo has just burnt his fingers
picking a chestnut out of the ashes. He turns very red,

but he is too proud to cry. Angelo's hands and feet are so hard he does not feel the pointed rocks that break the turf in the forest, nor does he fear the young snakes, as plenty as lizards, in the warm nooks. All yesterday Angelo had run up and down to look for chestnuts, on his naked feet. He dared not mount into the trees, for that would be stealing; but he leaped, and skipped, and slid when a russet-coated chestnut caught his eye. Gigi was with him, trusted to his care by Pipa, with many objurations and terrible threats of future punishment should he ill-use him.

Ah! if Pipa knew!—if Pipa had only seen little Gigi lonely in the woods, and heard his roars for help! Angelo, having found Gigi troublesome, had tied him by a twisted cord of grass to the trunk of an ancient chestnut. Gigi was trepanned into this thralldom by a heap of flowers artful Angelo had brought him—purple crocuses and cyclamens, and Canterbury bells, and gaudy pea-stalks, all thrown before the child. Gigi, in his little torn petticoat, had swallowed the bait, and flung himself upon the bright blossoms, grasping them in his dirty fingers. Presently the delighted babe turned his eyes upon cunning Angelo standing behind him, showing his white teeth. Satisfied that Angelo was there, Gigi buried himself among the flowers. He crowed to them in his baby way, and flung them here and there. Gigi would run and catch them, too; but suddenly he felt something which stopped him. It was a grass cord which Angelo had secretly woven standing behind Gigi—then had made it fast round Gigi's waist and knotted it to a tree. A cloud came over Gigi's jolly little face—a momentary cloud—when he found he could not run after the flowers. But it soon passed away, and he squatted down upon the grass (the inveigled child), and again clutched the tempting blossoms. Then his little eyes peered round for Angelo to play with him. Alas!—Angelo was gone!

Gigi sobbed a little to himself silently, but the treacherous flowers had still power to console him; at least, he could tear them to pieces. But by-and-by when the sun mounted high over the tops of the forest-clad mountains, and poured down its burning rays, swallowing up all the shade and glittering like flame on every leaf, Gigi grew hot and weary. He was very empty, too; it was just the time that Pipa fed him. His stomach craved for food. He craved for Pipa, too, for home, for the soft pressure of Pipa's ample bosom, where he lay so snug.

Gigi looked round. He did not sob now, but set up a hideous roar, the big tears coursing down his fat cheeks, marking their course by furrows in the dirt and grime. The wood echoed to Gigi's roars. He roared for mammy, for daddy (Angelo Gigi cannot say, it is too long a word). He kicked away the flowers with his pretty dimpled feet, the false flowers that had betrayed him. The babe cannot reason, but instinct tells him that those painted leaves have wronged him. They are faded now, and lie soiled and crumpled, the ghosts of what they were. Again Gigi tries to rise and run, but he is drawn roughly down by the grass rope. He tries to tear it asunder, in vain; Angelo had taken care of that. At last, hoarse and weary, Gigi subsided into terrible sobs, that heave his little breast. Sobbing thus, with pouting lips and heavy eyes, he waits his fate.

It comes with Angelo!—Angelo, leaping downward through the checkered glades, his pockets stuffed with chestnuts. Like an angel with healing in his wings, Angelo comes to Gigi. When he spies him out, Gigi rises, unsteady on his little feet—rises up, forgetting all, and clasps his hands. When Angelo comes near, and stands beside him, Gigi flings his chubby arms about his neck, and nestles to him.

Angelo, when he sees Gigi's disfigured face and sodden eyes, feels his conscience prick him. With his pockets

14

full of chestnuts he pities Gigi; he kisses him, he takes
him up, and bears him in his arms quickly toward home.
The happy child closes his weary eyes, and falls asleep on
Angelo's shoulder.	Pipa, when she sees Angelo return—
so careful of his little brother—praises him, and gives him
a new-baked cake.	Gigi can tell no tales, and Angelo is
silent.

While Pipa sweeps and sings, Angelo and Gigi are
roasting these very chestnuts on a heap of ashes under the
window outside.	Enrica sat near them—a little apart—on
a low wall, that bordered the summit of the cliff.	The
zone of mighty mountains rose sharp and clear before her.
It seemed to her as if she had only to stretch out her hand
to touch them.	The morning lights rested on them with a
fresh glory ; the crisp air, laden with a scent of herbs,
came circling round, and stirred the curls upon her pretty
head.	Enrica wore the same quaintly-cut dress, that swept
upon the ground, as when Nobili was there.	She had no
other.	All had been burnt in the fire.	Sitting there, she
plucked the moss that grew upon the wall, and watched
it as it dropped into the abyss.	This was shrouded in
deepest shadow.	The rush of the distant river in the val-
ley below was audible.	Enrica raised her head and lis-
tened.	That river flowed round the walls of Lucca.	Nobili
was there.	Happy river !	Oh, that it would bear her to
him on its frothy current !—Surely her life-path lay straight
before her now !—straight into paradise !	Not a stone is
on that path ; not a rise, not a fall.

"In a week I will return," Nobili had said.	In a week.
And his eyes had rested upon her as he spoke the words in
a mist of love.	Enrica's face was pale and almost stern,
and her blue eyes had strange lights and shadows in them.
How came it that, since he had left her, the world had
grown so old and gray ?—that all the impulse of her nature,
the quick ebb and flow of youth and hope, was stilled and

faded out, and all her thoughts absorbed into a dreadful longing? She could not tell, nor could she tell what ailed her; but she felt that she was changed. She tried to listen to the prattle of the two children—to Pipa singing above:

> "Come out! come out!
> Never despair!
> Father and mother and sweetheart,
> All will be there!"

Enrica could not listen. It was the dark abyss below that drew her toward its silent bosom. She hung over the wall, her eyes measuring its depths. What ailed her? Was she smitten mad by the wild tumult of joy that had swept over her as she stood hand-in-hand with Nobili? Or was she on the eve of some crisis?—a crisis of life and death? Oh! why had Nobili left her? When would he return? She could not tell. All she knew was, that in the streaming sunlight of this wondrous morning, when earth and heaven were as fair as on the first creation-day, without him all was dark, sad, and dreary.

CHAPTER II.

A FOOTSTEP was heard upon the gravel. The dogs shut up in the cave scratched furiously, then barked loudly. Following the footsteps a bareheaded peasant appeared, his red shirt open, showing his sunburnt chest. He ran up to the open door, a letter in his hand. Seeing Enrica sitting on the low wall, he stopped and made her a rustic bow.

"Who are you?" Enrica asked, her heart beating wildly.

"Illustrissima," and the man bowed again, "I am Giacomo—Giacomo protected by his reverence Fra Pacifico. You have heard of Giacomo?"

Enrica shook her head impatiently.

"Surely you are the Signorina Enrica?"

"Yes, I am."

"Then this letter is for you." And Giacomo stepped up and gave it into her outstretched hand. "I was to tell the illustrissima that the letter had come express from Lucca to Fra Pacifico. Fra Pacifico could not bring it down himself, because the wife of the baker Pietro is ill, and he is nursing her."

Enrica took the letter, then stared at Giacomo so fixedly, before he turned to go, it haunted him many days after, for fear the signorina had given him the evil-eye.

Enrica held the letter in her hand. She gazed at it (standing on the spot where she had taken it, midway between the door and the low wall, a glint of sunshine striking upon her hair, turning it to threads of gold) in silent ecstasy. It was Nobili's first letter to her. His name was in the corner, his monogram on the seal. The letter came to her in her loneliness like Nobili's visible presence. Ah! who does not recall the rapture of a first love-letter!—the tangible assurance it brings that our lover is still our own —the hungry eye that runs over every line traced by that dear hand—the oft-repeated words his voice has spoken stamped on the page—the hidden sense—the half-dropped sentences—all echoing within us as note to note in chords of music!

Enrica's eyes wandered over the address, "To the Noble Signorina Enrica Guinigi, Corellia," as if each word had been some wonder. She dwelt upon every crooked line and twist, each tail and flourish, that Nobili's hand had traced. She pressed the letter to her lips, then laid it upon her lap and gazed at it, eking out every second of suspense to its utmost limit. Suddenly a burning curiosity possessed her to know when he would come. With a gasp that almost stopped her breath she tore the cover open. The paper shook so violently in her unsteady hand that the lines seemed to run up and down and dance. She could distinguish nothing. She pressed her hand to her forehead, steadied herself, then read:

"ENRICA: When this comes to you I am gone from you forever. You have betrayed me—how much I do not care to know. Perhaps I think you less guilty than you are. Of all women, my heart clung to you. I loved you as men only love once in their lives. For the sake of that love, I will still screen you all I can. But it is known in Lucca that Count Marescotti was your accepted lover

when you promised yourself to me. Also, that Count
Marescotti refused to marry you when you were offered by
the Marchesa Guinigi. From this knowledge I cannot
screen you. God is my witness, I go, not desiring by my
presence or my words to reproach you further. But, as a
man who prizes the honor of his house and home, I cannot
marry you. Tell the marchesa I shall keep my word to
her, although I break the marriage-contract. She will find
the money placed as she desired.

" MARIO NOBILI.

" PALAZZO NOBILI, LUCCA."   .

Little by little Enrica read the whole, sentence by sentence. At first the full horror of the words was veiled.
They came to her in a dazed, stupid way. A mist gathered
about her. There was a buzzing in her ears that deadened
her brain. She forced herself to read over the letter again.
Then her heart stood still with terror—her checks burned
—her head reeled. A deadly cold came over her. Of all
within that letter she understood nothing but the words,
" I am gone from you forever." Gone!—Nobili gone!
Never to speak to her again in that sweet voice!—never
to press his lips to hers!—never to gather her to him in
those firm, strong arms! O God! then she must die! If
Nobili were gone, she must die! A terrible pang shot
through her; then a great calmness came over her, and
she was very still. "Die!—yes—why not?—Die!"

Clutching the letter in her icy hand, Enrica looked
round with pale, tremulous eyes, from which the light has
faded. It could not be the same world of an hour ago.
Death had come into it—she is about to die. Yet the sun
shone fiercely upon her face as she turned it upward and
struck upon her eyes. The children laughed over the chestnuts spluttering in the ashes. Pipa sang merrily above
at the open window. A bird—was it a raven?—poised

itself in the air; the cattle grazed peacefully on the green slopes of the opposite mountain, and a drove of pigs ran downward to drink at a little pool. She alone has changed.

A dull, dim consciousness drew her forward toward the low wall, and the abyss that yawned beneath. There she should lie at peace. There the stillness would quiet her heart that beat so hard against her side—surely her heart must burst! She had a dumb instinct that she should like to sleep; she was so weary. Stronger grew the passion of her longing to cast herself on that cold bed—deep, deep below—to rest forever. She tried to move, but could not. She tottered and almost fell. Then all swam before her. She sank backward against the door; with her two hands she clutched the post. Her white face was set. But in her agony not a sound escaped her. Her secret—Nobili's secret—must be kept, she told herself. No one must ever know that Nobili had left her—that she was about to die —no one, no one!

With a last effort she tried to rush forward to take that leap below which would end all. In vain. All nature rushed in a wild whirlwind around her! A deadly sickness seized her. Her eyes closed. She dropped beside the door, a little ruffled heap upon the ground, Nobili's letter clasped tightly in her hand.

> " My love he is to Lucca gone,
>   To Lucca fair, a lord to be,
> And I would fain a message send,
>   But who will tell my tale for me ? "

sang out Pipa from above.

> " All the folk say that I am brown ;
>   The earth is brown, yet gives good corn ;
> The clove-pink, too, although 'tis brown,
>   In hands of gentlefolk is borne.

" They say my love is brown ; but ho
Shines like an angel-form to me ;
They say my love is dark as night,
To me he seems an angel bright ! "

Not hearing the children's voices, and fearing some trick
of naughty Angelo against the peace of her precious Gigi,
Pipa leaned out over the window-sill.   " My babe, my babe,
where art thou ? " was on her lips to cry ; instead, Pipa gave
a piercing scream.   It broke the mid-day silence.   Argo
barked loudly.

" Dio Gesù ! " Pipa cried wildly out.   " The signorina,
she is dead !   Help ! help ! "

CHAPTER III.

MANY hours had passed. Enrica lay still unconscious upon her bed, her face framed in her golden hair, her blue eyes open, her limbs stiff, her body cold. Sometimes her lips parted, and a smile rippled over her face; then she shuddered, and drew herself, as it were, together. All this time Nobili's letter was within her hand; her fingers tightened over it with a convulsive grasp.

Pipa and the cavaliere were with her. They had done all they could to revive her, but without effect. Trenta, sitting there, his hands crossed upon his knees, his eyes fixed upon Enrica, looked suddenly aged. How all this had come about he could not even guess. He had heard Pipa's screams, and so had the marchesa, and he had come, and he and Pipa together had raised her up and placed her on her bed; and the marchesa had charged him to watch her, and let her know when she came to her senses. Neither the cavaliere nor Pipa knew that Enrica had had a letter from Nobili. Pipa noticed a paper in her hand, but did not know what it was. The signorina had been struck down in a fit, was Pipa's explanation. It was very terrible, but God or the devil—she could not tell which— did send fits. They must be borne. An end would come. She had done all she could. Seeing no present change,

Trenta rose to go to the marchesa. His joints were so stiff he could not move at all without his stick, and the furrows which had deepened upon his face were moistened with tears.

"Is Enrica no better?" the marchesa asked him, in a voice she tried to steady, but could not. She trembled all over.

"Enrica is no better," he answered.

"Will she die?" the marchesa asked again.

"Who can tell? She is in the hands of God."

As he spoke, Trenta shot an angry scowl at his friend— he knew her so well. If Enrica died the Guinigi race was doomed—that made her tremble, not affection for Enrica. A word more from the marchesa, and Trenta would have told her this to her face.

"We are all in the hands of God," the marchesa repeated, solemnly, and crossed herself. "I believe little in doctors."

"Still," said Trenta, "if there is no change, it is our duty to send for one. Is there any doctor at Corellia?"

"None nearer than Lucca," she replied. "Send for Fra Pacifico. If he thinks it of any use, a man shall be dispatched to Lucca immediately."

"Surely you will let Count Nobili know the danger Enrica is in?"

"No, no!" cried the marchesa, fiercely. "Count Nobili comes back here to marry Enrica or not at all. I will not have him on any other terms. If the child dies, he will not come. That at least will be a gain."

Even on the brink of death and ruin she could think of this!

"Enrica will not die! she will not die!" sobbed the poor old cavaliere, breaking down all at once. He sank upon a chair and covered his face.

The marchesa rose and placed her hand upon his shoulder. Her heart was bleeding, too, but from another cause.

She bore her wounds in silence. To complain was not in the marchesa's nature. It would have increased her suffering rather than have relieved it. Still she pitied her old friend, although no word expressed it; nothing but the pressure of her hand resting upon his shoulder. Trenta's sobs were the only sound that broke the silence.

"This is losing time," she said. "Send at once for Fra Pacifico. Until he comes, we know nothing."

When Fra Pacifico's rugged, mountainous figure entered Enrica's room, he seemed to fill it. First, he blessed the sweet girl lying before him with such a terrible mockery of life in her widely-opened eyes. His deep voice shook and his grave face twitched as he pronounced the "Beatus." Leaning over the bed, Fra Pacifico proceeded to examine her in silence. He uncovered her feet, and felt her heart, her hands, her forehead, lifting up the shining curls as he did so with a tender touch, and laying them out upon the pillow, as reverently as he would replace a relic.

Cavaliere Trenta stood beside him in breathless silence. Was it life or death? Looking into Fra Pacifico's motionless face, none could tell. Pipa was kneeling in a corner, running her rosary between her fingers; she was listening also, with mouth and eyes wide open.

"Her pulse still beats," Fra Pacifico said at last, betraying no outward emotion. "It beats, but very feebly. There is a little warmth about her heart."

"San Riçardo be thanked!" ejaculated Trenta, clasping his hands.

With the mention of his ancestral saint, the cavaliere's thoughts ran on to the Trenta chapel in the church of San Frediano, where they had all stood so lately together, Enrica blooming in health and beauty at his side. His sobs choked his voice.

"Shall I send to Lucca for a doctor?" Trenta asked, as soon as he could compose himself.

" As you please. Her condition is very precarious; nothing can be done, however, but to keep her warm. That I see has been attended to. She could swallow nothing, therefore no doctor could help her. With such a pulse, to bleed her would be madness. Her youth may save her. It is plain to me some shock or horror must have struck her down and paralyzed the vital powers. How could this have been ? "

The priest stood over her, lost in thought, his bushy eyebrows knit; then he turned to Pipa.

" Has any thing happened, Pipa," he asked, " to account for this ? "

" Nothing your reverence," she answered. " I saw the signorina, and spoke to her, not ten minutes before I found her lying in the doorway."

" Had any one seen her ? "

" No one."

" I sent a letter to her from Count Nobili. Did you see the messenger arrive ? "

" No; I was cleaning in the upper story. He might have come and gone, and I not seen him."

" I heard of no letter," put in the bewildered Trenta. " What letter ? No one mentioned a letter."

" Possibly," answered Fra Pacifico, in his quiet, impassible way, " but there was a letter." He turned again to interrogate Pipa. " Then the signorina must have taken the letter herself." Slightly raising his eyebrows, a sudden light came into his eyes. " That letter has done this. What can Nobili have said to her ? Did you see any letter beside her, Pipa, when she fell ? "

Pipa rose up from the corner where she had been kneeling, raised the sheet, and pointed to a paper clasped in Enrica's hand. As she did so, Pipa pressed her warm lips upon the colorlesss little hand. She would have covered the hand again to keep it warm, but Fra Pacifico stopped her.

"We must see that letter; it is absolutely needful—I her confessor, and you, cavaliere, Enrica's best friend; indeed, her only friend."

At a touch of his strong hand the letter fell from Enrica's fingers, though they clung to it convulsively.

"Of course we must see the letter," the cavaliere responded with emphasis, waking up from the apathy of grief into which he had been plunged.

Fra Pacifico, casting a look of unutterable pity on Enrica, whose secret it seemed sacrilege to violate while she lay helpless before them, unfolded the letter. He and the cavaliere, standing on tiptoe at his side, his head hardly reaching the priest's elbow, read it together. When Trenta had finished, an expression of horror and rage came into his face. He threw his arms wildly above his head.

"The villain!" he exclaimed, "'Gone forever!'—'You have betrayed me!'—'Cannot marry you!'—'Marescotti!'"

Here Trenta stopped, remembering suddenly what had passed between himself and Count Marescotti at their interview, which he justly considered as confidential. Trenta's first feeling was one of amazement how Nobili had come to know it. Then he remembered what he had said to Baldassare in the street, to quiet him, that "it was all right, and that Enrica would consent to her aunt's commands, and to his wishes."

"Beast!" he muttered, "this is what I get by associating with one who is no gentleman. I'll punish him!"

A blank terror took possession of the cavaliere. He glanced at Enrica, so life-like with her fixed, open eyes, and asked himself, if she recovered, would she ever forgive him?

"I did it for the best!" he murmured, shaking his white head. "God knows I did it for the best!—the dear, blessed one!—to give her a home, and a husband to protect her. I knew nothing about Count Nobili.—Why did you not tell me, my sweetest?" he said, leaning over the bed, and addressing Enrica in his bewilderment.

Alas! the glassy blue eyes stared at him fixedly, the white lips were motionless.

The effect of all this on Fra Pacifico had been very different. Under the strongest excitement, the long habit of his office had taught him a certain outward composure. He was ignorant of much which was known to the cavaliere. Fra Pacifico watched his excessive agitation with grave curiosity.

"What does this mean about Count Marescotti?" he asked, somewhat sternly. "What has Count Marescotti to do with her?"

As he asked this question he stretched his arm authoritatively over Enrica. Protection to the weak was the first thought of the strong man. His great bodily strength had been given him for that purpose, Fra Pacifico always said.

"I offered her in marriage to Count Marescotti," answered the cavaliere, lifting up his aged head, and meeting the priest's suspicious glance with a look of gentle reproach. "What do you think I could have done but this?"

"And Count Marescotti refused her?"

"Yes, he refused her because he was a communist. Nothing passed between them, nothing. They never met but twice, both times in my presence."

Fra Pacifico was satisfied.

"God be praised!" he muttered to himself.

Still holding the letter in his hand, the priest turned toward Enrica. Again he felt her pulse, and passed his broad hand across her forehead.

"No change!" he said, sadly—"no change! Poor child, how she must have suffered! And alone, too! There is some mistake—obviously some mistake."

"No mistake about the wretch having forsaken her,"

interrupted Trenta, firing up at what he considered Fra Pacifico's ill-placed leniency. "Domine Dio! No mistake about that."

"Yes, but there must be," insisted the other. "I have known Nobili from a boy. He is incapable of such villainy. I tell you, cavaliere, Nobili is utterly incapable of it. He has been deceived. By-and-by he will bitterly repent this," and Fra Pacifico held up the letter.

"Yes," answered Trenta, bitterly—"yes, if she lives. If he has killed her, what will his repentance matter?"

"Better wait, however, until we know more. Nobili may be hot-headed, vain, and credulous, but he is generous to a fault. If he cannot justify himself, why, then"—the priest's voice changed, his swarthy face flushed with a dark glow—"I am willing to give him the benefit of the doubt —charity demands this—but if Nobili cannot justify himself"—(the cavaliere made an indignant gesture)—"leave him to me. You shall be satisfied, cavaliere. God deals with men's souls hereafter, but he permits bodily punishment in this world. Nobili shall have his, I promise you!"

Fra Pacifico clinched his huge fist menacingly, and dealt a blow in the air that would have felled a giant.

Having given vent to his feelings, to the unmitigated delight of the cavaliere, who nodded and smiled—for an instant forgetting his sorrow, and Enrica lying there—Fra Pacifico composed himself.

"The marchesa must see that letter," he said, in his usual manner. "Take it to her, cavaliere. Hear what she says."

The cavaliere took the letter in silence. Then he shrugged his shoulders despairingly.

"I must go now to Corellia. I will return soon. That Enrica still lives is full of hope." Fra Pacifico said this, turning toward the little bed with its modest shroud of white linen curtains. "But I can do nothing. The feeble

spark of life that still lingers in her frame would fly forever if tormented by remedies.   I have hope in God only."
And he gave a heavy sigh.

Before Fra Pacifico departed, he took some holy water
from a little vessel near the bed, and sprinkled it upon Enrica.   He ordered Pipa to keep her very warm, and to
watch every breath she drew.   Then he glided from the
room with the light step of one well used to sickness.

Cavaliere Trenta followed him slowly.   He paused
motionless in the open doorway, his eyes, from which the
tears were streaming, fixed on Enrica—the fatal letter in
his hand.   At length he tore himself away, closed the door,
and, crossing the sala, knocked at the door of the marchesa's
apartment.

.   .   .   .

In the gray of the early morning of the second day,
just as the sun rose and cast a few straggling gleams into
the room, Enrica called faintly to Pipa.   She knew Pipa
when she came.   It seemed as if Enrica had waked out of
a long, deep sleep.   She felt no pain, but an excessive
weakness.   She touched her forehead and her hair.   She
handled the sheets—then extended both her hands to Pipa,
as if she had been buried and asked to be raised up again.
She tried to sit up, but—she fell back upon her pillow.
Pipa's arms were round her in an instant.   She put back
the long hair that fell upon Enrica's face, and poured into
her mouth a few drops of a cordial Fra Pacifico had left for
her.   Pipa dared not speak—Pipa dared not breathe—so
great was her joy.   At length she ventured to take one of
Enrica's hands in hers, pressed it gently and said to her in
a low voice :

"You must be very quiet.   We are all here."

Enrica looked up at Pipa, surprised and frightened ;
then her eyes wandered round in search of something.
She was evidently dwelling upon some idea she could not

express. She raised her hand, opened it slowly, and gazed at it. Her hand was empty.

"Where is—?" Enrica asked, in a voice like a sigh—then she stopped, and gazed up again. distressfully into Pipa's face. Pipa knew that Count Nobili's letter had been taken by Fra Pacifico. Now she bent over Enrica in an agony of fear lest, when her reason came and she missed that letter, she should sink back again and die.

With the sound of her own voice all came back to Enrica in an instant. She closed her eyes, and longed never to open them again! "Gone! gone! forever!" sounded in her ears like a rushing of great waters. Then she lay for a long time quite still. She could not bear to speak to Pipa. His name—Nobili's name—was sacred. If Pipa knew what Nobili had done, she might speak ill of him. That Enrica could not bear. Yet she should like to know who had taken his letter.

Her brain was very weak, yet it worked incessantly. She asked herself all manner of questions in a helpless way; but as her fluttering pulses settled, and the blood returned to its accustomed channels, faintly coloring her cheek, the truth came to her. Insulted!—abandoned!—forgotten! She thought it all over bit by bit. Each thought as it rose in her mind seemed to freeze the returning warmth within her. That letter—oh, if she could only find that letter! She tried to recall every phrase and put a sense to it. How had she deceived him? What could Nobili mean? What had she done to be talked of in Lucca? Marescotti—who was he? At first she was so stunned she forgot his name; then it came to her. Yes, the poet—Marescotti—Trenta's friend—who had raved on the Guinigi Tower. What was he to her? Marry Marescotti! Oh! who could have said it?

Gradually, as Enrica's mind became clearer, lying there so still with no sound but Pipa's measured breathing, she

felt to its full extent how Nobili had wronged her. Why
had he not come himself and asked her if all this were true?
To leave her thus forever! Without even asking her—oh,
how cruel! She believed in him, why did he not believe
in her? No one had ever yet told her a lie; within herself
she felt no power of deceit. She could not understand it in
others, nor the falseness of the world. Now she must learn
it! Then a great longing and tenderness came over her.
She loved Nobili still. Even though he had smitten her so
sorely, she loved him—she loved him, and she forgave him!
But stronger and stronger grew the thought, even while
these longings swept over her like great waves, that Nobili
was unworthy of her. Should she love him less for that?
Oh, no! He was unworthy of her—yet she yearned after
him. He had left her—but in her heart Nobili should forever sit enthroned—and she would worship him!

And they had been so happy, so more than happy—
from the first moment they had met—and he had shattered
it! Oh, his love for her was dead and buried out of sight!
What was life to her without Nobili? Oh, those fore-
bodings that had clung about her from the very moment
he had left Corellia! Now she could understand them.
Never to see him again!—was it possible? A great pity
came upon her for herself. No one, she was sure, could
ever have suffered like her—no one—no one. This thought
for some time pursued her closely. There was a terrible
comfort in it. Alas! all her life would be suffering now!

As Enrica lay there, her face turned toward the wall,
and her eyes closed (Pipa watching her, thinking she had
dozed), suddenly her bosom heaved. She gave a wild cry.
The pent-up tears came pouring down her cheeks, and sob
after sob shook her from head to foot.

This burst of grief saved her—Fra Pacifico said so when
he came down later. "Death had passed very near her,"
he said, "but now she would recover."

ON the evening of that day the marchesa was in her own room, opening from the sala. The little furniture the room contained was collected around the marchesa, forming a species of oasis on the broad desert of the scagliola floor. A brass lamp, placed on a table, formed the centre of this habitable spot. The marchesa sat in deep shadow, but in the outline of her tall, slight figure, and in the carriage of her head and neck, there was the same indomitable pride, courage, and energy, as before. A paper lay on the ground near her; it was Nobili's letter. Fra Pacifico sat opposite to her. He was speaking. His deep-set luminous eyes were fixed on the marchesa. His straight, coarse hair was pushed up erect upon his brow; there was at all times something of a mane about it. His cassock sat loosely about his big, well-made limbs; his priestly stock was loosed, showing the dark skin of his throat and chin. In the turn of his eye, in the expression of his countenance, there were anxiety, restlessness, and distrust.

"Yes—Enrica has recovered for the present," he was saying, "but such an attack saps and weakens the very issues of life. Count Nobili, if not brought to reason, would break her heart." She was obstinately silent. The balance of her mind was partially upset. "'I shall never

sce Nobili again,' was all she would say to me. It is a
pity, I think, that you sent the cavaliere away to Lucca.
Enrica might have opened her mind to him."

As he spoke, Fra Pacifico crossed one of his legs over
the other, and arranged the heavy folds of his cassock over
his knees.

"And who says Enrica shall not see Nobili again?"
asked the marchesa, defiantly. "Holy saints! That is my
affair. I want no advice. My honor is now as much concerned in the completion of this marriage as it was before
to prevent it. The contract has been signed in my presence. The money agreed upon has been paid over to me.
The marriage must take place I have sent Trenta to Lucca to make preliminary arrangements."

"I rejoice to hear it," answered Fra Pacifico, his countenance brightening. "There must be some extraordinary
mistake. The cavaliere will explain it. Some enemies of
your family must have misled Count Nobili, especially as
there was a certain appearance of concealment respecting
Count Marescotti. It will all come right. I only feared
lest the language of that letter would have, in your opinion,
rendered the marriage impossible."

"That letter does not move me in the least," answered
the marchesa haughtily, speaking out of the shadow. She
gave the letter a kick, sending it farther from her. "I care
neither for praise nor insult from such a fellow. He is but
an instrument in my hand. He has, however, justified my
bad opinion of him. I am glad of that. Do you imagine,
my father," she added, leaning forward, and bringing her
head for an instant within the circle of the light—"do you
imagine any thing but absolute necessity would have induced
me to allow Count Nobili ever to enter my presence?"

"I am bound to tell you that your pride is un-Christian,
my daughter." Fra Pacifico spoke with warmth. "I cannot permit such language in my presence."

The marchesa waved her hand contemptuously, then contemplated him, a smile upon her face.

"I have long known Count Nobili. He has the faults of his age. He is impulsive—vain, perhaps—but at the same time he is loyal and generous. He was not himself when he wrote that letter. There is a passionate sorrow about it that convinces me of this. He has been misled. The offer you sanctioned of Enrica's hand to Count Marescotti, has been misrepresented to him. Undoubtedly Nobili ought to have sought an explanation before he left Lucca; but, the more he loved Enrica, the more he must have suffered before he could so address her."

"You justify Count Nobili, then, my father, not only for abandoning my niece, but for endeavoring to blast her character? Is this your Christianity?" The marchesa asked this question with bitter scorn; her keen eyes shone mockingly out of the darkness. "I told you what he was, remember. I have some knowledge of him and of his father."

"My daughter, I do not defend him. If need be, I have sworn to punish him with my own hand. But, until I know all the circumstances, I pity him; I repeat, I pity him. Some powerful influence must have been brought to bear upon Nobili. It may have been a woman."

"Ha! ha!" laughed the marchesa, contemptuously. "You admit, then, Nobili has a taste for women?"

Fra Pacifico rose suddenly from his chair. An expression of deep displeasure was on his face, which had grown crimson under the marchesa's taunts.

"I desire no altercation, marchesa, nor will I permit you to address such unseemly words to me. What I deem fitting I shall say, now and always. It is my duty. You have called me here. What do you want? How can I help you? In all things lawful I am ready to do so. Nay, I will take the whole matter on myself if you desire."

As he spoke, Fra Pacifico stooped and raised Nobili's crumpled letter from the floor. He spread it out open on the table. The marchesa motioned to him to reseat himself. He did so.

"What I want?" she said, taking up the priest's words. "I will tell you. When I bring Count Nobili here"—the marchesa spoke very slowly, and stretched out her long fingers, as though she held him already in her grasp— "when I bring Count Nobili here, I want you to perform the marriage ceremony. It must take place immediately. Under the circumstances the marriage had better be private."

"I shall not perform the ceremony," answered Fra Pacifico, his full, deep voice ringing through the room, "at your bidding only. Enrica must also consent. Enrica must consent in my presence."

As the light of the lamp struck upon Fra Pacifico, the lines about his mouth deepened, and that look of courage and of command the people of Corellia knew so well was marked upon his countenance. A rock might have been moved, but not Fra Pacifico.

"Enrica shall obey me!" cried the marchesa. Her temper was rising beyond control at the idea of any opposition at such a critical moment. She had made her plan, settled it with Trenta; her plan must be carried out. "Enrica shall obey me," she repeated. "Enrica will obey me unless instigated by you, Fra Pacifico."

"My daughter," replied the priest, "if you forget the respect due to my office, I shall leave you."

"Pardon me, my father," and the marchesa bowed stiffly; "but I appeal to your justice. Can I allow that reprobate to break my niece's heart?—to tarnish her good name? If there were a single Guinigi left, he would stab Nobili like a dog! Such a fellow is unworthy the name of gentleman. Marriage alone can remove the stain he has cast upon Enrica. It is no question of sentiment. The marriage is essential to the honor of my house. Enrica must be *called* Countess Nobili, whether Nobili pleases it or not. Else how can I keep his money? And without his money—" She paused suddenly. In the warmth of speech the marchesa had been actually led into the confession that Nobili was necessary to her "I have the contract," she added. "Thank Heaven, I have the contract! Nobili is legally bound by the contract."

"Yes, that may be," answered Fra Pacifico, reflectively, "if you choose to force him. But I warn you that I will put no violence on Enrica's feelings. She must decide for herself."

"But if Enrica still loves him," urged the marchesa, determined if possible to avoid an appeal to her niece—"if Enrica still loves him, as you assure me she does, may we not look upon her acquiescence as obtained?"

Fra Pacifico shook his head. He was perfectly unmoved by the marchesa's violence.

"Life, honor, position, reputation, all rest on this marriage. I have accepted Count Nobili's money; Count Nobili must accept my niece."

"Your niece must nevertheless consent. I can permit no other arrangement. Then you have to find Count Nobili. He must voluntarily appear at the altar."

Fra Pacifico turned his resolute face full upon the marchesa. Her whole attitude betrayed intense excitement.

"Your niece must consent, Count Nobili must appear voluntarily before the altar, else the Church cannot sanction the union. It would be sacrilege. How do you propose to overcome Count Nobili's refusal?"

"By the law!" exclaimed the marchesa, imperiously.

Fra Pacifico turned aside his head to conceal a smile. The law had not hitherto favored the marchesa. Her constant appeal to the law had been the principal cause of her present troubles.

"By the law," the marchesa repeated. Her sallow face glowed for a moment. "Surely, Fra Pacifico—surely you will not oppose me? You talk of the Church. The Church, indeed! Did not the wretch sign the marriage-contract in your presence? The Church must enable him to complete his contract. In your presence too, as priest and civil delegate; and you talk of sacrilege, my father! Chè! chè! Dio buono!" she exclaimed, losing all self-control in the conviction her own argument brought to her—"Fra Pacifico, you must be mad!"

"I only ask for Enrica's consent," answered the priest. "That given, if Count Nobili comes, I will consent to marry them."

"Count Nobili—he shall come—never fear," and the marchesa gave a short, scornful laugh. "After I have been to Lucca he will come. I shall have done my duty. It is all very well," added the marchesa, loftily, "for low people to pair like animals, from inclination. Such vulgar motives have no place in the world in which I live. Persons of my rank form alliances among themselves from more elevated considerations; from political and prudential motives; for the sake of great wealth when wealth is required; to shed fresh lustre on an historic name by adding to it the splendor of another equally illustrious. My own marriage was arranged for this end. Again I remind you, my father, that nothing but necessity would have forced me to permit a usurer's son to dare to aspire to the hand of my niece. It is a horrible degradation—the first blot on a spotless escutcheon."

"Again I warn you, my daughter, such pride is unseemly. Summon Enrica at once. Let us hear what she says."

The marchesa drew back into the shadow, and was silent. As long as she could bring her battery of arguments against Fra Pacifico, she felt safe. What Enrica might say, who could tell? One word from Enrica might overturn all her subtle combinations. That Fra Pacifico should assist her was indispensable. Another priest, less interested in Enrica, might, under the circumstances, refuse to unite them. Even if that difficulty could be got over, the marchesa was fully alive to the fact that a painful scene would probably occur—such a scene as ought not to be witnessed by a stranger. Hence her hesitation in calling Enrica.

During this pause, Fra Pacifico crossed his arms upon his breast and waited in silence.

"Let Enrica come," said the marchesa at last; "I have no objection." She threw herself back on her seat, and doggedly awaited the result.

Fra Pacifico rose and opened a door on the other side of the room, communicating with the vaulted passage which had connected the villa with the tower.

"Who is there?" he called. (Bells were a luxury unknown at Corellia.)

"I," answered Angelo, running forward, his eyes gleaming like two stars. Angelo sometimes acted as acolyte to Fra Pacifico. Angelo was proud to show his alacrity to his reverence, who had often cuffed him for his mischievous pranks; specially on one occasion, when Fra Pacifico had found him in the act of pushing Gigi stealthily into the marble basin of the fountain, to see if, being small, Gigi would swim like the gold-fish.

"Go to the Signorina Enrica, Angelo, and tell her that the marchesa wants her."

As long as Enrica was ill, Fra Pacifico went freely in and out of her room; now that she was recovered, and had risen from her bed, it was not suitable for him to seek her there himself.

15

WHEN Angelò knocked at Enrica's door, Pipa, who was with her, opened it, and gave her Fra Pacifico's message. The summons was so sudden Enrica had no time to think, but a wild, unmeaning delight possessed her. It was so rare for her aunt to send for her she must be going to tell her something about Nobili. With his name upon her lips, Enrica started up from the chair on which she had been half lying, and ran toward the door.

"Softly, softly, my blessed angel!" cried Pipa, following her with outstretched arms as if she were a baby taking its first steps. "You were all but dead this morning, and now you run like little Gigi when I call to him."

"I can walk very well, Pipa." Enrica opened the door with feverish haste. "I must not keep my aunt waiting."

"Let me put a shawl round you," insisted kind Pipa. "The evening is fresh."

She wrapped a large white shawl about her, that made Enrica look paler and more ghost-like than before.

"Nobody loves me like you, Pipa — nobody — dear Pipa!"

Enrica threw her soft arms around Pipa as she said this. She felt so lonely the tears came into her eyes, already swollen with excessive weeping.

"Who knows?" was Pipa's grave reply. "It is a strange world. You must not judge a man always by what he does."

Enrica gave a deep sigh. She had hurried out of her room into the sala with a headlong impulse to rush to her aunt. Now she dreaded what her aunt might have to say to her. The little strength she had suddenly left her. The warm blood that had mounted to her head chilled within her veins. For a few moments she leaned against Pipa, who watched her with anxious eyes. Then, disengaging herself from her, she trod feebly across the floor. The sala was in darkness. Enrica stretched out her hands before her to feel for the door. When she had found it she stopped terrified. What was she about to hear? The deep voice of Fra Pacifico was audible from within. Enrica placed her hand upon the handle of the door—then she withdrew it. Without the autumn wind moaned round the corners of the house. How it must roar in the abyss under the cliffs! Enrica thought. How dark it must be down there in the blackness of the night! Like letters written in fire, Nobili's words rose up before her—"I am gone from you forever!" Oh! why was she not dead?—Why was she not lying deep below, buried among the cold rocks?—Enrica felt very faint. A groan escaped her.

Fra Pacifico, accustomed to listen to the almost inaudible sounds of the sick and the dying, heard it.

The door opened. Enrica found herself within the room.

"Enrica," said the marchesa, addressing her blandly (did not all now depend upon her?)—"Enrica, you look very pale."

She made no reply, but looked round vacantly. The light of the lamp, coming suddenly out of the darkness, the finding herself face to face with the marchesa, dazzled and alarmed her.

Fra Pacifico took both Enrica's hands in his, drew an arm-chair forward, and placed her in it.

"Enrica, I have sent for you to ask you a question," the marchesa spoke.

At the sound of her aunt's voice, Enrica shuddered visibly. Was it not, after all, the marchesa's fault that Nobili had left her? Why had the marchesa thrown her into Count Marescotti's company? Why had the marchesa offered her in marriage to Count Marescotti without telling her? At this moment Enrica loathed her. Something of all this passed over her pallid face as she turned her eyes beseechingly toward Fra Pacifico. The marchesa watched her with secret rage.

Was this silly, love-sick child about to annihilate the labors of her life? Was this daughter of her husband's cousin, Antonio—a collateral branch—about to consign the Guinigi name to the tomb? She could have lifted up her voice and cursed her where she stood.

"Enrica, I have sent for you to ask you a question." Spite of her efforts to be calm, there was a strange ring in her voice that made Enrica look up at her. "Enrica, do you still love Count Nobili?"

"This is not a fair question," interrupted Fra Pacifico, coming to the rescue of the distressed Enrica, who sat speechless before her terrible aunt. "I know she still loves him. The love of a heart like hers is not to be destroyed by such a letter as that, and the unjust accusations it contains."

Fra Pacifico pointed with his finger to Nobili's letter lying where he had placed it on the table. Seeing the letter, Enrica started back and shivered.

"Is it not so, Enrica?"

The little blond head and the sad blue eyes bowed themselves gently in response. A faint smile flitted across Enrica's face. Fra Pacifico had spoken all her mind, which she in her weakness could not have done, especially with her aunt's dark eyes riveted upon her.

"Then you still love Count Nobili?" The marchesa accentuated each word with bitter emphasis.

"I do," answered Enrica, faintly.

"If Count Nobili returns here, will you marry him?"

As the marchesa spoke, Enrica trembled like a leaf. "What was she to answer?" The little composure she had been able to assume utterly forsook her. She who had believed that nothing was left but to die, was suddenly called upon to live!

"O my aunt," Enrica cried, springing to her feet, "how can I look Nobili in the face after that letter? He thinks I have deceived him."

Enrica stopped; the words seemed to choke her. With an imploring look, she turned toward Fra Pacifico. Without knowing what she did Enrica flung herself on the floor at his feet; she clasped his knees—she turned her beseeching eyes into his.

"O my father, help me! Nobili is my very life. How can I refuse what is my very life? When Nobili left me, my first thought was to die!"

"Surely, my daughter, not by a violent death?" asked Fra Pacifico, stooping over her.

"Yes, yes," and Enrica wrung her hands, "yes, I would have done it—I could not bear to live without him."

A look of sorrow and reproach darkened Fra Pacifico's brow. He crossed himself. "God be praised," he exclaimed, "you were saved from that wickedness!"

"My father"—Enrica extended her arms toward him— "I implore you, for the love of Jesus, let me enter a convent!"

In these few and simple words Enrica had tried all her powers of persuasion. The words were addressed to the priest; but her blue eyes, filled with tears, gathered them-

selves upon the marchesa imploringly. Enrica awaited her
fate in silence. The priest rose and gently replaced her on
her chair. All the benevolence of his manly nature was
called forth. He cast a searching glance at the marchesa.
Nothing betrayed her feelings.

"Calm yourself, Enrica," Fra Pacifico said, soothingly.
"No one seeks to hurry or to force you. But I could
not for a moment sanction your entering a convent. In
your present state of mind it would be an unholy and an
unnatural act."

Although outwardly unmoved, never in her life had the
marchesa felt such exultation. Had Fra Pacifico seconded
Enrica's proposal to enter a convent, all would have been
lost! Still nothing was absolutely decided. It was possible Fra Pacifico might yet frustrate her plans. She ventured another question.

"If Count Nobili meets you at the altar, you will not
then refuse to marry him?"

There was an imperceptible tremor in the marchesa's
voice. The suspense was becoming intolerable to her.

"Refuse to marry him? Refuse Nobili? No, no, I can
refuse Nobili nothing," answered Enrica, dreamily. "But
he will not come!—he is gone forever!"

"He will come," insisted the marchesa, pushing her advantage skillfully.

"But will he love me?" asked the tender young voice.
"Will he believe that I love him? Oh, tell me that!—
Father Pacifico, help me! I cannot think." Enrica pressed
her hands to her forehead. She had suffered so much, now
that the crisis had come she was stunned, she had no power
to decide. "Dare I marry him?—Ought we to part forever?" A flush gathered on her cheek, an ineffable longing shone from her eyes. More than life was in the balance—not only to Enrica, but to the marchesa—the mar-

chesa, who, wrapped within the veil of her impenetrable reserve, breathlessly awaited an answer.

Fra Pacifico showed unmistakable signs of agitation. He rose from his chair, and for some minutes strode rapidly up and down the room, the floor creaking under his heavy tread. The life of this fragile girl lay in his hands. How could he resist that pleading look? Enrica had done nothing wrong. Was Enrica to suffer—die, perhaps—because Nobili had wrongfully accused her? Fra Pacifico passed his large, muscular hand thoughtfully over his clean-shaven chin, then stopped to gaze upon her. Her lips were parted, her eyes dilated to their utmost limit.

"My child," he said at last, laying his hand upon her head with fatherly tenderness—"my child, if Count Nobili returns here, you will be justified in marrying him."

Enrica sank back and closed her eyes. A great leap of joy overwhelmed her. She dared not question her happiness. To behold Nobili once more—only to behold him—filled her with rapture.

"What is your answer, Enrica? I must hear your answer from yourself."

The marchesa spoke out of the darkness. She shrank from allowing Fra Pacifico to scrutinize the exultation marked on her every feature.

"My aunt, if Nobili comes here to claim me, I will marry him," answered Enrica, more firmly. "But stop"—her eye had meanwhile traveled to the letter still lying on the table—a horrible doubt crossed her mind. "Will Nobili know that I am not what he says there—in that letter?"   •

Enrica could bring herself to say no more. She longed to ask all that had happened about Count Marescotti, and how her name had been mixed up with his, but the words refused to come.

"Leave that to me," answered the marchesa, imperiously. "If Count Nobili comes to marry you, is not that proof enough that he is satisfied?"

Enrica felt that it must be so. A wild joy possessed her. This joy was harder to bear than the pain. Enrica was actually sinking under the hope that Nobili might return to her!

Fra Pacifico noticed the gray shadow that was creeping over her face.

"Enrica must go at once to her room," he said abruptly, "else I cannot answer for the consequences. Her strength is overtaxed."

As he spoke, Fra Pacifico hastily opened the door leading into the sala. He took Enrica by the hand and raised her. She was perfectly passive. The marchesa rose also; for the first time she came into the full light of the lamp. Enrica stooped and kissed her hand mechanically.

"My niece, you may prepare for your approaching marriage. Count Nobili will be here shortly—never fear."

The marchesa's manner was strange, almost menacing. Fra Pacifico led Enrica across the sala to her own door. When he returned, the marchesa was again reading Count Nobili's letter.

"A love-match in the Guinigi family!" She was laughing with derision. "What are we coming to?"

She tore the letter into innumerable fragments.

"My father, I shall leave for Lucca early to-morrow. You must look after Enrica. I am satisfied with what has passed."

"God send we have done right!" answered the priest, gloomily. "Now at least she has a chance of life."

"Adieu, Fra Pacifico. When next we meet it will be at the marriage."

Fra Pacifico withdrew. Had he done his duty?—Fra Pacifico dared not ask himself the question.

CHAPTER VI.

TEN days after the departure of the marchesa, Fra Pacifico received the following letter:

"REVEREND AND ESTEEMED FATHER : I have put the matter of Enrica's marriage into the hands of the well-known advocate, Maestro Guglielmi, of Lucca. He at once left for Rome. By extraordinary diligence he procured a summons for Count Nobili to appear within fifteen days before the tribunal, to answer in person for his breach of marriage-contract—unless, before the expiration of that time, he should make the contract good by marriage. The citation was left with the secretary at Count Nobili's own house. Maestro Guglielmi also informed the secretary, by my order, that, in default of his—Count Nobili's—appearance, a detailed account of the whole transaction with my niece, and of other transactions touching Count Nobili's father, known to me—of which I have informed Maestro Guglielmi—would be published—upon my authority—in every newspaper in all the cities throughout Italy, with such explanations and particulars as I might see fit to insert. Also that the name of Count Nobili, as a slanderer and a perjurer, should be placarded on all the spare walls of Lucca, at Florence, and throughout Tuscany. The secretary denies any knowledge of his master's present ad-

dress.   He declared that he was unable, therefore, to communicate with him.

" In the mean time a knowledge of the facts has spread
through this city.   The public voice is with us to a man.
Once more the citizens have rallied round the great Guinigi
name.   Crowds assemble daily before Count Nobili's palace.
His name is loudly execrated by the citizens.   Stones have
been thrown, and windows broken ; indeed, there are threats
of burning the palace.   The authorities have not interfered.
Count Nobili has now, I hear, returned privately to Lucca.
He dares not show himself, or he would be stabbed; but
Count Nobili's lawyer has had a conference with Maestro
Guglielmi.   Cavaliere Trenta insisted upon being present.
This was against my will.   Cavaliere Trenta always says
too much.   Maestro Guglielmi gave Count Nobili's lawyer
three days to decide. At the expiration of that time Signore
Guglielmi met him again.   Count Nobili's lawyer declared
that with the utmost difficulty he had prevailed upon his
client to make good the contract by the religious ceremony
of marriage.   Let every thing therefore be ready for the
ceremony.   This letter is private.   You will say nothing
further to my niece than that Count Nobili will arrive at `
Corellia at two o'clock the day after to-morrow to marry
her.   Farewell.

" Your friend and well-wisher,

" MARCHESA GUINIGI."

The morning of the third day rose gray and chill at
Corellia.   Much rain had fallen during the night, and a
damp mist streamed up from the valleys, shutting out the
mighty range of mountains.   In the plains of Pisa and
Florence the October sun still blazed glorious as ever on
the lush grass and flowery meadows—on the sluggish
streams and the rich blossoms.   There, the trees still rus-
tled in green luxuriance, to soft breezes perfumed with

orange-trees and roses. But in the mountain-fastnesses of the Apennines autumn had come on apace. Such faded leaves as clung to the shrubs about the villa were drooping under the weight of the rain-drops, and a few autumnal flowers that still lit up the broad borders lay prostrate on the earth. Each tiny stream and brawling water-course—even mere little humble rills that dried up in summer—now rushed downward over rocks and stones blackened with moss, to pour themselves into the river Serchio. In the forest the turf was carpeted with yellow leaves, carried hither and thither by the winds. The stems and branches of the chestnuts ranged themselves, tier above tier, like silver pillars, against the red sandstone of the rocks. The year was dying out, and with the year all Nature was dying out likewise.

Within the villa a table was spread in the great sala, with wine and such simple refreshments as the brief notice allowed. As the morning advanced, clouds gathered more thickly over the heavens. The gloomy daylight coming in at the doors, and through the many windows, caught up no ray within. The vaguely-sailing ships painted upon the wall, destined never to find a port in those unknown seas for which their sails were set—and that exasperating company opposite, that through all changes of weal or woe danced remorselessly under the greenwood—were shrouded in misty shadows.

Not a sound broke the silence—nothing save the striking of the clock at Corellia, bringing with it visions of the dark old church—the kneeling women—and the peace of God within. Even Argo and his friends—Juno and Tuzzi, and the bull-dog—were mute.

About twelve o'clock the marchesa arrived from Lucca. In her company came the Cavaliere Trenta and Maestro Guglielmi. Fra Pacifico was in waiting. He received them with grave courtesy. Adamo, arrayed by Pipa in his Sunday clothes, with a flower behind his ear, and Silvestro, stood uncovered at the entrance. Once, and once only, Silvestro abstained from addressing his mistress with his usual question about her health.

Maestro Guglielmi was formally presented to Fra Pacifico by the punctilious cavaliere, now restored to his usual health and spirits. The cavaliere had arrayed himself in his official uniform—dark-purple velvet embroidered with gold. Not having worn the uniform, however, for more than twenty years, the coat was much too small for him. In his hand he carried a white staff of office. This served him as a stick. Coming up from Lucca, the cavaliere had reflected that on him solely must rest the care of imparting some show of dignity to the ceremony about to take place. He resolved that he would be equal to the occasion, whatever might occur.

There was a strange hush upon each one of the little group met in the sala. Each was busy with his own thoughts. The marriage about to take place was to the marchesa the resurrection of the Guinigi name. To Fra Pacifico it was the possible rescue of Enrica from a life of suffering, perhaps an early death. To Guglielmi it was the triumph of the keen lawyer, who had tracked and pursued his prey until that prey had yielded. To the cavaliere it was simply an act of justice which Count Nobili owed to Enrica, after the explanations he (Trenta) had given to him through his lawyer, respecting Count Marescotti— such an act of justice as the paternal government of his master the Duke of Lucca would have forced, upon the strength of his absolute prerogative, irrespective of law. The only person not outwardly affected was the marchesa. The marchesa had said nothing since her arrival, but there was a haughty alacrity of step and movement, as she walked down the sala toward the door of her own apartment, that spoke more than words.

No sooner had the sound of her closing door died away in the echoes of the sala than Trenta, with forward bows both to Fra Pacifico and the lawyer, requested permission to leave them, in order to visit Enrica. Guglielmi and Fra Pacifico were now alone. Guglielmi gave a cautious glance round, then walked up to the table, and poured out a tumbler of wine, which he swallowed slowly. As he did so, he was engaged in closely scrutinizing Fra Pacifico, who, full of anxiety as to what was about to happen, stood lost in thought.

Maestro Guglielmi, whose age might be about forty, was a man, once seen, not easily forgotten—a tall, slight man of quick subtile movements, that betrayed the devouring activity within. Maestro Guglielmi had a perfectly colorless face, a prominent, eager nose, thin lips, that perpetually unclosed to a ghostly smile in which the other features took no part; a brow already knitted with those fine wrinkles indicative of constant study, and overhanging eyebrows that framed a pair of eyes that read you like a book. It would have been a bold man who, with those eyes fixed on him, would have told a lie to Maestro Guglielmi, advocate in the High Court of Lucca. If any man had so lied, those eyes would have gathered up the light, and flashed it forth again in lightnings that might consume him. That they were dark and flaming, and greatly dreaded by all on whom Guglielmi fixed them in opposition, was generally admitted by his legal compeers.

"Reverend sir," began Maestro Guglielmi, blandly, stepping up to where the priest stood a little apart, and speaking in a metallic voice audible in any court of law, be it ever so closely packed—"it gratifies me much that chance has so ordered it that we two are left alone." Guglielmi took out his watch. "We have a good half-hour to spare."

Fra Pacifico turned, and for the first time contemplated

the lawyer attentively. As he did so, he noted with surprise the power of his eyes.

"I earnestly desire some conversation with you," continued Guglielmi, the semblance of a smile flitting over his hard face. "Can we speak here securely?" And the lawyer glanced round at the various doors, and particularly to an open one, which led from the sala to the chapel, at the farther end of the house. Fra Pacifico moved forward and closed it.

"You are quite safe—say what you please," he answered, bluntly. His frank nature rose involuntarily against the cunning of Guglielmi's look and manner. "We have no spies here."

"Pardon me, I did not mean to insinuate that. But what I have to say is strictly private."

Fra Pacifico eyed Guglielmi with no friendly expression.

"I know you well by repute, reverend sir"—with one comprehensive glance Guglielmi seemed to take in Fra Pacifico mentally and physically—"therefore it is that I address myself to you."

The priest crossed his arms and bowed.

"The marchesa has confided to me the charge of this most delicate case. Hitherto I have conducted it with success. It is not my habit to fail. I have succeeded in convincing Count Nobili's lawyer, and through him Count Nobili himself, that it would be suicidal to his interests should he not make good the marriage-contract with the Marchesa Guinigi's niece. If Count Nobili refuses, he must leave the country. He has established himself in Lucca, and desires, as I understand, to remain there. My noble client has done me the honor to inform me that she is acquainted with, and can prove, some act of villainy committed by his father, who, though he ended his life as an eminent banker at Florence, began it as a money-lender at Leghorn. Count

Nobili's father filled in a blank check which a client had incautiously left in his hands, to an enormous amount, or something of that kind, I believe. I refused to notice this circumstance legally, feeling sure that we were strong enough without it. I was also sure that giving publicity to such a fact would only prejudice the position of the future husband of the marchesa's niece. To return. Fortunately, Count Nobili's lawyer saw the case as I put it to him. Count Nobili will, undoubtedly, be here at two o'clock." Again the lawyer took out his watch, looked at it, and replaced it with rapidity. "A good deal of hard work is comprised in that sentence, 'Count Nobili will be here!'" Again there was the ghost of a smile. "Lawyers must not always be judged by the result. In this case, however, the result is favorable, eminently favorable."

Fra Pacifico's face deepened into a look of disgust, but he said nothing.

"Count Nobili once here and joined to the young lady by the Church, *we must keep him.* The spouses must pass twenty-four hours under the same roof to complete and legalize the marriage. I am here officially, to see that Count Nobili attends at the time appointed for the ceremony. In reality, I am here to see that Count Nobili remains. This must be no formal union. They must be bound together irrevocably. You must help me, reverend sir."

Maestro Guglielmi turned quickly upon Fra Pacifico. His eyes ran all over him. The priest drew back.

"I have already stretched my conscience to the utmost for the sake of the lady. I can do nothing more."

"But, my father, it is surely to the lady's advantage that, if the count marries her, they should live together, that heirs should be born to them," pleaded Guglielmi in a most persuasive voice. "If the count separates from his wife after the ceremony, how can this be? We do not live in the days of miracles, though we have an infallible pope. Eh, my father? Not in the days of miracles." Guglielmi gave an ironical laugh, and his eyes twinkled. "Besides, there is the civil ceremony."

"The Sindaco of Corellia can be present, if you please, for the civil marriage."

"Unfortunately, there is no time to call the sindaco now," replied Guglielmi. "If Count Nobili remains the night in company with his bride, we shall have no difficulty about the civil marriage to-morrow. Count Nobili will not object then. Not likely."

The lawyer gave a harsh, cynical laugh that grated offensively upon the priest's ear. Fra Pacifico began to think Maestro Guglielmi intolerable.

"That is your affair. I will undertake no further responsibility," responded Fra Pacifico, doggedly.

"You cannot mean, my father, that you will not help me?" And Guglielmi contemplated Fra Pacifico fixedly with all the lightnings he could bring to bear upon him. To his amazement, he produced no effect whatever. Fra Pacifico remained silent. Altogether this was a priest different from any he had ever met with—Guglielmi hated priests—he began to be interested in Fra Pacifico.

"Well, well," was Guglielmi's reply, with an aspect of intense chagrin, "I had better hopes. Your position, Fra Pacifico, as a peace-maker—as a friend of the family—however"—here the lawyer shrugged his shoulders, and his eyes wandered restlessly up and down the room—"however, at least permit me to tell you what I intend to do."

Fra Pacifico bowed coldly.

"As you please," was his reply.

Maestro Guglielmi advanced close to Fra Pacifico, and lowered his voice almost to a whisper.

"The circumstances attending this marriage are becoming very public. My client, the Marchesa Guinigi, considers her position so exalted she dares to court publicity. She forgets we are not in the middle ages. Ha! ha!" and Guglielmi showed his teeth in a smile that was nothing but a grin—"publicity will be fatal to the young lady. This the marchesa fails to see; but I see it, and you see it, my father."

Fra Pacifico shook himself all over as though silently rejecting any possible participation in Maestro Guglielmi's arguments. Guglielmi quite understood the gesture, but continued, perfectly at his ease:

"The high rank of the young lady—the wealth of the count—a marriage-contract broken—an illustrious name libeled—Count Nobili, a well-known member of the Jockey Club, in concealment—the Lucchese populace roused to fury—all these details have reached the capital. A certain royal personage"—here Guglielmi drew himself up pompously, and waved his hand, as was his wont in the fervor of a grand peroration—"a certain royal personage, who has reasons of his own for avoiding unnecessary scandal (possibly because the royal personage causes so much himself, and considers scandal his own prerogative)"—Guglielmi emphasized his joke with such scintillation as would metaphorically have taken any other man than Fra Pacifico off his legs—even Fra Pacifico stared at him with astonishment—"a certain royal personage, I say—earnestly desires that this affair should be amicably arranged—that the republican party should not have the gratification of gloating over a sensational trial between two noble families (the republicans would make terrible capital out of it)—a certain personage desires, I say, that the affair should be arranged—amicably arranged—not only by a formal marriage —the formal marriage, of course, we positively insist on— but by a complete reconciliation between the parties. If this should not be so, the present ceremony will infallibly lead to a lawsuit respecting the civil marriage—the domicile—and the cohabitation—which it is distinctly understood that Count Nobili will refuse, and that the Marchesa Guinigi, acting for her niece, will maintain. It is essential, therefore, that more than the formal ceremony shall take place. It is essential that the subsequent cohabitation—"

" I see your drift," interrupted downright Fra Pacifico, in his blunt way; "no need to go into further details."

Spite of himself, Fra Pacifico had become interested in the narrative. The cunning lawyer intended that Fra Pacifico should become so interested. What was the strongfisted, simple-hearted priest beside such a sophist as Macstro Guglielmi!

" The royal personage in question," continued Guglielmi, who read in Fra Pacifico's frank countenance that he had conquered his repugnance, "has done me the high honor of communicating to me his august sentiments. I have pledged myself to do all I can to prevent the catastrophe of law. My official capacity, however, ends with Count Nobili's presence here at the appointed hour."

¯At the word " hour " Guglielmi hastily pulled out his watch.

" Only a few minutes more," he muttered. " But this is not all. Listen, my father."

He gave a hasty glance round, then put his lips close to the priest's ear.

" If I succeed—may I say *we?* " he added, insinuatingly—"if *we* succeed, a canonry will be offered to you, Fra Pacifico; and I " (Guglielmi's speaking eyes became brilliantly emphatic now)—"I shall be appointed judge of the tribunal at Lucca."

" Pshaw ! " cried Fra Pacifico, retreating from him with an expression of blank disappointment. " I a canon at Lucca ! If that is to be the consequence of success, you must depend on yourself, Signore Guglielmi. I decline to help you. I would not be a canon at Lucca if the King of Italy asked me in person."

Guglielmi, whose tactics were, if he failed, never to show it, smiled his falsest smile.

"Noble disinterestedness!" he exclaimed, drawing his delicate hand across his brow. "Nothing could have raised your reverence higher in my esteem than this refusal!"

To conceal his real annoyance, Maestro Guglielmi turned away and coughed. It was a diplomatic cough, ready on all emergencies. Again he consulted his watch.

"Five minutes more, then we must assemble at the altar. A fine will be levied upon Count Nobili, if he is not punctual."

"If it is so near the time, I must beg you to excuse me," said Fra Pacifico, glad to escape.

Fra Pacifico, walked rapidly toward the door opening into the corridor leading to the chapel. His retreating figure was followed by a succession of fireworks from Guglielmi's eyes, indicative of indignation and contempt.

"He who sleeps catches no fish," the lawyer muttered to himself, biting his lips. "But the priest will help me —spite of himself, he will help me. A health to Holy Mother Church! She would not do much if all her ministers were like this country clod. He is without ambition. He has quite fatigued me." ·

Saying this, Maestro Guglielmi poured out another glass of wine. He critically examined the wine in the light before putting it to his lips; then he swallowed it with an expression of approbation.

CHAPTER VII.

THE chapel was approached by a door communicating with the corridor. (There was another entrance from the garden; at this entrance Adamo was stationed.) It was narrow and lofty, more like a gallery than a chapel, except that the double windows at either end were arched and filled with stained glass. The altar was placed in a recess facing the door opening from the corridor. It was of dark marble raised on steps, and was backed by a painting too much blackened by smoke to be distinguished. Within the rails stood Fra Pacifico, arrayed in a vestment of white and gold. The grand outline of his tall figure filled the front of the altar. No one would have recognized the parish priest in the stately ecclesiastic who wore his robes with so much dignity. Beside Fra Pacifico was Angelo transformed into an acolyte, wearing a linen surplice—Angelo awed into perfect propriety—swinging a silver censer, and only to be recognized by the twinkling of his wicked eyes (not even Fra Pacifico could tame them). To the right of the altar stood the marchesa. Maestro Guglielmi, tablets in hand, was beside her. Behind, at a respectful distance, appeared Silvestro, gathered up into the smallest possible compass.

As the slow moments passed, all stood so motionless—all save Angelo, swinging the silver censer—they might have passed for a sculptured group upon a marble tomb. One—two—struck from the old clock in the Lombard Tower at Corellia. At the last stroke the door from the garden was thrown open. Count Nobili stood in the doorway. At the moment of Count Nobili's appearance Maestro Guglielmi drew out his watch; then he proceeded to note upon his tablets that Count Nobili, having observed the appointed time, was not subject to a fine.

Count Nobili paused on the threshold, then he advanced to the altar. That he had come in haste was apparent. His dress was travel-stained and dusty; the locks of his abundant chestnut hair matted and rough; his whole appearance wild and disordered. All the outward polish of the man was gone; the happy smile contagious in its brightness; the pleasant curl of the upper lip raising the fair mustache; the kindling eye so capable of tenderness. His expression was of a man undergoing a terrible ordeal; defiance, shame, anger, contended on his face.

There was something in the studied negligence of Count Nobili's appearance that irritated the marchesa to the last degree of endurance. She bridled with rage, and exchanged a significant glance with Guglielmi.

Footsteps were now heard coming from the sala. It was Enrica, led by the cavaliere. Enrica was whiter than her bridal veil. She had suffered Pipa to array her as she pleased, without a word. Her hair was arranged in a coronet upon her head; a whole sheaf of golden curls hung down from it behind. There were the exquisite symmetry of form, the natural grace, the dreamy beauty—all the soft harmony of color upon her oval face—but the freshness of girlhood was gone. Enrica had made a desperate effort to be calm. Nobili was under the same roof—in the same room—Nobili was beside her. Would he not show some

sign that he still loved her?—Else why had he come?—
One glance at him was enough. Oh! he was changed!—
She could not bear it. Enrica would have fled had not
Trenta held her. The marchesa, too, advanced a step or
two, and cast upon her a look so menacing that it filled
her with terror. Trembling all over, Enrica clung to the
cavaliere. He led her gently forward, and placed her beside Count Nobili standing at the altar. Thus unsupport-
ed, Enrica tottered—she seemed about to fall. No hand
was stretched out to help her.

Nobili had turned visibly pale as Enrica entered. His
face was averted. The witnesses, Adamo and Silvestro,
ranged themselves on either side. The marchesa and
Maestro Guglielmi drew nearer to the altar. Angelo
waved the censer, walking to and fro before the rails.
Pipa peeped in at the open doorway. Her eyes were red
with weeping. Pipa looked round aghast.

"What a marriage was this! More like a death than
a marriage! She would not have married so—not if it
had cost her her life—no music, no rose-leaves, no dance,
no wine. None had even changed their clothes but the
cavaliere and the signorina. And a bridegroom like that!
—a statue—not a living man! And the signorina—
poverina—hardly able to stand upon her feet! The signorina would be sure to faint, she was so weak."

Pipa had to muffle her face in her handkerchief to drown
her sobs. Then Fra Pacifico's impressive voice broke the
silence with the opening words of exhortation.

"Deus Israel sit vobiscum."

"Gloria patri," was the response in Angelo's childish
treble.

Enrica and Nobili now knelt side by side. Two lighted
tapers, typical of chaste love, were placed on the floor beside them on either hand. The image of the Virgin on the
altar was uncovered. The tall candles flickered. Enrica

and Nobili knelt side by side—the man who had ceased to love, and the woman who still loved, but who dared not confess her love!

As Fra Pacifico proceeded, Count Nobili's face hardened. Was not the basilisk eye of the marchesa upon him? Her lawyer, too, taking notes of every look and gesture?

"Mario Nobili, wilt thou have this woman to be thy wife?" asked the priest. Turning from the altar, Fra Pacifico faced Count Nobili as he put this question.

A hot flush overspread Nobili's face. He opened his lips to speak, but no words were audible. Would the words not come, or would Nobili at the last moment refuse to utter them?

"Mario Nobili, wilt thou have this woman to be thy wedded wife?" sternly repeated Fra Pacifico, fixing his dark eyes upon him.

"I will," answered Nobili. Whatever his feelings were, Nobili had mastered them.

For an instant Nobili's eye met Enrica's. He turned hastily away. Enrica sighed. Whatever hopes had buoyed her up were gone. Nobili had turned away from her!

Fra Pacifico placed Enrica's hand in that of Nobili. Poor little hand—how it trembled! Ah! would Nobili not recall how fondly he had clasped it? What kisses he had showered upon each rosy little finger! So lately, too! No—Nobili is impassive; not a feature of his face changes. But the contact of Nobili's beloved hand utterly overcame Enrica. The limit of her endurance was reached. Again the shadow of death was upon her—the shadow that had led her to the dark abyss.

When Nobili dropped her hand; Enrica leaned forward upon the edge of the marble rails. She hid her head upon her arms. Her long hair, escaped from the fastening, shrouded her face.

"Benedicat vos omnipotens Deus!" spoke the deep voice of Fra Pacifico.

He made the sign of the cross. The address followed. The priest's last words died away in sonorous echoes. It was done. They were man and wife!

Fra Pacifico had by no outward sign betrayed what he felt during the discharge of his office; but his conscience sorely smote him. He asked himself with dismay if, in helping Enrica, he had not committed a mortal sin? Hitherto he had defended Count Nobili; now his whole soul rose against him. "Would Nobili say nothing in justification?" Spite of himself, Fra Pacifico's fists clinched themselves under his vestments.

But Nobili was about to speak. He gave a hurried glance round the circle—upon Enrica kneeling at the altar; with the air of a man who forces himself to do a hateful penance, he broke silence.

"In the presence of the blessed sacrament"—his voice was thick and hoarse—"I declare that, after the explanations given, I withdraw my accusations. I hold that lady, now Countess Nobili"—and he pointed to the motionless mass of white drapery kneeling beside him—"I hold that lady innocent in thought and life. But I include her in the just indignation with which I regard this house and its mistress, whose agent she has made herself to deceive me."

Count Nobili's kindling eye rested on the marchesa. She, in her turn, shot a furious glance at the cavaliere.

"'Explanations given!' Then Trenta had dared to exonerate Enrica! It was degrading!"

"This reparation made," continued Count Nobili—"my name and hand given to her by the Church—honor is satisfied: I will never live with her!"

Was there no mercy in the man as he pronounced these last words? No appeal? No mercy? Or had the marchesa driven him to bay?

The marchesa!—Nobili's last words had shattered the whole fabric of her ambition! Never for a moment had the marchesa doubted that, the marriage once over, Nobili would have seriously refused the splendid position she offered him. Look at her!—She cannot conceal her consternation.

"I invite you, therefore, Maestro Guglielmi"—the studied calmness of Nobili's manner belied the agitation of his voice and aspect—"you, Maestro Gugliclmi, who have been called here expressly to insult me—I invite you to advise the Marchesa Guinigi to accept what I am willing to offer."

"To insult you, Count Nobili?" exclaimed Guglielmi, looking round. (Guglielmi had turned aside to write a few hurried words upon his tablets, torn out the leaf, and slipped it into the marchesa's hand. So rapidly was this done, no one had perceived it.) "To insult you? Surely not to insult you! Allow me to explain."

"Silence!" thundered Fra Pacifico standing before the altar. "In the name of God, silence! Let those who desire to wrangle choose a fitter place. There can be no contentions in the presence of the sacrament. The declaration of Count Nobili's belief in the virtue of his wife I permitted. I listened to what followed, praying that, if human aid failed, God, hearing his blasphemy against the holy sacrament of marriage, might touch his heart. In the hands of God I leave him!"

Having thus spoken, Fra Pacifico replaced the Host in the ciborium, and, assisted by Angelo, proceeded to divest himself of his robes, which he laid one by one upon the altar.

At this instant the marchesa rose and left the chapel. Count Nobili's eyes followed her with a look of absolute loathing. Without one glance at Enrica, still immovable, her head buried on her arms, Nobili left the altar. He
16

walked slowly to the window at the farther end of the chapel. Turning his back upon all present, he took from his pocket a parchment, which he perused with deep attention.

All this time Cavaliere Trenta, radiant in his official costume, his white staff of office in his right hand, had remained standing behind Enrica. Each instant he expected to see her rise, when it would devolve on him to lead her away; but she had not stirred. Now the cavaliere felt that the fitting moment had fully come for Enrica to withdraw. Indeed, he wondered within himself why she had remained so long.

"Enrica, rise, my child," he said, softly. "There is nothing more to be done. The ceremony is over."

Still Enrica did not move. Fra Pacifico leaned over the altar-rails, and gently raised her head. It dropped back upon his hand—Enrica had fainted.

This discovery caused the most terrible commotion. Pipa, who had watched every thing from the door, screamed and ran forward. Fra Pacifico was bending over the prostrate girl, supported in the arms of the cavaliere.

"I feared this," Fra Pacifico whispered. "Thank God, I believe it is only momentary! We must carry her instantly to her room. I will take care of her."

"Poor, broken flower!" cried Trenta, "who will raise thee up?" His voice came thick, struggling with sobs. "Can you see that unmoved, Count Nobili?" Trenta pointed to the retreating figure of Fra Pacifico bearing Enrica in his arms.

At the sound of Trenta's voice, Count Nobili started and turned around. Enrica had already disappeared.

"You will soon give her another bridegroom—he will not leave her as you have done—that bridegroom will be Death! To-day it is the bridal-veil—to-morrow it will be the shroud. Not a month ago she lay upon what might

have been her death-bed. Your infamous letter did that!"
The remembrance of that letter roused the cavaliere out of
himself; he cared not what he said. "That letter almost
killed her. Would to God she had died! What has she
done? She is an angel! We were all here when you
signed the contract. Why did you break it?" Trenta's
shrill voice had risen into a kind of wail. "Do you mean
to doubt what I told you at Lucca? I swear to you that
Enrica never knew that she was offered in marriage to
Count Marescotti—I swear it!—I did it—it was my fault.
I persuaded the marchesa. It was I. Enrica and Count
Marescotti never met but in my presence. And you revenge yourself on her? If you had the heart of a man, you
could not do it!"

"It is because I have the heart of a man, I will not
suffer degradation!" cried Nobili. "It is because I have
the heart of a man, I will not sink into an unworthy tool!
This is why I refuse to live with her. She is one of a
vile conspiracy. She has joined with the marchesa against
me. I have been forced to marry her. I will not live with
her!"

Count Nobili stopped suddenly. An agonized expression came into his face.

"I screened her in the first fury of my anger—I
screened her when I believed her guilty. Now it is too
late—God help her!" He turned abruptly away.

Cavaliere Trenta, whose vehemence had died away as
suddenly as it had risen, crept to the door. He threw up
his hands in despair. There was no help for Enrica!   .

All this time Maestro Guglielmi's keen eyes had noted
every thing. He was on the lookout for evidence. Persons under strong emotions, as a rule, commit themselves.
Count Nobili was young and hot-headed. Count Nobili
would probably commit himself. Up to this time Count
Nobili had said nothing, however, that could be made use

of. Guglielmi's ready brain worked incessantly. If he could carry out the plan he had formed, he might yet be a judge within the year. Already Guglielmi feels the touch of the soft fur upon his official robes!

After the cavaliere's departure, Guglielmi advanced. He had been standing so entirely concealed in the shadow thrown by the altar, that Nobili had forgotten his presence. Nobili now stared at him in angry surprise.

"With your permission," said the lawyer, with a low bow, accosting Nobili, "I hope to convince you how much you have wronged me by your accusation."

"What accusation?" demanded the count, drawing back toward the window. "I do not understand you."

Guglielmi was the marchesa's adviser; Count Nobili hated him.

"Your accusation that 'I am here to insult you.' If you will do me the honor, Count Nobili, to speak to me in private"—Guglielmi glanced at Silvestro, Adamo, and Angelo, peering out half hid by the altar—"if you will do me this honor, I will prove to you that I am here to serve you."

"That is impossible," answered Nobili. "Nor do I care. I leave this house immediately."

"But allow me to observe, Count Nobili," and Maestro Guglielmi drew himself up with an air of offended dignity, "you are bound as a gentleman to retract those words, or to hear my explanation." (Delay at any price was Guglielmi's object.) "Surely, Count Nobili, you cannot refuse me this satisfaction?"

Count Nobili hesitated. What could this strange man have to say to him?

Guglielmi watched him.

"You will spare me half an hour?" he urged. "That will suffice."

Count Nobili looked greatly embarrassed.

" A thousand thanks !" exclaimed Guglielmi, accepting his silence for consent. "I will not trespass needlessly on your time. Permit me to find some one to conduct you to a room."

Guglielmi looked round—Angelo came forward.

" Conduct Count Nobili to the room prepared for him," said the lawyer. "There, Count Nobili, I will attend you in a few minutes."

CHAPTER VIII.

WHEN the marchesa entered the sala after she had left the chapel, her steps were slow and measured. Count Nobili's words rang in her ear: "I will not live with her." She could not put these words from her. For the first time in her life the marchesa was shaken in the belief of her mission.

If Count Nobili refused to live with Enrica as his wife, all the law in the world could not force him. If no heir was born to the Guinigi, she had lived in vain.

As the marchesa stood in the dull light of the misty afternoon, leaning against the solid carved table on which refreshments were spread, the old palace at Lucca rose up before her dyed with the ruddy tints of summer sunsets. She trod again in thought those mysterious rooms, shrouded in perpetual twilight. She gazed upon the faces of the dead, looking down upon her from the walls. How could she answer to those dead; for what had she done? That heroic face too with the stern, soft eyes—how could she meet it? What was Count Nobili or his wealth to her without an heir? By threats she had forced Nobili to make Enrica his wife, but no threats could compel him to complete the marriage.

As she lingered in the sala, stunned by the blow that

had fallen upon her, the marchesa suddenly recollected the penciled lines which Guglielmi had torn from his tablet and slipped into her hand. She drew the paper from the folds of her dress and read these words:

"*We are beaten if Count Nobili leaves the house to-night. Keep him at all hazards.*"

A sudden revulsion seized her. She raised her head with that snake-like action natural to her. The blood rushed to her face and neck. Guglielmi then still had hope?—All was not lost. In an instant her energy returned to her. What could she do to keep him? Would Enrica—Enrica was still within the chapel. The marchesa heard the murmur of voices coming through the corridor. No, though she worshiped him, Enrica would never lend herself to tempt Nobili with the bait of her beauty—no, even though she was his wife. It would be useless to ask her. "Keep him—how?" the marchesa asked herself with feverish impatience. Every moment was precious. She heard footsteps. They must be leaving the chapel. Nobili, perhaps, was going. No. The door to the garden, by which Nobili had entered the chapel, was now locked. Adamo had given her the key. She must therefore see them when they passed out through the sala. At this moment the howling of the dogs was audible. They were chained up in the cave under the tower. Poor beasts, they had been forgotten in the hurry of the day. The dogs were hungry; were yelping for their food. Through the open door the marchesa saw Adamo pass—a sudden thought struck her.

"Adamo!"

"Padrona." And Adamo's bullet-head and broad shoulders fill up the doorway.

"Where is Count Nobili?"

"Along with the lawyer from Lucca."

"He is safe, then, for the present," the marchesa told herself.

Adamo could not speak for staring at his mistress as she stood opposite to him full in the light. He had never seen such a look upon her face all the years he had served her. She almost smiled at him.

"Adamo," the marchesa addresses him eagerly, "come here. How many years have you lived with me?"

Adamo grins and shows two rows of white teeth.

"Thirty years, padrona—I came when I was a little lad."

"Have I treated you well, Adamo?"

As she asks this question, the marchesa moves close to him.

"Have I ever complained," is Adamo's answer, "that the marchesa asks me?"

"You saved my life, Adamo, not long ago, from the fire." The eager look is growing intenser. "I have never thanked you. Adamo—".

"Padrona"—he is more and more amazed at her—"she must be going to die! Gesù mio! I wish she would swear at me," Adamo thought. "Padrona, don't thank me— Domine Dio did it."

"Take these"—and the marchesa puts her hand into her pocket and draws out some notes—"take these, these are better than thanks."

Adamo drew back much affronted. "Padrona, I don't want money."

"Yes, yes, take them—for Pipa and the boys"—and she thrusts the notes into his big red hands.

"After all," thought Adamo to himself, "if the padrona is going to die, I may as well have these notes as another."

"I would save your life any day, padrona," Adamo says aloud. "It is a pleasure."

" Would you ? " the marchesa fell into a muse.

Again the dogs howled. Adamo makes a motion to go to them.

" Were you going to feed the dogs when I called to you ? " she asks.

" Padrona, yes. I was going to feed them."

" Are they very hungry ? "

" Very—poverini ! they have had nothing since this morning. Now it is five o'clock."

" Don't feed them, Adamo, don't feed them." The marchesa is strangely excited. She holds out her hand to detain him.

Adamo stares at her in mute consternation. " The padrona is certainly going mad before she dies," he mutters, trying to get away.

" Adamo, come here ! " He approaches her, secretly making horns against the evil-eye with his fingers. " You saved my life, now you must save my honor."

The words came hissing into his ear. Adamo drew back a step or two. " Blessed mother, what ails her? " But he held his tongue.

The marchesa stands before him drawn up to her full height, every nerve and muscle strained to the utmost.

" Adamo, do you hear?—My honor, the honor of my name. Quick, quick ! "

She lays her hand on his rough jacket and grasps it.

Adamo, struck with superstitious awe, cannot speak. He nods.

"The dogs are hungry, you say. Let them loose without feeding. No one must leave the house to-night. Do you understand ? You must prevent it. Let the dogs loose."

Again Adamo nods. He is utterly bewildered. He will obey her, of course, but what can she mean ?

" Is your gun loaded ? " she asks, anxiously.

"Yes, padrona."

"That is well." A vindictive smile lights up her features. "No one must leave the house to-night. You understand? The dogs will be loose—the guns loaded.—Where is Pipa? Say nothing to Pipa. Do you understand? Don't tell Pipa—"

"Understand? No, diavalo! I don't understand," bursts out Adamo. "If you want any one shot, tell me who it is, padrona, and I will do it."

"That would be murder, Adamo." The marchesa is standing very near him. Adamo sees the savage gleam that comes into her eyes. "If any one leaves the house to-night except Fra Pacifico, stop him, Adamo, stop him. You, or the dogs, or the gun—no matter. Stop him, I command you. I have my reasons. If a life is lost I cannot help it—nor can you, Adamo, eh?"

She smiles grimly. Adamo smiles too, a stolid smile, and nods. He is greatly relieved. The padrona is not mad, nor will she die.

"You may sleep in peace, padrona." With the utmost respect Adamo raises her hand to his lips and kisses it. "Next time ask Adamo to do something more, and he will do it. Trust me, no one shall leave the house to-night alive."

The marchesa listens to Adamo breathlessly. "Go—go," she says; "we must not be seen together."

"The signora shall be obeyed," answers Adamo. He vanishes behind the trees.

"Now I can meet Gugliclmi!" The marchesa rapidly crosses the sala to the door of her own room, which she leaves ajar.

CHAPTER IX.

THE room to which Angelo conducts Count Nobili is on the ground-floor, in the same wing as the chapel. It is reached by the same corridor, which traverses all that side of the house. Into this corridor many other doors open. Pipa had chosen it because it was the best room in the house. From the high ceiling, painted in gay frescoes, hangs a large chandelier; the bed is covered with red damask curtains. Such furniture as was available had been carried thither by Pipa and Adamo. One large window, reaching to the ground, looks westward over the low wall.

The sun is setting. The mighty range of mountains are laced with gold; light, fleecy cloudlets float across the sky. Behind rise banks of deepest saffron. These shift and move at first in chaos; then they take the form as of a fiery city. There are domes and towers and pinnacles as of living flame, that burn and glisten. Another moment, and the sun has sunk to rest. The phantom city fades; the ruddy background melts into the gray mountain-side. Dim ghost-like streaks linger about the double summits of La Pagna. They vanish. Nothing then remains but masses of leaden clouds soon to darken into night.

On entering the room, Count Nobili takes a long breath,

gazes for a moment on the mountains that rise before him, then turns toward the door, awaiting the arrival of Gugli-elmi. His restless eye, his shifting color, betray his agitation. The ordeal is not yet over; he must hear what this man has to say.

Maestro Guglielmi enters with a quick, brisk step and easy, confident bearing ; indeed, he is in the highest spirits. He had trembled lest Nobili should have insisted upon leaving Corellia immediately after the ceremony when it was still broad daylight. Several unforeseen circumstances had prevented this—Enrica's fainting-fit; the discussion that ensued upon it between Nobili and the old chamberlain—all this had created delay, and afforded him an appropriate opportunity of requesting a private interview. Besides, the cunning lawyer had noted that, during that discussion in the chapel with Cavaliere Trenta, Nobili had evinced indications of other passions besides anger—indications of a certain tenderness in the midst of his vehement sense of the wrong done him by the marchesa. But, what was of far more consequence to Guglielmi was, that all this had the effect of stopping Nobili's immediate departure. That Guglielmi had prevailed upon Nobili to enter the room prepared for him—that he had in so doing domiciled himself voluntarily under the same roof as his wife—was an immense point gained.

All this filled Maestro Guglielmi with the prescience of success. With Nobili in the house, what might not the chapter of accidents produce ? All this had occurred, too, without taking into account what the marchesa herself might have planned, when she had read the note of instructions he had written upon a page of his tablets. Guglielmi thought he knew his friend and client the Marchesa Gui-nigi but little, if her fertile brain had not already created some complication that would have the effect of preventing Count Nobili's departure that night. The instant—the

immediate instant—now lay with himself. He was about
to make the most of it.

When Guglielmi entered the room, Count Nobili received him with an expression of undisguised disgust.
Summoned by Nobili in a peremptory tone to say why he
had brought him hither, Guglielmi broke forth with extraordinary volubility. He had used, he declared, his influence with the marchesa throughout for his (Count Nobili's) advantage—solely for his advantage. One word from
him, and the Marchesa Guinigi would have availed herself
of her legal claims in the most vindictive manner—exposed
family secrets—made the whole transaction of the marriage public—and so revenged herself upon him that Count
Nobili would have no choice but to leave Lucca and Italy
forever.

"All this I have prevented," Guglielmi insisted emphatically. "How could I serve you better?—Could a
brother have guarded your honor more jealously? You
will come to see and acknowledge the obligation in time—
yes, Count Nobili—in time. Time brings all things to
light. Time will exhibit my integrity, my disinterested
devotion to your interests in their true aspect. All little
difficulties settled with my illustrious client, the Marchesa
Guinigi (a high-minded and most courageous lady of the
heroic type), established in Lucca in the full enjoyment of
your enormous wealth—with the lovely lady I have just
seen by your side—the enlightened benefactor of the city
—the patron of art—the consoler of distress—a leader of
the young generation of nobles—the political head of the
new Italian party—bearing the grandest name (of course
you will adopt that of Guinigi), adorning that name with
the example of noble actions—a splendid career opens before you. Yes, Count Nobili—yes—a career worthy of
the loftiest ambition!

"All this I have been the happy means of procuring

for you. Another advocate might have exasperated the marchesa's passions for his own purposes; it would have been most easy. But I," continued Guglielmi, bringing his flaming eyes to bear upon Count Nobili, then raising them from him outward toward the darkening mountains as though he would call on the great Apennines to bear witness to his truth—"I have scorned such base consideration. With unexampled magnanimity I have brought about this marriage—all this I have done, actuated by the purest, the most single-hearted motives. In return, Count Nobili, I make one request—I entreat you to believe that I am your friend—"

(Before the lawyer had concluded his peroration, professional zeal had so far transported him that he had convinced himself all he said was true—was he not indeed pleading for his judgeship ?)

Guglielmi extended his arms as if about to *embrace* Count Nobili !

All this time Nobili had stood as far removed from him as possible. Nobili had neither moved nor raised his head once. He had listened to Guglielmi, as the rocks listen to the splash of the seething waves beating against their side. As the lawyer proceeded, a deep flush gradually overspread his face—when he saw the lawyer's outstretched arms, he retreated to the utmost limits of the room. Guglielmi's arms fell to his side.

" Whatever may be my opinion of you, Signore Avvocato," spoke the count at length, contemplating Guglielmi fixedly, and speaking slowly, as if exercising a strong control over himself—"whether I accept your friendship, or whether I believe any one word you say, is immaterial. It cannot affect in any way what is past. The declaration I made before the altar is the declaration to which I adhere —I am not bound to state my reasons. To me they are overwhelming. I must therefore decline all discussion with you. It is for you to make such arrangements with your client as will insure me a separation. That done, our paths lie far apart."

Who would have recognized the gracious, facile Count Nobili in these hard words? The haughty tone in which they were uttered added to their sting.

We are at best the creatures of circumstances—circumstances had entirely altered him. At that moment, Nobili was at war with all the world. He hated himself—he hated and he mistrusted every one. Gugliclmi was not certainly adapted to restore faith in mankind.

Legal habits had taught Maestro Guglielmi to shape his countenance into a mask, fashioned to whatever expression he might desire to assume. Never had the trick been so difficult! The intense rage that possessed him was uncontrollable. For the first moment he stood stolidly mute. Then he struck the heel of his boot loudly upon the stuccoed floor—would he could crush Count Nobili thus!—crush him and trample upon him—Nobili—the only obstacle to the high honors awaiting him! The next instant Guglielmi was reproaching himself for his want of control—the next instant he was conscious how needful it was to dissemble. Was he — Guglielmi — who had flashed his sword in a thousand battles, to be worsted by a stubborn boy? Outwitted by a capricious lover? Never!

"Excuse me, Count Nobili," he said, overmastering himself by a violent effort—"it is a bitter pang to me, your devoted friend, to be asked to become a party to an act fatal to your prospects. If you adhere to your resolution, you can never return to Lucca—never inhabit the palace your wealth has so superbly decorated. Public opinion would not permit it. You, a stranger in the city, are held to have ill-used and abandoned the niece of the Marchesa Guinigi." Nobili looked up; he was about to reply. "Pardon me, count, I neither affirm nor deny this accusation," continued Guglielmi, observing his movement; "I am giving no opinion on the merits of the case. You have now espoused the lady. If for a second time you abandon her, you will incur the increased indignation of the public. Reconsider, I implore you, this last resolve."

The lawyer's metallic voice grew positively pathetic.

"I will not reconsider it!" cried Count Nobili, indignantly. "I deny your right to advise me. You have brought me into this room for no purpose that I can comprehend. What have I in common with the advocate of my enemy? I desire to leave Corellia. You are detaining me. Here is the deed of separation"—Nobili drew from his breast-pocket the parchment he had perused so attentively in the chapel—"it only needs the lady's signature. Mine is already affixed. Let me tell you, and through you the Marchesa Guinigi, without that deed—and my own free will," he added in a lower tone, "neither you nor she would have forced me here to this marriage; I came because I considered some reparation was due to a young lady whose name has been cruelly outraged. Else I would have died first! If the lady I have made my wife desires to make any amends to me for the insults that have been heaped upon me through her, let her set me free from an odious thralldrom. I will not so much as look upon one who has permitted herself to be made the tool of others to deceive me. She has been treacherous to me in business—she has been treacherous to me in love—no, I will never look upon her again! Live with her?—by God! never!"

The pent-up wrath within him, the maddening sense of wrong, blaze out. Count Nobili is now striding up and down the room insensible to any thing for the moment but the consciousness of his own outraged feelings.

As Count Nobili waxed furious, Maestro Guglielmi grew calm. His busy brain was concocting all sorts of expedients. He leaned his chin upon his hands. His false smile gave place to a sardonic grin, as he watched Nobili—marked his well-set, muscular figure, his easy movements, the graceful curve of his head and neck, his delicate, regular features, his sunny complexion. But Nobili's face without a smile was shorn of its chief charm: that smile, so bright in itself, brought brightness to others.

"A fine, generous fellow, a proper husband for any lady in Italy, whoever she may be," was Guglielmi's reflection, as he watched him. "The young countess has taste. He is not such a fool either, but desperately provoking—like all boys with large fortunes, desperately provoking—and dogged as a mule. But for all that he is a fine, generous-hearted fellow. I like him—I like him for refusing to be forced against his will. I would not live with an angel on such terms." At this point Guglielmi's eyes exhibited a succession of fireworks; his long teeth gleamed, and he smiled a stealthy smile. "But he must be tamed, this youth—he must be tamed. Let me see, I must take him on another tack—on the flank this time, and hit him hard!"

Nobili has now ceased striding up and down the room. He stands facing the window. His ear has caught the barking of several dogs. A minute after, one rushes past the window—raised only by a few stone steps from the ground— a formidable beast with long white hair, tail on end, ears erect, open-mouthed, fiery-eyed—this is Argo—Argo let loose, famished—maddened by Adamo's devices—Argo rushing at full speed and tearing up a shower of gravel with his huge paws. Barking horribly, he disappears into the shrubs. Argo's bark is taken up by the other dogs from all round the house in various keys. Juno the lurcher gives a short low yelp; the rat-terrier Tuzzi, a shrill, grating whine like a rusty saw; the bull-terrier, a deep growl. In the solemn silence of the untrodden Apennines that rise around, the loud voices of the dogs echo from cliff to cliff, boom down into the abyss, and rattle there like thunder. The night-birds catch up the sound and screech; the frightened bats circle round wildly.

At this moment heavy footsteps creak upon the gravel under the shadow of the wall. A low whistle passes through the air, and the dogs disappear.

"A savage pack, like their mistress," was Count Nobili's thought as his eyes tried to pierce into the growing darkness.

Night is coming on. Heavy vapors creep up from the earth and obscure the air. Darker and denser clouds cover the heavens. Black shadows gather within the room. The bed looms out from the lighter walls like a funeral catafalque.

A few pale gleams of light still linger on the horizon. These fall upon Nobili's figure as he stands framed in the window. As the waning light strikes upon his eyes, a presentiment of danger comes over him. These dogs, these footsteps—what do they mean?

Again a wild desire seizes him to be riding full speed on the mountain-road to Lucca, to feel the fresh night air upon his heated brow; the elastic spring of his good horse under him, each stride bearing him farther from his enemies. He is about to leap out and fly, when the warning hand of the lawyer is laid upon his arm. Nobili shakes him off, but Guglielmi permits himself no indication of offense. Dejection and grief are depicted on his countenance. He shakes his head despondingly; his manner is dangerously fawning. He, too, has heard the dogs, the footsteps, and the whistle. He has drawn his own conclusions.

"I perceive, Count Nobili," he says, "you are impatient."

This was in response to a muttered curse from Nobili.

"Let me go! A thousand devils! Let me go!" cried

the count, putting the lawyer back. "Impatient! I am maddened!"

"But not before we have settled the matter in question. That is impossible! Hear me, then, Count Nobili. With the deepest sorrow I accept the separation you demand on the part of the marchesa; you give me no choice. I venture no further remark," continues Guglielmi meekly, drilling his eyes to a subdued expression.

(His eyes are a continual curse to him; sometimes they will tell the truth.)

"But there is one point, my dear count, upon which we must understand each other."

In order to detain Nobili, Guglielmi is about to commit himself to a deliberate lie. Lying is not his practice; not on principle, for he has none. Expediency is his ·faith, pliancy his creed; lying is inartistic, also dangerous. A lie may grow into a spectre, and haunt you to your grave, perhaps beyond it.

Guglielmi felt he must do something decisive, or that exalted personage who desired to avoid all scandal not connected with himself would be irretrievably offended, and he, Guglielmi, would never sit on the judicial bench. Yet, unscrupulous as he was, the trickster shuddered at the thought of what that lie might cost him.

It is my duty to inform you, Count Nobili "—Guglielmi is speaking with pompous earnestness—he anxiously notes the effect his words produce upon Count Nobili—"that, un-less you remain under the same roof with your wife to-night, the marriage will not be completed; therefore no separation between you will be legal."

Nobili turned pale. He struck his fist violently on the table.

"What! a new difficulty? When will this torture end?"

"It will end to-morrow morning, Count Nobili. To-

morrow morning I shall have the honor of waiting upon
you, in company with the Mayor of Corellia, for the civil
marriage. , Every requisition of the law will then have been
complied with."

Maestro Guglielmi bows and moves toward the door.
If by this means the civil marriage can be brought about,
Guglielmi will have clinched a doubtful act into a legal
certainty.

"A moment, Signore Avvocato"—and Nobili is following Guglielmi to the door, consternation and amazement
depicted upon his countenance. "Is this indeed so?"

Nobili's manner indicates suspicion.

"Absolutely so," answers the mendacious one. "To-
morrow morning, after the civil marriage, we shall be in
readiness to sign the deed of separation. Allow me in the
mean time to peruse it."

He holds out his hand. If all fails, he determines to
destroy that deed, and protest that he has lost it.

"Dio Santo!" ejaculates Nobili, giving the deed to
him—"twenty-four hours at Corellia!"

"Not twenty-four," suggests Guglielmi, blandly, putting the deed into his pocket and taking out his watch with
extraordinary rapidity, then replacing it as rapidly; "it is
now seven o'clock. At nine o'clock to-morrow morning the
deed of separation shall be signed, and you, Count Nobili,
will be free."

CHAPTER X.

AT that moment Fra Pacifico's tall figure barred the doorway. He seemed to have risen suddenly out of the darkness. Nobili started back and changed color. Of all living men, he most dreaded the priest at that particular moment. The priest was now before him, stern, grave, authoritative; searching him with those earnest eyes—the priest—a living protest against all he had done, against all he was about to do!

The agile lawyer darted forward. He was about to speak. Fra Pacifico waved him into silence.

"Maestro Guglielmi," he said, with that sonorous voice which lent importance to his slightest utterances, "I am glad to find you here. You represent the marchesa.—My son," he continued, addressing Count Nobili (as he did so, his face darkened into a look of mingled pain and displeasure), "I come from your wife."

At that word Fra Pacifico paused. Count Nobili reddened. His eyes fell upon the floor; he dared not meet the reproving glance he felt was upon him.

"My son, I come from your wife," repeated Fra Pacifico.

There was a dead silence.

"You saw your wife borne from the altar fainting. She was mercifully spared, therefore, hearing from your own

lips that you repudiated her. She has since been informed
by Cavaliere Trenta that you did so. I am here as her
messenger. Your wife accepts the separation you desire."

As each sentence fell from the priest's lips his countenance grew sterner.

"Accepts the separation! Gives me up!" exclaimed
Nobili, quite taken aback. "So much the better. We are
both of the same mind."

But, spite his words, there were irritation and surprise
in Nobili's manner. That Enrica herself should have consented to part from him was altogether an astonishment!

"If Countess Nobili accepts the separation"—and he
turned sharply upon Guglielmi—"nothing need detain
you here, Signore Avvocato. You hear what Fra Pacifico
says. You have only, therefore, to inform the Marchesa
Guinigi. Probably her niece has already done so. We
know that they act in concert." Count Nobili laughed
bitterly.

"The marchesa is not even aware that I am here," interposed Fra Pacifico. "Enrica is now married—she acts
for herself. Her first act, Count Nobili, is one of obedience
—she sacrifices herself to you."

Again the priest's deep-set eyes turned reprovingly upon
Count Nobili. Dare the headstrong boy affect to misunder-
stand that he had driven Enrica to renounce him? Guglielmi remained standing near the door—self-possessed,
indeed, as usual, but utterly crestfallen. His very soul
sank within him as he listened to Fra Pacifico. Every
thing was going wrong, the judgeship in imminent peril,
and this devil of a priest, who ought to know better, doing
every thing to divide them!

"Signore Guglielmi," said Nobili, with a significant
glance at the open door, "allow me to repeat—we need
not detain you. We shall now act for ourselves. Without
reference to the difficulties you have raised—"

"The difficulties I have raised have been for your own good, Count Nobili," was Guglielmi's indignant reply. "Had I been supported by"—and he glanced at Fra Pacifico—"by those whose duty teaches them obedience to the ordinances of the Church, you would have saved yourself and others the spectacle of a matrimonial scandal that will degrade you before the eyes of all Italy."

Count Nobili was rushing forward, with some undefined purpose of chastising Guglielmi, when Fra Pacifico interposed. A quiet smile parted his well-formed mouth; he shrugged his shoulders as he eyed the enraged lawyer.

"Allow me to judge of my duty as a priest. Look to your own as a lawyer, or it may be the worse for you. What says the motto?—'Those who seek gold may find sand.'"

Guglielmi, greatly alarmed at what Fra Pacifico might reveal of their previous conversation, waited to hear no more; he hastily disappeared. Fra Pacifico watched the manner of his exit with silence, the quiet smile of conscious power still on his lips. When he turned and addressed Count Nobili, the smile had died out.

Before Fra Pacifico can speak, the whole pack of dogs, attracted by the loud voices, gather round the steps before the open window. They are barking furiously. The smooth-skinned, treacherous bull-dog is silent, but he stands foremost. True to his breed, the bull-dog is silent. He creeps in noiselessly—his teeth gleam within an inch of Nobili. Fra Pacifico spies him. With a furious kick he flings him out far over the heads of the others. The bull-dog's howl of anguish rouses the rest to frenzy. A moment more, and Fra Pacifico and Count Nobili would have been attacked within the very room, but again footsteps are heard passing in the shadow. A shot is fired close at hand. The dogs rush off, the bull-dog whining and limping in the rear.

Count Nobili and Fra Pacifico exchange glances. There is a knock at the door. Pipa enters carrying a lighted lamp which she places on the table. Pipa does not even salute Fra Pacifico, but fixes her eyes, swollen with crying, upon Count Nobili.

"What is the matter?" asks the priest.

"Riverenza, I do not know. Adamo and Angelo are out watching."

"But, Pipa, it is very strange. A shot was fired. The dogs, too, are wilder than ever."

"Riverenza, I know nothing. Perhaps there are some deserters about. We are used to the dogs. I never hear them. I am come from the signorina."

At that name Count Nobili looks up and meets Pipa's gaze. If Pipa could have stabbed him then and there with the silver dagger in her black hair she would have done it, and counted it a righteous act. But she must deliver her message.

"Signore Conte"—Pipa flings her words at Nobili as if each word were a stone, with which she would have hit him—"Signore Conte, the marchesa has sent me. The marchesa bids me salute you. She desired me to bring in this light. I was to say supper is served in the great sala. She eats in her own room with the cavaliere, and hopes you will excuse her."

Before the count could answer, Pipa was gone.

"My son," said Fra Pacifico, standing beside him in the dimly-lighted room, "you have now had time to reflect. Do you accept the separation offered to you by your wife?"

"I do, my father."

"Then she will enter a convent." Nobili sighed heavily. "You have broken her heart."

There was a depth of unexpressed reproach in the priest's look. Tears gathered in his eyes, his deep voice shook.

"But why if she ever loved me"—whispered Nobili into Fra Pacifico's ear as though he shrank from letting the very walls hear what he was about to say—   .

"If she loved you!" burst out Fra Pacifico with rising passion—"if she loved you! You have my word that she loved you—nay, God help her, that she loves you still!"

Fra Pacifico drew back from Nobili as he said this. Again Nobili approached him, speaking into his ear.

"Why, then, if she loved me, could she join with the marchesa against me? Was I not induced by my love for her to pay her aunt's debts? Answer me that, my father. Why did she insist upon this ill-omened marriage?—a proceeding as indelicate as it is—"

"Silence!" thundered Fra Pacifico—"silence, I command you! What you say of that pure and lovely girl whose soul is as crystal before me, is absolute sacrilege. I will not listen to it!"

Fra Pacifico's eyes flashed fire. He looked as if he would strike Count Nobili where he stood. He checked himself, however; then he continued with more calmness: "To become your wife was needful for the honor of Enrica's name, which you had slandered. The child put herself in my hands. I am responsible for this marriage—I only. As to the marchesa, do you think she consults Enrica? The hawk and the dove share not the same nest! No, no. Did the marchesa so much as tell Enrica, when she offered her as wife to Count Marescotti?"

At the sound of Marescotti's name Nobili's assumed composure utterly gave way. His whole frame stiffened with rage.

"Yes—Marescotti—curse him! And I am the husband of the woman he refused!"

"For shame, Count Nobili!—you have yourself exonerated her."

"Enrica must have been an accomplice!" cried Nobili,
17

transported out of himself. Count Marescotti's name had exasperated him beyond control.

"Fool!" exclaimed Fra Pacifico. "Will you not listen to reason? Has not Enrica by her own act renounced all claim to you as a wife? Is not that enough?"

Nobili was silent. Hitherto he had been driven on, goaded by the promptings of passion, and the firm belief that Enrica was the mere tool of her aunt. Now the same facts detailed by the priest placed themselves in a new light. For the first time Nobili doubted whether he was entirely justified in all that he had done—in all that he was about to do.

Meanwhile Fra Pacifico was losing all patience. His manly nature rose within him at what he considered Nobili's deliberate cruelty. Inflexible in right, Fra Pacifico was violent in face of wrong.

"Why did you not let her die?" he exclaimed, bitterly. "It would have saved her a world of suffering. I thought I knew you, Mario Nobili—knew you from a boy," he added, contemplating him with a dark scowl. "You have deceived me. Every word you utter only sinks you lower in my esteem."

"It would indeed have been better had we both perished in the flames!" cried Nobili in a voice full of anguish —"perished—locked in each other's arms! Poor Enrica!" He turned away, and a low sob burst from his heart of hearts. "The marchesa has destroyed my love!—She has blighted my life!" Nobili's voice sounded hollow in the dimly-lighted room. At last Nobili was speaking out— speaking, as it were, from the grave of his love! "Yes, I loved her," he continued dreamily—"I loved her! How much I did not know!"

He had forgotten he was not alone. The priest was but dimly visible. He was leaning against the wall, his massive chin resting on his hand, listening to Nobili. Now, hearing what he said, Fra Pacifico's anger had vanished. After all, he had not been mistaken in his old pupil! Nobili was neither cruel nor heartless; but he had been driven to bay! Now he pitied him, profoundly. What could he say to him? He could urge Nobili no more. He must work out his own fate!

Again Nobili spoke.

"When I saw her sweet face turned toward me as she entered the chapel, I dared not look again! It was too late. My pride as a man, all that is sacred to me as a gentleman, has been too deeply wounded. The marchesa has done it. She alone is responsible. *She* has left me no alternative. I will never accept a wife forced upon me by *her*—never, by Heaven! My father, these are my last words. Carry them to Enrica."

Count Nobili's head dropped upon his breast. He covered his face with his hands.

"My son, I leave you in the hands of God. May He lead you and comfort you! But remember, the life of your wife is bound up in *your* life. Hitherto Enrica has lived upon hope. Deprived of hope, *she will die.*"

When Nobili looked up, Fra Pacifico was gone.

CHAPTER XI

The time had now come when Count Nobili must finally make up his mind. He had told Fra Pacifico that his determination was unaltered. He had told him that his dignity as a man, his honor as a gentleman, demanded that he should free himself from the net-work of intrigues in which the marchesa had entangled him. Of all earthly things, compliancy with her desires most revolted him. Rather than live any longer the victim either of her malice or her ambition, he had brought himself to believe that it was his duty to renounce Enrica. Until Fra Pacifico had entered that room within which he was again pacing up and down with hasty strides, no doubt whatever had arisen in his mind as to what it was incumbent upon him to do: to give Enrica the protection of his name by marriage, then to separate. Whether to separate in the manner pointed out by Guglièlmi he had not decided. An innate repulsion, now increased by suspicion, made him distrust any act pressed upon him by that man, especially when urged in concert with the marchesa.

Every hour passed at Corellia was torture to him. Should he go at once, or should he remain until the morning?—sign the deed?—complete the sacrifice? Already what he had so loudly insisted on presented itself now to him in the light of a sacrifice. Enrica loved him still—he believed Fra Pacifico. The throbbing of his heart as he thought of her told him that he returned that love. She was there near him under the same roof. Could he leave her? Yes, he must leave her! He would trust himself no longer in the hands of the marchesa or of her agent. Instinct told him some subtle scheme lay under the urgings of Guglielmi—the dangerous civilities of the marchesa. He would go. The legal separation might be completed elsewhere. Why only at Corellia? Why must those formalities insisted on by Guglielmi be respected? What did they mean? Of the real drift of the delay Nobili was utterly ignorant. Had he asked Fra Pacifico, he would have told him the truth, but he had not done so.

To meet Enrica in the morning; to meet her again in the presence of her detested aunt; to meet her only to sign a deed separating them forever under the mockery of mutual consent, was agony. Why should he endure it?

Nobili, wrought up to a pitch of excitement that almost robbed him of reason, dares not trust himself to think. He seizes his hat, which lay upon the table, and rushes out into the night. The murmur of voices comes dimly to him in the freshness of the air out of a window next his own. A circle of light shines on the glistening gravel before him. There must be people within—people watching him, doubtless. As the thought crosses his mind he is suddenly pinned to the earth. Argo is watching for him—stealthy Argo—Argo springs upon him silently from behind; he holds him tightly in his grip. The dog made no sound, nor does he now, but he has laid Nobili flat on the ground. He stands over him, his heavy paws planted upon his chest, his open jaws and dripping tongue close upon his face, so close, that Nobili feels the dog's hot breath upon his skin. Nobili cannot move; he looks up fixedly into Argo's glaring, bloodshot eyes. His steady gaze daunts the dog. In the very act of digging his big fangs into Nobili's throat Argo pauses; he shrinks before those human eyes before which the brutish nature quails. In an instant Nobili's strong hands close round his throat; he presses it until the powerful paws slacken in their grip—until the fiery eyes are starting from their sockets.

Silent as is the struggle the other dogs are alarmed—they give tongue from different sides. Footsteps are rapidly approaching—the barrel of a gun gleams out of the darkness—a shot is fired—the report wanders off in endless reverberation among the rocks—another shot, and another, in instant succession, answer each other from behind the villa.

With a grasp of iron Nobili holds back gallant Argo—Argo foaming at the mouth; his white-coated chest heaving, as if in his last agony! Yet Argo is still immovable—his heavy paws upon Nobili's chest pressing with all his weight upon him!

Now the footsteps have turned the corner! Dim forms already shape themselves in the night mist. The other dogs, barking savagely, are behind—they are coming—they are at hand! Ah! Nobili, what can you do now?—Nobili understands his danger. Quick as thought Nobili has dealt Argo a tremendous blow under the left ear. He seizes him by his milk-white hair so long and beautiful, he flings him against the low wall almost insensible. Argo falls a shapeless mass. He is stunned and motionless. Before the shadow of Adamo is upon him—before the dogs' noses touch him—Nobili is on his feet. With one bound he has leaped through the window—the same from which the voices had come (it has been opened in the scuffle)—in an instant he closes the sash! He is safe!

Coming suddenly out of the darkness, after the great force he had put forth, Nobili feels giddy and bewildered. At first he sees nothing but that there is a light in the centre of the room. As his eyes fix themselves upon it the light almost blinds him. He puts his hand to his forehead, where the veins had swollen out like cords upon his fair skin. He puts up his hands to shade his dazzled eyes before which clouds of stars dance desperately. He steadies himself and looks round.

Before him stands Enrica !

By Pipa's care the bridegroom's chamber had been chosen next the bride's when she prepared Count Nobili's room. Pipa was straightforward and simple in her notions of matrimony, but, like a wise woman, she had held her tongue.

Nobili and Enrica are alone. A furtive glance passes between them. Neither of them moves. Neither of them speaks. The first movement comes from Enrica. She sinks backward upon a chair. The tangle of her yellow hair closes round her face upon which a deep blush had risen at sight of Nobili. When that blush had died out she looked resigned, almost passionless. She knew that the moment had come which must decide her fate. Before they two parted she would hear from the lips of the man she loved if they were ever to meet again ! Her eyes fell to the ground. She dared not raise them. If she looked at Nobili, she must fling herself into his arms.

Nobili, standing on the same spot beyond the circle of the light, gazes at Enrica in silence. He is overwhelmed by the most conflicting emotions. But the spell of her beauty is upon him. His pulses beat madly. For an instant he forgets where he is. He forgets all but that Enrica is before him. For a moment ! Then his brain clears. He remembers every thing—remembers—oh, how bitterly !—that, after all that has passed, his very presence in that room is an insult to her ! He feels he ought to go— yet an irresistible longing chains him to the spot. He moves toward the door. To reach it he must pass close to

Enrica. When he is near the door he stops. The light shows that his clothes are torn—that there is blood upon his face and hands. In scarcely articulate words Nobili addresses her.

"Enrica—countess, I mean "—Nobili hesitates—" pardon this intrusion.—You saw the accident.—I did not know that this was *your* room."

Again Nobili pauses, waiting for an answer. None comes. Would she not speak to him ? Alas ! had he deserved that she should ? Nobili takes a step or two toward the door. With one hand upon the lock he pauses once more, gazing at Enrica with lingering eyes. Then he turns to leave the room. It is all over !—he had only to depart ! A low cry from Enrica stops him.

"Nobili," Enrica says, "tell me—oh ! tell me, are you hurt ? "

Enrica has risen from the chair. One hand rests on the table for support. Her voice falters as she asks the question. Nobili, every drop of whose blood runs fevered in his veins, turns toward her.

"I am not hurt—a scratch or two—nothing."

"Thank God ! " Enrica utters, in a low voice.

Nobili endeavors to approach her. She draws back.

"As I am here "—he speaks with the utmost embarrassment—" here, as you see, by accident "—his voice rests on the words—" I cannot go—"

As Nobili speaks he perceives that Enrica gradually retreats farther from him. The tender delight that had come into her eyes when he first addressed her fades out into a scared look—a look like a defenseless animal expecting to receive a death-wound. Nobili sees and understands the expression.

His heart smites him sorely. Great God !—has he become an object of terror to her ?

"Enrica ! "—she starts back as Nobili pronounces her

name, yet he speaks so softly the sound comes to her almost like a sigh—"Enrica, do not fear me. I will say no word to offend you. I cannot go without asking your pardon. As one who loved you once—as one who loves—" He stops. ˙What is he saying?—"I humbly beseech you to forgive me. Enrica, let me hear you say that you forgive me."

Still Enrica retreats from him, that suffering, saint-like look upon her face he knows so well. Nobili follows her. He kneels at her feet. He kneels at the feet of the woman from whom, not an hour before, he had demanded a separation!

"Say—can you forgive me before I go?"

As Nobili speaks, his strong heart goes out to her in speechless longings. If Enrica had looked into his eyes they would have told her that he never had loved her as now! And they were parted!

Enrica puts out her hand timidly. Her lips move as if to speak, but no sound comes. Nobili rises; he takes her hand within both his own. He kisses it reverently.

"Dear hand—" he murmurs, " and it was mine!"

Released from his, the dainty little hand falls to her side. She sighs deeply. There is the old charm in Nobili's voice —so sweet, so subtile. The tones fall upon her ear like strains of passionate music. A storm of emotion sweeps across her face. She has forgotten all in the rapture of his presence. Yes!—that voice! Had it not been raised but a few hours before at the altar to repudiate her? How can she believe in him? How surrender herself to the glamour of his words? Remembering all this, despair comes over her. Again Enrica shrinks from him. She bursts into tears and hides her face with her hands.

Enrica's distrust of him, her silence, her tears, cut Nobili to the soul. He knows he deserves it. Ah!—with her there before him, how he curses himself for ever having

doubted her! Every justification suddenly leaves him.
He is utterly confounded. The gossip of the club—Count
Marescotti and his miserable verses—the marchesa herself
—what are they all beside the purity of those saint-like
eyes? Nera, too—false, fickle, sensual Nera—a mere thing
of flesh and blood—he had left her for Nera! Was he
mad?

At that moment, of all living men, Count Nobili seemed
to himself the most unworthy! He must go—he did not
deserve to stay!

"Enrica—before I leave you, speak to me one word of
forgiveness—I implore you!"

As he speaks their eyes meet. Yes, she is his own Enrica—unchanged, unsullied!—the idol is intact within its
shrine—the sanctuary is as he had left it! No rude touch
had soiled that atmosphere of purity and freshness that
floated like an aureole around her!

How could he leave her?—if they must part, he would
hear his fate from her own lips. Enrica is leaning against
the wall speechless, her face shaded by her hand. Big tears
are trickling through her fingers. Unable to support herself she clings to a chair, then seats herself. And Nobili,
pale with passion stands by, and dares not so much as to
touch her—dares not touch her, although she is his wife!

In the fury of his self-reproach, he digs his hands into
the masses of thick chestnut curls that lie disordered about
his head.

Fool, idiot!—had he lost her? A terrible misgiving
overcomes him? It fills him with horror. Was it too late?
Would she never forgive him? Nobili's troubled eyes, that
wander all over her, ask the question.

"Speak to me—speak to me!" he cries. "Curse me—
but speak to me!"

At this appeal Enrica turns her tear-bedewed face toward him.

"Nobili," she says at last, very low, "would you have gone without seeing me?"

Nobili dares not lie to her. He makes no reply.

"Oh, do not deceive me, Nobili!" and Enrica wrings her hands and looks piteously into his face. "Tell me—would you have come to me?"

It is only by a strong effort that Nobili can restrain himself from folding Enrica in his arms and in one burning kiss burying the remembrance of the miserable past. But he trembles lest by offending her the tender flower before him may never again expand to the ardor of his love. If Fra Pacifico has not by his arguments already shaken Nobili's conviction of the righteousness of his own conduct, the sight of Enrica utterly overcomes him.

"Deceive you!" he exclaims, approaching her and seizing her hands which she did not withdraw—"deceive you! How little you read my heart!"

He holds her soft hands firmly in his—he covers them with kisses. Enrica feels the tender pressure of his lips pass through her whole frame. But, can she trust him?

"Did I not love you enough?" she asks, looking into his face. She gently disengages her hands from his grasp. There is no reproach in her look, but infinite sorrow. "Can I believe you?" And the soft blue eyes rest upon him full of pathetic pleading.

An expression of despair comes into Nobili's bright face. How can he answer her? How can he satisfy her when he himself has shaken her trust? Alas! would the golden past never come again? The past, tinted with the passion of ardent summer?

"Believe me?" he cries, in a tone of wildest passion. "Can you ask me?"

As he speaks he leans over her. Love is in his voice—his eyes—his whole attitude. Would she not understand him? Would she reject him?

Enrica draws back—she raises her hand in protest.

"Let me again"—Nobili is following her closely—"let me implore your forgiveness of my unmanly conduct."

She presses her hands to her bosom as if in pain, but not a sound comes to her lips.

"Believe me," he urges, "I have been driven mad by the marchesa! It is my only excuse."

"Am I?" Enrica answers. "Have I not suffered enough from my aunt? What had she to do between you and me? Did I love you less because she hated you? Listen, Nobili"—Enrica with difficulty commands her voice—"from the first time we met in the cathedral I gave myself to you—you—you only."

"But, Enrica—love—you consented to leave me. You sent Fra Pacifico to say so."

The thought that Enrica had so easily resigned him still rankled in Nobili's heart. Spite of himself, there is bitterness in his tone.

Enrica is standing aloof from him. The light of the lamp strikes upon her golden hair, her downcast eyes, her cheeks mantling with blushes.

"I leave you!"—a soft dew came into Enrica's eyes as she fixed them upon Nobili—a dew that rapidly formed itself into two tears that rolled silently down her cheek—"never—never!"

Spite of the horrors of the past, these words, that look, tell him she is his! Nobili's heart leaps within him. For a moment he is breathless—speechless in the tumult of his great joy.

"Oh! my beloved!" he cries, in a voice that penetrates her very soul. "Come to me—here—to a heart all your own!" He springs forward and clasps her in his arms. "Thus—thus let the past perish!" Nobili whispers as his lips touch hers. Enrica's head nestles upon his breast. She has once more found her home.

A subdued knock is heard at the door.

"Sangue di Dio!" mutters Nobili, disengaging himself from Enrica—"what new torment is this? Is there no peace in this house? Who is there?"

"It is I, Count Nobili." Maestro Guglielmi puts in his hatchet face and glaring teeth. In an instant his piercing eyes have traveled round the room. He has taken in the whole situation—Count Nobili in the middle of the floor—flushed—agitated—furious at this interruption; Enrica—revived—conscious—blushing at his side. The investigation is so perfectly satisfactory that Maestro Guglielmi cannot suppress a grin of delight.

"Believe me, Signore Conte," he says, advancing cautiously a step or two forward into the room, a deprecating look on his face—"believe me—this intrusion"—Guglielmi turns to Enrica, grins again palpably, then bows—"is not of my seeking."

"Tell me instantly what brings you here?" demands Nobili, advancing. (Nobili would have liked beyond measure to relieve his feelings by kicking him.)

"It is just that"—Guglielmi cannot refrain from another glance round before he proceeds—(yes, they are reconciled, no doubt of it. The judgeship is his own! Evviva! The illustrious personage—so notoriously careful of his subjects' morals—who had deigned to interest himself in the marriage, might possibly, at the birth of a son and heir to the Guinigi, add a pension—who knows? At this reflection the lawyer's eyes become altogether unmanageable) —"it is just that," repeats Guglielmi, making a desperate effort to collect himself. "Personally I should have declined it, personally; but the marchesa's commands were absolute: 'You must go yourself, I will permit no deputy.'"

"Damn the marchesa! Shall I never be rid of the marchesa?"

Nobili's aspect is becoming menacing. Maestro Guglielmi is not a man easily daunted; yet once within the
room, and the desired evidence obtained, he cannot but
feel all the awkwardness of his position. Greatly as Guglielmi had been tickled at the notion of becoming himself
a witness in his own case, to do him justice he would not
have volunteered it.

"The marchesa sent me," he stammers, conscious of
Count Nobili's indignation (with his arms crossed, Count
Nobili is eying Guglielmi from head to foot). "The mar-
chesa sent me to know—"

Nobili unfolds his arms, walks straight up to where Guglielmi is standing, and shakes his fist in his face.

"Do you know, Signore Avvocato, that you are commit-
ting an intolerable impertinence? If you do not instantly
quit this room, or give me some excellent reason for remaining, you shall very speedily have my opinion of your conduct
in a very decided manner."

Count Nobili is decidedly dangerous. He glares at
Guglielmi like a very devil. Guglielmi falls back. The
false smile is upon his lips, but his treacherous eyes express
his terror. Guglielmi's combats are only with words, his
weapon the pen; otherwise he is powerless.

"Excuse me, Count Nobili, excuse me," he stammers.
He rubs his hands nervously together and watches Nobili,
who is following him step by step. "It is not my fault—I
give you my word—not my fault. Don't look so, count; you
really alarm me. I am here as a man of peace—I entreated
the marchesa to retire to rest. I represented to her the
peculiar delicacy of the position, but I grieve to say she
insisted."

Nobili is now close to him; his eyes are gathered upon
him more threateningly than ever.

"Remember, sir, you are addressing me in the presence
of my wife—be careful."

What a withering look Nobili gives Guglielmi as he says this! He can with difficulty keep his hands off him!

"Yes—yes—just so—just so—I applaud your sentiments, Count Nobili—most appropriate. Now I will go."

Alarmed as he is, Guglielmi cannot resist one parting glance at Enrica. She is crimson. Then with an expression of infinite relief he retreats to the door walking backward. Guglielmi has a strong conviction that if he turns round Count Nobili may kick him, so, keeping his eyes well balanced upon him, he fumbles with his hands behind his back to find the handle of the door. In his confusion he misses it.

"Not for worlds, Signore Conte," says Guglielmi, nervously passing his hand up and down the panel in search of the door-handle—"not for worlds would I offend you! Believe me—(maledictions on the door—it is bewitched!)"

Now Guglielmi has it! Safely clutching the handle with both his hands, Guglielmi's courage returns. His mocking eyes look up without blinking into Nobili's, fierce and flashing as they are.

"Before I go"—he bows with affected humility—"will you favor me, count, and you, madame" (Guglielmi is clutching the door-handle tightly, so as to be able to escape at any moment), "by informing me whether you still desire the deed of separation to be prepared for your signature in the morning?"

"Leave the room!" roars Count Nobili, stamping furiously on the floor—"leave the room, or, Domine Dio!—'

Maestro Guglielmi had jumped out backward, before Count Nobili could finish the sentence.

"Enrica!" cries Nobili, turning toward her—he had banged-to the door and locked it—"Enrica, if you love me, let us leave this accursed villa to-night! This is more than I can bear!"

What Enrica replied, or if Enrica ever replied at all, is, and ever will remain, a mystery!

CHAPTER XII.

OII BELLO!

An hour or two has passed. A slow and cautious step, accompanied with the tapping of a stick upon the stone flags of the floor, is audible along the narrow passage leading from the sala to Pipa's room. It is as dark as pitch. Whoever it is, is afraid of falling, and creeps along cautiously, feeling by the wall.

Pipa, expecting to be summoned to her mistress—Pipa, wondering greatly indeed what Enrica can be about, and why she does not go to bed, when she, the blessed dear, was so faint and tired, and crying—oh, so pitifully!—when she left her—Pipa, leaning against the door-post near the half-open door, dozing like a dog with one eye open in case she should be called—listened and looked out into the passage. A figure is standing within the light that streams out from the door, a very well-remembered figure, stout and short—a little bent forward on a stick—with a round, rosy face framed in snowy curls, a world of pleasant wickedness in two twinkling eyes, on which the light strikes, and a mouth puckered up for any mischief.

"Madonna!" cries Pipa, rubbing her eyes—"the cavaliere! How you did frighten me! I cannot bear to hear footsteps about when Adamo is out;" and Pipa gazes up and down into the darkness with an unpleasant consciousness that something ghostly might be watching her.

"Pipa," says the cavaliere, putting his finger to his nose

and winking palpably, " hold your tongue, and don't scream when I tell you something. Promise me."

" O Gesù !" cries Pipa in a loud voice, starting back, forgetting his injunction—" is it not about the signorina ? "

" Hold your tongue, Pipa, or I will tell you nothing."

Pipa's head is instantly close to the cavaliere's, her face all eagerness.

" Yes, it is about the signorina—the countess. She is gone ! "

" Gone ! " and Pipa, spite of warning, fairly shouts now " gone!" at which the cavaliere shakes his stick at her, smiling, however, benignly all the time. " Holy mother ! gone! O cavaliere! tell me—she is not dead ? "

(Ever since Pipa had tended Enrica lying on her bed, so still and cold, it seemed reasonable to her that she might die at any instant, without warning given.)

" Yes, Pipa," answers the cavaliere solemnly, his voice shaking slightly, but he still smiles, though the dew of rising tears is in his merry eyes—" yes, dead—dead to us, my Pipa—I fear dead to us."

Pipa sinks back in speechless horror against the wall, and groans.

" But only to us—(don't be a fool, Pipa)"—this in a parenthesis—" she is gone with her husband."

Pipa rises to her feet and stares at Trenta, at first wildly, then, as little by little the hidden sense comes to her, her rosy lips slowly part and lengthen out until every snowy tooth is visible. Then Pipa covers her face with her apron, and shakes from head to foot in such a fit of laughter, that she has to lean against the wall not to fall down. " Oh bello ! " is all she can say. This Pipa repeats at intervals in gasps.

" Come, Pipa, that will do," says the cavaliere, poking at her with his stick—" I must get back before I am missed —no one must know it till morning—least of all the marchesa and Guglielmi. They are shut up together. The

marchesa says she will sit up all night. But Count Nobili
and his wife are gone—really gone. Fra Pacifico managed
it. He got hold of Adamo, who was running round the
house with a loaded gun, all the dogs after him. Take
care of Adamo when he comes back to-night, Pipa. He is
fastening up the dogs, and feeding them, and taking care
of poor Argo, who is badly hurt. He is quite mad, Adamo.
I never saw a man so wild. He would not come in. He
said the marchesa had told him to shoot some one. He
swore he would do it yet. He nearly fought with Fra
Pacifico when he forced him in. Adamo is quite mad.
Tell him nothing to-night; he is not safe."

Pipa has now let down her apron. Her bright olive-
complexioned face beams in one broad smile, like the full
moon at harvest. She is still shaking, and at intervals
gives little spasmodic giggles.

"Leave Adamo to me" (another giggle); "I will man-
age him" (another). "Why, he might have shot the signorina's husband—the fool!"

This thought steadies Pipa for an instant, but she bursts
out again. "Oh bello!"—Pipa gurgles like a stream that
cannot stop running; then she breaks off all at once, and
listens. "Hush! hush! There is Adamo coming, cavaliere
—hush! hush! Make haste and go away. He is coming
—Adamo; I hear him on the gravel."

"Say nothing until the morning," whispers the cavaliere. "Give them a fair start. Ha! ha!"

Pipa nods. Her face twitches all over. As Cavaliere
Trenta turns to go, Pipa catches him smartly by the shoulder, draws him to her, and speaks into his ear:

"To think the signorina has run away with her own
husband! Oh bello!"

THE END.

CHRISTIAN REID'S NOVELS.

VALERIE AYLMER. 8vo. Paper, price, $1.00; cloth, $1.50.

"One of the best and most readable novels of the season."—*Philadelphia Post.*
"The story is of marked and sustained interest."—*Chicago Journal.*
"The author is one of the rising and brilliant lights of American literature."—
Portland Argus.
"The story is very interesting, and admirably written."—*Charleston Courier.*

MORTON HOUSE. With Illustrations. 8vo. Paper, price, $1.00;
cloth, $1.50.

"For the sake of our literature we trust that the author will not pause in her new
career, which certainly opens with the bravest promise."—*Christian Union.*
"There is intense power in many of the scenes."—*New York Evening Mail.*
"Marked by great force and originality."—*Philadelphia Age.*
"Interesting from beginning to end."—*Eclectic Magazine.*
"It is, long, very long since we have read an American novel of any thing like
equal merit."—*Philadelphia Press.*

MABEL LEE. With Illustrations. 8vo. Paper, price, $1.00;
cloth, $1.50.

"A story of absorbing interest."—*St. Louis Republican.*
"A tale of vivid interest; full of natural, striking characterization."—*Banner of
the South.*
"The story is one of thrilling interest."—*New York Express.*
"A capital picture of Southern character and society."—*Boston Gazette.*
"No American author of to-day charms us so much."—*Portland Argus.*

EBB-TIDE. With Illustrations. 8vo. Paper, price, $1.00; cloth,
$1.50.

"'Ebb-Tide' is a story of power and pathos, and will be much admired."—*Boston
Commonwealth.*
"Scenes and incidents portrayed with vividness and skill."—*Boston Traveller.*
"The plot is interesting and well developed, and the style is both spirited and
clear."—*Boston Gazette.*

NINA'S ATONEMENT, and Other Stories. With Illustrations.
8vo. Paper, price, $1.00; cloth, $1.50.

"To readers in want of a book with which to while away an after-dinner hour, or
cheat railway traveling of its tedium, we commend this collection of stories and nov-
ellettes."—*N. Y. Arcadian.*

A DAUGHTER OF BOHEMIA. 1 vol. Illustrated. Paper,
price, $1.00; cloth, $1.50.

"Those who have followed the course of this remarkable story through APPLETONS'
JOURNAL will need no fresh incentive to induce them to read it in book-form; and to
those who have not thus followed it there remains an opportunity for real mental enjoyment which we almost envy them. It is emphatically thus far one of the best novels
of the season."—*The Golden Age.*
"It is a novel of brilliancy and attractiveness in its conversation and style generally, on a par with the writer's previous books."—*N. Y. Evening Mail.*

D. APPLETON & CO., Publishers,

549 & 551 BROADWAY, N. Y.

ROMANCE

OF

OLD COURT-LIFE IN FRANCE.

By FRANCES ELLIOT,

AUTHOR OF "THE ITALIANS," ETC.

WITH ILLUSTRATIONS BY ALFRED FREDERICKS.

Large 8vo, cloth, $2.00; paper, $1.50.

Cincinnati Times.

" In a most entertaining manner the romantic history of France, since the sixteenth century, is related. The authoress tells us that, in all she has written, she has sought carefully to work into her dialogue each word and sentence recorded of the individual, every available trait or peculiarity of character, to be found in contemporary memoirs, and every tradition that has come down to us. She has thereby made a most readable book. It is very handsomely gotten up, and is finely illustrated."

Philadelphia Ledger.

"A remarkably rich and delicate imagination weaves about the persons of the French nobility a charm of refinement."

Worcester Daily Spy.

"This is an historical novel of the time of Louis XIII. of France. In combining history with romance, the author has been unusually successful."

Philadelphia Age.

"We do not recall any English book that presents so comprehensive and accurate a sketch of the loves, intrigues, and events, which agitated the old court-life in France."

Hartford Times.

" To those who are familiar with the French memoir-writers, the most agreeable of histories, or with the series of historical novels in which the elder Dumas rivaled Walter Scott, this book will revive many memories of court history, adventures, and intrigues. To others, who are not conversant with those departments of French literature, this volume will be a new revelation. It begins with Francis I., who lost, as he said, every thing but honor at the battle of Pavia."

Quincy Whig.

"The period of French history embraced in the work before us extends from the reign of Francis I., through that of Le Grand Monarque, Louis XIV., and deals with characters whose memory is inseparably connected with the history of France—the famous Catherine de Medici, Mazarin, Mesdames Montespan and Maintenon, and many others. Historical facts are treated with great fidelity, and in an excellent and attractive style, and the numerous illustrations and the letter-press are superior to those of most works of the kind."

D. APPLETON & CO., Publishers, 549 & 551 *Broadway, N. Y.*

MEMOIRS OF GENERAL WILLIAM T. SHERMAN,

WRITTEN BY HIMSELF. Complete in Two Volumes. With a Military Map showing the Marches of the Armies under General Sherman's Command, inserted in a pocket at the end of the second volume; size, 30 by 47 inches. Small 8vo, 400 pages each. Price, in Blue Cloth, $5.50; Sheep, $7.00; Half Morocco, $8.50; Full Morocco, $12.00.

"These memoirs are by far the most interesting and important contribution yet made to the military history of the Rebellion by any of the leading actors in the great struggle. The staggering blows which General Sherman dealt to the Confederacy have secured him the undying gratitude of his countrymen, while the brilliancy which he displayed as a strategist, and the surpassing ability which he developed as a commander, entitle him to rank among the most distinguished leaders that the world has produced. The personal history of so marked a man must always possess extraordinary interest. When it is related by the man himself, and in that peculiarly racy style which General Sherman's letters and speeches have made familiar to the public, it becomes not only absorbing but fascinating. The march from Atlanta began on the morning of November 15th. General Sherman's narrative of this whole movement is of romantic interest. Some of his descriptions are not only picturesque but thrilling in their eloquence. And interspersed are well-told incidents, many of them full of genuine humor, which give unusual vivacity to the story. In military annals the narrative is unique, but it must be read in its entirety to be appreciated. The terse, clear, vigorous English in which the memoirs are written is one of their greatest charms. This fitly reflects the intense personality of the man. The straightforward, spirited narrative will enable a grateful country better to appreciate the immense value of the services which General Sherman rendered it in the critical period through which he helped guide it, and it will also aid others than Americans in forming a clearer estimate of the tremendous struggle in which the author of these memoirs bore so distinguished a part."—*N. Y. Times.*

"An autobiography so unreserved as this of General Sherman, printed during the lifetime of the writer, would certainly be an unsafe procedure for one who had the least need of any assistance from humbug. The author of these memoirs is a man who can afford to be seen as he is. Strip him of his epaulets, his brass buttons, and his cocked hat, and he still appears a valiant, able, and distinguished person. Indeed, it is quite necessary that he should be stripped of these accoutrements. We need to see him amid the camp-fires of Georgia, or on the march with his wagon-trains and foraging-bummers. So much for the picturesque and external man. But there is no need that he should conceal the mind behind all this. General Sherman has told his story with the most entire unreserve, and the story is one which Americans will be proud to read. We cannot help a feeling of satisfaction in being of the same race and the same country with such a man. We have here a picture of a person, resolute yet cautious, bold yet prudent, confident yet modest; a man of action to his finger-ends, yet withal something of a poet; we see all through the book the evidences of a chivalrous mind and of an intellect of singular force and precision. . . . We have spoken of Sherman as, in some sort, a poet. All through these great campaigns, while his whole mind is absorbed with the events he is conducting, he nevertheless appears to take a poet's joy in the spectacle of his battle-fields and moving armies. His enthusiasm will be shared by his readers. That passage in which he speaks of his last look on Atlanta, and tells us how it brought to his mind 'many a thought of desperate battle, of hope and fear,' has an eloquence which no mere writer of books can reach. The skill to write in that way is not taught in Blair or Whately."—*N. Y. Evening Post.*

"Sherman shows that he can wield the pen as well as the sword. His style is as much his own as that of Cæsar or Napoleon. It is a winning style. We see a gifted man telling his life in a plain, artless fashion, but with a trenchant rhetoric. Whenever an opinion is demanded he gives it. His picture of the early days in California is as graphic as a chapter from Sir Walter Scott. Now and then there are criticisms upon his contemporaries which will provoke comment; but, plainly enough, Sherman means what he says. This is the value of the work. We are glad the General has written it. In many cases it throws new light upon the Rebellion. Only by such light can the full measure of that momentous time be taken. And, whatever criticisms may be made upon the book, we honor the General for having given us so graphic and just a history of events in which he himself was so illustrious and successful an actor."—*N. Y. Herald.*

D. APPLETON & CO., Publishers, 549 & 551 Broadway, N. Y.

Mrs. Warfield's New Novel.

MIRIAM MONFORT.

BY THE AUTHOR OF "THE HOUSEHOLD OF BOUVERIE."

One 12mo Volume. Price, $2.00.

The *N. Y. Evening Post* says of "Miriam Monfort:" "Mrs. Warfield's new novel has freshness, and is so far removed from mediocrity as to entitle it to respectful comment. Her fiction calls for study. Her perception is deep and artistic, as respects both the dramatic side of life and the beautiful. It is not strictly nature, in the general sense, that forms the basis of her descriptions. She finds something deeper and more mystic than nature in the sense in which the term is usually used by critics, in the answer of the soul to life —in the strange, weird, and lonesome music (though now and then broken by discords) of the still small voices with which human nature replies to the questions that sorely vex her. She has the analytic capacity in the field of psychology, which enables her to trace phenomena in a story without arguing about them, and to exhibit the dramatic side of them without stopping to explain the reasons for it. In a word, her hand is as sure as that of a master, and if there were more such novels as this simple semi-biographical story of Miriam Monfort, it would not be necessary so often to put the question, 'Is the art of fiction extinct?'"

The *Cincinnati Daily Gazette* says: "'Miriam Monfort,' which now lies before us, is less sensational in incident than its predecessor, though it does not lack stirring events—an experience on a burning ship, for example. Its interest lies in the intensity which marks all the characters good and bad. The plot turns on the treachery of a pretended lover, and the author seems to have experienced every emotion of love and hate, jealousy and fear, that has inspired the creations of her pen. There is a contagion in her earnestness, and we doubt not that numerous readers will follow the fortunes of the beautiful but much-persecuted Miriam with breathless interest."

The *All Day City Item* says: "It is a work of extraordinary merit. The story is charmingly told by the heroine. It is admirable and original in plot, varied in incident, and intensely absorbing in interest; besides, throughout the volume, there is an exquisite combination of sensibility, pride, and loveliness, which will hold the work in high estimation. We make a quotation from the book that suits the critic exactly. 'It is splendid; it is a dream, more vivid than life itself; it is like drinking champagne, smelling tuberoses, inhaling laughing-gas, going to the opera, all at one time.' We recommend this to our young lady friends as a most thoughtfully and delightfully written novel."

D. APPLETON & CO., Publishers,

549 & 551 BROADWAY, NEW YORK.

BRESSANT.

A NOVEL.

By JULIAN HAWTHORNE.

1 vol., 12mo.   Cloth.............................. ....Price, $1.50

From the London Examiner.

"We will not say that Mr. Julian Hawthorne has received a double portion of his father's spirit, but 'Bressant' proves that he has inherited the distinctive tone and fibre of a gift which was altogether exceptional, and moved the author of the 'Scarlet Letter' beyond the reach of imitators.

"Bressant, Sophie, and Cornelia, appear to us invested with a sort of enchantment which we should find it difficult to account for by any reference to any special passage in their story."

From the London Athenæum.

"Mr. Hawthorne's book forms a remarkable contrast, in point of power and interest, to the dreary mass of so-called romances through which the reviewer works his way. It is not our purpose to forestall the reader, by any detailed account of the story; suffice it to say that, if we can accept the preliminary difficulty of the problem, its solution, in all its steps, is most admirably worked out."

From the Pall Mall Gazette.

"So far as a man may be judged by his first work, Mr. Julian Hawthorne is endowed with a large share of his father's peculiar genius. We trace in 'Bressant' the same intense yearning after a high and spiritual life, the same passionate love of nature, the same subtlety and delicacy of remark, and also a little of the same tendency to indulge in the use of a half-weird, half-fantastic imagery."

From the New York Times.

"'Bressant' is, then, a work that demonstrates the fitness of its author to bear the name of Hawthorne. More in praise need not be said; but, if the promise of the book shall not utterly fade and vanish, Julian Hawthorne, in the maturity of his power, will rank side by side with him who has hitherto been peerless, but whom we must hereafter call the 'Elder Hawthorne.'"

From the Boston Post.

"There is beauty as well as power in this novel, the two so pleasantly blended, that the sudden and incomplete conclusion, although ending the romance with an abruptness that is itself artistic, comes only too soon for the reader."

From the Boston Globe.

"It is by far the most original novel of the season that has been published at home or abroad, and will take high rank among the best American novels ever written."

From the Boston Gazette.

"There is a strength in the book which takes it in a marked degree out of the range of ordinary works of fiction   It is substantially an original story.   There are freshness and vigor in every part."

From the Home Journal.

"'Bressant' is a remarkable romance, full of those subtle touches of fancy, and that insight into the human heart, which distinguish genius from the mere clever and entertaining writers of whom we have perhaps too many."

D. APPLETON & CO., Publishers, New York.

D. APPLETON & CO.

Have recently published,

GOOD-BYE, SWEETHEART!

By RHODA BROUGHTON,

AUTHOR OF "RED AS A ROSE IS SHE," "COMETH UP AS A FLOWER," ETC.

One Vol., 8vo. Paper covers..............Price, $0.75.
      "   12mo. Cloth.................... "   1.50.

"Good-bye, Sweetheart!" is certainly one of the brightest and most entertaining novels that has appeared for many years. The heroine of the story, Lenore, is really an original character, drawn only as a woman could draw her, who had looked deeply into the mysterious recesses of the feminine heart. She is a creation totally beyond the scope of a man's pen, unless it were the pen of Shakespeare. Her beauty, her wilfulness, her caprice, her love, and her sorrow, are depicted with marvellous skill, and invested with an interest of which the reader never becomes weary. Miss Broughton, in this work, has made an immense advance on her other stories, clever as those are. Her sketches of scenery and of interiors, though brief, are eminently graphic, and the dialogue is always sparkling and witty. The incidents, though sometimes startling and unexpected, are very natural, and the characters and story, from the beginning to the end, strongly enchain the attention of the reader. The work has been warmly commended by the press during its publication, as a serial, in APPLETONS' JOURNAL, and, in its book-form, bids fair to be decidedly THE novel of the season.

D. A. & Co. have now ready, New Editions of

COMETH UP AS A FLOWER......................Price, 60 cents.
NOT WISELY, BUT TOO WELL....................Price, 60 cents.
RED AS A ROSE IS SHE...........................Price, 60 cents.
BY THE SAME AUTHOR.